THE

BRIGHTEST

SUN

THE BRIGHTEST SUN

ADRIENNE BENSON

PARK
ROW
BOOKS

Recycling programs
for this product may
not exist in your area.

ISBN-13: 978-0-7783-3127-8

The Brightest Sun

ParkRowBooks.com
BookClubbish.com

Printed in U.S.A.

My parents, who cracked the world open for me so stories could spill out. My brother, who somehow made them all seem funny. And TCKs everywhere, who grow wild in the spaces between. This is for you.

THE

BRIGHTEST

SUN

PART I

FROM A DIFFERENT TRIBE

One of the old women severed the umbilical cord and passed the tiny body, slippery and warm, up into Leona's arms. It felt unnatural to hold the baby; the infant seemed too small somehow, almost weightless. Leona rolled carefully onto her side and settled the baby next to her. The brand-new hands splayed and stretched blindly in the dim air. Dust motes floated in the crack of light coming through the one palm-sized window cut from the mud walls. Leona watched as the dust swirled. She wished she had a bigger window. She craved light and air. For the first time in the almost twelve months she'd been in Kenya, she yearned for things she'd left home in America. She wanted clean lines and shiny surfaces, nurses in sensible shoes and the comfort of hospital machinery whirring and clicking and dripping around her. For a minute, she even wanted her mother.

The small body wiggled beside her and a sound came out— staccato like the bleating of a newborn goat. It was a tenuous sound, hesitant, an experiment with an uncertain outcome. The tiny lips pursed in anticipation of what only Leona could give. It was a girl, Leona saw. She squeezed her eyes against the coming tears and tried to roll over onto her stomach. She wanted to bury her face in darkness. She was so tired. She felt a sob in her throat and then a sound filled the dark room. It was her scream, she understood, although she couldn't feel her mouth opening or the reverberation of air. She only heard the sound of keening fill the space around her head and saw Simi and the Maasai attendants jerk their faces up and look at her, then glance at one another, concerned. Simi reached across the baby's back to take Leona's hand, but Leona shook her friend off and brought her hands to her face. She tried to press them over her mouth tightly enough to stop the sound. Her insides were glass, shattering in the shell of her skin. This baby was born of loneliness—the desperate kind that arises in people who live among foreigners; who don't share language or gestures.

Leona arrived at the manyatta in a little, dented Renault 4 she purchased, with cash, from a departing French expatriate who she'd met her first night in Nairobi. She drove the distance between Nairobi and Loita hesitantly. It was her first time in Africa and the small car didn't feel like it would offer protection from lions or elephants or any other wild game that might lurk in the yellow savannah grassland she drove through. The drive terrified her so much that she promised herself to stay in the manyatta and only use the car for emergencies. But after a few weeks the dry dust made Leona's skin itch, and the nearest water source, a little tributary of the Mara River, was low and thick, too muddy to bathe in. Leona didn't miss much from home, but she did miss the feeling of a shower, the water soaking her hair and skin. She couldn't stand the way her skin felt, the way her body stank. She wanted a hot shower. She wanted to immerse herself in soap and water, to scrub her hair and fingernails and wash the spaces between her toes. Her yearning to be clean was visceral.

So, only six weeks after her arrival, she packed an overnight bag and drove to Narok to spend the night at the Chabani Guest House. The hotel was small and cheap, mostly used by safari guides and the occasional shoestring tourist or traveling Peace Corps volunteer. But it was clean, and with electricity, running water and a real, if old, mattress, it felt luxurious to Leona. The sky outside was darkening and cool when she arrived. The purple dusks in Kenya were short; night came quickly. Leona turned on all the lights in her room, and laughed at how easily they flicked into brightness. The manyatta had no electricity. After she scrubbed the dirt from her skin and scalp and stood under the warm, rusty water until it ran cold, she dressed in clean clothes, the one set she hadn't worn yet, saved in the bottom of her suitcase. Until now, she'd only smelled it occasionally. The scent of the American detergent lingered in the fibers and reminded her of home.

She felt new and lighter somehow, cracked free of her dusty shroud. With the smell of floral shampoo still lingering in her hair, Leona went down to the hotel's café to order a drink.

The bar was wooden-walled and dark. The only light came from a string of colored Christmas tree bulbs—the big ones people back home wrapped around outside tree branches—and a disco ball revolving slowly above a central space where people could dance. There were no dancers that night. Maybe it was still too early.

Leona chose the bar stool farthest away from the only other customers, a white couple, both about her age, maybe a little older. Leona didn't like small talk so she avoided making eye contact with the two. But she hadn't seen other white people for weeks, and she found herself unable to keep from glancing up at them. The two were clean; both neatly dressed, which made Leona think they might be tourists. But the woman turned slightly, and Leona recognized the logo of a well-known anti-poaching foundation on the front of her T-shirt. The woman was pretty. Petite and blonde with a sunburned spot on her nose and rosy pink cheeks, she watched the man intently as he spoke, his body movements fluid as he gestured with his arms, acting out the story he was telling her. The man was attractive, square shouldered and blond with large, tan hands. Leona forced herself to look away and focused her concentration on gathering the right collection of Swahili words to order a beer. She felt the sudden lightness of joy when the barkeep slid a sweating, brown Tusker bottle her way. She didn't bother asking for a glass.

The beer—after so long without alcohol—made her feel luminous and unencumbered. The couple laughed loudly and Leona glanced at them again. The blonde woman was standing, holding out a bill, which the man waved away. He turned to the barkeep and said something in rapid-fire Swahili. Then he turned back to the woman and laughed again. Leona heard him say, "Now you'll have to meet me again, next one's on you."

Leona watched him watch the woman walking out of the bar. She wondered if anyone had ever watched her with that intensity.

Halfway through her second beer, she found she didn't mind when the blond man slid his stool closer to hers and offered to buy her another drink. As they talked, the ease of English after the weeks and weeks of only rudimentary Maa made Leona giddy. Normally a reserved, quiet person, she felt almost drunk with the millions of words she could so easily pluck from her head and toss out, like confetti.

"You're a flirt," she said. "Your girlfriend barely left."

"I am a flirt." He nodded, smiling. "But you're wrong. She's not my girlfriend. I met her here tonight. Interesting girl, though. Working on antipoaching—elephant protection."

They purposely avoided names. It didn't come up at first, names hadn't mattered, and anyway Leona, after weeks of being a curiosity among the Maasai, wanted the anonymity. As an anthropologist, she constantly had to study, observe and ask questions. Now, with this man, she wanted to suspend words and curiosity and talk. Later, alcohol erased the curiosity of names, and the next morning, slow and headachy, Leona felt exposed. She wasn't new to sex, she'd had a couple of boyfriends during her college and grad school years, but they drifted into, and then out of, her life like ghosts. She'd never, though, slept with someone she'd just met, and under the weight of her headache and nausea, she was ashamed of what she'd done. She wanted to disappear. Sex was a fraught thing. Hard for her to indulge in, an unsettling mix of pleasure and fear.

The man was breathing evenly and heavily next to her, and she had to very carefully slide from under his arm and out of bed. She found her clothes and dressed quickly. But the door creaked when she opened it, and she heard his voice, sleepy and rough. "Going to leave without a goodbye?"

"I have to go back," she whispered.

"You mean you have to come back to bed," he said, patting the empty mattress beside him.

Leona turned back to the door and grasped the handle again, pulling it open. When it clicked shut behind her, she raced down the hall to her own room and tossed her shampoo, razor and yesterday's clothes in her bag. She'd planned to stay in Narok for the day. She wanted to have the hotel do her laundry, and indulge in a big breakfast with coffee. But now she changed her mind. She was embarrassed. She hated feeling out of control, and she was ashamed of herself for letting it happen. She lived by the mantra that it was best to be alone—less difficult, less complicated. She didn't want to see the man again, or look him in his eyes. She thought she'd see her own shame there, reflected back at her.

Outside the hotel, the morning street was almost empty, but already the air smelled like wood smoke, frying dough and rotting produce. She opened the trunk of her car and tossed her bag in.

"Is it me, or are you running out on your hotel bill?" a voice called, and when Leona turned, he was there. He was dressed and his feet were shoved into unlaced boots. "I have to go up to Solai today. Can't put it off. But I'll come to the manyatta as soon as I'm done there. I'll find you."

Leona felt the bubbling up of terror deep inside her. It was always this way. Even in college, and graduate school, it wasn't the sex that made her most frightened, but the aftermath. The first time she'd seen a therapist, it only took thirty minutes of talking through her background before the therapist said, "It sounds like you're not sexually frigid, but emotionally cut off." She'd never gone back for another appointment.

"No," she said, "don't bother with that." She inhaled consciously. The panic made her breathing shallow, the imaginary walls that closed in around her made her lungs tense and ineffective. The man was standing close, looking down at her. His eyes were calm, and his face open. She could smell him—warm skin and sleepy breath.

"No, I want to," he said. "I had fun with you last night. No reason we can't see one another again, is there?"

There was always this dread when a man wanted to get to know her. She wasn't normal in this way. Other women her age wanted boyfriends, wanted to marry. The idea set off an alarm in Leona's mind. It always had. She could share physical intimacy, but the notion of allowing herself to want anything else, to be vulnerable in any other way, tore her in two—yearning and revulsion. She wanted to be normal and allow someone to love her, and to return love, but the fear was always too great, and it always won.

She couldn't look at the man's face when she answered. Instead, she glanced sideways, pretending to watch a mangy dog rolling in the dust. "I'm not interested in a relationship," she said. It was her typical line, worn thin from use. She wondered if it sounded as implausible to him as it did to her.

"Who said anything about a relationship?" the man asked.

His lips turning up into a grin that made Leona's pulse quicken. "I'm just talking about seeing you again. Maybe reprising our night." He raised his eyebrows suggestively. He was flirting. Leona felt that hollow ache she always felt at moments like this; the ache of wanting something she was far too terrified to actually reach for.

"I have a boyfriend." That always worked. Even so, Leona didn't wait to see if his face changed, or if his voice hardened into understanding.

She turned, climbed into her car and slammed the door shut. She might have heard him calling, but she couldn't be sure. She sped off as fast as she could toward the manyatta. She didn't look back. She didn't glance into the rearview and see him standing next to his truck watching her leave. She didn't want to think about how she'd feel if he never really came looking for her.

Now, with the baby beside her in her little mud-walled hut, she had no desire to speak. She wept with fatigue and terror as the dark women hunkered at her side, murmuring and running their rough fingers along her arms and across the new baby's head.

"You must let her nurse," the Maasai midwife said. She reached over and pulled Leona's T-shirt up, freed her aching breast and clasped it firmly, rubbing the nipple on the baby's new mouth.

"Now it's empty, but the baby will bring the milk."

Leona wanted to cringe at the unfamiliar fingers on her breast and at the mewling little thing next to her. The baby was blindly flailing, her mouth open hopefully, trying to burrow into Leona's flesh like a chigger. Leona closed her eyes. She only wanted to sleep. The midwife grasped Leona's breast again, flattened it in her hand and inserted it firmly into the baby's mouth. Leona felt a strange sensation and opened her eyes. The baby was connected to her and its desperate little mouth was pulling on Leona's flesh. A shudder of alarm rippled through her and she bit her lip against the scream she could feel rising in her mouth again. She couldn't be a mother.

At first when Leona noticed her missing period, she was relieved. The task of finding enough privacy and water to wash herself—let alone driving all the way to Narok to buy supplies—was something she dreaded. When the bleeding didn't appear, as it should have, Leona was happy. It was all the changes in diet and the syncing with the other women, she assumed. But then it didn't come again, and again.

When it dawned on her that she was pregnant, it was like she'd been diagnosed with a fatal disease. Her thoughts obsessively circled back to it, again and again. She couldn't concentrate on work and she couldn't sleep. Every time she closed her eyes, the tide of dread and distress washed through her. She spent hours flipping through the medical manual she'd brought with her in a desperate search for a remedy. The book offered no way to flush this thing out of her.

By the time she sought out the *laiboni*, the witch doctor and spiritual leader of the community, she hadn't slept for nearly a week. The *laiboni* was a wizened elder who sucked his few remaining teeth when he saw Leona and never seemed to understand her halting Maa. As the village doctor, he had a special role here and knowledge of traditional medicines Leona was dying to include in her work. But he was a stubborn interviewee, and Leona suspected he was wary of her presence in the village. She'd been delicately trying to gain his trust, not asking too much of him yet, instead hoping that the other villagers would assure him of her intentions. Being too direct with the old man might cement his unfavorable opinion. But now Leona was desperate.

"*Sopa*," she greeted him, ducking her head as a gesture of respect. He was sitting alone under an acacia tree just outside the village enclosure. He lethargically waved a bead-handled cow tail in front of his face to keep the flies from setting into his eyes. He murmured his own greeting back but said nothing else. Leona lowered herself to the ground in front of him and crossed her legs. She batted a few lazy flies away and tried to decide what to say. Her phrase book lay in her lap, and she flipped through it. Where were the words she needed?

"Hello, my friend." A voice above Leona pulled her from the book. Simi stood above her, smiling. Simi was the third and youngest wife of the secular village leader's son. She had been educated in the local school up to sixth grade, and was the only woman in the village who spoke English. Simi wasn't absolutely fluent, but had enough for most basic conversations and, more important, had the curiosity and dedication to interpret Leona's explanations and hand gestures. Simi had a sense of the things Leona needed to learn to live in the manyatta, and was never shy about teaching them. She'd been the one, early in Leona's stay here, to grasp Leona's hand and guide her outside the village to the shallow riverbed, dry now, and indicate that Leona should come to this spot when she needed to relieve herself. Simi helped Leona buy the few kitchen items she needed—the large pot, or *suferia*, for boiling water, the frying pan, the tins of sugar and tea—and taught Leona how to keep the embers in her fire pit alive all day. She was the one who Leona talked to like a friend. But Leona couldn't bear to be honest now. Not about this. Especially not about this.

"*Sopa, Simi,*" Leona said. She used the Maa word for hello, even though Simi preferred speaking English whenever possible. "I am researching the doctor's work today. Can you help translate?"

Simi hunkered and spoke quickly to the old man. He nodded and waved his cow tail faster.

"What do you want to know?"

Simi relayed Leona's question without a blink. Leona was surprised. Maasai looked askance at premarital sex, and Leona knew her situation might cost her the relationships she'd built here.

"It's for my book," she assured Simi. And then she asked her to translate the detailed questions she had about the plant, where it was found and how much was used. Was it ingested or topical?

Later, when the old man stood up and shuffled home for tea, Simi turned to look at Leona. Leona tried to tell if Simi's eyes held anger or sadness and, if so, for whom?

"You should have asked only me. I could tell you this information. Now it is possible that the others in the village will discover your secret."

"Simi, it's not for me," Leona whispered, suddenly on the verge of exhausted tears. "It's for the book."

But Simi's face was serious now, and she leaned close to Leona's ear and whispered, "You have a baby...inside?"

Leona started as if her friend had slapped her. She looked down at Simi's slim fingers resting on her arm. She glanced up at Simi's face and then away again. What should she say? Knowing that Simi might disapprove or, worse, that she'd be reminded of her own pain made Leona frantic with embarrassment and anxiety.

"The man," Simi whispered, her eyes serious and steady, "did he force you?"

Leona couldn't stop the tears. Her eyes filled up and she used the heels of both hands to press into her eyes. "I'm sorry, Simi, I'm so sorry."

Leona considered two things: it was not acceptable for unmarried women to have children out of wedlock and, because of that taboo, her status as a foreigner would be the only thing to prevent the community from banishing her. She thought of the precarious position Simi herself was in—married for three years with no children of her own. Would Simi's desperation and the irony of the situation make her angry? That was a risk. Leona's work here was going well, and she couldn't bear the idea of leaving. She couldn't bring herself to claim rape, but she could lie.

"My husband," she said. It was not unusual for Maasai spouses to live apart.

"You never told me you had a husband," Simi stated. Her voice was quiet, but Leona felt it like a warm current deep below cool water. Simi knew she wasn't married. Simi knew this baby belonged to nobody, but she wouldn't betray Leona's secret.

"Your husband, he must be a strong man." Simi smiled a small, sad smile. "He is living so far away in America, and still he can give you a baby!"

"Simi, I can't have a baby." Leona searched for a reason that Simi would understand, a lie to cover a truth that Simi would never really be able to understand. "My body is broken. It's dangerous for me to deliver a child." This was a reason a Maasai woman would see as reasonable. Not the other, not the choice Leona made to sleep with a stranger.

Later, after the village was quiet and dark and most families had settled around their fires in their little huts, Simi slipped through Leona's door. She held a blue plastic bag filled with leaves.

"I found this for you near the river. Put some inside where the baby is." And then she slipped outside again.

The leaves were rough and uncomfortable, and Leona worried they would somehow make her sick, poison her for her stupidity. But she slipped a few inside herself several times a day and waited for the relief of blood. It never came. Instead, her breasts began to hurt, she found herself thirsty and her jeans grew tighter and tighter. It was too late.

Leona considered driving to Nairobi to check herself into the hospital for the birth, but it was easier for her to force forgetfulness, and eventually she lost track of the days. There was work to do here. It had been a dry year and the year before had been dry, too. The Maasai in Loita were worried; cattle and goats had begun to get thin. Some of the baby goats had already died, their mothers too emaciated to produce enough milk. Years ago, the Maasai were free to go wherever the good grazing land was. In times of drought, they moved their herds a hundred and seventy miles to Nyeri, in the central highlands, where grass stayed greener and rains were more common. Under British rule, though, the government limited their movements and, with British settlers setting up their own farms, Maasai land was reduced further. The final nail in the coffin of the traditional Maasai way of life was the wildlife preserves. In the 1970s, citing the need for land and wildlife conservation, great swathes of Maasai land were designated as game parks. Grazing was prohibited.

Leona's work was centered on discovering and mitigating the effects of the government-imposed strictures on the traditionally nomadic Maasai people in Western Kenya. She had the idea that if she could prove that the Maasai culture was changing, and that those changes would negatively impact Kenya in general, it would add fuel to the argument that the government should allow the Maasai more movement, more chances to keep herds healthy and more chances to survive. Her study was vital, life and death, and Leona took it that way—without the option of other grazing land, this culture could disappear as fast and as easily as the rivers and streams were drying.

She had no idea how pregnant she actually was. Thinking about how much time had passed made her panic, so she forced herself not to think about it, let alone plan for it. She hadn't seen a doctor; she hadn't had checkups. She spent the months trying to ignore her growing belly and forcing all thoughts of the future out of her head. She felt sick when the movements started—the tugging and sliding of her insides felt like a punishment. She watched Simi watching her grow, and when she let Simi place a hand on her moving belly, she wished fervently that the roles were reversed. After a while, the other women around her noticed, and that was a relief. They offered to help carry water and sent their own children to collect wood for Leona's fire. And so it settled in—the silence, the forced ignorance. Leona worked constantly: watching the people around her and taking careful notes. The people in the village knew that she was there to observe their culture and way of life so she could write about them, maybe help them with the grazing problem. They knew her research meant she observed them and wrote in the notebook she always had with her, and that she asked questions incessantly about everything she saw. Leona began to draft what she planned to turn into her book, an academic study of the shifting cultural norms of the Loita Maasai brought on by laws limiting their nomadic heritage. She concentrated all her efforts on looking outward, and purposely pushed away what was happening inside.

That's why her baby was born in the way of Maasai babies—in her dim *inkajijik*, the small hut made from thin branches covered with mud and dung. Only the embers in the fire pit lighted the birth, and when the baby's eyes opened, they opened to a halo of wood smoke. The first face the baby saw was brown and wrinkled and adorned with strings of beads sewn onto strips of leather. The first sounds she heard were the women ululating four times to alert the village to the birth of a girl, their calls echoed by the lowing of cows.

Three days after the baby was born, Leona was curled around the infant on her bed. She was still so tired. She must have dropped off because the sound of a car engine and the shouts of people greeting one another outside slipped through her sleep. She lay still, for a moment forgetting everything, and grasped at the feeling of peace. It evaporated the moment she recognized one of the voices outside. When the tall blond man dipped his shoulders and neck to fit through her little door, she wasn't altogether surprised. If he heard the story of an American giving birth, he'd know who it was. A white woman having a baby in a Maasai village would be big news. There was nobody else it could be. That he came, though, shocked her. She assumed he'd avoid further contact, eschew responsibility. But there he was, and for a moment Leona was stunned into silence.

"How are you?" he said. His English words, though flattened by his British-Kenyan accent, were startling in their familiarity. Leona tried to discern his reaction to the birth from his voice, whether or not he was angry. She concentrated hard, but her vision felt fuzzy and her thoughts flipped too quickly to pin down and consider. He was so handsome, and she remembered how her body stretched toward him that night, like a plant craving light. Even now, a part of her pulled toward him. She thought of how it felt to be pressed into him, how her head had spun with alcohol and need and how she'd wanted him, and how he'd wanted her, too. But the person she was that night in the Chabani Guest House, the woman who'd used flowery shampoo and worn her tightest jeans, the woman who had not walked away when the blond stranger spoke to her…that wasn't the real Leona. It wasn't her, she reminded herself as she looked up at the man. Her cheeks reddened and she wished, for the millionth time, that she could erase the previous months and erase that night and erase that rare, stupid version of herself.

The man leaned down and studied the sleeping baby.

"A girl?" he whispered, and reached out as if he wanted to touch the baby with his fingertips to check if she was real, but he stopped before finger met cheek. He glanced at Leona's face and then away again. She couldn't read him. He folded his lanky body and knelt on the dirt floor next to where she lay, up on the raised bed of rawhide stretched and dried to stiffness on a frame of sticks.

Watching the man now, here, in her home, Leona realized that although she had no idea what he was called, she knew a lot of other things about him. He'd grown up on a cattle ranch in Solai—close to Maasailand—and had a profound understanding of the Maasai and a fluency in their ways. He knew many of the elders in Leona's manyatta. This was what had impressed Leona the night they met and caused her to feel that unfamiliar yearning stretch through her. He made her feel comfortable, so she didn't hesitate when he gently picked her hand up off the bar and told her to follow him to his room. She liked his coarse blond hair and his sunburned, peeling arms that wrapped around her in the night, and his wide, calloused fingers rough on her breasts. While it was dark and they were breathing together that night, she let herself think about how it might be to have a man of her own—one she wanted—to lie with every night. She hadn't wanted that before, but under the darkness of that night the thought was as exciting as it was terrifying.

In the weeks after she'd met him, though she knew she'd been clear to him, brutally so, perhaps, Leona found herself hoping through the hot, still days. She couldn't shake the suspicion that something was different. In the golden evenings when the sun pulled colors out of the sky and turned the landscape soft and blue, she scanned the horizon around the manyatta for the telltale clouds of dust a Land Rover would make if it were hurtling up the track toward her.

She hated herself a little more each day when it grew dark without him coming. And she hated him for causing her to hope that he'd ignore the way she'd brushed him off in Narok and come find her, anyway. The multiplying cells inside of her—his baby—had nothing to do with her confusing feelings about the man himself. This was her usual pain: wanting to be seen and loved but being utterly unable to let herself allow it. She accepted being alone, she liked it, but there was the occasional wondering. How would it be to share a life with a man? Maybe with this man? How would it feel to see him and to allow herself to be seen? Each evening when he didn't appear, she nursed her disappointment by listing the reasons it was better to be alone. She knew them by heart—and she knew that however many items she listed, there was really only one rea-son: her own fear. This made her hate herself, too.

The dust gathered in her hair and made her itch, but she didn't go back to Narok to shower. She lived with it, like the Maasai did. She was adjusting, she convinced herself, to the life of an embedded anthropologist. When she really understood she was pregnant, and it was long after she could do anything about it, she felt too paralyzed to make the effort to find out who the man was, exactly, and to let him know. She couldn't imagine the conversation they'd have to have, or the decisions they'd have to make. It was too much. She told herself over and over again that she didn't want a relationship, she preferred being in a place where everyone was different from her, where she could restrict her interactions and be just an observer. The man—the baby's father—wouldn't allow her to limit herself. He would require more than she felt she knew how to give. More than she wanted to give. Intimacy was a risky thing.

Now, here he was.

A Maasai woman, squatting in the shadows by the low embers of the fire pit, reached out and handed him a chipped enamel cup of chai. He took it and thanked her in Maa. He looked per-fectly relaxed, happy even, to be there. Leona was grateful Simi had gone to the river; surely she would have noticed Leona's discomfort. Surely she would have fit the pieces of the puzzle together. And what then? Leona felt a sudden anger burn in her chest—here was another man who walked in without permis-sion, who settled in her space with no regard to whether she wanted him there or not.

"Were you going to tell me?" the baby's father asked now.

Leona shut her eyes tightly. She answered in Maa.

"Go away. It's not your child."

"That's bullshit, and we both know it." He paused, then spoke so quietly Leona could barely hear him. "I didn't have a good father myself, but I think I'd like to try to be one." His voice cracked slightly. "Whether or not you want me in your life, the girl deserves a father in hers."

"You had a shitty father? Well, so did I," she said. "What makes you think you'd do a better job?"

She saw the man wince. His expression hardened. She knew she'd hit a nerve—she'd hurt him. She wasn't happy about that, but she sensed a shift in his attitude and felt relief. If she had to hurt him in order to get him to leave her alone, so be it.

To her surprise, he spoke again. "Give me a chance to be a better father than mine, or yours, apparently."

She felt hemmed in, strangled. Why wouldn't he just go? Like a trapped animal, she bit hard. "A father is the last thing this baby needs. I didn't tell you because I didn't want you to know, because I don't want her to suffer through a terrible childhood like I did. You're not going to change my mind."

Leona grew up watching the rain fall on the green, green grass in the yard of her parents' home in Beaverton, Oregon. Her father was a surgeon—never around during the day—and her mother was only a shadowy presence, less a mother than a waft of perfume in another room, always on the way out, always saying goodbye. Leona was left home with a housekeeper who lazily vacuumed the Persian rugs and huddled on the back deck in her blue uniform smoking secret cigarettes and blowing rings into the wet sky. Leona had no siblings, and was never encouraged to bring friends home or to go to parties, so she was ignored at school. Not bullied, not sought after, but invisible.

If she were ever asked to sum up her childhood in one word, she would have said *silent*. Silence was forced on her. Her father's infrequent presence was a dark thing, covered by night and a sleeping house. The crack of her bedroom door opening and the memory of rough skin pressed against Leona's cheek, the dank smell of his breath and his wet lips hissing in her ear, "Don't tell your mother. Don't say anything to anyone. You'll ruin it…you'll ruin me." Those nights Leona bit her soft inner cheeks bloody and raw to keep from making a sound.

Only once did she try to break the silence with her mother. Her father always left the house early, and at breakfast one day Leona unlocked her voice. Her mother smiled at her over her toast, and Leona whispered a phrase she'd chosen carefully, the canary in the mine. "Dad came into my room last night." The coffee bubbled loudly in the percolator, and Leona found that forever after, the sound made her anxious.

Her mother's pause lasted a lifetime. Leona dragged her fork through the egg yolks on her plate, afraid to look up.

"Your father is under a lot of pressure at work," her mother finally answered, and when Leona glanced up to explain what she meant, to spill it all out like a liquid from a broken bottle, she caught her mother's eye. There was a tiny flicker there, a lit candle, and then the curtain snapped tightly shut over it. A shutter firmly closed against a possible storm.

After that, Leona kept the secret locked away from everything else. In the daytime she sat through classes at school, concentrating hard, always finding the correct answer. In the evenings, she sat at the kitchen table doing homework while the maid ironed. Her mother came and went, came and went, off to Ladies Auxiliary meetings or the Junior League. Leona's insides turned to stone, but she never wondered if her mother noticed that her father couldn't look Leona in the eyes.

The invisibility—the pressure not to speak—became a habit. It saw her through high school and college and, later, through her doctoral program in sociocultural anthropology. Leona grew a jagged space—a broken section deep inside. She learned that people, especially the ones closest to her, weren't to be trusted.

She declared a major in anthropology because she felt she'd never learned to understand humans; her childhood had given her no great notion of how her own species worked. She was desperate to go as far away from her parents as she could. Leona wrote with skill and conviction and her Fulbright application was chosen. Three months later she was ensconced in a bathroom-sized mud-and-cow-dung *inkajijik*, in a manyatta filled with identical *inkajijiks*. They all circled the central livestock corral and were protected from lions and elephants by thorny acacia branches piled in a ring around the whole cluster. In the rare letters to her parents, Leona referred to her new home as a "gated community."

Dusty and crowded, the manyatta was noisy with the grunting of livestock that lived inside the circle of thorny branches, and the sounds of hyenas, wildebeests and the occasional lion from outside. The small door to her hut was open—as they all were—and she loved the voices she could hear almost always, even brighter in the night, from the tiny huts all around her. She loved the constant scent of other humans and the way the livestock made the air smell tangy. It surprised her at first that she even loved the lack of physical space in the Maasai culture and how a child climbed into her lap every time she sat down and how the other women included her without question in their daily lives. For the first time she felt seen. Eventually she realized her comfort came from the fact that she was foreign. The language barrier and the cultural differences gave her the perfect excuse to feign misunderstanding, to keep people at a manageable distance—not physically, perhaps, but emotionally. At home she couldn't hide this way. Her unwillingness to be vulnerable was an obvious thing, a scarlet letter people read as standoffish, odd. Here, her days were filled with sound and the presence of people, and she felt warm in it, relaxed, fully in charge of the depth and frequency of any emotional exchange.

But through everything—the meals she shared with the villagers, the long walks to the spring to collect water in her bucket, the rare rainstorms that saw her side by side with the other women in the village slapping fresh mud and soggy cow dung on the leaky *inkajijik* roof while rain poured down her back—she remembered the first rule of the anthropologist, Participate Only to Observe, and she held back the one thing she could: herself.

Here in Loita, people expressed curiosity about Leona. Women and children crowded into her little *inkajijik* to watch her. These women wanted to know about her father and her mother and her old life. It wasn't lost on Leona that her first experience of bonding with other women was in a language she didn't speak fluently and in a place half a world away from where she'd come.

She liked the questions the women asked, she liked the way they wanted to know her; it was novel and pleasant. Mostly, she loved that she could pick and choose her answers, and that they could never know what she held back—they couldn't force intimacy against her will. When she spoke to them about herself, she chose her words like picking fruit from a tree, selecting wisely—concentrating on telling them things that didn't hurt. She painted a picture of her life up to now that was simple and easy, a life that didn't make her sad. Mother, Father, school and work. She deflected the conversation when she had to. It was easy to edge away from dangerous memories by changing the subject to the differences between a Maasai home and an American one, or how American people dressed and what they ate. Only Simi pressed. Her curiosity was relentless, and she asked endless questions about life outside the village. Her brief education had given her a rare glimpse into the world, and she drank Leona's stories like water. Simi was different from the other women. She didn't loiter by the river gossiping, or tease the other women to make them laugh. She had several books, children's primers, really, that she'd kept from her days at school. Once she showed them to Leona. She proudly lifted them from a small basket tucked under her bed. She could read, she told Leona proudly—none of the other women in the village could.

After that, Leona selected a couple of novels she'd brought

with her—beloved classics. *The Call of the Wild* was Simi's favorite. Simi poured over the book. She'd sit under an acacia reading for hours, oblivious to the annoyance of the other women who called her lazy and proud. Her innate intelligence broke down the urge to judge things. She'd ask Leona to explain the words she didn't understand, like *snow*. She said she liked the way the dog was in charge, the loyalty he showed. She said she'd never thought that even Americans could be cruel to each other—in Kenya, America was seen as a perfect place where only good things happened.

It suited Leona to be emotionally removed from the commotion around her and to have the freedom to be on the outside looking in. Here, nobody expected any more than that from her. Back home, when another person did something Leona didn't comprehend, something that hurt or confused her, she felt a terrible sense of bewilderment, of sinking beneath the surface into a place where she couldn't breathe—the fear of not understanding what she felt she should have understood. Here, that panicked sense was gone. She didn't want to cross that line, to feel confused and misunderstood without a reason again.

Leona knew that in Maasailand, babies weren't recognized until they were three months old. Children are loved, but utilized, and the utility is treacherous. She'd seen babies die of disease before they took their first steps; she'd observed death rites for teenagers bitten by snakes, toddlers who fell into cooking fires and the bleeding body of a seven-year-old fatally mauled by a hyena while tending goats outside the village. It was prudent, Leona thought, to hold your children at arm's length when you lived the hard life of the Maasai. Anything could happen, after all. Life out here was fragile; you had to be tough. This is what she told herself when her baby was born. These were the thoughts in her head. She convinced herself it was good to keep distance between herself and the baby. She wrapped her leaky breasts tightly with a *kanga* and let another nursing mother in the village feed the baby. She let Simi take the baby to her house to sleep, and she let Simi carry the baby on her back during the walks to the river. This was the line that she drew between herself and her child.

Simi loved the baby. With no children of her own, she was free to adopt a baby who couldn't, for whatever reason, be cared for by its own mother. Leona knew that Simi was more of a mother to her child than she was. She also knew Simi's place in the village, as a childless wife, was precarious. She said yes when Simi asked to make it official; she consented to an adoption ceremony—the *laiboni* slaughtered a ram and both women ate the fat. That was the traditional process. Leona knew, in her own head, that her daughter would never really be Maasai, that she was, by her inherited DNA, privy to the perks of being American, but she felt better in an unexpected way. Her child had two parents now.

The Maasai elders gave the baby her first, sacred, name. The name only used by the parents, nobody else. *Nalangu*, they whispered to Leona, which meant "from a different tribe." And that's what the little pale baby looked like. A different tribe, an alien being that Leona observed; who she watched learn to roll over on a rawhide blanket, who she watched nursing from another woman's breast, who took her first steps in the red dust and dried dung of the manyatta. Leona watched the baby grow in the same way she watched all the babies of the village grow. She allowed her baby to go to Simi for comfort, and not come to her. She spoke to the baby in English, but she spoke to all the kids in English—their parents wanted them to learn. She convinced herself that nothing was different, that the nine months of her pregnancy never really happened and the terror she had felt through it all was just a bad dream.

At night, though, Leona often woke up sweating and terrified, her nightmares alive in her mind. She dreamed of her baby disappearing into a puff of smoke, or being carried away in the mouth of a lion, the wide tawny shoulders heaving as it leaped over the thorny fence, the shaggy blond mane curling slightly over the cold, yellow, animal eyes. Those nights she'd sit bolt upright and reach over to check for her baby's presence. The baby was never there. When she was awake, Leona hated the version of herself she saw in the nightmares; it wasn't the smoke or the lion that caused the frantic heart beating and the suffocating breath, but instead it was the vision of herself, just standing there watching, calmly stirring the chai in her dented enamel cup with her metal spoon, in concentric circles, over and over again, while her child vanished before her eyes. What kind of mother did nothing but watch?

Leona found peace and freedom in concentrating on her work. It was important, not just to her, but to the community. When a Maasai member of parliament gave a speech in Narok, Leona pulled him aside afterward and told him of her work, of her idea to convince the government to allow grazing privileges, at least during droughts. He'd been trying to forward a similar idea and asked Leona to send him her research. This forced Leona to focus more fully on her observations of specifics; current grazing patterns versus the ones the elders had known, old ways of dealing with drought versus the new ones. Leona began to visit other manyattas in the area, gathering observations and stories from the largest sampling she could. Those trips away from her baby didn't upset either one of them. Nalangu was perfectly content with Simi and her wet nurse; Leona was perfectly content not being a mother.

When Nalangu was one, it came time for her to be given a real name—one that could be said aloud, a name that she would keep. Leona allowed Simi to choose that name, and when the girl's hair was washed with milk and water, and then shaved, Leona watched, notebook and pen in hand. The new name Simi selected was *Adia*, gift. Like all the kids in the manyatta, she was the child of everyone—free to eat and sleep with any of the mothers, and so Leona's connection to Adia remained the same as her connection to all the babies around her; affectionate but removed, seen through a telescope, detailed but remote.

Since Maasai fathers played only a tiny role in the lives of their children, Adia's lack of one was barely a detail worth considering. By the time Adia turned three, Leona didn't think much about the girl's father. She'd succeeded in keeping him away. Leona was relieved, frankly, to let it go.

It was easy for Leona to concentrate on her work with all the mothers available to her daughter. And, because of that, it was easy for the days to slip into months, and even years. Occasionally, Leona drove to Nairobi to meet with her government contact. She provided him with the information she'd gathered, and he began taking it to the halls of parliament. Leona liked her trips to Nairobi. She was beginning to crave a city again, the intellectual stimulation of others like her. And she was finally making a name for herself. Other local anthropologists sought her out; she was becoming known in her field. And she rarely thought of Adia. She knew her daughter was safe in the manyatta under the watchful eyes of Simi and the other women.

During one trip to Nairobi, she was introduced to the head of the anthropology department at the University of Nairobi. He'd requested a meeting, and after they talked awhile, he offered her a position on his staff. Leona was thrilled. Now that she had evidence to support her theory that imposed grazing borders were disproportionately damaging to Maasai communities, she could take that to the lecture halls. She could talk to students about the way their own society was changing, and maybe help inspire a new generation of people committed to the work of helping nomadic people.

Leona thought of her daughter and considered her choices. She could mother the girl alone in Nairobi without the benefit of the village women. She thought back to the nightmares she'd had early on and how casually her nightmare self watched as the baby vanished. What an unsuitable mother she was. It occurred to her that she could leave Adia in the manyatta and come to Nairobi by herself. The manyatta was Adia's home, after all, and she had Simi.

Leona harbored a smoky vision of Adia as a teenager, bent over books in a real high school. That vision, she understood, would require her involvement as a mother. But that was a distant problem. Adia was too young for school, and she'd be safe and happy in the manyatta, at least for a while. She was barely three—far too young for Leona to have to worry about educating her.

The thought niggled at her mind and made her heart beat fast in her chest. She told the department head she needed time to think, to tie up a few loose ends in her research, but she knew her decision was made. The whole drive back to Loita she imagined the way it would feel to teach, to make more contacts in the higher realms of Kenyan government. She could feel excitement in her blood. She could do this; she could use her work, her skills, to help the people she'd come to love so much she'd practically given them her firstborn child.

She stopped for gas a few hours' drive from the manyatta, and, on a whim, decided not to wait. Leona liked to be resolute after making a decision. While the attendant washed the windshield, Leona asked to use the phone. The connection was fuzzy and unclear, but the department head understood. She accepted the position. She'd move to Nairobi soon. The new semester was only a few weeks away, and as she drove the final miles to the place she'd called home for over four years, Leona listed the things she'd need in her new life: a place to live in the city, clothes to wear for teaching (her old, torn jeans and cotton blouses wouldn't do); a bank account; an office with a decent computer. These thoughts distracted her as she rolled to a stop outside the manyatta enclosure. She registered the presence of more people than usual milling around but didn't think about

why they might be there. Her mind was full of other thoughts.
In her *inkajijik*, Leona looked around. She'd probably leave most
everything here. Simi could use it, and Adia. Absently, Leona
reached for a small pile of mail someone—Simi probably—left
on her bed. The mail came from Nairobi via Narok, and then
to a shop that doubled as a post office nearer the manyatta.
Usually, when she received mail, the shopkeeper would send
his son to deliver it to her directly. This mail must have come
while she was away.

When Leona wrote to her parents, she selected her words
carefully. She didn't keep Adia a secret, but she didn't write
much about her, either. In the letters, she explained only that
the father was not present and that the baby—a girl—was happy
and safe. As Adia grew, the letters Leona received from her parents became insistent. They'd started a bank account for the girl;
they'd rewritten their will. Her father, in particular, couldn't
imagine life in the manyatta. He couldn't stomach the idea of
his only grandchild—a little girl, for that matter—growing up
in the dirt, as he said, without the civility of nearby doctors and
things like electricity and running water. Leona forced herself
to open all of the letters and to read them. But each time a fat,
white envelope—half covered with stamps—appeared in the
manyatta, she felt her breath quicken and saw sparks of light
behind her eyes. She felt she was sinking. She wondered why
she'd bothered to tell them about Adia in the first place.

When she read the letters they wrote to her, the pain of her
childhood came back like the feeling of a phantom limb, or the
flashes of her remembered nightmares. But something surprised
Leona, too. Underneath the anger she had for her parents, and
the resentment, she fought an unexpected jealousy. The idea
of her parents showing concern for Adia when they had never
shown much for her was a notion that cut her. She planned to
never let them meet her child. She planned to never go back to
the wet silence of those Oregon skies or to the dead feeling of

being alone in a house with only the ticking of clocks and the hum of the refrigerator to remind her she was alive.

"And who is the father?" this most recent letter asked. "You must know. If nothing else, a girl deserves a father." It was this that forced a crack in Leona's long-held conviction about keeping a distance from the white Kenyan. The cruel joke that her own father—simultaneously brutal and absent—should imply that his granddaughter needed something he'd never given Leona sent a shiver up into a hidden spot in her brain. She pushed the thought away and tried to bury it. She told herself that Simi and the village were all Adia needed, at least for now. And yet the thought grew in her mind.

Her father, her parents, made Leona what she was—silent and isolated. During the torturous moments when the worry couldn't be pushed away, Leona wondered if she was giving her own daughter the same relationship her parents had given her—disconnected and cool. She hated the idea of that, and the guilt it filled her with, but she didn't know how to be different. Knowing she'd fail was why she'd never wanted to be anyone's mother in the first place. She was torn. When she watched Adia with the Maasai children, laughing and playing games, never alone and never silent, she was happy. Adia always had Simi. Leona told herself that Adia's childhood was better than her own. Adia would grow up with age-mates and friends, and the constant activity and watchful eyes of the entire village. It helped Leona to realize that, if her daughter grew up here, she would be nothing like she herself was. Leona tried to convince herself that giving her child a community, a feeling of belonging somewhere, was far more important than giving Adia herself as a mother.

This most recent letter, the one Leona read now after accepting the position at the university, was no different from the others. Leona crumpled it into the tiniest ball she could, tossed it in the fire pit, and went to find Simi.

As she stepped through her doorway and into the light, she noticed again the number of people in the manyatta. There was the *laiboni*, the spiritual leader, surrounded by the young *moran*, warriors, in the central area between the small houses. Newly initiated warriors crowded the manyatta. Their faces and their long braids were slicked with a mixture of bright red dirt and sheep fat. It made Leona feel light-headed when she realized that in the faces of these brand-new men—most only thirteen or fourteen—she recognized the rounded faces of little boys she'd first met four years ago. Now they were men. She'd been here for so long. She hadn't considered how it would hurt to leave them all behind. To leave Simi. The thought made her feel dizzy, and she wandered over to sit with the elders in the shade of a scraggly acacia tree.

"What's happening?" she asked one wizened woman.

"*Emurata,*" the woman answered.

When Leona first came to the manyatta, she forced herself to watch everything, all the rituals and ceremonies. Her work was to observe, without emotion, the daily life and events that reflected the beliefs of the people she wrote about. Her least favorite ritual was the girls' coming-of-age rite, the *emurata*. She found it impossible not to wince at the cutting of the flesh, and she found herself unable to keep from feeling a harsh judgment against the entire idea. Her resolve to observe everything without critique was tested every time she was audience to an *emurata*. After watching three of them, she convinced herself she had all the information she needed about the practice and stopped going to the ceremonies at all.

The ceremony had started and the *moran* began to dance. They stood in a circle, impossibly tall and impossibly thin, backs as straight as the spears they held. When they began their singing, they chanted *uh-uh-uh-uuuu-huh* and the straight-bodied jumping made their braids slap against their backs and the iron of their spear tips glisten in the sun—Leona knew the circumcision was about to start. She stood up and walked past the dancing *moran*. She wanted to be outside the village, far enough away so that the wind in the acacia trees would fill her ears instead of the sound of the rites.

Vaguely, as she made her way through the crowd, she glanced around for Adia. It was rare that she was alone with the girl, but she wanted that now. It occurred to her she would miss the daily interaction—as unsubstantial as it was—with her daughter. A tingle of worry nibbled at her from somewhere deep and hidden. Her parents' letter, the guilt it made her feel, pressed into her mind. She wanted to hurry, but she was caught between the desire to leave and the unfamiliar feeling of maternal responsibility leaking through her. Where was Adia?

Leona could tell the instant the knife met flesh by the sound of the deep-throated cry of the girl that rose from the squat dung-and-wattle structure and hovered in the air. An image flashed into Leona's mind of Adia, sprawled and bleeding. It couldn't be her, Leona knew. At three, Adia was far too young, but the image of her daughter being cut, now or years from now, set Leona's heart pounding. Someday Adia would be thirteen. Someday, if Leona did leave her here, Adia would think of the cutting as normal, as necessary. This would be her world. Maybe her father was right. The idea of giving him credit for parenting advice made Leona sick, but she couldn't ignore it. This was her daughter, after all. And then some tiny, unwelcome shoot of a poison plant took root in her mind—a thought she didn't want to think. As much as she hated them, there was a part of Leona that desperately wanted her parents' approval. They were happy to have a grandchild. It was the first thing Leona had done to inspire their pride.

Leona's head throbbed, and she felt a trickle of sweat beading down her back. Her heart was beating too fast now, she wanted to sit down, to be able to breathe slowly and pull her thoughts back to where she could contain them, control them.

Then the girl screamed again. Of course she screamed. Of course she writhed against the knife. And Leona, alert and wild with panic, bounded across the dusty paddock.

The quick absence of light when she bent into the ceremonial *inkajijik* made her stop and rub her eyes, but when she opened them, through the haze of smoke, she saw her small blonde daughter sitting ramrod straight in a gaggle of little girl age-mates, watching intently as the bleeding almost-woman curled in pain under the glinting blade. Leona's eyes watered, the wood smoke thick in the air. Through the tears, she thought she could see blood in the dust, little bands of soft flesh left behind.

In one fluid movement, Leona leaned over the embers in the fire pit and pulled her daughter up and out into the light, hissing through the smoke that choked in her throat as she dragged Adia, "You can't watch this. This is not for you... Not for you. Not for us."

Through her panic, Leona didn't see Simi approach, concerned, and when Adia turned away from Leona to pull herself toward the other woman, who grasped the girl's other arm, Leona responded by pulling harder. Flickers of her life as a child popped in her mind. It wasn't all bad. There was the summer camp she loved, the elderly neighbor lady who bought all her Girl Scout cookies one year after Leona admitted to being too shy to go door-to-door, the ice-cream truck in the summer, the smell of the Christmas tree in December and the Thanksgiving dinners they shared with friends who always brought Leona little presents. Was she stealing that life from Adia?

"You are not Maasai," Leona hissed. She saw Simi then, and their gazes held, both women clutching the girl who stood, sobbing, in the dust between them.

"I adopted her," Simi said.

Leona remembered the ram, and the fat she had eaten and

the relief it brought her to know she wasn't solely responsible for the baby. Simi had helped her. Surely, though, she hadn't meant forever? Surely Simi knew that Leona didn't really have to obey the traditions of a culture that wasn't her own?

"You are her second mother," Leona said, watching Simi's face carefully—there was nothing but alarm in her eyes. Adia twisted, trying to release herself, but instead stumbled.

"I am her first," Leona continued. "She has a family in America." She thought of the letter, of her parents' concern that Adia be educated, be allowed to live like an American. Leona wished there wasn't a minuscule part of her that didn't agree with them. She hated that, on some level, she knew they were right.

Adia jerked backward and fell. Leona kept her grip, but Simi, in an instinctual moment, leaned forward to break Adia's fall. In that second, Leona pulled Adia out of Simi's reach.

"Simi, she can't be a Maasai. I can't let that cutting happen to her."

Then her own daughter's voice, thick and raw, hysterical, rose above the manyatta like the call of an exotic bird, out of place, far from home. Whether she was screaming from the pain of Leona's tight grip around her upper arm, from the humiliation of being dragged out of the ceremony or from fear of the sudden and uncontrolled presence of a mother she hardly knew, Leona didn't know. She didn't care. Leona pulled Adia up and held her up against her hip. She knew that she had to get Adia away from here quickly, while the conviction was strong. She stumbled as fast as she could to where her car was parked.

"This is not your real life, Adia," Leona said over and over again. "You are not Maasai. You are like me. You are like me."

Leona's car was dented and rusted to the point of being colorless. Now, she pulled the back door open, grateful it was unlocked—her shaking hands could never have managed a key—pushed Adia into the back seat and clicked the child's seat belt firmly. She didn't say goodbye to the people she'd lived

with for so long, she didn't let Adia say goodbye. She was frantic to leave, driven by the thought that if she didn't go now, her
own fear would force her to change her mind again and leave
Adia behind. Simi was screaming frantically on her knees in the
dust, other women gathering by her, and one began running
toward the car. Leona slammed the driver's-side door shut so
violently that the window slid down into the door frame, off its
track, rendering it useless. She managed to fit the key into the
ignition and start the car. She popped the brake and hit the gas
pedal. Adia screamed and screamed, crying out for Simi as the
car bumped wildly on the lumpy, dusty road. She banged on the
window with her small fist and kicked the back of Leona's seat.

Leona felt like a kidnapper.

It was getting dark when the lights of Narok emerged on the
horizon. Leona hated driving at night. There were too many
hazards—broken-down trucks in the road you couldn't see until
it was too late to avoid them, elephants wandering, antelope
shocked into stillness right in front of you by the flash of your
headlights. Leona knew of too many car accidents to take it
lightly, and when she reached the cluster of buildings that made
up the Narok town, she shuddered the Renault to a stop in front
of the Chabani Guest House. She hadn't been here since the
night of Adia's conception. She felt a flutter of nerves. What if
he was here? What would she say? But the lobby was empty,
and when the attendant showed Leona to the nicest room—one
of only three with an en suite bath and more than one light to
read by—the hall was empty, too.

That night, Leona avoided the bar. Instead, she walked a
teary-eyed Adia to a café down the street. Adia, over and over
again, asked for Simi, for her mother.

"I want to stay with my mother," she said once. "Not with
you."

Leona lied and told the girl they'd go back home soon. She
ordered Adia french fries, grilled meat and ice cream. The nov-

elty of the ice cream worked. This is a vacation, she told her daughter. Back in the hotel, Adia consented to a shower and laughed at the feeling of water pouring over her head and down her back. When she climbed into bed, wet hair slicked against her neck, looking as small and pale as a grub, she asked Leona what the sheets were for? The pillow?

Her own daughter had never slept on a mattress. The thought shouldn't have been a surprise, but it shocked her. Leona flicked off the light and lay in the dark. She remembered her own childhood home, her father distant and silent, with hard, hard hands. She remembered what it felt like when she was a child and a stranger in her own life. She thought of the man who gave her Adia, a gift that terrified her into numbness for so long. The girl lay in the bed beside her, so close Leona could feel the rise and fall of her breathing, the tiny lungs; the warm air she expelled.

When Leona finally fell asleep, she fell asleep with Adia's soft hair under her chin and her arm wrapped around Adia's shoulders. There wasn't a nightmare that night. Leona's sleep was calm. She dreamed about the sky, clear and calm and infinite. It was the kind of sky she remembered from one long ago summer when she was a child, and the darkness hadn't bloomed inside her, and the endless rain hadn't come.

When Leona woke up it was barely light. A centipede trailed along the polished floor and Leona watched it disappear and reappear through the shadows. She absently smoothed back Adia's hair with her palm. They were in Narok now. The white Kenyan came here, Leona knew. He lived nearby. If they waited long enough, asked the right people the right questions, they could find him. Leona was sure of that. She felt a twinge inside of her somewhere, a place so deep she'd almost forgotten, silent and still but, finally, shivering with potential. The sky was getting lighter outside the window and there were squares of light on the wall opposite the bed. Leona twisted her back so she was facing her baby. She traced her finger along the small nose that looked like hers, the ears that reminded Leona of her own mother's. Then she recognized the feeling that was so tiny and so deep down between her bones. Hope was a seed inside of her.

A WOMAN LIKE A WILDERNESS

Simi's earliest memory was one she wished she could forget. Mostly she pushed it to the back of her mind and kept it trapped there in the dark. Sometimes, though, mostly while she slept, it slipped out of its confines and floated, ghostly, into her consciousness.

The details were no longer clear. In her memory, the *inkajijik* was chilly. That didn't make sense, Simi knew, because her mother was a good Maasai woman who always kept burning embers in her fire pit. She would never allow the fire to burn out or let the air chill. There would have been fire. But still, in Simi's adult mind, the memory was cold. It was a typical evening, happy and calm. She and her mother and brother sat by the fire. Simi and her brother were telling their mother about their day at school. Their mother loved hearing about school and was proud that she was sending both her children, not just her son.

Simi's family was rich in cattle and children. Her mother was her father's fourth wife. This was a lucky thing for Simi because by the time she was born he'd grown accustomed to the demands children placed on his time and his money. Mostly her father kept away from the children, and he only visited Simi's mother's house when he needed something. He spent his time with other elders under the shade of an acacia tree. One of his wives made honey beer, and he enjoyed that and spent most nights in her hut. Sometimes he liked the honey beer so much his speech slurred and his walking became erratic. Before the night when everything changed, Simi thought her father was funny when he was drunk. Afterward, it made her hate him.

Simi's mother was quiet and thoughtful; she didn't spend much time with the other women. Instead, in her free time she sat alone and made intricate beaded jewelry. Her designs were delicate and unique. They were so beautiful that people from other manyattas, some two or three days' walk away, began to seek out her creations. Sometimes they would trade a goat for a piece, sometimes they would pull a faded wad of shillings from their wraps. Simi's mother allowed the animals to wander with the others. She made no secret of them. The money, though, she hid. She saved it in an old tobacco tin she kept hidden in the dark space under the bed. When Simi turned seven, her mother bought a used school uniform and sent Simi to school. Simi's father didn't notice, or didn't care, that Simi left the manyatta each morning, dressed in a uniform she carefully kept pristine by washing it each week in the river and hanging it to dry over a small, thornless bush.

As the years passed, her mother earned enough money to buy Simi a new uniform, and she provided Simi with a clean exercise book each year. In all her eight years of school, Simi never missed a day. She walked in rain and dust, and through the torrent of taunts and names the boys tossed her way as she went. In the early years, she walked with other girls, but one by one they all left. They were circumcised, married and sent to live in their husband's villages. Every time another girl left, Simi fought dread that she would be next. But her mother kept sending her. Every evening when it grew dark and all the people withdrew to their houses, Simi and her brother showed their mother letters; they taught her how words were written. They taught her addition and subtraction and times tables. Those years, in Simi's mind, were the happiest. But, in the way daylight follows a dark night, the dark follows daylight, too.

Simi couldn't remember the details anymore. When her father entered, her brother was in the middle of speaking. What story was her brother telling? Simi only remembered that he stopped, mid-word, when their father burst into the hut. This is where her memory skipped from a feeling of contentment to one of fear.

"Where is the money?" Her father's voice. Angry and urgent. "You have been stealing money." His voice stank of honey beer.

Simi's mother was a good wife. Simi knew that. She'd never seen her mother disagree with her father. But now, Simi's mother turned to him and said quietly, "I have not taken your money. I have given you many sheep and goats."

Simi remembered sliding closer to her mother. She remembered the warmth from her mother's skin, and how suddenly it disappeared when her father leaned down and pulled her mother up.

"You are a liar, wife!"

Simi watched as her father dragged her mother from the hut. She couldn't move. Her brother jumped up and disappeared through the door. There was scuffling outside. Simi heard her mother make a guttural sound and then she heard a thud. Suddenly her father was back, standing above Simi. His red eyes, foul breath and the angry quivering of his lips made him look inhuman, like a monster or a wild beast.

He leaned down slowly and, when his face was only inches from Simi's, he growled.

"You, child, find me my money."

Later Simi would cry and wonder why she did what she did. But at that moment, her monster father took all the thoughts from her head. It was just an empty cave.

"It is there," she whispered, pointing under the cowhide bed.

Her father pivoted, still leaning low, and stretched a long arm out into the space under the bed. His face instantly changed when his fingers felt the tin box. He smiled wide, stood up, tucked the box under his arm and was gone.

Simi crept out of the hut. She thought her mother might be there, but she wasn't. It was dark and she could hardly see the sleeping cattle. Not even the stars were shining. Simi kept the fire alive, and knowing her mother would want something warm to drink when she returned, she put a pot of water on the fire for tea. She added the sugar and milk and took it off the heat when it boiled. The tea grew cool, and the milk formed a skin on top, and still her mother didn't return. Finally, unable to keep her eyes open, Simi curled up on the bed and fell asleep. She woke again when her mother returned and climbed into the bed next to her. Simi listened to her mother breathing for a long time. She was ashamed of what she'd done.

The next morning, Simi woke up early. Her mother was stirring chai in the pot and ladled out a hot cup that she handed to Simi. Her face was calm.

Simi watched her mother's face carefully, desperate to know if she was angry with Simi or if, Simi hoped, she understood the choice Simi made. She found it impossible to refuse her father. Surely her mother understood.

"It was your school money, Simi."

Shame bubbled up in Simi's mouth. It was impossible to drink her tea.

"I wanted you to learn so when you married, you could be smarter than your husband. A husband can beat his wife, he can take what she has, but he can never take the things she knows."

Simi stood up. It was almost time to leave for school. She glanced at the hook where her uniform hung. It was empty.

"Your father wanted that, too. I gave it to him."

The loss was a blow to her chest. Simi fought to find air to breathe.

Her mother continued, "He has also told the *laiboni* that you are to be cut."

How fast everything changed then. Simi was fifteen. Many of her age-mates were already women—circumcised and married and gone from her manyatta. The last several years were dry; Simi's father's herds had thinned, and the land grew hard. The bushes and trees the women cut for firewood and building were less and less plentiful. They had to walk farther to get them and, without tree and grass roots to hold the soil together, when it did rain, it merely turned the land to mud. All the seeds and tiny grasses were gone. Money was harder to find and, therefore, food less plenty. Simi would bring a bride price of at least two cows and two goats and one less mouth to feed.

Her mother changed. In the evenings, she didn't ask Simi's brother about what he was learning in school. Simi didn't ask him, either. She tasted bitterness every time she thought of him writing in his exercise book and learning things while she cut wood and washed clothes in the trickle of water that used to be a river. Instead, each night they sat quietly, staring into the fire and sipping tea.

The night before Simi's *emurata*, though, her mother took her hand and said, "I was a weak wife." Then she reached up and unlatched her favorite necklace from her own neck. It was a stunning piece, wide and flat and shimmering with beads in all shades of blue and green. Simi remembered watching her mother make it, painstakingly selecting the perfect bead to sew on next. It was the only piece she'd refused to sell. Simi felt her mother's rough hands slide the necklace around Simi's neck and fix the clasp shut.

"You are my daughter," her mother told her. "And now you are a woman and soon a wife. Your life will be like mine, but maybe not your children's. Maybe they will have a wider sky."

Simi looked at her feet. She knew her mother was still bitterly disappointed in her, in the way she'd ruined the dream her mother had had—to send Simi to school and delay marriage. This was a gesture that her mother had forgiven her, maybe, but had not forgotten.

Simi was resigned to marriage. Even with her schooling, it was inconceivable that she wouldn't follow the path of all the other women before her. She was lucky that the man who chose her was the son of the village elder, the one whose opinion mattered and to whom others paid respect. Her husband was a pleasant man and had an easy rapport with all his wives and his children. Simi was the third wife.

Simi was married for one year before her husband began asking if she was unlucky. He asked with pity in his eyes—a childless woman is a sign of chaos; disorder in the way the world always works. After all, of what importance is a woman without a child? A woman is to provide children; if she cannot give babies, what can she give?

There were things to be done in this situation. The weeklong silent praying to N'gai, the eating of lambs, the visit to the *oreteti* tree in the forest, the slaughtering of the ox, the dousing with milk and the eating of fat. For two years Simi consulted with the village doctor. Four times, she hoped. And four times the babies, unformed, left her. The other women, especially the other wives, looked at her through eyes tinged with suspicion. An unlucky woman could veil the whole village with her curse. And what was unluckier than a woman who couldn't bear children? God only made perfect things; imperfections were doled out in life only to the people who deserved them. A childless wife was an imperfection of the highest degree— a stunning slight from God. Some husbands cast out their infertile wives to save themselves from the stain of bad luck she might bring to the family. Some villages refused to allow unlucky women to stay.

Simi's husband didn't tell her the American was coming. She found out through his first wife, Isina, when the women all gathered at the river to wash their clothes.

"Why is the *muzungu* coming here?" someone asked. "To steal our men?" The women laughed.

"How will she live here when she cannot speak to us?" someone else asked.

Nalami, Isina's daughter, turned to Simi. Her hands were soapy with lye, and her palms red and chapped. She paused and then said slowly, "Simi, you will be the only one who will be able to talk to her." The other women nodded and murmured.

"Ooh, Simi." Loiyan cackled. She was the second wife, and although she often kept the women laughing with her jokes and her brassy interactions with the men, she had a meanness that could flare up with little warning. In the beginning, Simi was frightened of Loiyan, but she wasn't anymore. Still, she didn't like Loiyan—she thought of her as she did a snake, more dangerous because the strike was often unexpected.

"Ooh, Simi." Loiyan stood tall and tipped her head back. "You will be too important. You will be an American yourself." Loiyan pranced in place, pretending to be a white woman.

"You don't look like an American," Simi said, "you look like a sick hippo." All the women laughed, and Loiyan sucked her teeth and hunkered down again to rinse her pile of clothes in the slow-moving river.

Simi was excited by the news of the *muzungu*. When her husband came to her the next night, Simi handed him a cup of chai and asked him why the American was coming.

"She wants to study us, the way we do things."

Simi was surprised. She couldn't imagine why anyone would be curious about the lives they led in the manyatta. She couldn't imagine why an American would come all the way here just to watch them.

She had seen white people before, but never up close. Usually she saw them behind the glass of a vehicle window, through a film of dust billowing from under the slow-rolling tires as she stood by the side of the road. Often, the white faces on the other side of the glass stared at her, too, with eyes as wide and curious as hers. Sometimes, if the windows were open, the white people would lift their hands and call "Hello!" It always thrilled Simi when this happened. English was her best subject at school, and hearing words she'd practiced over and over again coming from the mouths of strangers was exciting. She loved the way learning a different language had made her feel free—like she had a key to a new life. When she waved and called "Hello" into the van's dusty wake, she felt important. English was her connection to the world outside, and now, though her school days were long past, she was proud of her knowledge. Her mother was right; nobody could take away the things she knew.

In the early days, the American hardly spoke. She wandered like a ghost through the dust in the manyatta and started at the movements of the cattle. Simi watched her closely. She felt too shy to talk to the white woman at first, but she also worried that if the American stayed frightened and out of place, she would leave. Simi desperately wanted her to stay. She watched how the other Maasai women crowded into the American's little house—one they'd constructed for her the day she arrived— and just sat there, watching the strange woman and gossiping among themselves. Finally Simi slipped in with them one afternoon and watched the white woman trying to light a fire in her fire pit. There were no embers there, and Simi quickly got up and fetched a bright coal from her own house and brought it back. She sifted it into the American's fire pit, added a few twigs and dry grasses and blew it all into a flame.

"You must keep some fire alive all the time," she said quietly. "We let it burn, just a little, even at night. We must always have our own fire, miss."

The white woman smiled. "You speak English! Thank God!

I've been needing you!" Simi felt herself flush, and she knew the other women were watching. She thought she heard Loiyan sucking her teeth.

"Please," the American said, "tell me your name. Mine is Leona."

From that moment, Leona was always near Simi. "Help me, Simi," Leona would say, and the questions that followed were endless and wide-ranging—from how many handfuls of tea to toss into boiling water for chai, to how a man selects a wife. Simi grew bolder in her English, and lost her shyness with Leona. She scolded Leona the time Leona forgot to dip her head when greeting an elder, and warned her never to walk far from the manyatta in the evenings, when the shadows grew long and the hyenas and leopards stirred from their dens. With Leona next to her at the river, washing their clothes together, Simi found Loiyan left her alone. It wasn't enjoyable to tease Simi anymore when Simi had a friend to speak to in a language Loiyan couldn't understand.

Simi came to understand that Leona's life back in America was completely different from the life they all lived here. Leona showed them photos of enormously tall buildings, expanses of grass so green it almost hurt their eyes to see it.

"Where are the cattle?" Simi asked when she saw the grass. "They must be too fat to walk!"

The images were breathtaking—it was hard to imagine they were real. Leona explained to Simi that not only did America look vastly different from Loita, but that life there—everything from clothing to speech to thoughts themselves—were unlike those here. Simi knew that some of the other women, ones who had never gone to school and seen a photo in a book, didn't understand how to grasp the images and ideas Leona introduced them to; their minds were so firmly here that they could not see things differently. Simi could, though. She'd read stories about people different from herself and knew that the Maasai

way wasn't the only way people lived. The images in the pictures and the stories Leona told were like dreams. They flickered in her mind and flashed against the reality she saw around
her constantly, two worlds—one inside herself, and one outside, like hot flames that burned blue and orange and red all at
the same time.

In the evenings, Leona would come to Simi's house. Her Maa
was improving. Often, they practiced together. Leona would
look through her notebooks and ask Simi questions about things
she'd seen that day, and note ages and names of the people in
the village. In return, Leona would teach Simi American slang.
Simi loved the feel in her mouth that the new words gave her,
and took to peppering her Maa with "That's cool!" and "For
real?" Other nights they'd drink tea and just stare into the fire
quietly. One night, after Leona had been in the manyatta for
several weeks, she sat on a low stool next to Simi. Simi threaded
beads onto a strip of leather for a bracelet. It was dark outside,
and chilly. "You don't have children," Leona stated.

Simi was relaxed in Leona's presence but this statement—
vocalized so clearly and directly—shocked her. It was unexpected, too bold for Simi's comfort. She started and spilled
some tea in her lap. It was hot and it stung. Her eyes welled,
and she glanced across the bright embers of the fire and saw
Leona watching her. There was no malice in Leona's face. Part
of Simi wanted to bury the subject forever, but another part
was desperate to talk about the pain, release it to someone else
in a way she couldn't with the other women. Leona's face was
clear, her eyes blank.

"How long have you been married?" Simi heard Leona's
question and shifted uncomfortably.

"Three years," Simi answered.

"It's a problem to be a wife without a child?" Leona was
speaking as if she had her notebook and pen with her, but Simi
saw she had neither.

Simi answered in English. To say the words in her language made them hurt more coming out. "We say that a woman who hasn't given birth is like a wilderness. A woman or a man with children to remember them can never die. But a person like me? When I am gone, nobody will remember."

"In America people can choose to have a baby or not," Leona said. "But even so, there are people who want to but can't. This is something that happens everywhere, Simi. Have you seen a doctor?"

Simi didn't answer. She was tingling with discomfort now. There was no way to explain it all to Leona. Her pain was not something for an American notebook, something to be inscribed with a pen on paper. Simi's bitter frustration about not having a child, and her fear of the repercussions, were not something she would ever let see the light of day. She tried to keep herself from even thinking of them. How could sharing the story in words even scratch the surface of Simi's disappointment and terror at the way her own body betrayed her? She was grateful when, after a long silence, Leona smiled and said she was tired, and then stood up to leave.

With Leona in the manyatta, Simi's daily life changed. Her ability to communicate was a link between the American and the others. She had a certain power she'd never felt before. Even the men saw it. They approached Simi carefully with their questions about Leona, and the conversations Leona had with the villagers all happened with Simi hunkered close by, interpreting for both parties, not just the words themselves, but the ideas and feelings behind them. For the first time since Simi understood the fact of her infertility, she felt her fear loosen. Leona was her anchor. Even with her bad luck, they couldn't send her away while they needed her so much. They were grateful for Simi's education now. There were educated men in the village who spoke English, but because Simi was a woman, she had easier access to Leona. A man couldn't spend so much time with a woman who wasn't his wife without eyebrows being raised.

Leona joined the women daily at the river, and the women taught her to bang her clothes against the rocks and rub the bar of White Star soap until it frothed. It made the hours of banging and rubbing and rinsing clothes go faster when Leona was there. Simi was sorry, in some deep way, that she wasn't the only woman who could have a companionship with Leona. Leona was beginning to make friends with many of the other women, but she was grateful that Leona seemed happy here, content. She wanted Leona to stay for a long time.

"Simi," Leona whispered one day when they were resting their soapy hands. "I think Loiyan is pregnant."

It was something Simi knew already, but she glanced up at Loiyan, anyway. The folds of the other woman's wraps strained a bit under the swell of her belly. Simi swallowed a hot ember of jealousy. Loiyan already had three children. Two of them boys.

"Isn't it true that a childless wife can adopt a baby of another woman?" Leona was whispering her words, but also speaking in English, not Maa. The conversation, Simi understood, was one Leona wanted to keep secret.

"Yes," Simi answered simply. The possibility had crossed her mind a thousand times. To be regarded a mother didn't absolutely have to mean bearing your own child. "It happens often." Leona opened her mouth to speak again, but Simi already understood the subtext of Leona's question, and answered it before Leona could clarify.

"Unless the reason for the adoption is that the mother died, the women have to be as close as sisters."

Later the thoughts of adoption—and the seeming impossibility of it—crowded Simi's mind like the scuffling cattle in the paddock—pushing against each other and refusing to let her sleep. Her husband was rich with children. Loiyan's three and seven from his first wife, Isina. Now another baby was coming, and still, she herself had nothing.

A few months after Leona arrived, Simi found her squatting next to the *laiboni*, struggling to make conversation. Simi offered to translate, and when she heard the questions Leona asked, she felt herself shaking. Her skin went cold, and her vision blurred. She recognized a feeling of deeply embedded anger, but there was something else, as well—a sense of betrayal. N'gai had betrayed her, and now Leona had, too, by so easily achieving, and not even wanting, the one thing Simi desperately desired.

That evening Simi left the enclosure. She walked until she couldn't see the acacia tree fencing, and she couldn't hear the sounds of people. It was near dusk, and this was dangerous. Simi didn't want to be seen, though. She needed time alone, and she didn't want to talk. She stood at a place where the land dipped down toward a stream, now dry, but where shrubs and grasses were thicker. She saw a family of zebra, munching calmly, and she felt safer—they didn't sense a predator nearby. Near where she stood, she saw a young green shrub, the one they used to treat stomachaches. They always needed this plant, so she began plucking leaves, tying them up in the end of her *kanga* as she did. It was later, when she returned home to heat up tea, that she had her idea. Leona hadn't learned to tell one plant from another, so Simi tossed a handful in a crumpled plastic bag and made her way to Leona's house. These leaves would do nothing, Simi knew. And as she handed them to Leona, she imagined the baby clinging tightly to the dark insides of Leona's body. Simi's own muscles clenched at the idea of that fullness. If only. If only.

It was early one morning—before dawn, even the cattle and goats were still asleep—when Leona's cry broke the dark sky into two. Simi heard it. It woke her from her dream and sent a rushing shiver down her spine. It was time. She wrapped her *kanga* around her shoulders to stave off the cool air and crossed the enclosure to Leona's house. The midwife was already there, and some other women, too. Everyone loved to participate in a birth. There was Loiyan with her own new infant—another boy—snuggled fast asleep in a wrap tied tightly against his mother's back.

Leona was lucky. The birth was an easy one, and the midwife had no trouble releasing the baby from Leona's body and into the world. The cord was cut and the new baby—a tiny, pale girl—was placed in Leona's arms.

There were women who didn't take to their babies. Simi had seen it happen before, but never with someone who didn't also have the wild-eyed look of the cursed. Leona's reaction frightened Simi. After the baby was placed in Leona's arms, Leona made a wailing like an animal. Her mouth opened, and her eyes closed, and the cry was from a deep place Simi never suspected Leona had inside of her.

Leona tried to nurse the infant, but within days she pushed the baby away and wrapped a *kanga* tightly around her breasts to stop the milk from coming. It wasn't uncommon for mothers to be unable to nurse—it happened on occasion, and another nursing mother could always step in and help. But Leona could nurse. The few times she tried, her milk came strong and plentiful. Simi could see that the baby was able to drink her fill and that Leona's breasts were swollen and ripe. Simi never heard of a woman who could nurse but wouldn't. There was a sharp feeling in Simi's belly when she saw the way Leona treated the baby.

Simi told herself she was helping Leona when she began caring for the baby herself, and when she arranged for a wet nurse. The wet nurse had five other children, one only a few days older than Nalangu, so she didn't mind when Simi handed her the pink baby for feedings. A few weeks later, when Leona's interest in her baby hadn't increased, Simi asked her husband for a ram to make the adoption official. His wife's adopting Leona's baby was a good thing, and although he found Nalangu's color unappealing, he was happy to provide the animal. All his wives should have children, and this would bring luck to Simi and the community. Even if the child was the color of a bald baby aardvark. Simi divided the ram's fat into two portions. Leona was still gray and quiet, and Simi told Leona the fat would make her body strong again after the depletion of pregnancy. After all, that was the truth. Leona never asked why Simi bundled off the other portion of fat. Simi told herself that Leona must know the procedure for adopting. She'd been here for so long now, taking notes on everything. Surely they'd talked about this.

Simi loved being a mother. Her place in the village was cemented. Loiyan didn't tease her anymore, and her husband no longer looked worried when he came to her at night. Simi was part of things now—safely protected from the wilderness of a life without a child.

Simi didn't choose Nalangu's name, but it sounded like the hand of fate reaching out to give Simi what she'd wanted for so long. Until now, she'd felt like a member of a different tribe herself. Now she and this new person were together, they had each other and that would allow them both to be included. Simi knew Leona watched Simi and the baby together with a sense of relief. Leona's skin grew pink again, and the hollowness in her eyes filled out. She seemed happy. By the time Nalangu turned one, and it was time to give her a proper name, Simi didn't ask Leona what she thought. The mother could decide this one, and Simi chose Adia, "gift," because that was what this child was.

Later, Simi wondered why the clouds came that particular day, and what it was she'd done to deserve renewed punishment. She was a good person, a good mother to Adia. She took all the necessary steps to ensure that N'gai—God—was satisfied with her. Leona had been going to other manyattas often lately. She also traveled to Nairobi. Simi could sense that her friend's attachment to the village was waning. Simi was ashamed that the notion of Leona leaving brought her relief. There were times she wondered if her baby would feel more like hers if Leona were gone. The link they had—Leona and Adia—simply through the color of their skin, was too obvious. People outside the village, people who didn't know, assumed the wrong connection. When Leona was gone, it would be easier.

It was a day like any other, hot and clear and dusty. They needed rain, but they always needed rain. It was a special day, too. The *emurata* was a glad day for the village, and the *moran* were gathering. There was no way Simi could have known that Leona's mothering urge, so long dead, would choose this day to rear its head and strike.

It was past noon, and the sun was flat and hot and stared down at the village with its burning face when suddenly Simi heard Adia's scream. She recognized her girl's voice like her own and, with her heart pounding in her chest, she leaped up from where she'd been sitting with some other women and raced across the village. She expected to see a snake or a leopard or some terrible creature hurting her daughter. Instead, she saw Leona dragging her baby—*her* baby—from the *emurata* hut. Leona's face, usually blank, was a riot of clouds like the darkest of rainy seasons. Her eyes were glassy—those of a cursed woman—and they lit upon Adia like flames. Leona's English was fast and rough and too angry for Simi to grasp completely, but her intention was clear. She was taking Adia away.

Instinctively, like any mother would, Simi reached out to pull her daughter back from the abyss. Adia shouted her name, "Yeyo! Mother!" She clutched at Simi's hand.

Adia screamed, *"Tung'wayeni!"* at Leona, "Don't touch me!"

And the girl tried to wrest her arm from Leona's grip. Simi saw the terror in her daughter's eyes and tried to make Leona look at her—she tried to get the American to calm down, to speak in a way Simi could understand.

But when she did, her words echoed Simi's darkest fear. "Adia, you are my daughter!" Leona said in a cold and measured voice—finally speaking so that Simi could take it in.

"You are mine. You are mine."

Adia stumbled, and Simi's muscles fell slack with shock, and her grip released from Adia's arm. Then the girl was gone. Simi fell to the ground. The other women gathered around her, but she couldn't answer their questions.

Simi watched her daughter's anguished face through a screen of dust and then through the smudged window of Leona's car as it pulled away. As the car grew smaller and smaller, Simi gathered her energy and drew herself up from the ground. She chased after the car, kicking up dust and cutting her feet on the sharp stones. She followed Leona's car until she couldn't anymore, and then she fell to earth like a rock. She looked up once to see the tiny car far in the distance, and then, like all the white people she'd seen before, they disappeared.

When the dust died away and the earth beneath her grew cold, Simi lifted her head. The evening was coming, and she could hear the sounds of the village far behind her. The *emurata* was finished, and the children were bringing the goats and cattle back from their grazing. Something—she couldn't name the motivation, because every cell inside her wanted to die— forced her to stand and shuffle back through the enclosure and into her house. It was dangerous to be outside the manyatta at night. She could be attacked by a leopard, a lion, and eaten. It was the smallest part of her that pushed her to avoid that by retreating to her home. She bent to enter and fell into her bed. The fire needed tending, but she couldn't make herself care. Simi's longing for her daughter came in painful waves that made her feel as if her body was burning on the inside. How could this be real? She was desperate to relive that last moment when she held Adia's arm and watched as the terrified girl was pulled from her grasp. How could she have let it happen? How could a mother let her child—her only child—be taken? God was right not to bless her body with her own children—she was not fit to be a mother.

Over the next few days, Simi was broken. She could only lie in her bed. The other women—even Loiyan—came into her hut to see how she was. They kept watch, boiled chai in the *suferia*, and tried, constantly, to make Simi open her mouth to drink, to swallow, to take the small sustenance that the sugar and tea and milk might give her. The women whispered to each other as they watched her. Simi didn't speak. She couldn't open her mouth, not to answer the women and not to drink the tea; she could hardly open her eyes.

She remembered the time after Adia's birth, and how Leona had sunk into herself, barely speaking, barely eating. A thought crossed her mind that this was Adia's mark—that her mothers were destined to share a kind of darkness. And then she remembered that Adia had been pulled away from her; she was nobody's mother—not anymore. It was that thought that made her stomach heave, and she leaned over and retched. Because she hadn't eaten for days, it was nothing but bitter, sticky foam she coughed out. She watched as it disappeared, slowly absorbed into the dirt of the floor. The women in her hut tsked and sucked their teeth.

Late that night, Simi woke up. Her hut was empty. The other women had gone home. That was a relief. Her stomach growled. Her mouth still didn't want food, but her belly called for it. She stretched her weak legs and slid off the bed. Even though she'd barely sipped water in the last few days, she had a desperate need to urinate. The cattle in the manyatta enclosure lowed softly and shook their great heads as Simi slipped past them. There were fewer than there used to be, Simi noted. The drought was bad again. It seemed the pattern was changing—a year of good rains and hope, followed by several years of dry land and dry skies, starving animals and hungry people.

It struck Simi just then that nothing was certain. Not ever. Not even the continuation of the life she'd always lived. More and more Maasai men were abandoning cattle herding and moving to Nairobi to seek work. There were manyattas where no men lived at all, only women and children, all the husbands and sons having left for new opportunities. Everything was changing.

Simi squatted down and felt the relief of emptying her bladder. It felt good to be outside, to breathe the cool night air and look up at the stars. It was a clear night, not one cloud to tease her with the possibility of rain, but none to obscure the universe above her, either. The moon was new. It was a curved edge, as sharp and clean as a scythe. The Maasai myth said that the sun and the moon were married. Olapa, the moon, was short-tempered and, during a fight one day, she wounded her husband. To cover his wound, he began shining more brightly than anything else. To punish his wife, he struck out one of her eyes. Now, Simi thought, as she slowly stood up, her body weak from lack of food, the sun was punishing all of them by shining too hard, never allowing rain clouds to form.

The moon, the wounded wife, was lucky, Simi thought. She'd only had an eye taken. Simi remembered her mother always said nobody could take an education from her. That was true, but her mother never told her that everything else could be taken; a body part, grazing grasses for the cattle, a way of life and a daughter.

WATER IN A DRY PLACE

Nairobi lay in the highlands, but Narok was on the floor of the Rift Valley, and when Jane's plane cruised over the valley's edge and the land fell away in a great crack, she stared out the window and searched for her first glimpse of the elephants. Kenya was red. The terrain was rusty and volcanic—the dust made from layers and layers of ancient lava, dried to a crust and ground down by time. The earth looked like gaunt stretches of skin seen through a magnifying glass—gray-brown and pocked, with the scabby outcroppings of rock and the dried blood of the barely damp riverbeds.

Kenya was new to Jane. Africa was new. Her flight from Washington had come in for its bumpy landing at Jomo Kenyatta airport in Nairobi less than twenty-four hours ago, and now she was about to touch down in her new home. Her eyes were raw with fatigue, and her skin felt dry and grimy. She pressed her face to the tiny plane window and tried not to blink. She didn't want to miss any of this first introduction to her new home. She didn't know what she was supposed to see. She'd been told that the drought was severe, that all of eastern Africa was drying out, dying. The rivers were low and water was precious.

Jane traced her interest in elephants back to a day at the National Zoo. She was six, and her brother, Lance, was four months old. Her mother had Lance strapped in a front pack, snuggled against her chest. This made her walk slowly under the weight of the baby. Jane wanted to hurry, to run from one animal to another, taking everything in at once. She knew if Lance weren't there, they would have been able to walk faster, and it made her angry with the baby. Her mother led Jane over the zoo's winding pathways, and when they reached the elephant enclosure, she let Jane step up onto the lowest rung of the metal fence. The elephants had just been fed, and they rooted through the bales of hay and grasses with their trunks. They waved their enormous ears gently, like the tails of the tropical fish her father kept in the tank in his study. Jane heard her mother sigh with pleasure. The gentle motion of the animal's trunks up and down between hay and tiny mouth, and the rolling motion of their jaws, gave them a delicacy that made Jane laugh and clap her hands. Jane's mother wrapped her arm around Jane's shoulders, and her breath was warm and sweet in Jane's ear. Jane could feel her mother's joy at the sight of them.

"Aren't they lovely?" she asked. "They're very maternal creatures. I read that somewhere." She leaned down and kissed the top of Jane's head. "Very maternal, just like I am."

Jane's mother was sick for a long time before she died. Jane was ten when the diagnosis came, Lance was four. At first nothing changed. There were doctor's appointments and days when her mother was too tired to cook dinner so her father brought home McDonald's instead. But mostly it was the same as it always had been, and Jane began to believe it would always be this way. On the tired days, Jane would come home after school and curl up on the couch next to her mother and do homework. Lance would lie on the carpet watching TV and eating

Cheerios one by one from a plastic bowl. But by the time Jane was twelve, there were more and more tired days. She turned thinner than any grown-up Jane had ever seen, and she was always cold. She began coughing and spitting up blood into a bright green bandanna she kept shoved up the sleeve of the nubby brown sweater she always wore. The sounds of the wet coughs scared Jane, and she found herself avoiding her mother; instead of sitting next to her on the couch, Jane spent the hours between school and dinner in her bedroom. Once she heard her mother calling her in that thin, weak, dying voice. When Jane came down the stairs, her mother was standing at the bottom of the flight, clutching the newel post to steady herself.

"I understand it's hard to watch me, Jane," her mother said. "And I know you love me and if you need this time alone, take it. But we have to talk about Lance. You're his sister. That gives you some responsibility." Jane didn't hear what her mother said next, because she'd already turned and raced back up the steps. She slammed her door as loudly as she could, and after that, she always pretended she couldn't hear when her mother called.

There was an open casket at the funeral. Jane's father left Lance with a babysitter and wanted to leave Jane home, too, but she begged and cried and finally he relented. Her mother's body was ravaged by disease, but someone had put foundation on her face, blush on her cheeks. Jane thought she looked beautiful, and that she would like the blush and the rosy color of the lipstick they'd put on her. But it struck Jane that just under the powders and the creams her mother's face was gone. That is, it was intact and Jane could see it all—eyes, lips and the familiar way her mother's ears curved and the diamond studs in her lobes that she wore every day. But they didn't add up to her anymore. Her mother was an empty shell—like the ones cicadas left behind in late summer, only this one resembled the person Jane loved most in the world. The unfairness of that moment, the trickery, made Jane burst into sobs so loud and incessant her grandmother had to lead her away.

The house was quiet after her mother died. Jane hated it. She missed the singular sounds of her mother's movement, the way she slowly climbed the stairs and shuffled along the hallways in her slippers. Jane even missed the ugly sounds of the coughing. Most of all, though, she missed how it felt before she hated herself. She replayed all those recent afternoons when she'd avoided the sounds her mother's sickness made, and instead closed her bedroom door. She would do anything to have those afternoons back. She didn't bother with homework, but she did take up her old place on the couch—napping there after school and then, again, after dinner. Sleep was the only way she could turn off her mind.

Her father must have noticed that Jane didn't do anything except sleep, and one evening, a few months after the funeral, he looked at her across the dinner table and he said, "Life goes on. She'd want us to be happy." As far as Jane could remember, that was the last they'd spoken of the grief they all stumbled through alone.

Lance grew silent. Far quieter than a boy his age should be. He spent hours draped in an armchair in the family room, watching TV. He barely spoke to Jane.

Her father started smoking and spent evenings in his study, watching his fish and blowing rings of smoke up toward the ceiling. "You shouldn't be near all this smoke," he'd say when Jane was lonely after dinner and wanted to be near him. "I'll come and find you later, tuck you in. We can talk then." But he rarely remembered, and Jane eventually stopped trying. She felt like a shadow, visible, but of no substance, and it frightened her. It felt like fading away. Some days she thought she might just disappear.

Two years later her father was married again, and the only thing Jane had left of her mother was a pile of photos and some ugly antique furniture that traced the maternal line back for generations. Her father's new wife was kind to Jane and Lance, but she hated to "wallow," as she said, in the memories of their life before, of Jane's father's other wife.

When her father remarried, Jane and Lance lost their mother all over again, in Jane's mind; by picking a new wife, he erased her mother further. The new wife moved into their house, opened the windows, banished the fish tank and aired out the smoky study in favor of a guest room and a small, barking dog. Soon, all the photos that included Jane's mother were gone, piled into boxes in the attic with her books and the antique furniture Jane would inherit when she grew up and had a house of her own.

It was true that her father was happier, and his new wife was kind and funny and cooked dinners every night so they could sit around the table "like a family should." Lance watched TV less, and smiled more, and all of this made Jane grateful. But she couldn't push past the notion that this woman was an intruder in their house, in their lives, and that this new family they had formed was just a weak facsimile of what it should have been.

Jane was in graduate school before Lance began showing signs of his own sickness. Her master's program in conservation biology was difficult. Jane struggled with math—the tricks of statistics and probability eluded her. She had to work hard, and this gave her a ready excuse to ignore her father's calls, to listen to, but not return, his messages saying that Lance was seeing things that weren't there and talking to empty corners. One message sounded as if her father were about to cry—a depth of emotion Jane hadn't even seen from him after her mom died. That was the message saying that Lance was sent home from college because of a violent outburst and was under psychiatric care.

She'd never mentioned the conversation her mother tried to have about Lance, the one where Jane was supposed to agree to be a good big sister. And now she never would—being a responsible sister to a normal little boy was one thing, but Lance was an adult man now, with psychological issues. The calls and the urgency in her father's voice made Jane increasingly desperate to flee.

Within days of arguing her thesis, Jane applied to the Elephant Foundation. Her adviser knew the foundation's director, and Jane was hired. She went home for the first time in months to tell her dad. Lance was at home at the time, but Jane remembered the message her father left her, telling her they might have to put Lance in a home, right before her thesis was due, and how she'd listened to it once and then deleted it. Now she saw that her father's face was pinched. He looked older than he should. At dinner one night, when his new wife was in the kitchen, filling plates with dessert, Jane told him she was leaving, soon, for Kenya.

"Wow," he said, nodding. "That's far away...but you'll be happy."

His blasé attitude made Jane illogically angry. It was her choice to leave, to go as far away from home as she could. She was the one leaving him, leaving Lance and the new wife. He should be angry, or sad. But he didn't seem to care, and he didn't beg her to stay. She'd always be just a small, annoying shadow in his smoky study, or a child with grief so big it made his new wife uncomfortable. Jane wasn't surprised by his reaction, but the vicious rush of anger and the grief she tasted on her tongue stunned her. She'd almost forgotten it was there, secret tinder she kept hidden away.

"Before one, two years ago...this was green," Muthega, the Kikuyu guide hired by the Elephant Foundation, told her when he parked the Land Rover and fumbled for the keys to her new front door. He'd waited on the airstrip of the tiny Narok airport for her plane to land, and he was standing there, in a khaki shirt with the foundation's logo emblazoned on the chest pocket holding a handwritten sign with her name on it, when she'd

disembarked. It made Jane laugh; there was only one other passenger on the little plane.

"Are you sure you're here for me?" Jane had joked, but Muthega just nodded solemnly and hoisted her suitcase onto his shoulder.

Jane's house in Narok was a two-room building, low and
squat and slapped together with rough, gray concrete. Just to the
south were the dusty streets and the warren of other flat-topped
concrete buildings of Narok, but north was nothing but dry
grassy savannah edging the Maasai Mara game reserve, and the
distant line of trees that clung to the bank of the Mara River.
The yard space around the house was bare dirt, with a little dry
scrub grass and one lone pink bougainvillea that climbed the
wall next to the front door and grasped the earth below it in a
constant struggle for water.

Now Jane looked around the dry patch of land that was her
new yard. The high concrete wall surrounding her plot of land
distracted her. It was at least six feet tall, and the top edge glinted
with shards of broken bottles.

"For thieves," Muthega said, following her eyes with his own.
"It can be dangerous for you here."

Jane thought of the dingy little town they'd driven through
to reach this house. It seemed quiet and charming, in a dusty
way, not particularly dangerous. Anyway, she'd keep the gate
locked, she told herself, and better to be safe than sorry. She
didn't dwell on the thought; she was desperate to get out into
the bush.

Muthega's job was to drive her to where the elephants were.
He did his best to track their movements. Elephants are creatures of habit and in the dry season their daily range is somewhat limited. Once Jane tracked them long enough, she could
calculate the specifics of different groups. And once she and
Muthega had figured that out, they'd situate bush cameras in
the areas the various elephant groups were likely to congregate.

Timing was critical; once the wet season came, the elephant groups would migrate much farther afield and be nearly impossible to track. Muthega smoked cigarettes that smelled like burning rubber, but Jane was glad to have him around because he had watched the elephants in this area for years, and because he wore a rifle slung over his shoulder. It was for people, not game, he told Jane. It was the people who made her uneasy; it was people who she was here to combat. The presence of Muthega's gun was comforting.

The foundation's war on poaching was waged in three ways: the collection of DNA samples from elephant dung, which would help other researchers pinpoint sources of illegal ivory; the logging of traps, poacher sightings and slaughtered elephants on a GPS; and the placing of elephant cams in areas most heavily used by the animals. The foundation hadn't tried the cameras here before, but there had been a successful pilot program in Sumatra, where faces of three poachers were caught so clearly on the cameras that within days of posting Wanted posters promising financial rewards, they'd all been jailed. Jane brought ten remotely operated cameras with her from the foundation headquarters in Washington. She was responsible for safeguarding the expensive equipment, and because the elephant cameras would bring a high price if stolen and sold, Muthega's gun was necessary.

Jane and Muthega followed the elephants by tracking their footprints in the dust. Often they saw them at the edge of the Mara River, where the water was low and groggy and ran thickly, more solid than liquid. The edges of the river were gray with silt, and the elephants had to lumber farther and farther from shore to find spots deep enough to settle into and drink from during the hottest hours of the afternoon. This left them exposed for Jane to count and study, but exposed, also, to the poachers.

Smaller streams and tributaries, and the springs far from the river, had dried up to nothing more than trickles. The last good rainy season was two years ago, and now crowds of eland, gazelles, zebras and giraffes migrated off their habitual feeding grounds, away from their usual watering holes. The river teemed with game in numbers it couldn't possibly sustain, and daily Jane and Muthega saw the dead—gazelles dropped in their tracks, bony and starving, set upon by hyenas and eaten alive, their bones and gristle left behind, fodder only for the vultures and the marabou storks who held their ground as Jane and Muthega drove by.

Muthega and Jane didn't talk much. He smoked constantly, and scanned the horizon. It kept him busy, and to make conversation, Jane felt, would be too distracting. She told herself he needed to keep his focus on the signs of elephants and hints of poachers. Jane put her feet on the dashboard and studied the unfamiliar landscape. When they did speak to each other it was brief exchanges about the land, the animals they saw, how the lack of water affected the game, and the dead. The dead, always the dead, in little leather piles of hoofs and bones, the only parts left after the feasting and the incessant sun.

Jane had a cistern at home, filled up biweekly by a water truck. She had no idea where her water came from, and never wondered. She conserved it as much as she could, bathing only every two days. It never occurred to her to ask Muthega about his family, if they had enough, or if the people in the town worried about the endless drought. Jane only thought of the thirsty, skeletal game. She saw the women of Narok clustered daily by the drying river, washing clothes and filling up cans and buckets and calabashes to carry home. Often when they crossed the river at the low, wooden bridge closest to town, Muthega slowed the Land Rover for the women who thronged there. They gathered in groups, their heads weighted with basins of clothes to rub with bricks of lye and then rinse in the sluggish river. There were always tiny children with them who splashed in the water and flickered like dark flames in the mud. Muthega greeted the women in Swahili, his smile breaking open and his tongue clicking his teeth to punctuate his words. The throngs of women around the car made Jane uncomfortable. They watched her during the exchanges, and sometimes they gestured at her, and Jane knew Muthega was answering questions about who she was and why she was here. None of the women spoke directly to Jane. They just watched her.

Sometimes, when they crossed the river in the evening, returning to town for the night, Muthega stopped and let some of the women climb up in the back seat with their basins of laundry, which smelled like the sun, and the buckets they'd filled. It felt too crowded then. The women pushed and laughed behind Jane, their knees bruising her through the back of her seat and their joking, singsong voices saying things Jane couldn't understand. She wanted to tell Muthega not to pick up the women, but she didn't know how to phrase it in a way that wouldn't seem unkind. How could she explain that the women made her feel unseen all over again, or that watching the toddlers walk home in the care of older siblings made her sick with guilt? It was seeing these little children take care of each other that made her guilt unfurl. She'd flown halfway around the world just to escape her family, her obligation to care for her brother.

One morning, less than a month after she arrived in Narok, Muthega tapped the Land Rover horn outside Jane's gate. He always came early and today was no different. The sun hadn't risen. It was a navy blue dawn, cool and clear.

"The poachers were nearby last night. The dead one is just by the river. I will show you," Muthega said.

The sky lightened as they drove, silently, into the scrubland on the opposite side of the river. But still, when Muthega waved his hand to indicate the body was nearby, Jane saw only a dusky gray, curved rock. It looked like a boulder lying there in the flat grassland. Then she saw the carrion. Vultures circled the sky and marabou storks stood by, as still as fence posts but for the way they tipped back their heads to swallow their mouthfuls of meat. They didn't scatter when the truck rumbled up next to them, but merely stepped back a few paces on their backward-kneed legs, more annoyed by the presence of humans than afraid. The sky-hung vultures retreated to the upper branches of the nearest acacias. Muthega jerked the Land Rover into Park and reached behind him to pull his rifle from the back seat. He double-checked it was loaded and climbed out. Jane assumed he suspected the poachers were still close.

"Coming?" he asked, slamming his door. "We must gather the evidence."

The flesh that burst from the bloody hacked holes in the animal's face was bright pink. Against the sullen brown of the earth it looked unreal, plastic. The dead elephant was young, Jane could tell instantly, in the prime of his life. Likely he'd only recently left his family clan to find a mate. He'd been shot first and then hacked through with machetes to harvest the parts poachers would sell—tusks, tail and feet. The rest of him was left for the feeding frenzy of hyenas, jackals and wild dogs that slunk out of the underbrush, and the rancid-beaked vultures and storks that floated in from wherever they'd been lurking to feast on fresh meat.

Muthega climbed up onto the elephant's shoulder and pulled the giant ears up to search for a tag.

"This one I think is Twiga," he said.

They had seen Twiga just days before, feeding on the bark of a baobab tree a few miles to the north of here. When Muthega told Jane his name that day, she had laughed. "He's named 'giraffe'?" she asked.

Muthega complimented her on a new Swahili word learned, and told her that when Twiga was younger, still in his mother's clan and unnamed, he'd been seen stretching his trunk as far as he could up the side of a nearly bare tree to pull down the few remaining leaves.

"Like a *twiga!*" Muthega explained.

Jane closed her eyes and pulled her bandanna from the pocket of her shorts. She tied it tightly around her nose and mouth. The flesh wounds on the animal were fresh, the blood on the ground still sticky, and the iron smell of raw meat hung in the air.

Muthega laid a calloused hand with wide, flat fingernails on her upper arm.

"Miss Jane," he said slowly, as if she hadn't been trained in this already, "you must photograph the body for the records, collect samples for the DNA and measure him."

Then he let go of Jane's arm and left her standing, dizzy, next to the body. She watched him walk out into the surrounding scrub bush so, she assumed, he could look for tracks or evidence of the people who'd killed Twiga. But instead he set his gun down under an acacia and hunkered on his heels. He pulled a cigarette from his shirt pocket.

Jane glanced down at the raw place where Twiga's face used to be and it felt like looking at someone she once loved. She'd seen photos of poached elephants before, of course, and had worked on collecting DNA samples from elephant dung and tusk fragments during an internship in Sumatra. But this, the reality of a healthy, beautiful animal in the midst of the drought that was killing so many others…felled by the brutal force of humans, stunned her more than she thought it would. A rage swelled up in Jane. "Goddammit!" she muttered. "What the fuck is wrong with these people? What kind of abhorrent sub-human asshole does this?"

Jane reached down to pull a tiny flake of severed tusk from the ground. She placed it carefully in a plastic vial. She gathered a skin scraping and a marble-sized piece of dung. She took measurements to determine the rough age of the animal and the size the tusks might have been. She did her work—what she'd come here to do. She could feel that her face was twisted and hot, and tears and snot were soaking the bandanna. Flies, awakened by the rising sun and attracted to the smell of blood, buzzed in waves around her head, settling on her arms and cheeks, licking thirstily at the tears hung in the corners of her eyes. Jane waved her arms fruitlessly. It was getting hot, and the meat was beginning to smell. Muthega's cigarette smoke caught in a gasp of the breeze and mixed with the smell of meat. Her stomach rolled over in her belly and she bit her lip, forbidding herself to vomit.

Sweat dribbled down her forehead, and when she rubbed it with her hand, a flake of dirt fell in her eye. It hurt and she cursed and cried out. Muthega hunkered and smoked, just watching her. She hated him then. The way he just sat there, emotionless. He didn't care, Jane thought, and she wanted to smack him, to see him feel pain, to watch him cry. She felt the flicker of that angry ember she had forgotten was in her, and the rage spilled out like blood.

"Goddammit, Muthega! At least get off your ass to get the fucking measuring tape! There's one in my bag—in the trunk. Sample collection jars, too. Jesus Christ!"

"Okay, Miss Jane, okay," he said laconically.

Jane pulled her small digital camera out of the pocket in her shorts and pointed and clicked, pointed and clicked through her tears. First she photographed Twiga, what remained of him, for the foundation's records. Then she pointed the lens at Muthega as he rummaged through the trunk of the car for the measuring tape. He'd placed it on Twiga's hind leg, and then he'd sat down again. She would go to her boss in Nairobi. She would have Muthega fired for not even trying to trail the poachers, for avoiding the responsibility of helping her get the information they needed from the body. Jane snapped picture after picture of him hunkered there, in the dust, a calm look on his face and smoke circling his head.

He smiled up at her as she clicked and cried. He said in a voice so calm it made Jane want to kill him, "Anger will not bring Twiga back to life, Miss Jane."

Then he stuffed the end of his cigarette into an anthill and stood up. "If you have finished with the work, we can go now."

Jane watched the body as they drove away. The vultures and the storks slipped back through the sky and began their feast. There would be nothing left soon, Jane thought. "Take me home again, Muthega," she said. "I need to deal with the samples." She wanted to be alone now; she didn't want to have to talk to Muthega or watch him sucking on his cigarettes. She didn't want him to see her crying.

That night she climbed into her little wooden bed early. She wanted sleep to blot out the day. It was late when the smell of them woke her, the African smell of wood fire and meat, dust and sweat. She kept her body still but cracked one eye. Her front door was open and she could see the sky, a shade lighter than the dark of her room. She heard the low murmur of their voices through the dark. They'd come for the cameras, she thought. She kept them in a tin trunk locked with a padlock. Her heart choked her and panic took over. She wished she had Muthega's gun.

In a single movement, Jane pulled herself from under her sheets and ran. She had no desire to fight or to defend the few things she kept in the house; even the cameras weren't worth her life. She made for the open space beneath the sky. She thought the air might save her, or the land. The wall around her garden was tall and too smooth to climb. She turned and ran for the gate.

Jane was halfway across the bare yard before she was caught. Dry, calloused hands jerked her forearm and she fell. The voice attached to the hands grunted and spoke rapid-fire Swahili, and then she felt fingers around the back of her neck, pressing her face into the ground. She couldn't understand the Swahili. It was too fast and her vocabulary too small. Jane thought there was a familiarity to one voice, though, a growl, a shudder of smoke in the throat.

It seemed like hours before they were gone. She heard them rummaging through her little house, going through her things. She heard the smashing of glass—the outdoor elephant cameras, she knew—on her concrete floor. But why had they broken them? The thought occurred to her that they'd be of no value to sell now. So, what did they want? There was nothing else to steal. Even her little digital camera, which would bring the men a couple of hundred dollars in the market, wasn't in the house. It was in the truck. Jane kept it in the glove compartment so she'd have it if she ever needed it. Finally, they crossed the yard to leave. One voice spoke to Jane in halting English. "Next time we kill you, too." Jane lay there for a long time. She was terrified that if she moved they would come back, or that if she looked up, she would see nothing but the flash of a blade slicing toward her.

The light came in the Kenyan way—quickly, like a shade pulled up. Jane finally sat up. Her whole body hurt. She wondered if she was bleeding. There was a puddle of her own saliva in the dirt where the men had pressed her face. Jane felt bits of dirt on her tongue.

Jane pulled herself up, knees cracking as she bent them straight. She focused only on her next step. She thought of nothing else. She was frozen and terrified that, if she stirred her mind in any direction, what had happened would crush her.

Luckily, there was space on the afternoon flight from Narok to Nairobi. When the plane landed, Jane took a taxi from the airport directly to the Elephant Foundation's main office on Wayaki Way. She focused on reporting Muthega to the regional director, a large Kenyan man called Johnno, famous for his lifelong dedication to elephants and his harsh indictment of poachers.

Jane hated that she cried, again, when she told Johnno the story.

"Muthega and his friends, they were the ones," Jane sobbed.

She described the smell of the bodies, the rough hands and the familiar phlegmy voice. She showed them the photos on the tiny screen of her camera. There was Muthega, how guilty he was! Just sitting there.

"It had to have been him," Jane said. "He obviously doesn't care about the elephants and he is in league with the poachers. He wanted the cameras destroyed."

Johnno answered, "We cannot have criminals working for us like that. Sorry, so sorry we had to learn this way."

Jane thought she would feel stronger when she reported Muthega, when she set in motion the wheels that would punish him for what he did to her, to the elephants. Johnno told Jane it had happened before—poachers bribing protectors to look the other way. Ivory was a lucrative trade, and it paid to hand out bribes for easier access to the animals.

"But Muthega," he said, "Muthega surprises me. He's been an excellent, trustworthy employee for years. We've only recently given him a substantial raise. This drought, though… Everyone is desperate. People's children are dying."

He shook his head, disappointed, as betrayed as Jane was.

Later that afternoon Johnno drove Jane to the US Embassy to file a report. The marine who inspected her passport looked like a boy from home. The carpeted hallways, the smiling portraits of the president and the familiar accents Jane heard around her made her dizzy with longing—how she wanted to go home.

It was a man about her age who helped her fill out the paperwork to lodge a criminal complaint. He was tall with dark hair, and when she told him what happened, his brow furrowed and he winced. Jane thought she heard him curse under his breath. When the paper was filled out, he pulled a business card from inside his desk and reached over to hand it to Jane. Under the seal of the United States was his name in gold letters—Paul O'Reilly.

"I don't know if you were planning to go back to Narok to work, or back to the States, but you'll have to stay around Kenya for a few weeks, maybe a few months," he said. "Authorities will want to question you. Don't worry, I'll help you. Call me." He smiled and Jane felt dizzy again. She slipped the card into her backpack.

Jane stayed in a hotel in Nairobi that night. She showered until the water turned cold, scrubbing and scrubbing and wishing to turn herself inside out to be able to clean every part of her of the memory of those men. Then she crawled into bed and she slept and dreamed about her mother. In the dream, Jane was an elephant and her mother was chasing her, and every time Jane turned around to see if her elephant mother was there, she saw the flash of a machete through the dust she'd kicked up behind her as she ran.

The hotel phone woke her.

"Muthega," Johnno said immediately. "Are you sure he was among the men who assaulted you? Did you absolutely see him?"

"I heard him," Jane said. "I thought I did."

Jane remembered the smell of the men, meaty and smoky. She wondered if Johnno ever smelled that way.

"Is there any way, any way at all—" he said this gently, apologetically "—that you could be mistaken? You see," he went on, "the Narok police have found a body. They think it may be him, but it's too maimed to tell. Hacked with a machete the same way the poachers hack apart the elephants—face and feet and hands."

Jane listened, both to Johnno and to her own heart, banging in her chest. Johnno kept talking, his voice small and sharp through the phone, a needle to her brain.

"Some of the other locals are saying Muthega was targeted. He'd made enemies of the poachers recently—instead of staying away like he'd done before, letting them do their business unimpeded, he'd been watching them closely, taking photos of suspects in the town while they drank beer. He'd been taking names."

Jane thought of Muthega the day they watched Twiga through the barren trees, the way his voice softened when he told her Twiga's name and the reason for it. Jane thought of how he always spoke quietly and made little clicking sounds when they drove together, slowly, through the herds of Thomson's gazelles because they were too fatigued to move like they should have and he didn't want to scare them. Jane thought of his smile and his easy banter with the women by the river, the bits of hard candy he'd sometimes hand out to the children. She thought of his possible wife and how she had never asked if he had one or if she could meet his family. She'd never treated Muthega like a colleague, not like the people she'd worked with in offices back home.

Then she remembered that tiny, critical word—*too*. Jane heard one of the men say "too"—he spat it at her like a stone. "Next time we kill you, too." Jane hadn't forgotten that word when she told Johnno her story. But it referred to Twiga, the elephant. Jane had been sure of that. "Next time we'll kill you as we did the elephant." That's how she'd explained it to Johnno. She hadn't considered any other angle. She was angry and scared and wanted Muthega punished.

The rain came that night. It beat the windows and dimmed the streetlights. When it moved on and left nothing but heavy, dripping trees, cool air and pools of water in the streets, the winged termites released themselves from their subterranean caves and spun through the air in frantic, pale clouds. They beat against Jane's window in a desperate attraction to the bedside light she had turned on. Jane watched them flicker and dive, flicker and dive, until finally they fell away when the sky turned to dawn.

In the morning, she called her father. She had no idea what time it was back home, but the phone rang only twice before his new wife answered, sleepy but happy to hear Jane's voice.

"Jane? Your dad's been wondering when we might hear from you! We're dying to hear all about it, let me get him…he's in the bathroom."

Jane heard what sounded like the phone dropping from her stepmother's hands, and then a voice calling through the halls of the house she remembered so well.

"Honey, it's Jane! Come quick!"

Then her father's voice, low and soothing, said, "Janie! So glad, so glad to hear your voice! We miss you. We've been gathering things to send you in a care package. But we haven't finished. Is the address you gave us still the right one?"

Jane imagined the house. The warm kitchen with the old blue table where she always ate breakfast—weekdays cereal and every Sunday waffles that Jane and Lance would pool in syrup.

Jane tried to keep the tears out of her voice when she spoke. "I miss you, too, Dad. I miss you both. How's Lance?" This time, when her father described Lance's progress, and how the new medication helped with his moods, and how his new psychiatrist was brilliant, Jane listened. In her mind she saw Lance at five or six, sitting at the dining room table alone, eating the peanut butter sandwich she'd slapped together for his dinner so quickly that the slices of bread didn't line up. She thought of how he looked up that evening and asked her to read to him. Had she even bothered to answer before leaving him there, alone, and shutting herself back in her bedroom? Even then, when he was just a regular kid, she'd been a terrible sister. She'd made him a shadow, a vague annoyance, as she thought her father had done to her. How unfair that was.

"Dad," Jane said when her father paused. "I called to ask you something. It's important. You've made a will, right? You've made me his guardian if something happened to you? I'm next in line. He's my brother, and I want to help."

Jane flew to Narok that afternoon. She was terrified to go back to the place where she had been both victim and perpetrator, but she had to—one more time.

She slipped the card out of her backpack and studied it again. Paul O'Reilly. She assumed she'd still have to be questioned in the case. She'd have to go back to Nairobi and meet him again soon—tell him the whole story and maybe help find the people who did this to Muthega. There were no papers to accuse the faceless men she didn't know, but she'd do what she could to find them.

The tiny plane cruised over the edge of the Rift Valley, and the earth fell away below. The scroll of the land spread out below Jane, empty and pale. The rains had swelled the river and its banks were dark with dampness. The plane banked steeply and suddenly the land swung out of Jane's view, replaced with nothing but sky, darkening into evening, and another storm's arrival. When the plane tipped back and leveled, Jane looked down again. The land was too dark to see details now. It had turned into shadows and long, ill-defined shapes where the river once was. Jane thought of the local women standing in their muddy courtyards, holding their faces and their buckets to the sky. The plane was a winged termite, released from the dry, tight earth. And Jane was one, too—flinging herself into the darkening sky, desperate for softening earth, desperate for light.

NAROK

Leona had lied to the white Kenyan, and now it was time to tell him the truth and ask him to help her. She hated needing help, and with every breath she fought the instinct to give up, to go back to the manyatta and let Adia have her old life, no matter what that meant for her future.

The expression on Simi's face when they left the manyatta that day flashed in Leona's mind. What on earth had she done? Simi was the one who'd mothered Adia all these years; she was the one who protected the girl. Leona felt weak. No matter what, she would go back, she would tell Simi that she was sorry, she would let Simi know that she'd always be a mother to Adia, even if Adia lived in Nairobi or Solai or somewhere else. She vowed to keep the connection between her daughter and Simi alive.

Leona felt frozen somehow now that she'd made the sudden decision to move out of the manyatta. She wasn't Maasai, and the white Kenyan wasn't, either. Leona thought about the white Kenyan's family, and in her imagination he'd had the perfect childhood; one foot in the customs of his European heritage, and the other firmly in the ways of this place. Leona couldn't think of a better solution for her girl, but her thoughts were unsettled, confused. She felt unable to make a decision bigger than what to eat for dinner or when to make Adia take a shower. Narok was a small town—most people knew each other at least by sight—but it was far bigger than the manyatta, and that allowed Leona the illusion of anonymity. That, for now, was a relief.

In the manyatta, Leona was peripheral to Adia. The girl had moved with a constantly shifting school of manyatta children, all between the ages of two and seven, who swirled in and out of the individual *inkajijiks* like tides. All the mothers there were fine-tuned to the concept of benign neglect; that was the Maasai way.

In that sense, Leona knew, her version of new motherhood was vastly different and perhaps completely opposite to that of her own mother's, who birthed Leona in a bright Portland hospital while Leona's father drank coffee in the lobby. Leona's maternal grandparents lived an hour's drive away, but Leona was told, later, that they never came to stay after she was born; they never helped Leona's mother ease into the first days with the new baby. Being a mother was immediately a lonely thing. Leona's mother hadn't taken to the role, or the isolation. As soon as she could, she hired the nanny and the housekeeper. She'd never had another baby. The similarities Leona was beginning to see between herself and her mother made Leona feel bruised deep inside. She'd never wanted the comparison. It was the main reason she hadn't wanted children of her own. She was from a long line of mothers who didn't mother. And now, here she was.

In Narok, motherhood became central to Leona for the first time. It became a lonely and alien way of being. She was uncomfortable directing Adia's every move, and she wasn't used to being the girl's only source of entertainment. Time stretched out thin and slow, and even Leona's body seemed to move as if through deep water. The daily ritual was her job, while her position in Nairobi sat waiting. She wouldn't leave until she made a decision about Adia's father. She'd called the department head and assured him she still wanted the job, but lied about why she'd have to delay her start. There was a new piece of information she was tracking down—old stories of days when Maasai crossed into Tanzania for grazing. She didn't know if he believed her, but he said he'd hold the job for one semester. The university could wait.

Now, since they arrived in Narok less than two weeks ago, every day was the same. Breakfast at the café next to the hotel was first. Adia ate piles of sweet dough in the form of greasy, fried *mandazis*, and Leona drank cup after cup of hot chai. She hoped that if she drank enough of the sweet tea, the caffeine would eventually bring her back to life; speed up her blood again, throw a spark into the damp ash she'd become. Without her work, she didn't know who she was, and she could feel that the absence of purpose was making her depressed, empty. But she had to push that aside. She had to find Adia's father. Everything else had to wait.

For the first two weeks in Narok, Leona went to the bar daily. She described what she remembered of the white Kenyan to anyone who would listen. Often her audience were at their most unsuspecting, tired from their day and only wanting to order a beer, and when she pulled at their shirtsleeves or nudged their shoulders, they looked at her askance, suspicious. She knew someone, eventually, would know who she was describing, and also that her behavior would be talked about, but she kept her voice low; she murmured like a spy. Rumors blew like the dust around here, and she didn't want the white Kenyan to know anything before she could look him in the eyes.

She wondered if she'd recognize the man if he walked in. She'd only seen him twice, after all. The drunken, sweaty night of Adia's conception and then again only days after Adia's birth three years ago, when she was exhausted and terrified and had lied to him to make him disappear. She wondered if Adia looked like him and if, when she saw him, she'd know it instantly.

It was an aid worker's driver who finally gave her what she needed. One morning at the end of their second week in Narok, Leona saw a set of waxy Chinese crayons and a lined exercise book in the window of Narok's only stationery store and, on a whim, she pulled out a small wad of shillings and bought them. Leona didn't know what was normal for a three-year-old American, but she knew Adia missed her manyatta friends. She'd never been without a gaggle of age-mates, and Leona hoped the crayons and paper, which Adia had never used before, would help make the sitting and waiting more bearable. Back at the bar, Adia proudly showed the bartender her new gifts, and just as Leona was instructing the child on how to hold a crayon, she felt a tapping on her shoulder.

"Madam." The voice was gruff and wrapped in the scent of beer. "You are looking for Mister John?"

Leona spun around so fast the crayon she was holding flew across the room and rolled under a distant table. Adia screeched and hopped off her stool, then scrabbled on the floor to retrieve it. The speaker was a tall, muscular man around her age, she figured. He had scarification marks on his cheeks that told Leona he wasn't Maasai. Perhaps Kikuyu, she thought. He wore a khaki safari suit with a badge that said, "The Mara Lodge—Driver."

"Mr. John?" Leona tried to keep her face impassive. Suddenly she was frightened. Maybe it was a mistake to find him.

"Yes, Mister John, from Solai. Wilson—" here the man indicated a bar regular, slumped in a chair in a dark corner "—Wilson told me you were looking for Mister John. I know him."

"Is he here?" Leona asked, her voice unintentionally high.

"No. I am also from Solai. I can tell you how to go."

He nodded at the bartender, asked for another Tusker and, when it was slid across the polished surface to him, tipped his dusty hat toward Leona. She would pay.

He used Adia's blue crayon to draw a rough map in the little exercise book. Then he ripped out the page and handed it to Leona.

"You can go there by car in one day. But the road is bad, so if it is raining, you cannot make it." He swigged back a long drink of beer.

Leona was grateful for the checks her parents enclosed in their letters. Her Fulbright fellowship was long expired and the stipend from it had dried up. The only money she earned anymore was the pittance her articles received when they were published, and the promise of an advance on the book. In the manyatta, money hadn't mattered. There was nothing to spend it on. But in Narok everything cost. She fished a two-hundred-shilling note of her father's money out of her wallet and handed it over to the dusty man standing next to her. He answered with a solemn nod and placed the blue crayon carefully back in the box. Leona folded up the paper with the blue crayon map and slipped it into her bag.

Occasionally, Kamau, the guide who had drawn the map, came back to the bar she still visited. She didn't ask after the white Kenyan, John, anymore, though. She had the information she needed and now only had to decide how to deal with it. Those days she watched Kamau across the room, and when he looked over she always waved. She didn't want to talk to him, wasn't attracted to him in any way, but Kamau's presence gave her a connection to John. John. His name. She could hold it in her lips and write it down on paper if she wanted to. She could give it to Adia. But it felt unnatural to say it out loud, slightly uncomfortable, like wearing a heavy jacket on a warm day. The tenuous connection to Kamau was the only kind of relationship she could manage right now. Her thoughts were too ragged and her indecision was a living thing inside her, like cancer.

One afternoon Kamau caught her by the arm as she made her way out of the ladies' room.

"Have you followed my map, madam? Have you gone to Solai?"

"No," Leona lied easily. "My car is in the garage. Have to wait."

Then she felt a shiver of terror when he answered, "I can take you there. I am going to visit my father. I can take the car of my boss."

Kamau turned and waved at a friend across the room. As he walked away, he shouted back to Leona, "I will find you here in two days, and we can go to Solai."

It was late that night when a pounding on the door woke Leona from a dead sleep.

"Miss, you have a call," the yawing night attendant said.

Years ago, when she first arrived, she'd given the Guest House phone number to her parents. For emergencies only, she said, and she assumed they'd never call, or that if they did, she wouldn't even get the message. As Leona stumbled sleepily to the lobby, she realized this phone call was the first she'd ever received here.

Leona hadn't heard her mother's voice since she left the US. The familiarity—even after all this time, surprised her so much she almost didn't hear her mother breaking the news.

"I wasn't there," her mother's voice echoed over the phone, the time difference and bad phone service making her sound tinny and strange, like she was phoning from a distant planet.

"Why didn't you tell me he was dying? You've been writing me letters—you've been in contact. You just decided to tell me now?" Leona asked, wondering if her voice sounded odd to this woman she hadn't spoken to for almost four years; wondering if she should be crying. She didn't feel like crying. She didn't feel anything, except far away.

"He didn't want to speculate if you'd come or not," her mother answered, blunt to the core.

She added, in case it hadn't been clear, "He thought you wouldn't come anyway, and he didn't want to spend his last days watching for you and hoping."

Leona wondered how she was supposed to respond.

"In any case, nobody was there at the time of death. It was just after 2:00 a.m. He'd sent me home. Either he wanted to die alone, or he didn't expect it to happen so fast. Who can say?"

Leona wondered how it would be to die alone. If, with your last intake of breath—knowing the darkness was closing in— you would yearn to reach out, to feel your hand touching someone else's, to have your last sight be that of a human face, someone who knew you. She wondered if her father felt regret and wanted to make a deathbed apology. But maybe he'd just pushed the memory of what he used to do to her so far back in his brain that he couldn't retrieve it anymore. She felt a flaring up of terrible joy when she realized that her absence at his deathbed meant she wasn't there to forgive him. She couldn't have stood looking in his eyes and seeing anything—remorse or, worse, lack of it.

"Anyway, we need to plan a funeral. He's cremated, so there's no real hurry. We want to schedule it when you can come. You and the girl. It's time to come home, Lee."

For a second Leona was stunned by the use of her childhood name. Nobody had called her that for so long. She felt her eyes fill with tears. That place wasn't home. It never had been. She thought of the bed where her daughter was now, stretched out crossways, fast asleep. Adia's skin was nut-brown and her hair a halo of knots and golden curls. She looked nothing like Leona. She wore only a pair of little boy's underwear. A goatskin brace-let hugged her tiny wrist. Her small bare feet were thick with calluses and grime. Leona bought her a pair of rubber-tire shoes in the Narok market, but Adia hated wearing them, and when the left one went missing under suspicious circumstances, Leona didn't bother replacing it.

In Leona's memories, her childhood home was a cool, gray and silent place. It was a place of carpets and leather-bound books, meals around a table with the sound of scraping silver. She tried to picture barefoot Adia in her old school, following rules. She tried to see wild-haired Adia at her mother's dinner table eating with antique forks and knives, drinking from a crystal glass. She couldn't imagine it. She wondered if maybe where you were born informed your cells or if the air your mother breathed while you swam inside her contributed to your body, to your mind. Maybe the place in which a person was conceived set in motion that person's own unique history. If so, Adia was a child of dust and the smell of wood fire and livestock. Leona could never make her leave this behind.

Now, she hung up the phone and went back to her room. She lay down in the hard Chabani Guest House bed with her daughter curled up next to her. She had a sensation of spinning away.

Leona didn't sleep after the conversation with her mother. When Adia woke up just as the sun was breaking over the horizon, Leona's head felt as heavy and unwieldy as a boulder. She desperately wanted to stay in bed with her eyes closed. She was exhausted and filled with spinning thoughts about her father, but she was also uncomfortable going to the bar now that Kamau had offered to drive her up to John's farm. She didn't want to see him, to have to brush off his offer of the drive or, worse yet, work up the courage to tell him the truth—that she was too scared to see John. But Adia had gotten used to their daily task, had befriended the bartender and the cooks and insisted, after breakfast, that they go about the day as they always did. Leona tried to rouse her brain and her body by showering in cold water, but she still felt slippery somehow, greasy both inside and out. She felt sad, too. And that was unexpected. She wondered if she'd miss her father, his presence on the planet, even though it had been so long since she'd seen him, and even though she recognized she didn't feel tenderness toward him, nor love. But she saw she was fatherless now.

It rarely rained those days. The bottom of the Rift Valley was desolate and dry. It was the sound of wind through rough, yellow grasses and a constant film of dust on sweaty skin. That year, though, the drought was worse than usual. It had gone on too long. The previous two rainy seasons were sparse. The deep water tables never completely filled, and the Mara River and its tributaries lagged low and thick, the usual waterline nearly forgotten. A storm a week or so ago brought rain that fell hard. The children danced and laughed and drenched themselves in it. As she watched them, she thought it meant hope. But it was a one-off storm. Heavy and solid, but too hard, and it had washed away the topsoil and left little behind. Then it disappeared again, and the mud dried back to dust and the rivers—dangerous with flash floods for a few days—shrunk to trickles again. Another storm was expected, though. Soon, the people said. Leona assumed it was only wishful thinking, because the sky looked like it always did to her. The locals said they saw something different in it, a heaviness maybe, a slight deepening of color in the clouds that looked promising. People were waiting. All along the slogging rivers women waded deeper and deeper to wash their laundry, the gazelles and elephants coming closer and closer—their fear of humans mitigated by their desperate thirst.

When Leona finally got out of her shower and dressed and gathered the energy to take Adia back to the Chabani bar, she noticed there were more people standing in the streets than usual. It seemed more crowded somehow, more active. People called to each other from open shop doors and children buzzed past with intent.

"Maybe today's the day it'll rain," Leona said, leaning down to take hold of Adia's hand. "Maybe people are excited."

Leona had never seen Adia scared, and it dawned on her suddenly that Adia was alone, too. Fatherless, like she was now or, she thought grimly, "father-lost" in Adia's case. Nothing stood between the girl and the world but she herself, the reluctant mother. The enormity of that was more of a shock than her father's death.

"Lee, he left you everything."

The phone again, late at night. Her mother. By Leona's watch it was 3:35 a.m. and the knocking at the door pulled her from a dark and murky sleep. She blinked her eyes and rubbed them.

"I can wire some money to you for the tickets. When are you coming? We have to move forward with arrangements.

"I'm sorry, Lee." Her mother hummed through the phone, when Leona began to cry. She assumed Leona's tears were ones she shared. "It must be hard to be so far away from family now. At this time."

Her father's service would be formal, everyone in black, and everyone speaking in hushed voices. The priest would stand in his bright white robes among the enormous flower arrangements. Leona remembered the smell of her grandmother's service. She'd never forget the urns full of lilies and roses. She'd loved those flowers before that day, but the cloying smell in the church made her so sick with their heavy perfume that she still couldn't bear to be near them.

"I can't come." Leona couldn't make her voice any louder than a whisper. She felt that if she said it quietly enough, she could imagine that she hadn't said it at all. She could imagine away this conversation; this severing of ties. If she went there now those rainy skies would cling to her. She doubted she'd be able to escape and come back to Kenya; she'd get stuck. Adia would be foreign there, foreign and fatherless.

"Lee." Her mother's voice was hardening like mud left in

the sun. "You will regret not coming. No matter what went on between the two of you. Please."

When she hung up the phone and padded back to her room, she didn't try to sleep. She knew she wouldn't be able to. Instead, she walked over to the window. Her mother's words shocked her. What her mother said meant that she knew. She knew the whole time Leona was being violated by her father. She knew and she'd never done a thing to stop it. Leona bit her lip so she wouldn't scream and wake Adia. She wanted to open the window and scream and cry and shake the night with her anger and her hopelessness. She would never be able to punish him now. His death clipped her tongue, forced her silence.

The window was barred on the outside, so thieves and monkeys couldn't get in. Glass louvers on the inside could be closed against rain or dust. Burgundy strips of cloth hung from a wooden rod, the limp fabric masquerading as curtains. Leona pulled the cloths aside and turned the rusty handle that opened the louvers wide. She needed air. Outside the wind stirred the branches on the flame tree and made the petals on the bougainvillea flutter. There was a moon, and it was bright and perfect, and it turned everything—the dry grasses, the walls of the buildings, the roofs and the cars out there—a mournful gray. It wasn't silver, but instead the shades of a black-and-white film, color drained away but everything as visible and as lit as at midday. Leona felt a shift in the air and noticed a cold edge to the night. Yes, she thought, the rain is coming again. The rain would come and it would make the air wet and heavy and delicious for the plants and the people, but it would make the road to Solai impassable. Her little car wouldn't be able to manage flooded roads or deep muddy ruts. It had to be now. Time was short.

She pulled her jeans off the dresser and slid herself into them. She wrapped her hair in a bandanna and went to the bathroom to wash her face and brush her teeth. She packed the toiletries she'd purchased into a plastic bag and added Adia's crayons and paper, and the few pieces of clothing she'd bought in Narok to replace what they'd left behind.

It would be light soon, and they would have to go immediately. Her shoulder bag sat on the chair next to the dresser and Leona retrieved it. As quietly as she could, she dumped the contents on the end of the bed and felt through it all, putting the things back in one by one. Her wallet, her keys, a hair clip, a small notebook. There wasn't much. And then she felt the scrap of paper. It was folded over and over and she walked to the window to see it better in the moonlight. The line drawings didn't look blue now, the crayon Kamau used may as well have been black, but there it was, the map he'd carefully drawn.

Leona put the map in her pocket and then sat on the bed, legs stretched out in front of her. When the moon went down again, when the sun came up, the lines on the map would be blue again. She'd be able to follow them. She'd hurry, before the rain came.

JUJU

Liberia sits on the curve of West Africa's spine. Ocean currents fold and twist around the coast that stretches from the tropical jungles of Congo all the way up to the dry desert sands of Morocco. The year before, pushing opposite those ocean currents on a night flight from Washington, DC, Jane and Paul moved here. Monrovia was Paul's second Foreign Service post.

Liberia was bright with a sun that pushed down on everything below it, a sun that burned in an instant, a sun that made Jane light-headed and even chilled her to the bone if she sat in it too long. Liberia was sweat that rolled down her back, tacked her shirt to her skin, filled up her ears and dripped into her eyes. Liberia was tropical storms that would suddenly bunch up the sky in huge, black clouds to crumple what had been a flat hot day into a driving rain, which, just as suddenly, would stop. Liberia was the constant taste of salty ocean air from the surf that roiled on the sand just on the other side of the garden wall, the incessant drone of the air-conditioner. It was the constant motion of living things: mold, centipedes, beetles and plants that grew up thick and green and so fast Jane could almost see them moving, fed by the sun and rain. It was sitting, day after day, waiting for Paul to come home. Liberia was mystery, too. It was black magic and juju and things that sounded like they could never be true, but which were, things as true as a finger on a trigger, things as true as blood.

She should have known. There were times early in their courtship when Paul and Jane barely saw one another. They started dating at the beginning of his Foreign Service career, when Jane was finishing her work with the Elephant Foundation—training her replacements, a husband and wife team, to take over where she and Muthega left off. When Paul's new assignment came in—Washington, DC—Jane moved back with him. Jane's father gave her away, and her stepmother was the matron of honor. Even Lance attended the wedding, sitting quietly the whole time, a dazed look on his face.

Jane remembered falling in love with Paul at a specific moment. She would always remember it. After Muthega's murder, Paul was the one who helped her file the report; he was the one who helped her pack up her little house in Narok. It wasn't those things, though, that made her love him. Instead, it happened the day he drove her to see Muthega's family's little house, tightly built with mud bricks and a shiny new tin roof. As they parked the car, Paul mentioned the nicer-than-average construction was probably thanks to Muthega's western, non-profit salary. The home's tidy profile belied the tangle of dogs, undergrowth and runny-nosed children that wrestled for attention in front of it.

"Baba Muthega ni wapi?" Paul asked when an elderly woman shuffled out of the house to greet them. Jane was impressed at the way Swahili simply rolled off Paul's tongue. She nervously poked at the dust with her shoe and shifted her bag from one shoulder to the other.

The inside of the house was murky and bare. An old man sat

curled on a mat in the corner, and the woman invited Paul and Jane to sit on a pair of low stools under the tiny, empty window.

Jane toyed with the hot cup of chai the woman—Muthega's mother, she assumed—handed her. Paul drained his cup of tea and began to speak.

Jane watched him talk, his language sure and fluent. She had learned enough Swahili to basically follow where he was in the narrative by noting the reactions of the old couple. They nodded and winced, whispered acknowledgments and wiped tears from their eyes.

"They know already, someone sent word last week."

Paul knew Jane would be relieved that she wasn't the one breaking the awful news.

"In fact, Muthega's wife and children are in Narok now, gathering his things and applying for a scholarship for his eldest daughter to go to the school there. A better school than the one here in Solai. Apparently she's smart—they want her to be educated."

"Paul, tell them I have money. She doesn't need a scholarship. There is money for them."

"Money?"

"It's money the foundation pays in…instances like this one. His back pay and some life insurance. Plus some I'm donating. I want his family to be okay… I know they relied on him."

Paul turned to Muthega's mother. *"Yeye ana fedha kwa ajili yenu. Katika benki katika Narok."*

"Not in the bank, Paul. I have it…here." Jane pulled her bag from her shoulder and rummaged through it, finally pulling forth a wad of dollar bills.

"Jane, that's a lot," Paul said quietly. "It's more cash than Muthega would have been able to get for them in his whole life. Sure you want to do that?"

"It's foundation policy," she blustered, but the look on Paul's face told her that he knew the bulk of the cash was her own.

Muthega's mother reached past Paul and plucked the money from Jane's hand, then turned and tossed it to the man lying prone on the mat.

They drove silently away from Muthega's house.

"You know his murder had nothing to do with you, right?" Paul finally said. "He's not the first to be murdered out here, and he won't be the last."

"I should have tried harder to get to know him," Jane answered. "I shouldn't have yelled at him, accused him… I should have been smarter. I was so…" She began weeping.

"It's just unfair. And now his whole family has to suffer."

Paul stopped the car then, and turned to face her. His face was serious. "Don't carry that guilt. You can't live in Africa—or anywhere in the developing world—if you feel guilty about what it is you have versus what it is the people around you have. You won't make it." His voice was almost angry. "This work, my work and yours, requires you to be tough. If you feel guilt for everything, you'll burn out."

Jane loved how Paul was voracious in his appetite for his work. He took every short-term assignment the State Department offered him, especially the ones nobody else wanted. He was a wonderful diplomat. He could talk to anyone. He could make anyone feel important, and he loved entertaining groups.

"Send me to the seventh circle of hell, and I'll have the devil lapping from my palm in no time," he'd say at events between swigs of beer. His bravery was attractive to Jane then. She didn't mind that his travels left her to attend parties alone and, in fact, she loved telling their friends where he was. "Paul? Oh, he's in Syria."

Jane and Paul had barely returned from their honeymoon when Paul accepted an unaccompanied yearlong tour in Angola, then he went to Mozambique, where land mines still studded the earth, and Jane worried every day that went by without a call from him. They wrote each other letters. He had R & R in Spain and made enough money to fly Jane out to meet him and book four-star hotels and order expensive wines at dinner. In the spaces between these visits, Jane concentrated on her own fledgling career as a biology teacher in a private high school and on the friendships she was forging. She spent long weekends with her father and stepmother and took turns visiting Lance. Life didn't change for her much, really. She preferred, in some regards, the way their new marriage was structured, and the long stretches of time she had to live alone. Her job was time-consuming, and often she graded tests into the night and felt relieved that there was nobody there to interrupt her. Marriage was a theoretical thing at that time in her life, a daydream. Even the ring on her finger didn't seem real.

In college, Paul minored in art history, focusing particularly on sacred African carvings. When he was offered the post in Monrovia, where Jane could finally join him, his first reaction was excitement at having a chance to see, in person, examples of carvings from the region.

"You can get a job there, if you want," he told Jane. "We'll meet people, have dinner parties." He made it seem like a partnership. But at the dinner parties they threw in Monrovia, he crowded their table with local intellectuals and foreign development workers who drank wine and ate the expensive imported cheeses Paul kept hidden in the fridge. Jane sat at the foot of the table patiently as he held court, regaling the guests with the stories he'd learned when he studied the sacred art—tales of the Leopard Society and the masks they used to frighten other tribes, and the masks he wanted to see, and the ones he was desperate to buy. She found it hard to edge the subjects into areas where she was an expert, where she could contribute. Nobody cared that she was a biologist, that or that she'd been an excellent teacher. Paul and the others were passionately worldly and could talk for hours about international politics and the issues of doing development work in third world nations. Jane knew little about those subjects.

Jane assumed that she would find a job in Liberia. People told her international schools were always looking for teachers, and that finding work would be easy. She even contacted an elephant conservation NGO that worked on antipoaching efforts in the Sapo National Park. But somehow after she arrived here, she felt sapped. She drove out to the American school once to meet with the principal, but their talk was awkward. She'd felt ill that day but forced herself to go. The whole time she sat in the office, making small talk and trying to seem capable and prepared, her head pounded and the vague feeling of needing to vomit hung in her belly. Later, the principal called her to say that although there were no full-time staff vacancies, she would be number one on the list of potential substitutes.

"Don't worry," he said. "This is tropical Africa, teachers will be calling in sick all the time." School had been in session for two months already. Jane knew that. He hadn't called her once. She wished she cared, but she didn't. The heat here weighed her down, drained her motivation. Occasionally she thought of Kenya, and she remembered how crisp the morning air was when she and Muthega would begin their day and the way the mourning doves cooed the sky awake just before dawn. She saved the details of Narok, of the Mara, in her mind, pulling them out now and then to examine. On some level, she realized that when they came to Liberia she'd expected it to be more like Kenya. The utter difference was a bruise of disappointment, and the hope she'd felt before they arrived here turned to lethargy. When she missed her period twice in a row, she felt vindicated. This had to be the reason for her exhaustion.

Holding her secret close, Jane spent her days reading and walking along the wide stretch of beach in front of their house. Occasionally, she'd slip into her bathing suit and sit in the sand on a towel, watching the surf. In the late afternoons, showered and changed, she'd dab perfume behind her ears, and wait for Paul to return. She was never alone; Mohammad was there, too. Silently wiping dust from the framed pictures on the wall, organizing the kitchen or chopping things for the dinner he'd cook for them. Evenings were Jane's favorite time of day. When Paul was home, he'd always turn on the stereo and the house would be filled with jazz. She and Paul would sit down for dinner, and Mohammad would light the candles and place their plates in front of them. Jane felt like royalty when Paul was there and it was just the two of them. And dinner was a time of anticipation, too, because Jane knew it was always then, in the later evening, when the Charlies would come.

The "Charlies" were roving groups of folk-art sellers that fascinated Paul. Jane never figured out what their name meant. Even Paul couldn't tell her. The Charlies bought their goods cheaply from villages in the densely forested up-country, packed everything into market bags and came to the capital city to sell them door-to-door to foreigners. They brought West Africa and all its dark secrets out of the jungles right up to Paul and Jane's back porch, rapping softly at the back door.

When the Charlies came, Jane and Paul slipped out the kitchen door, closing it tightly behind them to keep the air-conditioning in. The Charlies set low wooden stools on the polished concrete floor of the back porch. The things in the Charlies' bags were new to her, mostly unattractive in her opinion.

"I'm looking for a passport mask," Paul said one night, and the Charlies dug through their bags to draw out some examples of the small carvings, dark and delicate and as compact as shells.

"What are they for?" Jane asked.

The Charlie sitting nearest her turned and said, "The juju can come to you wh'n you are sleeping."

He was tall and had long fingers. He held a cigarette in one hand, and tipped his head back to spout white smoke into the darkness above their heads. It hung there like a ghost.

He continued. "If you can see the forest spirit, Gle, wh'n you are dreaming, you can tell the carver how that Gle was looking, and he will carve it for you like making a photo. When you dream, juju can come. It can tell you things you must know."

Jane looked at the masks Paul held; they were hardly bigger than his palm. One was a woman's face topped with intricately carved braided hair; the other was a man's with a pattern of tribal cuts fanned out across his wooden forehead. Jane wondered what those dreams whispered to their owners, and where the people who had commissioned the masks were now.

Paul went straight for the dark heart. He didn't turn away when the Charlies mentioned that one wooden figure had been placed under a dead body to help usher the man's spirit to a better place. It didn't faze him when they told him the mask he was holding had been steeped in the blood of a sacrificial goat and that's what gave it its strange, dark patina. Jane was different from her husband in this way: she liked the new things better. The freshly carved pieces that seemed unfettered by a history of use, those were the ones that Jane would have chosen. She was afraid of the darkness.

Mostly the Charlies concentrated on Paul—his authority and masculinity made Jane invisible—but that night one of them gave something to her, as well. He murmured, "Madam, just take a look." He pressed a necklace made of smooth, brown seeds into Jane's palm, then a carved wooden doll a little girl would have carried and dressed and named.

"It's nice, isn't it?" Jane ran her finger over the small wooden face, and felt the strands of fabric hair.

Paul glanced over and chuffed a small laugh. "Hon, that's nothing more than a village Barbie doll. It's not even old."

Jane smiled apologetically at the Charlie who'd offered her the doll and handed it back.

Nights when Jane sat next to Paul, watching him work, she felt she didn't understand him at all. When he'd stopped traveling without her, when they'd finally settled into a marriage where they were together more than they were apart, Jane assumed they'd cement the closeness they felt when they were first dating. In those early days, they'd sketched out a future together, they'd built the scaffolding of a marriage, and Jane hoped he would be one of best friends, true partners and lovers. But somehow, after they came to Liberia, they kept missing each other. Each was visible to the other but untouchable, like the images on a movie screen to the audience: she could see him, she could hear him, but he couldn't see her back. She waited for the right moment to tell him he was going to be a father. It would change everything, she knew. Put it all right and Paul would see her again.

Days were too quiet and too long, and when Paul came home in the evenings, she was too eager to see him. She had no stories to tell him about her quiet days, and instead she pelted him with questions. She was desperate for attention, and it made her ashamed. She'd never been like this before, and she didn't want to tell him about the baby while she felt so weak. If she did, he might worry, and that would risk cementing her like this in his eyes; a dependent, weak wife cast in the amber of his mind. At night she dreamed of Narok. Of elephants that walked on hacked and bleeding legs, of babies reaching their trunks up to nurse and sucking on nothing but blood. She woke from those dreams sweaty and terrified. She wanted nothing more than to protect this baby, her baby, the way she hadn't been able to protect Twiga or Muthega or her mother.

In Liberia there were tales of up-country tribes who lived by the rules of black magic and curses. There were stories of how drummers could talk to each other over miles of air, through miles of thick forest, with the drums they pounded. There were the masked stilt walkers who danced in the streets and stopped passersby to ask for money. If you didn't give them what they were looking for, they would use their juju against you. In Liberia it was impossible not to believe these stories. It was impossible not to believe in magic. Jane felt the juju would hurt her.

One night as Jane sat in the dark next to him, she heard Paul whistle low, through his teeth, "Oh, that's a fantastic piece!" She saw what he was reaching for and then shut her eyes tightly, but the mask couldn't be unseen. Two roughly carved eyeholes pierced a piece of dusky, gray wood. The nose was wide and straight, and the forehead split slightly, so that a scar ran down the hard, angry-looking brow. The crack had been mended with bits of wire that gave the effect of crude stitches. Under the nose was the slash of a mouth, stiffly open as if the wooden face were trying to scream, and embedded in the mouth were six or seven yellowed, cracked teeth.

"*C'est les vrai, vrai dents des gens, quoi,*" one of the foreign Charlies murmured proudly. Jane noticed another salesman edge away from the wooden face, refusing to look in its direction.

"It's a Dan mask," he whispered to Jane in a voice that made her quiver. "When the witchdoctor must put on curse. That one be the mask for killing someone." Paul didn't see the man leaning away from the mask. He didn't put it on and tease him with it, or tell him he shouldn't believe what he did.

Jane hated the mask. She hated Paul for buying it. She wondered how it was that he could look at the masks and the carvings the Charlies brought to them and say exactly when they were carved and by whom, and even why. He could spin stories of up-country ceremonies that made his friends at their dinner table gasp with glee and revulsion. But lately, when he looked at Jane, she didn't know what he saw. Jane knew he missed her independent self, the strong, curious scientist he'd fallen in love with. But she didn't know how to retrieve that old version of Jane. It scared her that Paul wasn't curious about her anymore.

The morning after Paul bought the mask, he excitedly installed a hook on the wall between the bathroom and the guest-room. He stepped back to make sure it was centered and straight. This time, he didn't ask Jane if she thought it would look nice there. At night, when Jane got up to use the bathroom, she edged past the mask with her eyes closed. During the day she avoided it as much as possible. She didn't want the hollow eyes to follow her; she didn't want to see the real teeth. She thought about the mask constantly. She wondered if the teeth had been plucked from a dead person or, worse, if they'd been broken out of someone alive, someone whose mouth would have filled with blood and empty spaces.

The president was shot in his sleep just before dawn and dis-membered by his own army. When the static on the speakers cleared and the radio announced the *coup d'état* in shouts and chants, the army had already declared victory. *"In the cause of the people,"* the voices on the radio shouted from the kitchen, *"the revolution continues."*

After the president's murder and the coup, the Charlies stopped coming. The army enforced a strict curfew—dusk to dawn, penalty of death. From the balcony overlooking the beach, Paul and Jane watched soldiers in their camouflage pants and torn T-shirts sleeping in the sand. Even during the day, when he went to work, Paul advised Jane not to walk down the beach.

"It's not that they want to hurt Americans," he assured her. "This is a local thing—it's not ours. But they're drunk and armed and not to be trusted."

He wanted this to make her feel better, safer. He smiled when he said it, even held her hand. But it made Jane feel even more foreign to this place, like a ghost that nothing—not the juju and not her husband—could see. She was an interloper—as foreign and displaced as a broken bead on the forest floor.

A week after the coup, thirteen ministers and cabinet members of the old ruling party were sentenced. The accusations were shouted on the radio, and the announcer's gleeful voice said, *"Justice will be served."* The announcement sent a shiver down Jane's spine, and she told Mohammad to turn the radio off. She didn't want bad news today; she didn't want to be sad or anxious. She'd been to the embassy doctor, who confirmed what Jane already guessed. She wasn't alone in her body. She held the secret close. She wanted to think of a special way to tell Paul the good news. She wanted this to be a moment that would make him really see her again—as his wife, as the mother to his unborn child.

In the predawn darkness the next morning, the shouts of soldiers on the beach woke Jane up. She tiptoed to the bedroom window and peeked out. By the slashing beam of flashlights, she saw a line of men unloaded from the back of a truck. They were led, single file, over the gray sand by a sinewy-armed man who wore his mirrored sunglasses even though the sky was dark. Waving a heavy-looking gun, he shouted at them to be quiet, to kneel where he pointed.

The sun rose and the telephone rang. Paul's boss needed him at the office; documents had to be secured, loose ends tied up. The political situation had turned, the army in charge was angry; they were murdering dissenters in the streets. Any minute there might be evacuation orders for Americans.

"This could go up in smoke," Jane heard Paul say into the phone, and she begged him not to leave the house. The day slid dangerously in front of her—too long for her to be alone with the terror she felt and the chaos outside—the drunken soldiers and the guns. The iron garden gate, and the elderly guard who sat in front of it all day, seemed too thin a line of defense.

"Just stay in the hallway," Paul implored Jane before he left. "Stay away from the windows—stray bullets!" He didn't want her looking out at the beach or sitting on the balcony where she could be exposed. She slid to the floor and leaned against the windowless wall. She could hear the radio on in the kitchen. Mohammad was listening to the news again. He was afraid, as well, and that made Jane even more frightened. Jane took a deep breath and rubbed the place where, inside of her, she imagined cells splitting and multiplying, and she was glad she hadn't told Paul. She didn't want the idea of the baby spoken aloud in the world yet. It was better for now, she thought, to keep even the words tucked safely in her mind.

Jane sat in the hallway, waiting for Paul to come home. It was hot and not light enough to read. Her muscles ached from not moving, and her skin felt sticky. The mask was there in the dark, inner hallway, too. She felt it staring down at her. She didn't want the mask near her baby, didn't want its empty eyes boring into her belly. It was an evil thing. The anger surprised her. It was drawn like water up a tree's roots; filling her veins with heat, making her heart beat faster and her face flush hot.

After the dim hallway, the sun was sharp in her eyes. She blinked and squinted and crawled out the balcony doors as quietly and as slowly as she could. She kept her body close to the floor. She didn't want anyone on the beach to notice her. The soldiers were everywhere. Some lay in the sand, others stood smoking in groups. When the breeze shifted, Jane could smell the acrid smoke. A few soldiers took turns pulling what looked like large tree branches out of the back of a truck.

None of the soldiers engaged the thirteen men still kneeling silently. They'd been in the same position since before dawn, and now the white sand glistened like ice under the high, hot sun. The ocean had shifted from the deep black of the early morning to jade green. The thirteen men waited, hunkered down and sweating.

Jane slid on her stomach away from the sliding balcony door

and past the wicker chaise she loved to sit in and read. She didn't want Mohammad to walk by the doors and see her. Edging her body under the rustling leaves of the potted palm, she watched the men on the beach through the decorative openings in the balcony's brick wall.

While she sat, thirteen thick tree branches were pulled from the truck and whittled into posts. The posts were set upright, anchored deeply in the sand. The thirteen waiting men were ordered in loud voices to peel off their shirts. The men were tied with green plastic rope to the posts. None of the men tried to escape, none of them screamed or begged for mercy. They simply stood, their hands tied to the wooden stakes behind them. They seemed tired, even bored. Jane imagined the terror they felt and how it could make them listless.

Jane was shocked by the sudden snap of thirteen bullets—one after the other, *BAM, BAM, BAM* in even intervals of split seconds. The bullets sounded distant to her, sliding high above the noise of the tide coming in. It was over quickly. Each bullet hit its mark. The bodies slumped, one by one, crumpled in upon themselves in puddles of blood that spread out in the sand and were absorbed into it. Jane couldn't breathe; she couldn't move. She sat there in the sun, her heart shattering in her chest. Her body shook involuntarily and her breath was short and ineffective. She clenched her palms over the beginning of the baby in her belly and she felt a new sensation of fear physically. It forced its way inside her; it coursed thickly through her blood; she felt it curling around her organs like a writhing, headless snake.

She must have screamed. It was Mohammad who found her. Mohammad who put his arm around Jane and helped her shaking legs find their way back inside to that shadowy stuffy hall. Mohammad who brought her a blanket and a glass of water, and Mohammad who held Jane's secret closely tucked away so that it never saw light. When Paul finally came home that evening,

Jane was curled like a snail on the floor, eyes tightly shut. She felt him crouching next to her and heard him breathing quietly as he tiptoed away. She wished he'd sit next to her and stay, that he'd smooth back the sweaty hair from her cheeks and tell her it would all be fine, just fine.

That night Jane and Paul picked at a cold dinner of leftovers at their dining room table. They kept the light off and lit candles. Throughout the meal, fear coiled in Jane's belly. She started at every loud sound and avoided making too much noise. She listened to Paul talking with one part of herself, and with the other part Jane listened to the silence beyond their walls, beyond their locked gate, beyond the sounds of surf on the beach, out to where the sun was sinking into the horizon in a puddle of disappearing light and the dark was rolling in.

Jane told Paul about the baby a few days later; she just blurted it out at breakfast, nothing special. He was thrilled; he couldn't wait to be a father. But he still didn't stay inside with her after dinner to watch a movie or talk. In the following weeks the government stabilized, the curfew lifted and the Charlies returned. They came up the steps and waited. Mohammad whispered, "Sir, they are here." But Jane didn't join Paul on the back porch anymore. She sat in the living room pretending to read, plugging her ears and forcing herself to breathe when she thought she heard the sound of bullets whizzing through the air on the beach. Before Jane drifted off to sleep at night, she didn't think about the mask anymore. Instead, she saw herself watching silently through the railings as those men in their droopy pants, with their glistening skin and bewildered eyes, were shot.

Jane didn't go to the beach anymore, either. On clear Saturdays, Paul would try to tempt her with the suggestion of ocean swimming, picnics on the sand, kite flying. She never agreed. She used the pregnancy as her excuse—she didn't feel well, she wanted to stay inside. He didn't know what she knew: that the ocean had licked blood from the shoreline, that the blood swirled in the water now; there were bullets; there were beads of flesh rotting under the sand. The beach was a decaying thing, marked by violence, and Jane didn't want any part of it—any molecules of sea or silica or even the air off the waves—to melt through her skin or lungs and dissolve into her baby. She had to be a wall now, between her baby and the tragic world they lived in.

GOD IS THE RAIN,
GOD IS THE SKY

The air was cooler in the hills, easier to breathe. Simi concentrated on that, the rhythm of her breath. She kept her eyes cast downward and tried not to think about the distance she'd come from the manyatta, or the length of the return journey. She walked as fast as she could, but she was still weak and empty and her legs felt heavy and slow. The prospect of a night out in the bush, alone, wasn't one she relished, so she didn't stop to rest her legs or to drink water. The path was rocky, and a long ago rain cut a deep track in the dirt. It was too narrow for her to walk in, so she tried to straddle it. Occasionally one foot would slip, causing her to stumble.

Around her, the world changed. Her path led upward, away from the yellow savannah spread out below her and up into the Loita hills. The scrub gradually became taller, and greener, and the plant life changed. After a while, Simi noticed she couldn't see down the escarpment into the savannah anymore. The trees along the path were too thick now, too tall. Even the sun was hidden behind them. Far above her tree branches rustled and shook with the weight of colobus monkeys that leaped between them, hooting warnings to each other as Simi crossed under them. Once, Simi looked up to see a mother colobus launch herself from one branch to another, the long, white fur stripes along her sides and tail streaming out behind her, while a tiny baby clung bravely to her breast. Even when the branches were still, Simi could feel the peering eyes of monkeys all around her. The forest breathed, and its heart beat; it was a unified body that lived and moved, its cells the countless creatures and plants that made it, and the rocks and the dirt and the air.

The part of the forest body Simi looked for was the large *oreteti* tree she'd visited six years ago when she first realized she might be barren. That time, she'd come with other women. They'd eaten fat and cleansed themselves with milk. They danced and sang songs and then each woman left an offering at the tree. Some of the women left calabashes of milk; one left a tin of sugar. Simi couldn't remember if all of the other women had later given birth, but she knew some had.

Even after six years, it was easy to find the tree. It was as wide as Simi's hut and stretched so far up that even when she tipped her head all the way back she couldn't see where the branches met the sky. This was an old tree. The *oreteti* begins as a seed dropped into the branches of another tree by a bird or a monkey. The seed breaks open and tiny roots grow. As the roots gather nutrients from their host, they grow bigger, and longer, and more plentiful, wrapping the host tree in python-sized roots that seem to descend from the sky itself. The host tree struggles to survive the *oreteti's* embrace, but eventually dies and rots away, leaving an enormous, intricate lattice of great roots that curl and crawl over one another as they push themselves higher and higher from the earth to the sky.

Simi knelt down in the soft earth at the base of the tree. She stilled her breathing and licked her dry lips. The *oreteti* commanded respect and reverence. It was through an *oreteti* tree's roots that N'gai handed the cattle from heaven into the care of the Maasai. The roots could also take prayers to N'gai, who shares a name with the rain and also the sun. Years ago, Simi put her faith in this tree. She danced and sang and made her own offering. But the tree hadn't taken her prayer to N'gai. Or N'gai hadn't wanted to give her what she sought. Instead, he'd only taunted her—giving her a full womb and then emptying it again and again, like water poured from a calabash. Then a baby had come. Not one grown in her own body, but a baby all the same. But that was a taunt, too, and now, like all the others, that baby was gone.

Simi stood. The tree loomed above her, its countless arms snaking in and around and over each other. In between the woven roots, Simi knew, was a dark, empty space where the host tree used to be. Last time she was here, her desperation made her brave. The other women implored her not to—there were surely snakes hiding there, they'd cried, maybe a leopard. But she'd slipped in between the roots and entered the tree's middle space. Now she remembered the feeling of peace that came over her then. She wasn't frightened that day. The other women chatted nearby, and their voices had been comforting. She was safe, she felt, in the belly of the sacred tree, and she lowered herself and sat on her haunches and prayed there, in the dark. The women's voices faded, and all she could hear was the sound of the leaves so far above her in that dark hollow. When her prayer ended, she'd reached up to her neck, unlatched the necklace of blue and green beads her mother had given her and laid it on the ground. Six years ago she'd offered her most valued possession in the hope that N'gai would bless her with children. She'd placed it directly in the heart of the *oreteti*. But N'gai hadn't blessed her. And now she wanted her offering back.

In the time since she was here with the other women, the tree had grown many more winding roots. The space she'd slipped through before was now crossed over by new growth that barred her entry. Simi carefully examined the tree. The side that faced the path was covered tightly, and around the other side, a tangle of undergrowth obscured the tree's base. Simi slipped her machete from the leather band around her waist. Her heart beat painfully in her chest. The forest was full of animals, from snakes to leopards, and any of them could be hiding in the bush. The bravery she felt with the other women was gone now.

Slowly Simi picked her way around the tree, sliding the branches and leaves out of her way with the blade of her machete. She examined the tree as she moved, looking for an opening she could access. It didn't take long to find one. It was off the ground, though—she'd have to sidle up the large roots, slide into the opening and then drop back onto the ground in the middle of the tree. It wasn't so high that the drop would hurt her, but it might be difficult to climb back out.

An image of the car, carrying her daughter and disappearing into a cloud of dust that choked her, flashed through her mind. What did she have to lose, anyway? Who would miss her? She told nobody she was leaving just after dawn that day. She told nobody where she was going. It didn't matter. Now, childless again and far past hope that she could ever conceive, she wouldn't be missed. In fact, she wasn't sure her husband wouldn't cast her out, anyway. An unlucky, cursed woman like her.

Simi took hold of the tree, one serpentine root in each hand, and hoisted herself up. She was weak from days without eating, and her arms barely held her. But she found footing on a lower root and pushed herself upward. The opening she wanted was just above her head. Once Simi grasped the root that formed the bottom edge of the space, it was easy for her bare feet to find secure places to stand, and slowly she worked her way up until her chest rested on the bottom of the open space. She leaned over and peered down into the center of the tree. It was quiet. No sound of an animal breathing. No dry rasp of a snake slithering below her. Dim light entered from the spaces between the filigree of roots, but there were puddles of shadows she couldn't see into. She wished she had fire to illuminate the space, but she didn't want to take the time to find the wood to make a spark. She knew if she found the necklace soon, and hurried back through the forest, she could be down the escarpment before dark. She could ask to stay at the nearest manyatta for the night.

So she moved quickly, pushing herself up and sliding the front of her body forward, then grasping the top edge of the opening and pulling her legs up so she was sitting on its edge, her back to the forest and her feet dangling into the darkness. She slid forward and dropped into the space. Her feet hit solid ground, and she braced herself for the sharpness of fangs in her ankle, or the slipping of a centipede against her toes. Nothing. She stood for a second, letting her eyes adjust to the minimal light, which fell in soft shafts, echoing the shapes the tangle of roots made all around her. She leaned her head back and looked up. The tree was taller than she remembered, the top invisible to her. The original roots, born in an upper branch of the host tree, were thicker than they were at the base, and so closely entwined they allowed no light to enter.

She waited to see if the feeling of calm she'd felt the first time she slipped into the heart of this tree would fill her again. Her head, whether light from lack of food and the long walk up the escarpment that day or from the dizzying effect of the light through the tree, spun. She knelt down in the dirt to steady herself and took a deep breath. The spinning slowed, and Simi looked around, hoping her eyes would adjust to the low light. She didn't think the necklace would be hard to find. She'd only placed it on the ground, not in a hole or in some divot of the trunk that would have grown taller and taken the necklace with it. Slowly, Simi leaned forward and stretched her arms out, carefully patting the ground all around her. Six years of dust had gathered here since last time, as a hopeful young wife, she came here in an act of faith. She'd assumed the offering would work, and that soon enough her empty belly would fill with children and her life would spin out the way she, her mother, her father and everyone else expected it to.

Remembering that hope, and the way it slowly gave way to disappointment, made Simi feel weak again. It had been upsetting enough to be unable to bear a child, but shouldering the expectations of generations of ancestors who expected her life to unfold in a certain way made it worse. It wasn't simply the absence of a baby, but also the absence of a place. Before Adia, Simi had lived with a constant undercurrent of fear. She never knew if she'd be forced to leave; if the others would begin to see her bad luck as catching—as a curse on all of them. And when Adia came to her, the fear vanished. She had a baby to love and a secure place in the community. She'd been just another mother, not someone to look at sideways and wonder about. Adia. Simi remembered the weight of Adia's infant body in her arms, the way Adia curled next to her as she slept and the way her little voice sounded when she spoke. Grief rolled over her with the force of a beast attacking her. She felt her chest collapse into the dirt. For an instant she thought it really was a big cat, and she imagined she could feel the creature's hot, fetid breath on her neck and its claws tearing her skin. She couldn't breathe. Her lungs constricted and terror filled her. Light popped behind her eyes, and heat flashed like fire across the surface of her skin. She thought she was dying, and she tucked her body around itself and held her head in her arms, the instinct for self-preservation too strong to deny.

She must have faded into sleep, because when she opened her eyes, it was completely dark. Every light had faded into blackness. She wiggled her toes, and felt the sensation along her legs, and stretched her arms wide. Everything moved just as it should. Simi was tired. Too tired to make the effort to rise. If darkness had fallen, she couldn't risk a walk back through the forest, anyway. She let her body relax again. Every piece of her was still. She made no movement except for the rising and falling of her breath. The panic was gone now; the fear had left. She only felt resigned. Her life wasn't what she'd planned. The children weren't coming. Adia was gone. There was nothing she could do about it. Her husband might or might not shun her, and she might or might not be mauled by a lion on her way to the river one day. Things happened all the time that were out of anyone's control.

She thought of the moon she'd observed the night before and how, underneath it, she'd noticed that the animals were dying again, the drought slowly killing them off, and how the woman had to go farther and farther to collect firewood and how men were leaving their traditions behind to find work and money in Nairobi. Her life wasn't the only one that didn't continue the pattern of all the lives that had come before. Nobody's future was written from the past. She remembered when Leona first arrived, she told Simi she wanted to help the Maasai hold on to their traditions by figuring out ways to graze their livestock in places the drought hadn't reached.

Thinking about Leona threatened despair, and to quell those dangerous thoughts, Simi shifted her body, just a bit, to relieve her hip bones of the ache the cold ground had sown in them. As she shifted, her left arm, still stretched out its full length, shifted, too. The fingers on her left hand moved, and under them Simi felt something that wasn't dirt. The dark was too thick to see the colors, but Simi felt the details. All the beads were there. The clasp still seemed to work. Simi sat up and fastened the necklace around her neck. Her mother had wanted Simi's life to be different. That's why she'd worked so hard to get Simi to school. She couldn't imagine her daughter not marrying or being cut, but she'd wanted her daughter to have a modern mind, to go one step further than the women of her own generation. How odd that a *muzungu* was working so hard to try to preserve their way of life, while Simi's own mother had injected change, however small.

Simi was grateful for her mother's vision. She thought that, if she'd had a daughter, she would have taken one step even further into the future. Her daughter, the one she didn't have, would get an education and Simi would make sure she finished. That's how she would keep her mother's vision passing into the future.

Simi wrapped her *shuka* tightly around her shoulders and, within the secure confines of the *oreteti*, curled herself into a ball. One last thought flipped into her mind before she drifted off— if she had that daughter and if she encouraged that daughter to finish secondary school, when would that girl be cut? Cutting signified a girl's readiness to marry, and usually she became a bride quickly afterward. Would she still be cut at thirteen, but wait to marry? Would a husband be willing to wait? Or, would the girl be cut after secondary school? It made an extraordinary picture in Simi's mind—an older girl, one of seventeen or eighteen, educated, having *emurata*. It didn't make sense; you might as well have a man nurse a baby or an old woman become a *moran*.

In the morning, the slow sun found its way back through the pattern of roots. Simi opened her eyes and the bits of light were like stars. The forest around her was already awake, the colobus monkeys were busy searching for breakfast and the birds called to each other, gossiping in the chilly air. Simi's back hurt from the way she'd curled up to sleep, but she was rested. She felt an emptiness that she hadn't felt in the previous few days. That is, she didn't feel happy, but she felt an absence of the deep grief Adia's leaving gave her. It was still there, she knew, but it had settled into a deeper place, the way a stone, after it's tossed into water, settles on the river's floor, leaving no traces of itself when the ripples smooth out.

It wasn't as hard as Simi expected to climb back out of the space in the tree, nor for her to start walking back toward her manyatta. And once she passed the outer edge of the forest and broke back into the open sky with the wide savannah stretched out below her, she paused and sat on a large stone. She unclasped the necklace and examined it. The beads were dirty—all those six years of dirt clustered in the spaces between them—but, as she had thought the night before, they were all there. Simi used the bottom edge of her *kanga* and rubbed at the beads, dislodging the dirt bit by bit. She rubbed until she could see the colors of the beads, blue for the sky and rain that should have come, green for the way the land would look if it did. When it was clean, she clasped it back around her neck and began her long walk home.

CHILDREN BECOME
THEMSELVES

There was a kind of unease stalking Jane, and it grew daily as her pregnancy bloomed. She couldn't decide whether to blame the mask, the murders she'd borne witness to or the history of her own blood. Thoughts of Lance and his disease haunted her. It was genetic, and the idea that it might infect the cells she was giving her baby terrified her. Without warning the feeling would leap on her back and dig its claws in, a jungle animal weighted with muscle and teeth and driven by an instinct not to let go. Jane didn't know how to fight the thing off and, instead, began to hide all day in her darkened bedroom, curtains drawn against the Liberian light, the air-conditioner rattling on its highest setting to drown out the sounds of the surf and the world going on—without Jane—outside.

For weeks, Mohammad slipped inside the bedroom only to place bowls of soup and bottles of boiled, filtered and chilled water on the bedside table. Jane would eat the things Mohammad cooked. She trusted him and his fastidious adherence to the rules of cleanliness. But she ate little else. Nothing fresh, nothing raw. The potential to make her baby sick by eating diseased produce or ingesting even a drop of untreated Liberian water hung over Jane constantly. Even her desire to shower was outweighed eventually by the terror that the unpotable tap water would somehow pass her lips. In the late afternoons, Paul returned from work, and when he was home, Jane climbed out of her bed and sat at the dining table with him to nibble dinner. She tried to be calm and happy around Paul, but the fear kept leaking out. All day long Jane counted squares on her calendar, calculating the day of conception and the day she was due. She wondered what her baby looked like week to week, she obsessed over the growth of her baby and was frightened to lose track. She compulsively checked off the days as they slid past. At thirty-two weeks the embassy would send her to the States to wait until Grace was born. Jane only had to hold on until then. At home, things would be clean and safe, and she would be able to breathe the air and drink the water again.

"I'm worried," Paul said one night. "You aren't doing well." His face was scared, and the concern Jane saw there was a chisel to her fear and broke it all open.

"I'm scared," Jane cried. "I can't stop being scared, and I keep thinking this is how my brother started." She couldn't stop crying, and the bursts of emotion kept her in tears until Paul finally convinced her to get back in bed. He curled next to her, stroking her hair until her sleep came.

Jane refused to leave the house at all and missed two appointments with the embassy doctor. Finally Paul arranged a ticket for her to fly home. He knew the albatross of a wife suffering the kind of mental distress Jane was experiencing would impact his career. The State Department would limit his choice of future posts, and he'd be a far less attractive employee to ambassadors if they found out. Unwilling to risk that, he told his boss that Jane wanted her mother to help with the preparations for the baby. His tour in Liberia was almost finished, anyway. He would join her just before the baby's due date. His next post was assigned—Washington, DC. They'd settle for a while.

"Back from Africa!" Those were her father's first words when she exited customs and saw him. He looked older than the last time she'd seen him. Older and somewhat fragile. Jane hugged him, and he said, "And pregnant! Sure it's not a voodoo baby?" He laughed.

Jane could still smell the salty Liberian air in her own hair, and when she opened her suitcase later, it released the scent of her Monrovia house—the slight tang of mildew she'd become used to and hadn't realized was so pervasive.

That night, Jane woke up sweating, breathing heavily. She lay completely still, eyes tightly shut, and listened hard. In her dream, someone was there in the room with her. Someone was watching from a corner as she slept. Someone's breath mingled with hers in the darkness of the bedroom. Slowly she gathered the courage to open one eye, then the other. The curtains were gauzy against the windows and since she'd kept them open for the air, they billowed out a bit with the night breeze. The streetlight, a few houses down, sent a cool white glow into the room. Even still, it took Jane a few minutes to remember where she was—in the guest bedroom of her parents' house in Fairfax. There was the heavy wooden dresser between the two windows and the chintz-covered armchair piled with things she'd begun to unpack. There was the cat, curved and silent as a comma in the bed beside her. They weren't touching, but Jane sensed the weight of the little body, the slight heat the cat gave off.

Jane tried to shake the dream from her head, but it left her breathless, with little shocks of terror that burst in her veins like fever. She wished her father hadn't joked about her "voodoo baby." Jane's genes were tainted; she knew that. Her father knew that, too. It wasn't something to joke about. The baby slid inside her and the movements were a comfort. This baby would be fine, Jane whispered to herself. Her brother was her brother, not her, and his demons wouldn't infect her or her baby. Jane told herself this over and over in a mantra of her own design. Finally, she turned onto her left side and the cat stretched her legs and purred, then shifted into a furry ball. Jane pressed her right hand to the stretched dome of her belly. This is how she held her unborn daughter and this is how she banished the nightmare and finally fell asleep once more.

She woke to an overcast sky and the promise of rain. For June it was cool in Virginia. She could hear someone in the kitchen downstairs, and a sudden memory of her childhood struck her. When Jane's mom was still healthy, she'd make a pot of tea and a pile of cinnamon toast for Jane every morning. Jane would sit at the blue kitchen table and eat. Jane's friends thought it was weird to drink tea. None of the other kids did. But Jane's mother made it sweet and milky, and Jane had a favorite cup, which she used every day. Jane couldn't remember what happened to that mug—dark blue with white flowering vines trailing around it.

Later that first morning, Jane joined her dad and stepmother in the kitchen. She poured herself a cup of coffee. "If I can borrow the car, I think I'll go today," Jane said. She'd showered and dressed but still felt bleary and light-headed from the jet lag and disturbed sleep. She hoped the coffee would help. "To see Lance."

Jane's father didn't answer. His face changed slightly—his mouth slid into a line, and his jaw clenched just enough that Jane noticed. Jane wanted to force the conversation, poke her father with words. This was the chasm between them now. Her father and stepmother kept a strict schedule of visits to Lance— they had to draw lines, they'd explained once, in order to protect themselves from pain. Jane knew that was true theoretically, but in her heart she had never understood how her father could turn his back on his only son. Although Jane had come to appreciate—even love—her stepmother, she also silently blamed her for the boundaries erected between Lance and their father. Her real mother would have done anything for Lance.

It was disconcerting to drive along streets that were wide and clean and empty. They were so different from the crowded and colorful streets in Monrovia. There she'd have to navigate puddles of oily water and stray dogs wrestling for scraps, and she'd have to share space with children selling single cigarettes and ladies hawking vegetables or dusty packages of biscuits and noodles. At every stoplight someone would rush to slap a wet soapy rag on her windshield in the hope of earning a few cents. There was a loneliness to these empty American streets. Jane was shocked to feel a tiny wave of nostalgia unfurl inside her. She never ever thought she'd find things to miss about Monrovia.

The place her brother lived now tried hard to look homey from the outside. There were bright flowers in pots on a wide front porch and cheerful green shutters on all the windows. But you had to sign in at a front desk where a man had a dozen screens that all showed different views. In them you could see hallways, people shuffling in grainy black-and-white. The people looked like specters. Jane signed the book the man indicated, and then she was buzzed through a metal door into one of the hallways. She thought the man at the desk was probably watching her now. She was a specter, too, like all the others.

After two years away, Jane was shocked by her brother's appearance. Thin and pale and hunched over in a metal folding chair, he stared up at a TV screen affixed high in a corner of the common room. Jane could hardly tell the women from the men, as slouched and hunched as they were, dressed nearly identically in dreary, loose cotton clothes that puddled around them. But she knew her brother, and at her first sight of his back, she recognized him out of all the others. Something about the lines of his body, the way he sat, the shape of his head. It all made him, the little brother she grew up both resenting and adoring in the years before her mother's death. He'd been a distraction in those early days when she wanted nothing more than to have her mother to herself. Later, he'd been a symbol of the reality that her mother was really dying—one she dodged by avoiding her mother's desire to talk about Jane's responsibility to Lance. But things changed again when Jane's father remarried. Then, Jane saw him as her ally, the one person left who connected her directly to her mother. As he'd gotten older, he'd made her laugh and dared her to climb trees and helped her, slowly, move past the heaviness of her grief. He was smart and funny and athletic. He was handsome, too. When, in the middle of his sophomore year in college, he'd had his first schizophrenic episode, the whole family was shocked. They racked their memories for signs they'd missed, quirks of moods, silent periods, brief moments of deep confusion. They never agreed on whether or not the signs had been there, and after a few years, it didn't matter anymore.

"He's okay, you can go to him," an orderly in bright green scrubs told Jane. She tried to ignore the other patients watching her as she crossed the room and knelt down on the linoleum next to her brother's chair.

"Hi, Lance, it's me. I'm back."

She didn't expect a reply, and she didn't get one. He was often quiet. The drugs kept his hallucinations at bay, but they also sent him spinning in a different direction—into a completely internal world. After his first breakdown, Lance moved home and began a strict regimen of medications and therapy. Her father watched him closely, hired the best psychologists and sought innovative treatments as he researched endlessly.

Her dad and stepmother poured money and time into Lance at just the time when they wanted a new kind of freedom. Lance's sickness took over every aspect of their lives for years. They couldn't leave him alone, couldn't travel and couldn't trust him to take care of himself. Lance didn't always respond to the medication, and when he forgot to take it or it stopped working, he could grow violent in an instant. By then, Jane was away at college. One day, not long after she'd come home to tell her dad she was leaving for Africa, she'd witnessed Lance switch from calmly eating lunch to grasping his father's head in a tight lock, only letting go when Jane and her stepmother leaped upon him, scratching and screaming and pulling him back. The next day, her father had Lance committed again.

"We can't put you in the face of that danger," he'd said. "You shouldn't have to be afraid in your own house." But Jane hadn't been afraid of Lance. Not ever. Instead, she felt only anger. She remembered the fight she'd had with them after Lance was gone. The things she'd accused them of—of using her as their reason to finally get rid of her brother.

Jane sat with Lance in the common room, with other patients watching them for several silent hours. Once, when she felt the baby moving, she grasped Lance's hand and pressed it to her belly. "That's your niece or nephew," she said, and she'd watched his face. His expression didn't change at all.

"He didn't talk," Jane said later that night at dinner. "Not even a word." She mentioned it only as something to say; she knew they didn't want to hear about Lance. They had locked him away in a mental compartment they only opened during their twice weekly, one-hour visits. But Jane wanted to talk. She still obsessed over her own mind and moods. The anxiety that had weighted her down for the last few months fed off the deep-seated fear that her own brain was as diseased as her brother's. Or, worse, that this baby of hers would inherit Lance's sickness. She was terrified of that and even more terrified that if that did happen, she would end up doing what her own father had—sending the child away and barely looking back.

Paul returned to her just in time. He'd packed the Monrovia house up and had all their freight directed to the States. He was exhausted when his plane landed, and Jane let him go right to bed. She opened his suitcases, though, and pulled out a couple of books he'd packed, a shirt or two and his toothbrush. She sniffed everything closely, both wanting and dreading a whiff of the place he'd come from.

Barely two days later, Grace was pulled from Jane under bright lights and a rush to the operating table. It wasn't what Jane expected, and she lay shivering with surprise and terror as the doctors cut her open. Paul's face was mostly hidden behind a neat blue mask, but Jane noticed the way his eyes looked—as if, for the very first time, he had no understanding of what was happening. There was nothing he could say, no way to control the outcome of the birth. Through the fear and the chill in Jane's body, she saw his eyes and they made her feel a bubble of sympathy under everything else. Paul was not in charge here. This was not his element, and even though Jane never wanted Grace born this way—she'd imagined a natural birth, free of drugs and scalpels and fear—she was oddly relieved to see Paul in this moment of vulnerability. This wasn't his to manage, none of it was. He wasn't in control, and for the first time in their relationship, Jane felt fear like heat from his skin. She'd never seen him raw like this. It made her feel vindicated, somehow. *Now you know*, she thought. *Now you know.*

When Grace was in her arms—wet and red as meat—she felt elated. Paul leaned down and kissed her temple, awe in his eyes replacing the fear. He hadn't looked at Jane with that expression for so long. She was new again for him—strong and capable. Already baby Grace changed everything.

For the first six weeks of Grace's life, the new family lived with Jane's parents. Paul spent days at the State Department, settling into his new position. Occasionally, Jane left Grace with her parents so she could visit Lance. He never spoke to her. He was a shell; the dark breathing creature of his brain, his real self, was hidden so deeply it couldn't come out.

One evening, a few days before they were set to move into the little house they'd rented in Arlington, Jane and her father packed Grace into the stroller and walked slowly through a nearby park. Together they watched the little children dig holes in the sand and shout from between the bars of an elaborate jungle gym. Mothers sat on benches, watching closely, occasionally offering up juice boxes and packets of pretzels or Goldfish crackers to the kids who buzzed back and forth to them, bees to flowers.

"I miss those days," Jane's father said. "When you and Lance were little and it was so very simple. It all changes fast. You just can't predict."

Jane didn't answer. She was stunned her father had said Lance's name. She hadn't heard it from his mouth in so long. The stroller wheels clicked against the seams in the sidewalk, and Jane's father breathed deeply. "It's not perfect, nothing ever is. Kids aren't yours to keep, in the end, Jane. You can't control every outcome. I tried to make a place for Lance, but I couldn't. It was too hard. We had to accept him the way he is. The Lance you knew? The Lance we loved? He's gone forever. It was our gift to him to finally acknowledge that. Children become themselves. You can't force an outcome just because you want to."

A few months later, Paul and Jane took Grace to get her passport photo. They didn't know when, but they would be posted overseas again, and even the baby needed official papers. Because Grace couldn't sit or stand for the photo, Jane had to hold her up. The photographer directed her to stand behind a thick, blue drape and push her hands out—still draped—to lift the baby up for the camera. Behind her dark curtain, Jane held tightly to Grace's wiggling body. Several weeks later, Paul brought the passport home with him from work. When Jane looked at it, she saw the beautiful round face of her beloved daughter. It was a good picture, and Jane filed it away with her own passport and Paul's and didn't think of it again.

Months later, when they were packing up for their next post, Paul pulled the three passports out and laid them on his dresser where they wouldn't be forgotten. This time, when Jane opened Grace's, her eyes were drawn to the space beyond Grace's soft, round head to the undefined, almost ghostly shape behind the blue curtain. For a second Jane thought maybe it hadn't been her back there, not her at all who lifted the baby's body dutifully up to the camera's eye. It couldn't be her who'd agreed to take this new and delicate thing so far away. And she felt the sensation of slipping on ice, uncontrolled and dangerous; there was no way to stop from falling. For an instant, she didn't even recognize herself.

SOLAI VALLEY

There it was again—a puff of dust.

Ruthie's heart beat fast. She licked her bottom lip, and wondered if she should put her boots back on. If it were John coming back, she'd want to meet him at the turnoff. The sun was sliding low, a pure white smudge in the pale blue sky. Twilight was coming. She should put the kettle on. John would want his tea.

Her eye had caught something out beyond the screen door, out beyond the paving-stone walkway that led from the house to the two concrete posts marking the entrance to the property. The front field was out that way, hardly a field now that the drought had erased the grasses and shrubbery bit by bit, leaving only the bones and hides of the cows she used to help tend.

She knew what it meant, that puff of dust. In the distance, where before everything went bad, trucks would rev their engines up that last hill, making for the barns where they'd load their beds with fresh milk and meat. No trucks had come for so long now.

She opened the screen door and stepped out onto the terrace. The stones were curved and warm under her stocking feet. How long it had taken Martin and the Kikuyu to make this terrace. Ruthie remembered the endless lines of sweating workers, bent under the weight of baskets filled with river stones Martin had them dig and then lay in the cement he'd carefully mixed. Every day the project grew. First, Ruthie agreed to have a small patio there, just enough for guests to stand on while knocking at the door. But then she had an image of them all sitting in wicker chaises on a large stone terrace, drinking Pimm's Cup in the evenings while the children played in the garden and the sun set—all the colors they would see in that wide-open sky where evening was short-lived but beautiful.

The chaises were gone, long ago rotted through and never replaced. So instead of sitting, Ruthie wrapped her arms around herself and stared out at the rutted dirt road, where the cloud of dust had become a small car.

Fifty years ago, when Martin proposed, the Solai Valley was ripe. Ruthie didn't hesitate when he asked her to marry him and move to the farm he'd bought here. Nairobi and the Club, her life in her parents' house, it all made Ruthie tired. She craved the land to the north and the way the space and the overwhelming sky made you feel small and free. It was in her bones, she argued to her parents, as both of them had been ranch children raised by British *émigrés* in the expanses of the Rift, and Ruthie herself spent her childhood summers on the farms in Loita and Nyeri where each pair of her grandparents had, at that time, still worked—eking out livings that sustained them until they died. And then the farms were sold. Her parents hadn't wanted either of them, and there was nobody else to pass them down to. The money Ruthie inherited from each sold farm was, in fact, the seed money for the house behind her now, for the barns, for the sheep dip and the Kikuyu school they'd built at the back of the acreage. Both were empty now, the concrete lining of the dip and the foundation of the school each as dried and cracked as the land.

What hope they'd had then, what visions of a beautiful earth-bound life filled with cows and milk and children of their own that would come back to farm on school holidays and work side by side with Ruthie and Martin and the Kikuyu.

They had had a few good years. At the beginning Ruthie was strong, and they had the patience to wait for the land to blossom with the corn they planted, the bananas and beans, and of course her daisies and herbs and the passion fruit vine she was training up a trellis in the back. They had that patience, and they had the open faces and clear eyes that made talking to each other so easy.

They had expected to work hard for the first few years. They had also expected that, eventually, things would be easier. That the rain wouldn't stop for so long, and that then, when it finally did come, it wouldn't be in such great deluges that it washed away topsoil and seedlings. They hadn't anticipated the darkness that fell into Ruthie after their first baby was born. How she would look at the tiny body asleep in her arms and have visions of leaving him under a bush for a hyena to eat, or the guilt she was racked with when the visions subsided.

"There's another one dead in the front field." Ruthie spoke quietly to herself now. "Another dead cow. This drought will be the death of all of us."

So deep in her own memories, Ruthie was startled enough to gasp when she heard a car door slam.

"Hello?"

The greeting came from a woman who stood beside a small and very dusty, dented car. Her accent was American, Ruthie noted, and her dark hair was pulled back into a long ponytail, but her head and face, well, all of her, was covered in a veil of the ochre dust the dry roads had spun up under her car tires. The woman wore jeans and a T-shirt, also covered in dust, and the same sandals made of car tires that the Maasai wore.

"Well, you're a right mess!" Ruthie couldn't think what else to say. She hadn't seen a *muzungu* stranger on her land for so long, for years and years. She swallowed the sudden bitter taste of disappointment that flooded her mouth. It wasn't John come back to see her. It wasn't John, just some lost aid worker or tourist needing directions.

"Are you John's mother?" the woman asked as she began approaching the stone terrace.

The words made sense. Ruthie understood each one separately, but strung together in this way, they confused her. She let the question sit. She did have a son. Was his name John? It was.

"Yes." Ruthie was suddenly aware of how alone she was. She couldn't afford the house staff anymore, not to mention the farmhands, so only Samuel had stayed on. He was as old as Ruthie was and, over the years he'd worked as their houseman, had married three wives one after the other and built a small house at the back of the land. Ruthie was glad he stayed; he and his son were the ones who helped Ruthie now, a few hours a week, with the house. Samuel still did her shopping, as well, down at the market. But she couldn't expect them to hear her if she screamed, not from this distance.

"My name is Leona. I'm wondering if your son is here? I met someone in Narok who told me this is where I might find him."

For a moment Ruthie felt her brain whirring in her head, trying to find the traction to organize the storm of thoughts blowing around like leaves in a windstorm. *Which son?* Ruthie wondered first, then she remembered, and then the confusion subsided.

"He's not here anymore." Ruthie spoke in a voice that wavered a bit, and then she cleared her throat. "What is it you want with him?"

The woman didn't answer Ruthie right away. She only stood there in her dusty jeans and rubber tire shoes and looked as perplexed as Ruthie felt. Then she turned and walked back to her car. Ruthie thought maybe she would get back in and drive away again, without another word. But instead, the woman opened the back door and leaned down. When she turned, in her arms, Ruthie saw, was a sleeping child.

Though covered with the same dust the mother was, and dressed only in a red *shuka* and several strands of beads, Ruthie could see the child was young—only three or so.

"What on earth have you got there?" Ruthie asked. "Why is this child dressed like a villager?"

Ruthie knew children were fragile. How often had she watched the Kikuyu children succumb to malaria and dysentery? It was common. But a white child? Ruthie felt her neck prickling with sweat. She squeezed her eyes closed. This couldn't happen again.

"No, no, no!" she scolded herself, pushing away the demon thought in her head. "This is not that. This is not that."

She opened her eyes and saw the younger woman's stricken face. Had she spoken aloud? It was so hard to remember anymore, what was in her head and what was outside. She spent the days speaking to nobody, and sometimes the words broke free from her mind and flew out into the world like birds from her mouth.

"She's not sick," Leona said. "She's only sleeping. It's been a long day. We drove from Narok. The road is worse than I expected. We didn't bring food for the trip, only a little water. It's gone now. I came here..." She paused, considering. Ruthie saw her eyes close and open again, shifting down to gaze at the grass. "I came to talk to your son. I wanted him to meet his daughter."

Ruthie's heart might have stopped just then. Her mind did. She could feel her thoughts, her lists, the memories she flipped through, even her ability to move, to speak, drain out of her. She turned into something frozen, instantly not a living thing. She forgot to breathe.

The American woman turned to look out at the road behind them. The dust had settled, and the horizon was clear and empty. The day sky was lifting itself up, tucking the final folds of light away and drawing out the colors of the land.

It was out of her control, this body was, Ruthie thought. As quickly as she'd been drained of life, she filled back up again. She didn't want to. She wanted to stay a stone thing, to die, to disappear from here.

Leona resumed talking, as if she hadn't noticed that Ruthie had died and come to life again right in front of her.

"I'm sorry, but are there villages near here? A town? I didn't see one on the Narok road, but maybe beyond here? Close?" Ruthie saw Leona looked worried. "I can't bear to drive back to Narok tonight. It's too dark—my daughter is too hungry. We need to find a place to eat and sleep."

"You'd best come in," Ruthie said, glancing down at the smooth face of the child. It was a girl. She couldn't remember when she'd last seen a white child that age. She yearned to reach out and touch the girl's cheek, her hair. Leona shifted the girl in her arms so that the small blonde head was nestled in the crook of her neck, and her hands were clasped under the child's legs. Ruthie turned, and Leona followed her back across the stone patio and up the steps into the house.

Ruthie hadn't had guests for years, and she felt herself becoming flushed and nervous when she glanced around and saw how her house might look to a stranger. The tight foyer, the faded chairs in the sitting room and the cobwebs that traced the upper corners of the walls. She felt a flash of annoyance at Samuel and his son. They had gotten lazy, hadn't they? Not bothering to do their best for an old woman.

"Sit," Ruthie said curtly, her annoyance shifting to the strange woman. Who was she and why had she come? "I'll make a pot of tea. I'm afraid—" Ruthie knew the lie was coming and did nothing to stop it "—the servants are off today."

Martin had designed the house so that all of the rooms in

the back looked out over the garden. Ruthie wanted a garden desperately. In her parents' Nairobi house, there were always fresh flowers in vases, newly plucked herbs hanging to dry in the kitchen, and enormous jacaranda and flame trees that burst into bloom and filled the windows with lavender and crimson. When Ruthie moved here, to this house, her first order of business was to create a garden in the back. She had it all in her head. She took her time to sketch out her plan, carefully labeling her drawings with the correct genus and plant names, and using her oil pastels to plan where the pinks would go, the gladiolas, the roses and the herbs. She wanted it to be perfect. But a drought that year had slipped its fingers one by one across the land.

At first Martin told her it would be best not to water the bougainvillea she was trying to train up the front of the house, between the windows, or the stands of glads she'd painstakingly transplanted from her mother's garden to soften the look of the entryway. How sad she'd been to watch them die. Then he said she should forget the garden entirely. "We don't have the resources now," he'd warned, "not the manpower or the water. We've got to put everything into the farm, the cattle."

Now Ruthie stood in her kitchen. The polished concrete floor was cold under her feet, and the window looked out over nothing but more scrub. A lone acacia in the middle distance was a flat smudge against the darkening sky. One or two stars emerged above it. It would be a clear night.

She heard sounds from the sitting room, a rustle and then voices—one small and thin, the other a woman's voice. The child was awake and the knowledge of that sent a frisson through Ruthie. She felt both terrified and thrilled at the opportunity to sit near a little one again, to watch the tiny hands move.

Only two tea bags left, but Ruthie used them both. Samuel would have to go to the market tomorrow. Only a tiny bit of milk, as well. Children liked milk. She wondered if she should pour it into the teapot or into a glass for the girl. She chose to save it just for the child and found a packet of digestive biscuits in a cupboard she hadn't opened in days. When had she put them there?

The girl was a dirty thing curled up like an animal next to her mother on Martin's chair. They shouldn't sit there, Ruthie thought. It was Martin's chair and he wouldn't like it. But she held her tongue.

"So, can I ask you where John is?" Leona looked up and sipped her tea.

Ruthie's teacup shivered in her hand, almost tipped.

"It's important that I speak to him." Leona glanced at the child when she said this and reached out to touch the girl's head. "He needs to know."

Ruthie paused. The edge of her cup grazed her bottom lip and she couldn't remember, for a second, what she was doing by holding it there, so close to her face that she could feel steam. What was that for?

Sometimes Ruthie knew she was sliding into forgetfulness. She would notice that she'd left the tap on and that precious water was escaping down the drain. She would wake up to where she was and turn the water off or close the refrigerator door or pull the ant-covered butter from the cupboard where she'd left it days before, having forgotten, for the moment, that butter should be kept where the ants couldn't get it. She watched this happen to her father, and she wasn't surprised by the lapses in memory she had, the confusion. She tried hard to think of only one thing at a time, to concentrate on what she was doing. She couldn't always, though, and the moments of lost thoughts were increasing.

The splash of milk from the child's cup broke into her thoughts. She'd dropped the glass and had leaped back from it while her mother fussed. "God, be more careful!"

"It's all right, girl, it's all right. There's a rag in the kitchen, down the hall," she directed Leona. "She's just a child, no need to scold."

It was much later, after she showed Leona to an empty bedroom and gave the girl some blankets to curl up with on the armchair that she realized she hadn't answered Leona's question.

Ruthie sometimes wondered when things changed. Was it watching her garden die? Seeing the parched land suck the life out of every living thing it could hold? She remembered clearly that it was around that time when the life, the smiles and jokes, had slid out of her Martin. He changed the same way the land did those first years. But when the rain came—finally, after three years—and things grew green again, Martin never turned back. His face was set by then. His eyes were tired, his arms were burned the color of dirt, and his anger at the land, at everyone and everything, never left. His anger would have come again anyway, Ruthie knew, just as the drought came back. They had two years of normal rains and then season after season that were dry as bones. They were doomed from the start of this farm; the weather never settled back into the patterns they'd depended on.

So they rarely sat on the wide terrace in the evening, having drinks and watching the children. Instead, Martin sat in his chair in the sitting room, where he drank whiskey, not Pimm's, and Ruthie learned to be quiet near him, to keep the babies from crying. She learned to watch the way he clenched and unclenched his hands, the way the new muscles in his forearms rose and fell like breathing.

Ruthie woke in the earliest part of the morning. The windows in her bedroom were thick with darkness and, way out there, somewhere, she could hear the whoop of a hyena. How she hated them. After the first baby was born, her blood turned thick with constant dread and terrible thoughts pushed into her brain like worms through dirt.

It was always a hyena. A hyena that snuffled the dirt for the new baby smell and sidled on his bloody paws up to where, in her mind, her baby lay, naked and prone, innocent and perfectly unaware. In the beginning, she had no control. The pictures in her head would flicker on—the hyena would come closer and closer and she would watch as it stopped, sniffing the baby's head and soft hair. Later she learned to force the images away by shouting. She'd let her anger take over instead, and that cut the visions short. The hyena stopped in his tracks, turning tail and slinking back into the underbrush. But her anger made her children slink, too. They would eye her warily, close their mouths and cry. How she hated herself then. How she wished she could find the words to explain that her temper was her only way to let them live.

In the end, it wasn't a hyena at all. But still, the sound of them, even after all these years, drove a spike of despair through her heart.

Leona woke after the sun was already above the horizon. The narrow bed Ruthie showed her to last night was hard, and the mosquito net had holes in it. All night she'd heard buzzing in her ears, and now she could see several mosquitoes resting on the interior of the net. They were thick with her blood. She turned her head and stretched her arms and legs. Her muscles hurt from hunching over the steering wheel all those long hours yesterday, fighting the bumps in the road. She sat up and pulled the useless net out from under the mattress. At least she could trap the creatures in here, hope they would die before the net was used again. And when would that be? The house looked like nobody ever came. The woman, Ruthie, seemed like she hardly ever saw another person.

Leona noticed as she threw her feet to the floor and stood up that the room was nearly empty. There was only the bed and the net, a small table with a lamp on it and, across from the bed, a white dresser. The dresser looked wildly out of place in the simple room in this derelict house. It reminded Leona of the kind of things in her parents' house, back in Oregon. It was shiny white, with curved edges, and perfectly round glass pulls on the drawers. There were painted flowers, faded now, but visible, along the drawer faces.

Curious, Leona walked to the dresser and slid her hands across the empty, smooth surface. The tips of her fingers remembered the feel of this kind of furniture, even though it had been years since she'd seen anything like it. The memory pulled something in her. She opened the top drawer, expecting to find nothing but dust or maybe silverfish. But instead she found it full. Tiny linen clothes, all folded perfectly in even piles, interspersed with the smallest pairs of shoes Leona had ever seen. There were three little brown pairs of soft leather, and one little white pair with ribbons for ties.

Leona picked up each pair of shoes one by one. She touched the soft fabric of the clothes and the delicate stitches in the knitted hats and sweaters. She never had clothes like this for her daughter. She had left all that behind when she moved to Kenya. Leona shoved the drawer shut and opened the next one. This one was empty except for a large photograph, framed in silver, turned facedown. Leona didn't hesitate to pick it up, to turn it over, and when she did she saw two little boys. One about three, she guessed, and one younger, barely sitting up. They were dressed in the things the drawer held—the linen overalls, the tiny shoes. Leona could clearly see her daughter in one of the faces. That must be him, she thought, as a baby.

Leona flipped the photograph back on its face and shut it in the drawer again. She remembered that she'd told Ruthie the truth, that it had escaped her mouth without her realizing it until it was too late. She wondered if Ruthie would even remember.

Ruthie lay still in her bed, listening to the air in the house around her. Strange how even the silence changed when someone else was in the house with her. She imagined she could hear the child breathing. The child. She pulled the thread of a vague memory in her brain, and like a magician's multicolored scarf pulled from a hat, the thought loosened and broke free. Her grandchild.

Ruthie sat up in bed and turned so her feet could find the floor. She had to see the child.

She didn't bother with the lights. She'd lived here long enough that she knew each divot in the concrete floor by heart. She padded down the hall and into the sitting room where the girl curled, fast asleep, in Martin's chair. A line of mosquito bites studded the girl's cheek. Should have made sure she had a net, Ruthie scolded herself. She grasped the edge of the blanket she'd directed Leona to cover the girl with last night, and tugged it back up to the child's chin. She paused with her hands on the blanket and lifted a finger to stroke the girl's cheek just above the reddened bumps. How soft it was, how curved. Ruthie quietly pulled a stool from the corner of the room and perched upon it. She watched the girl's eyelids shiver with dreaming.

Leona had said John was the father, and of course that was true. Of course. But deep down in Ruthie's bones, she recognized the imprint of her other son on this girl's face. The set of the eyes, the particular placement of the ears, the way the eyebrows swept gracefully up in the middle. She hadn't been able to look at the one remaining photo of Thomas for years and years, and watching the sleeping girl was nearly as painful. Had he been this age? Ruthie wondered. She couldn't remember; she wouldn't let herself remember. She slid off the stool and went to the kitchen to heat water for tea. It was only after she filled the kettle and turned on the flame that she remembered she had no tea. Shame. She'd have to see if Samuel had some. She had to feed her guests, of course.

So she left the kitchen to dress. She thought she could hurry to Samuel's little house and be home before the girl woke, but as she crossed the sitting room she caught sight of two blue eyes, wide-open and peering around the room curiously.

She didn't want her granddaughter to be frightened, so she spoke in a whisper. She held out her hand and said, "The sun's nearly up, girl. Come, I'll show you where I watch it being born." Without a word, the child slipped from under the blanket and stood up.

The sitting room was empty when Leona wandered through. She'd left her daughter curled on the chair last night fast asleep. Ruthie had given her a blanket to put over her and then shown Leona to bed. But the girl was gone, the blanket neatly folded, the chair vacant. Leona felt dread pour through her like a liquid spilling down her back.

"Hello?" she called down the hall toward where she assumed the other bedrooms were. There was no answer. Leona just heard the hiss of the kettle and, in the kitchen, found the stove on, the flame from the burner so high it licked halfway up the sides of the kettle, almost to the handle. She turned the burner off and glanced up to where the large window looked out over the yellow savannah. In the distance, she saw two figures walking slowly up a small hill. Ruthie was bent at the waist, leaning toward Adia. Leona saw her daughter reach up and take the old woman's hand. "Thank God," Leona thought, as she looked around the kitchen for the teapot, the tea and something to eat.

She found the teapot sitting on the windowsill, the cold dregs of last night's brew in the bottom. The box of tea bags was empty, however, and when Leona began opening cupboards to look for more, she found almost nothing. The wrapper from the biscuit package they'd eaten last night was in one cupboard, next to a quarter bag of flour infested with black weevils. In another cupboard was a full set of cups made from delicate china, painted with the softest pale pink flowers. There was a matching teapot and sugar bowl, too, and a curved milk pitcher of china so fine, Leona thought she could see through it. But that was it. The other cupboards held a few rough pottery mugs—the ones they used last night, still dirty, Leona noticed, and a few plates and random pieces of cutlery. The fridge was nearly as bad. In the back were a couple of slices of bread in a bag and an empty jar of marmalade.

Leona was starving. They'd left Narok yesterday just after a breakfast of *ugali* and chai, and stopped a few hours later in a tiny, unnamed town for *mandazis* and more tea. But then, apart from the weak tea and the biscuits they'd eaten here last night, they'd had nothing. Well, Leona thought, she'd simply fill up the water bottles and head out. It would only be a couple of hours until the next town, or at least a village, where they could ask for food.

She couldn't see Ruthie and her daughter anymore, but around the back of the house she found the path up the hill where she'd seen them last. The air was cool, and she heard a hoopoe in an acacia tree nearby calling its own name. God, she thought, how amazing it would be to live here, to have this empty space be the backyard, the hills in the distance your daily view, the sounds of the creatures all around you. Nobody, no people for miles.

Leona walked up a long bare track that meandered from the house up a steadily rising hill through the grasses—someone had used this very path so many times that the foliage just here had stopped growing. Leona wondered whose feet had worn it down.

At the top of the hill Leona saw her daughter and Ruthie. They were sitting on a stone bench under a spreading baobab larger than any Leona had ever seen. The tree's broad branches were thick with green leaves, and the shadow it threw was dark and wide. When she neared them, they both turned, and for an instant Leona saw them in each other; the way Ruthie's lips curved at the edges was in her daughter's face, the way each of their necks rose, long and elegant, from their shoulders.

Leona scooped her daughter up, and sat down on the bench in her place, the girl in her lap, facing Leona's chest, small arms around Leona's neck. There were headstones at her feet, Leona saw. That's what Ruthie was showing the girl.

"Who are they?" Leona asked Ruthie, tightening her hold on her daughter.

"It's her family," Ruthie answered. Leona's heart skipped. It was too late to pretend anymore. Ruthie had heard; she knew.

"Where is John?" Leona asked again. In her imagination, she'd come here and found him, they'd talked it all through and he'd accepted, happily, his role as a father. On the drive up yesterday, Leona daydreamed a joyous reunion of father and daughter, of settling her daughter into a new home where John could raise her as Leona expected he'd been raised—in a family of happy ranchers, connected to the earth and each other. And then, Leona had imagined, she would be free again. Free to settle into academic life in Nairobi with nobody to worry about but herself. She wanted Ruthie to tell her John was coming back, that he lived in this beautiful place and they could wait for a while and then he'd be here.

Ruthie tried to answer. She worked to make her mouth move in the way that would tell Leona what she needed to know. But instead she heard the sound of the snuffling animal, smelled the rotten hyena breath on her face, saw the baby under the bush, unknowing, still loving her, his mother, still instinctively connected to her, still unaware of the ways a mother could betray her child.

Her head filled with pictures she couldn't organize, and among them was the one she dreaded the most, the split hairbreadth when she'd tried to run from Martin, and his breathing muscles, his stony face, his whiskey and his rock-hard fists. She'd run from the house that night; it wasn't dark yet, but where did she think she would go? She couldn't remember that, but she remembered how she'd flipped on the engine in the farm truck and revved it loudly. She remembered the hysteria she felt that night, the desperate need to fly away into another world, away from the desolate land and the sullen man she found herself with. She remembered that she left her children behind. She threw the truck in Reverse, hit the gas and only then looked back.

It was little John's face in the rearview mirror that she couldn't forget. The O of his mouth, the fear in his eyes. For the shortest second, Ruthie thought his rapidly approaching figure was running after her because he didn't want her to leave him behind, didn't want her to leave. He'd only just started walking, was unsteady on his feet and slow. But Thomas was older. He'd darted out after her when the only thing she could hear was the whooshing of desperation in her ears, her need to escape.

She didn't see him running behind her to help John, she didn't see him. She saw John's eyes, those saucers of terror, before she felt the bump under the truck tire.

Everything had changed the day Thomas died. It all had changed that day, like an earthquake that jarred everything out of position, and nothing ever went back right. She didn't attempt escape again. Martin finally succumbed to cirrhosis, and although she tried her best, the farm was left to decay. John had moved to Nairobi by then, and one by one the servants and farmhands had drifted away to jobs that would pay.

In her head Ruthie opened her mouth to tell Leona the truth. She heard herself say, "John is dead."

Leona felt it physically; the news hit her in the solar plexus. She winced at the pain and gasped. The door she'd counted on being opened slammed shut. John was the family she'd counted on for Adia, and the aunts and uncles and cousins she imagined him having. But there was none of that, just this doddering old woman. Adia couldn't stay here. Leona wanted to ask how John had died and when, and whether he'd left behind other children or a wife, but she couldn't form the words. Ruthie's face was pinched and sad. Leona didn't want to prolong the suffering of making the old woman remember. What did it matter, anyway?

"What will you do?" Ruthie asked. She wanted to hold the girl's hand again, walk with her down the hill and take her home.

Leona shook her head slowly. She had no idea what to say. She had no idea what she'd do. "Go home, I guess," she answered, and a blank page spread out in her mind. The ease of moving back to the manyatta tempted her. She could leave the girl there. Simi would be thrilled, would mother her better than she could herself. Then she could forget everything. But she knew she wouldn't do that, and so the question went unanswered. Where would home be?

"Home to America," Ruthie stated. That was a good idea. It would be better for the child there, she expected.

They didn't stay under the baobab much longer after that. Leona helped Ruthie walk back down the track through the grasses and reminded her not to leave the kettle on, the flame up too high. Leona was torn, she told herself over and over again as she fought the road back to Narok, about leaving such a fragile woman alone in such a wild place. But she couldn't possibly stay. She was stung with disappointment and hemmed in by the hot breath of indecision. What now? She'd made a plan; she'd tried to execute it. Now there were too many new decisions to make, too many new things to consider.

Ruthie had watched the dust die down on the road after Leona drove away with the girl and she was alone again. She stood by the window long after the car had disappeared and her hips began to ache with the strain of standing. She couldn't decide if what she'd told Leona was what she'd really meant to say.

Samuel came that evening with her groceries. He came nearly

every day to check on her, and sometimes brought fresh food with him. He told her not to try to cook by herself; in her hands, the food ended up in the wrong places, burned or rotting, improperly stored or cooked. He would do it, he implored. And so he came that evening laden with bags from the market, and he placed the milk and eggs in the fridge and the biscuits and tea in the cupboard. He was sweeping ants off the counter when Ruthie thought to reach out and grasp him by the arm. He turned and looked at her, and she noticed the film over his eyes, the gray curls in his hair, his thin, old voice.

"I've misled her, Samuel. The American woman."

"Madam, sit please," Samuel whispered. "You are tired. There is nobody here, no American."

Ruthie knew he hadn't seen Leona, hadn't seen the little girl, her granddaughter. The house Samuel lived in with his family was beyond the hill, out of sight.

"They were here, Samuel. My granddaughter and her mother. I've told them John is dead. He's the girl's father. She looks like our family, exactly like Thomas." Ruthie took a deep breath.

"But you must tell them I meant my Martin is dead, my Martin and my Thomas. They are the ones who've gone. John is the one she wanted, of course. John, in Nairobi. I don't know why I said what I did. You must help me. You have to remember to tell her if she comes back, or to tell him. You must."

When the dark fell, Ruthie watched Samuel leave her house. He'd made her tea, fried an egg for her and laid it carefully on toast. The house felt more empty than usual. She wished they had stayed, her granddaughter and the American.

That night, late, Ruthie watched from her bedroom window as the moon slid up the sky. It would be a bright night. The moon would illuminate the open land behind the house; it would keep hyenas in the shadows. It would spill on the gravestones under the baobab and shine down on the faces of her dead.

She thought about Samuel telling his son to go into the market tomorrow to call John in Nairobi. She needed him to come. John would come. He was a good son; the one who lived.

CHILDREN ARE THE BRIGHT MOON

Leona drove without stopping. The dust from the road billowed thickly through the windows and covered Adia, who was stretched out and sleeping on the back seat. Leona glanced at her hands on the wheel. They looked like clay—as if she was a still, carved statue. She felt like one, too—still and cold and unable to think. She just drove. Even the potholes and the bumps and ruts in the road didn't concern her. She let the car bounce and dip and bang, and she didn't slow down until she saw the buildings of Nakuru town in the distance. She wished it wasn't so close, and she regretted not driving more slowly. In Nakuru the road split—the southeastern route led up the edges of the Rift Valley escarpment to Nairobi, and the southern route led back to Narok and, beyond that, to the manyatta. Nakuru meant a decision.

Leona lifted her foot off the accelerator and let the little car stop. It seemed so silent when the engine died. She watched the dust sink from the air around her, and then opened her door and stepped out of the car. Her legs felt rubbery and weak from the combination of sitting still for so long and the constant vibrations of the engine through her muscles. She shook one leg, and then the other, and then walked up the road a few steps. The sky was empty and clear, and Leona had the sensation she might be able to just walk into it. She could pull the blue around her like a blanket and sleep. The image made her smile. How long had it been since she last felt relaxed?

"Mama?" Adia's voice was small and sleepy through the space between them. Leona felt her heart seize up—just the tiniest bit—when she heard the voice. Were mothers supposed to feel that—what was it, disappointment?—when they heard their babies call to them? Simi had always looked thrilled to see Adia. Leona thought hard, but couldn't remember ever seeing Simi look tired or annoyed when Adia wanted her. "Yeyo." Adia called Simi "mother." Although Adia called Leona mama, when the girl said them, the two words for the same thing sounded different to Leona's ears. When Adia said *yeyo*, the word was softer somehow, less foreign to Adia's tiny lips.

Leona walked back to the car and opened the back passenger door for her daughter to climb out. "Go pee if you have to," she said, and then the choice was made without her even making it—the words just came out—so easily they surprised her when she heard them. "It'll be another couple of hours driving until we see Simi." Adia's face, still sleepy and layered with the fine, red dust of the road, lit up as brightly as Leona had ever seen it. She couldn't take the words back now. She settled behind the steering wheel again. Her legs still felt stiff, and her neck was sore, though Leona felt lightness in her chest she hadn't felt before. There were solutions to every problem.

They'd been gone just over two weeks. A tiny amount of time, but Leona thought the manyatta looked different. As they drove closer, the light began to darken in the sky, and the silhouettes of the squat, curved houses looked cold and shadowy. Leona knew that inside the huts fires were crackling and hot, sweet tea was boiling. But the image didn't make her feel warm and secure as it had before. Instead, she thought of the dense smoke in the huts and the low chairs that made her knees ache when she lowered herself onto them.

Adia, however, became more animated as the village drew closer and closer, and when Leona finally brought the car to a stop, Adia flew from the back seat like a bird and was off—just a tiny figure silhouetted against the darkening sky—and then disappeared into the enclosure.

Leona sat in the still car. The windows were open, and the air was filled with the smells she'd loved and lived with for so long: wood smoke and cattle and meat roasting on a fire and, underneath it all, the sharp smell of dust in the grasses and the wind; a distinctly African smell. The wave of emotion she felt suddenly took Leona by surprise. It was the exhaustion, she told herself as the tears came. Leona hardly ever cried. The heavy feeling in her chest and the tears themselves were a shock to her, but more of a surprise was the feeling of longing. She wondered how it was possible to long for something you hadn't left yet. Preemptive nostalgia, she decided. She was ready to leave—she wanted to leave, but in so many ways she would miss this life, this manyatta, these people. She would miss Adia. She drew in a deep breath and wiped her eyes on her sleeve. The car door, slamming shut behind her, sounded too sharp for this soft place.

First, Leona went to her old home. Nobody was in the central corral, just the lowing cattle, methodically chewing their cuds. They shook their heads as Leona threaded her way through them. Of course her fire was out. She couldn't remember if she'd extinguished it before she left that afternoon, or if it had gone out naturally. Either way, the hut was dark and chilly, and the coals in the fire pit sooty and dead. She fished her key fob out of her jeans pocket and found the tiny flashlight attached. Its light was too small to make out much, but she ran it over the contents of the little room with the hope she'd see a box of matches. She usually kept some, but she couldn't see any now—

not on the little wooden shelf she kept her cups and plates on, not on the overturned box she used as a bedside table. She was wary about fumbling around in the dark too much. Snakes were always a possibility since the place had been empty of people for so long, scorpions, too. Instead, she swallowed her dread, and turned to head back toward the corral.

It was hard for Leona to think about that afternoon. On one hand she accepted that, at least in her mind, she'd acted in Adia's best interest. She'd wanted to provide a different life for the girl, one her own parents would approve of, and one that might be more secure. But shame rose in her chest now. The look on Simi's face haunted Leona. Simi, who had been a friend and confidant; really, her only friend and confidant. Simi, who had loved Adia in a way that Leona hadn't—couldn't. How could she have hurt her friend that way? Dreading the confrontation, but needing fire, and wanting to get it over with, she crossed to Simi's house and ducked in the door. The air inside was acrid and stale. Simi hadn't been taking care of the fire, or cooking much. That was obvious. The embers glowed tiny and orange in the very bottom of the fire pit, they would die soon, but in the pale glow they gave, Leona could make out two figures twined together on the rawhide bed across from her. One thin woman, wrapped in a *shuka* and shaking with sobs, and one little blonde girl.

Leona knelt on the dirt floor and blew into the coals; she tossed in a few bits of kindling she found there and emptied Simi's bucket of water into the *suferia*. She busied herself without speaking; finding Simi's tin of tea, the sugar in a twisted piece of newspaper and a small jug of milk someone had recently left.

When the tea was ready, Leona ladled it into three cups. Only then did she clear her throat and speak. "I've made tea. Simi, Adia, we have to talk."

She handed a cup to both Adia and Simi, and then sipped from her own. She wished she knew what to say.

"Simi, I'm sorry." It was a good start, a necessary one. "Adia loves you, and I love you, and you're an excellent mother to her. Much better than I am."

Simi stayed quiet. Leona noticed how comfortable her daughter looked, curled in Simi's lap, the mug held carefully in her hand. Leona wondered again, for the hundredth time, how on earth she could have pulled these two apart.

"I am her mother, too, though. And even though Adia lives like a Maasai and thinks she's a Maasai, she isn't. The fact is…" Leona grasped for what to say next.

"The fact is that she is an American, and that brings good things, good opportunities." And here her voice veered into pleading. "I haven't been a mother to her, not like you have. I can only really give her two things—education and an opportunity to be American if she wants. I'll probably never be as good a mother as you are, Simi. That's why I hope we can agree to both be mothers to her. You for here, and me for Nairobi, and one day maybe for America."

Simi looked down at Adia, who had drained her cup and now lay with her head in Simi's lap, her legs stretched out to the side.

Simi was quiet. Leona felt a rustle of panic. If Simi refused, what would she do?

But then Simi shifted Adia off her lap and stood up. She knelt down and pulled a box from underneath the bed. From that, she lifted a traditional, wide necklace. In the firelight, the beads glinted and shone. It was beautiful. Even to Leona's untrained eye, it was obvious the work was delicate and perfect.

"When I knew I couldn't have my own baby, I gave this to N'gai. I hoped he would accept it and make me pregnant, but he didn't."

She looked up and Leona saw that Simi's eyes were clear and her gaze unapologetic. "I gave you leaves that I knew wouldn't work to make you bleed your baby out. I knew that she would live inside of you. I wanted her here more than you did."

Leona hated to cry, and the threat of a sob made her want to escape back into the darkness of her own little hut. Simi had never spoken to her this sternly, and maybe anticipating Leona's instinct to run, she placed her hand on Leona's arm.

"I took the necklace back from him. I lied to you and I stole my offering back—all for this child."

Leona didn't like the way the shame felt on her skin, like an itchy heat rash. But she forced herself to stay still, to endure the words she knew were true.

"You ask if we can both be her mother? I have always been her mother. If you wish for my daughter to go to school in Nairobi or in America, I will find a way to let her go."

Leona didn't answer. She was exhausted. Her body felt weak and worn out. She took the last swig of tea and tried not to catch Simi's eye as she stood up. She didn't want Simi to see how upset she was.

But Simi reached over again and touched Leona's pant leg. "Look at her," she said. When Leona looked up, Simi's eyes were gentle. "Two mothers can be better than one." Leona sighed deeply and tried to shake away her sadness.

"Look at our daughter," Simi said in a voice more proud than Leona had ever heard her use.

Leona looked down at the blonde head of her child. She was surprised that when she opened her mouth and said, "She's fast asleep," her own voice was warm and hopeful.

Leona woke the next morning in her cold, fireless house to the sounds of children playing a game, and she heard Adia's laughter. Leona stretched, rubbed her eyes and looked around the house where Adia was born. Then she pulled on her jeans and left. She didn't know when she'd be back.

Simi was up and different from the shadow she'd been last night. Leona, too, felt a sense of calm she hadn't felt in weeks. She was relieved she'd made this decision. Simi had already been to the river for water and had a pot of *ugi* boiling over the fire.

"Eat," she commanded Leona, handing over a bowl of the hot porridge. "It's a long drive to Nairobi."

Leona didn't wait long to leave. She found Adia playing outside the manyatta and gave her a hug. The little girl's body hummed with energy, and Leona knew she was desperate to escape back to her game. She released her daughter and watched as the girl bounded out of sight. Simi walked to the car with Leona and the two women stood together for a long, silent moment.

"I'll come back on as many weekends as possible, and holidays. When she turns six, I'll take her with me and enroll her in the school there. The one where she'll meet other American children," Leona said. She needed to watch Simi agree to this again in the light of day. She needed to make absolutely certain the other woman understood. "So, when she turns six, she'll come live with me."

Simi nodded. "Leona," she said, "you know I wanted to finish school. I would never stop my daughter from being educated."

"And no talk of *emurata* for her—ever. I don't even want her attending them." This was most important.

"Even though I'll take her to Nairobi when she's still too young, she'll be back and forth here a lot as she gets older, and I don't want her ever thinking she'll be cut. She cannot ever begin to want it, to think she needs it."

Leona had to trust that Simi would not put the notion in Adia's mind. The girl needed to know, all along, that she would never be joining her age-mates in that ceremony.

"Simi, you'll have to make it clear, not just to Adia, but to the elders."

Simi hadn't reconciled the image she'd had of an older girl, one who'd been to school, being cut. She had no idea how that would work, or if she could keep Adia from feeling the weight of that tradition. But her mouth opened, and she said what she needed to say.

"I swear to you, Leona, she will never think it's going to happen to her. She will never think she needs it."

Leona climbed in her car and closed the door. The window was still broken—permanently rolled down—so Leona stretched out her hand and clasped Simi's. The women looked at each other and Simi said, "Sometimes a child needs two mothers."

Leona didn't answer. She was ripe with more sadness, but also she felt a sense of relief. She was doing her best with what she had. Adia needed a family, and now she had one. Simi needed a child, and now she had one. Leona, well, she needed her work and her freedom, and her solitude. At least for a while longer.

As she shifted the car into Reverse, she leaned out the window one more time and waved at Simi, who still stood, her hand shading her eyes, the silver on her beaded necklaces glinting in the morning sun. It was a Kenyan sun; the kind she loved best—the brightest sun Leona had ever seen. Leona turned the car toward the road, and then she was gone.

THE BAOBAB IN SOLAI

John wasn't expecting anything other than the usual weekly update. "How's the old girl, then, Daniel? Still hanging on?"

But Daniel, the houseman's son, didn't assure John that his mother was okay, still forgetful, still confused, but okay. Instead, he sighed into the phone and clucked his tongue.

"Your mother, she is telling stories now, Mister John. My father is worried. Yesterday, your mother told him that an American *memsahib* came to the house. That she had a small girl with her. She said it was your daughter."

John lowered his coffee cup. His hand shook.

"An American was at the ranch, Daniel? In Solai?" His voice was rough in his mouth. "She had a girl with her?"

"Mister John, that is what your mother told my father when he went to cook her dinner last night. He told me that she was very firm. She was clear. *Tell John the American came. Tell John she brought his daughter.* But I am telling you, Mister John, this cannot be true. I think your mother's mind is almost finished. We saw nothing. We saw nobody." The phone line crackled.

Despite being less than two hundred miles away, the phone connection from Solai to Nairobi was tenuous at best.

"No worries." John managed to hide the catch in his throat. "I'll come to see Mum. I'll check that she's okay."

Almost four years ago, he was well on his way to being drunk when the American woman entered the bar. The place was a dark, wooden-walled room lit primarily by Christmas lights strung all around and looped across the ceiling over the bar. The woman seemed comfortable, like she'd been there before. She wasn't a tourist; John could see that from the way she greeted the barman in a familiar way and the quiet mix of Swahili she sprinkled on her English.

He'd liked the way her slim legs looked in her faded jeans and the way her straight brown hair was pulled back from her face in a tight ponytail, but how one piece, slightly shorter than the rest, kept falling back across her forehead. He liked the clear and steady gaze she gave the bartender when she ordered her beer and the way she didn't seem at all self-conscious of being in a bar, a woman alone in the middle of southwestern Kenya.

But mostly, he had to admit, he was drawn to something else about her—the air she had, the way she sat in this still pool of just herself and the way her face was so clear and plain and yet… He'd recognized something in her, a kinship of the broken. She was not whole, somehow. She resonated with echoes of spaces inside her that he knew too well. She wasn't beautiful, definitely not the kind of woman he normally found himself attracted to, but she was of his kind. He knew her without speaking a word.

When the blonde American he'd been flirting with came back from the restroom and stood behind him, sliding her sunburned arms around his shoulders and pressing her breasts against his back, he slid loose and turned to face her.

"Now you'll have to meet me again, next one's on you."

The way her face fell punished him a little. He didn't like

hurting women's feelings, but it was better, he figured, to rip the Band-Aid off as quickly as possible. He stood up and walked down the bar to where the brunette sat. He slid onto the stool next to her.

"Nipe bia ya Tusker, Matthew."

She made no movement to acknowledge him, even when he surreptitiously edged his stool closer to hers. She made no half turn so that her knees would brush his, gave no sidelong glance as she tipped her glass of beer to her lips. He'd never met a woman so unaware of his presence. He raked the fingers of his right hand through his thick, blond hair. He kept it just slightly long, curling over his ears and at the nape of his neck. Women loved to toy with it—pulling gently at the curls over his temples and brushing it back from his eyes as if he were a child. They liked to feel as if they were helping him, taking care of the handsome and hapless man-child.

Not this one, though. She didn't move a muscle when he pulled his fingers through his hair or when he deliberately laid his hand down on the bar just an inch or two from the wet ring her glass left there. Instead, she flagged the barkeep and ordered another beer.

"It's on me, Matthew," John said loudly. "Get the lady a drink."

That's when she turned to face him. Her face was slender and she wore no makeup. Her eyes were clear and her gaze completely steady, no guile, no sense of nervousness or needing to flirt.

"Thanks," she said. "But you don't have to buy my drink."

"No worries. I saw you come in. You're not a tourist are you? What... Peace Corps? Development worker? Christ—" he paused and tipped his head back, squinted his eyes at her "—don't tell me you're a bloody missionary!" He grinned as he said it.

Women told him all the time that with his looks, he could call a person a bastard and it would sound like a compliment if he smiled when he said it. He registered the tiny movement in her brow, the slight softening of her mouth. It worked. She dipped her head and the errant tendril of hair fell from behind her ear and slipped across her cheek. Before he could think what he was doing, he lifted his hand to slide it back into position for her.

"Are you English?" she asked.

"Not for generations. Born in Nakuru, actually. Kenyan all the way back to my great-greats. They came here from England to farm and to fuck. The farms mostly went to shit, but they drank enough that they stopped caring." He flashed the smile again. "How about you? American?"

She nodded. "Pacific Northwest. Oregon."

"Well, we've established that I am home and that you are not. So what's your story? What brings you to the armpit's asshole here?"

"I live south of Narok. In Loita. I'm living in a manyatta there. You know…" She paused, and he watched her fingering the label on the bottle. Peeling and unpeeling the same corner, over and over. "I'm an anthropologist." She smiled and turned to face him straight on.

"So it's you, then? You're the *'muzungu Maasai'*? I've heard about you."

He took a deep drink from his bottle and waved at Matthew to bring a couple more. "I've been to your manyatta before. Hired *moran* from there. Years ago, before I hired a permanent staff of guides."

She smiled. "I have to admit, it's amazing to speak English like this. It's been forever since I've had a conversation in a language I know fluently."

She blushed and he watched the light—so tiny—click on behind her eyes.

He could hold his alcohol easily. His father's son. But hours later, when he laid his hand over the woman's and pulled her from her bar stool, he planted his lips on hers as she stood and he felt dizzy. Maybe that's why he'd not thought of his usual protections. It didn't occur to him. In his dank hotel room, he'd not thought at all. They were both just bodies being swept away down some fast-moving river, clinging together, trying not to drown. They were just movements, not thoughts and not words. They didn't speak once, but he felt her underneath him, her dark interior shifting and rising, turning itself over and outward, desperately seeking whatever light he could shed for her. His body, too, betrayed the usual spaces he liked to keep between himself and his women. He fell into her when he was finished and found himself drifting off to sleep, unable to move his arm from around her shoulders and not minding how close she was—her hair across his face and one naked breast rising and falling, all night long, under his palm.

They hadn't even exchanged names, he and that woman in the bar. It was something of a game they played. Flirtation. He asked her, and she'd answered with a series of Maasai nicknames, words that described her but didn't name her. He laughed, but when he asked again—seriously this time—she said she would tell him the next time they met. If there was a next time. He had to leave early that morning to drive up to Solai. It was time he checked on his mother, made sure the water was still on in the house and that Samuel hadn't given up and moved away. The woman, though, left even earlier. He woke to see her fully dressed with her ponytail tightly in place, trying to slip from his room.

He followed her outside in nothing but his jeans and his un-laced boots. The cool air made the hair on his arms prickle. He couldn't stand to see the woman leave. He wanted to kiss her again. He told her he'd track her down and for the first time with a woman, he meant it.

He told her that she'd be easy to find, even without a name she stuck out like snow in Tsavo.

Now, as he hung up his phone and replayed what Daniel had told him, he remembered the look her face had taken on when they stood there. It stilled, her eyes shuttered themselves and she'd looked up at him and said firmly that he shouldn't try to find her, that she wouldn't want to see him if he came to the manyatta. He nursed the feeling of having been stung all the way up to Solai.

So he didn't try to find her. The rejection he'd felt that morning was the one thing he'd always tried to avoid in relationships. He was the one who rejected, not the other way around. But then, months after their nameless tryst, he found himself back at the Chabani bar. Matthew slid a beer to him and laughed. "Did you hear about the *muzungu* lady with the baby in Loita? A pure white Maasai baby!"

And the blood in John's veins ran cold for an instant, and then he felt his heart slow—he breathed easily. Something bloomed inside of him like a flower.

He found her easily, just as he knew he would. It was curiosity that drove him there, and the easy excuse of needing to hire more *moran* to take a group of incoming tourists into the Nguruman forest. Part of him couldn't imagine it would really be her, that it would really be his child. A gaggle of kids led him across the dusty paddock, and then he ducked through a tiny door frame into a smoke-filled *inkajijik*. Her face surprised him. He tried to stay calm, and he accepted with a grateful smile the hot cup of chai a Maasai woman handed him.

But he was frightened. The woman on the rawhide platform barely resembled the woman from the bar. This woman's hair was lank and unwashed; it hung behind her ears like eucalyptus bark. Her skin was sallow and sunken. She looked unwell, he thought with some alarm, and he wondered what he should do. He felt responsible for her condition.

It was her eyes that frightened him the most. When he saw her first, they seemed blank, dead somehow. But as she registered his presence they shriveled and became as hard and brittle as glass. He stared into them, and asked the only thing he could think to ask, "Were you going to tell me?"

Because there was no question that the baby was his. His body was alive with the vibrations of instinct. His nerves and veins and bones all shifted toward the tiny, red-faced thing wrapped in a *kanga* and lodged firmly next to the women in the bed.

"It's not your child." She sounded cold. Her voice wasn't just angry but also absolutely dismissive.

It was a tone he recognized. It was the way his father spoke to him, and he felt himself instinctively turning away, as he'd learned to do. He felt physical pain in pulling the pieces of himself back into place, but he forced himself away, back out into the sunlight again.

Before John was born, his mother was beautiful, lean and graceful with gentle eyes and a delicate smile. His father was tall and well built with a wide smile and blond curls like John's own. There were photos in the house of these younger versions of his parents. Only Samuel noticed them, and only to dutifully pick them up every week, dust them carefully and put them down again. The people in the photos, the beautiful, happy, young people, were completely disconnected from the people John knew as his parents. His parents weren't happy. He'd never known them happy. There were photos of John, too, a few at least. But only one of the brother he once had, and that photo was hidden away in a drawer. John found it once accidentally. He was tiny when Thomas died and never thought to wonder why the hidden photo wasn't displayed.

Often John wondered if being the child of desperately unhappy parents was worse than being the child of merely uncaring ones, or even of being the child of no parents at all. Being orphaned, John suspected, would be freeing. Orphans, he assumed, could breathe. Not him. His breath was squeezed out of him by the suffocating triangle he and his parents formed.

He found space only away at school and in the expanse of his parents' ruined farm where his playmate was Daniel, the houseman's son, and he could spend the day pretending Daniel's small concrete house was his, the chickens and the goats and the laundry on the line, too. He could pretend Daniel's mother was his and that she loved him like a second son, a white son.

Times he'd spent at home were regimented. He always woke up early and joined his mother for a silent cup of tea in the kitchen, the floor cold under his bare feet and the sky outside a deep gray. When he heard his father stirring—padding heavily down the hall to the bathroom, clearing his throat and coughing while he pissed, long and heavy, and never quite in the bowl, John glanced at his mother. Every day at that time he saw the softness of her sleepy features gel into something hard, the shell covering the body of an animal too soft for the world.

"Bye, Mum," John always whispered, and then he was out the door, running barefoot over the still-cool dust, leaping over the shadows of anthills. He ran fast so he'd hear nothing but his breath growing more and more ragged as he ran, hard, toward the flickering lights and the smell of wood fire in Samuel's *shamba*, way, way back at the farthest edge of his parent's land.

When he was older, living in Nairobi and building his business, his father began to die. John dutifully returned to the farm to see him. Standing at his father's bedside late one afternoon, John watched the old man struggle for breath under sweaty sheets and a veil of skin gone gray and thin as a curtain over his bones. John couldn't think what to say. He merely listened to the wretched breathing, the sound of his father's struggle against death.

Samuel hired a couple of Kikuyu to dig the grave up on the hill under the enormous baobab, but John made a point of taking the shovel from one and jamming it into the earth himself, over and over again. He wanted to know how it felt to dig his father's grave. He dug until his shoulders burned and his eyes stung with sweat. The Kikuyu stepped back and watched. After some time they laid the other shovels down and hunkered on their heels, whispering to themselves and smoking. John finally stood straight, leaned the shovel against the trunk of the baobab and wiped his face on the tail of his shirt. The earth was pulled open, a wound that wouldn't heal, and next to the bleeding pile of red dirt was the tiny mound and miniature headstone that marked his brother's grave. John swallowed a desire to kneel down on the little grave and whisper a warning. If the dead could commune with one another, Thomas should prepare for the imminent arrival of his violent grave-mate.

At the funeral, his mother, Samuel's family and a few local farmers stood with the priest at the top of the hill behind the house. The day was overcast, and under the spreading branches of the baobab it was chilly and damp. Nobody cried. The grave was refilled, flowers placed on top and headstone installed. Now there were two grave markers—father and child.

When John was a boy, there were so many nights he lay awake in his bed and listened to the erratic thumping sounds of knuckles on flesh, punctuated by his mother's soft weeping. Once, when he was a teenager, she told him that she tried hard to make herself soft, to allow her body to absorb the blows, to relax enough that it would be quiet. Her great concern was only that the beatings not disturb John.

When John was thirteen, his maternal grandparents died, and his mother inherited a little stone house in the Nairobi suburb of Karen. At the time, she told him firmly that she would never sell it—she wanted him to have it when he was grown. The place stood empty for years, but John tried time and again to convince her to leave his father, move to the Karen house and let his father rot out here alone. The last time he tried to make her leave was during one of their early morning teas. It was a cold Christmas and the night before his father had flung

the decorated tree into a wall, sending delicate antique orna-
ments smashing onto the floor.

"Please, Mum," he said, gripping her hands over the kitchen
table. Neither he nor his mother had slept, and both were bleary
and nervous from lack of rest.

His mother jerked her hands from his. There was anguish in
her eyes he'd never seen. She looked terrified, as if, this time,
he were the one beating her.

"I tried to get away once, John. It killed your brother. I'll
never leave that baby again, and he can't come with us, can he?"

Her voice was ripe with secrets, and John was afraid to ask
her what she meant. She stopped talking, poured more tea and
they never again discussed the idea of her leaving.

After John finished school, he moved to Nairobi and started
his photo-safari business, which earned him good money. He
let a woman or two stay around for a while. There were two in
particular he lingered over. Both had wanted to marry him; they
dropped hints and introduced him to their parents and joked
to their friends—with him in earshot—that he better not get
used to the milk if he wasn't planning to buy the damn cow.
It wasn't marriage that frightened him away from the women,
ultimately. It was the expectation of children. His own mother
was all he knew of motherhood, and he couldn't, he wouldn't
turn a girl he loved into that. He considered it kinder to break
their hearts than their spirits.

And now. Now he'd gone and had a kid, anyway. And the
image of the broken woman lying in the dark *inkajijik* with her
glass-hard eyes and glass-hard voice haunted him. Had he poi-
soned her with the presence of his genes in her body? He didn't
consider looking for her after that day. He tried to put the fear-
ful new-mother face and his own craving to see his baby out
of his mind. He purposely avoided the area anywhere near that
manyatta. Instead, he hired *moran* from much farther away. He
thought of the baby and the woman less and less over the years.

How long had it been, three years? He did the math in his head, Christ, how time had flown. The girl would be three. Not a baby, but a walking, talking person. He wondered what her name was, if she looked at all like him.

Daniel's phone call left John anxious and unable to sleep, so long before dawn the next day, he loaded his bag into the cab of his truck and left Nairobi. He stopped for lunch in Narok, gassed up the truck at the BP station on the main road and then drove to the Chabani. He needed a beer. He told himself he needed a beer, needed food, needed to stretch his legs. But somewhere inside him a tuning fork was resonating, softly but clearly. He didn't want to admit he'd stopped here in the hope he'd catch a glimpse of a blonde-haired girl, a child with his face, maybe, one that might catch his eye and know—instinctually—just who he was.

"*Imekuwa ni muda mrefu,* Mister John," Matthew, the bartender, greeted John as he took a seat at the bar.

"It has been a long time, my friend," John answered. "Too long."

John wondered if Matthew knew why he was here, if he'd seen his daughter. He didn't have to wait long. Matthew popped the cap on a Tusker, and placed it on the bar.

"Your girl, my friend, she is looking like you."

John's heart beat fast. He didn't know if he was ready to see her, to face the nameless woman. But his blood streamed faster in his veins, and his heartbeat was so quick it was almost painful.

"Matthew, are they still here? In Narok?"

"No, Mister John. They were here for so long. Maybe two, maybe three weeks. Every day they would come here. They would sit just there." Here, he indicated a booth tucked into a dark back corner.

"*Memsahib* would drink tea all day long, and the child would play. The *memsahib* was looking for you. But now—" Matthew paused and popped open another beer "—they are gone. I haven't seen them for days."

"Well," John said, "I'm headed up to Solai to speak with my mother. Hope she'll tell me where they've gone."

The stars were blooming in the sky when John finally saw the lights of his mother's house on the horizon. He felt himself inadvertently slowing down, barely pushing the wheels of the truck through the ruts and pits in the road. For the last few years, every time he came here, there was a part of him that feared finding his mother's body stiff and cold on the floor of her house. He knew, theoretically, that Samuel and Daniel checked in on her faithfully, kept her fed and the house clean. He sent money to them from Nairobi every month to cover the expenses and to pay them for their time, but in his heart he couldn't believe they'd stay.

The truck shuddered to a stop outside the house, and he pulled the key out of the ignition, then leaned back and closed his eyes. He used to regret his childhood. He used to wish he could pretend it all away and grow up normal in a family that smiled at one another, talked about things, a family that wasn't marred by absence.

He thought of his family like a photograph—all of them in a row, in outdated clothes with outdated haircuts and a big black scribbled-on space where Thomas would have been. A permanent deletion whose ink stained all of them, long beyond the quick moment that marked the moment the family was ruined.

He opened his eyes and sighed, then pulled himself out of the truck and grabbed his duffel. The front door was open, and light spilled out through the screen. Moths and beetles buzzed and banged themselves against the door. He waved them away as he slid through the door, knowing most of them would find a way inside regardless. The edges of the screen were pulling out of the frame, and there was a large hole near the bottom. He sighed. Every time he came here, there was something to fix.

"Mum?" he called.

He was surprised not to see her in the hall, waiting, or asleep in the faded flowered chair in the living room. God, was this the time he'd find her body? His breath shortened, and he felt a chill climb through his veins.

"Mum?" His voice was shrill, and he took a breath. "Mum!"

She was nowhere. Her bed was made, the bathroom was dark and empty, the kitchen light was on, but there was no sign she'd been there, either.

John banged out the screen door again, paying no attention to the large rhino beetle that flew past his ear and into the house.

"Mum!" he called again.

Maybe she'd gone to see Samuel. It was not unusual for her to walk back across the field, over the hill and to the houseman's little compound. They'd all told her not to go at night, but they all knew her mind was failing, and whether or not she remembered the warnings was anybody's guess.

"Dammit," he muttered, opening the door of the truck again. He'd drive there.

His headlights bore down on the dusty ground, illuminating the sparse grasses and wizened acacia trees. Now and again tall crusts of chewed earth rose like towers—the anthills he used to leap on and crush underfoot, trying to destroy them before the ants could swarm his legs and bite.

Just ahead of him now was the hill. The family burial ground with the two headstones—one small and one large. The truck bounced over a rut and the light of his headlights leaped up for an instant and shone on a tiny, ghostly figure—his mother, her white puff of hair and pale housedress. She was so small, hunched there on the stone bench under the massive baobab—she was just bones, really, bones and skin under her long flowered dress. When did she get so old?

He stopped the truck but left the engine running and the lights on. He didn't want to spend the time retrieving his gun, and the lights would help keep hyenas and snakes at bay.

"Mum, you gave me a scare!" He walked up behind her and she turned to look at him, her face a tiny, white moon.

"I killed you both," she said.

John knew his mother was suffering from Alzheimer's or senility or some such thing that had slowly been erasing her mind. It was more than the incessant forgetfulness or the conversations she had with nobody but herself. Her mind was deteriorating; he had to face the fact that she was no longer able to care for herself enough to get by with only daily visits from Samuel. He could hardly bear to watch her speak this nonsense and act in ways that were both confusing to him and pathetic.

"You didn't kill anyone, Mum. You're having a spell."

"Do you remember your brother? No, he was too young."

"Don't remember, really. And there aren't any photos to remind me."

"I couldn't bear to look at his face in a photo. I only kept one, but I hid it."

John was horrified then that his mother began to cry. Her face folded in upon itself, and tears slid down her cheeks. Had he ever seen her cry? Even when his father hit her, even on the most miserable days, she was a stone.

"I never told you. I never told anyone. The only one who knew was your father. That's why he punished me. I deserved it."

"Jesus, Mum, what are you saying?"

"You are a father now. You know that, right?"

Her brain seemed clear. Her eyes, even through her tears, were wide-open and lacked the clouds that usually marked her moments of confusion.

"Don't do what I did. I tried to run away and it killed Thomas. I still feel the bump..."

Her breath heaved, and a cry rose like a night bird, a scream so deep inside her that he could almost see it pulling itself up through her body. She clenched her fingers into fists and pounded them on her knees.

"Mum, shh! It's okay..."

He put his arm around her shoulders. He hadn't touched her in so long, and her skin felt like paper, her bones like twigs. Her face was tipped up toward the stars, which, unhindered by any ambient light, spread out endlessly.

She paused in her cry for a breath, and then she shook her head and said calmly—he would always remember how calmly she spoke the secret out loud. It was a voice he'd never heard her use, strong and clean and honed to a sharp edge by the force she used to get it out.

"I have to tell you before I die. You have to know. I killed Thomas when I tried to run away. He came too close to the tire... I didn't see him. It was the farm truck, so high up, I couldn't see..." She trailed off, her voice spent and the tears rising again.

John's body felt frozen. His skin was cold and he shivered. His brother's death was always a shrouded thing, mysterious and frightening, and never spoken of. He hadn't ever wanted to know the details. He still didn't. How could she have lived with this?

He didn't say anything. His own heart throbbed in his chest.

"Now you're a father and I've killed you, too."

Startled, he glanced at her face. Tiny clouds were forming behind her eyes. She was disappearing again. This time, he felt relieved for her. Maybe in these moments she could forget or she could conjure another life in her head, one that wasn't so painful.

"The American came to give you your daughter. She tried to find you. She came all the way here with the girl."

"Yes, Mum, and I've come now, too. I want them to find me. You can tell me where they are, and I'll go there. Or maybe you told them to come back here? That you were calling me to come and meet them?" His voice was hopeful—he felt a flicker in his chest, a star fallen to infuse him with light.

"No, you see, that's what I mean. I killed you, as well. I told her you were dead. That she could never find you."

The star turned to ice in his neck. He glanced at her, not wanting to believe what he heard. Had she really told the woman he was dead? He couldn't bear to think he'd missed out on knowing his daughter forever just because of the lie his mother told. Dammit! He wanted to accuse her, to shout at her, to tell her that she had no right.

"How did you leave it with her? Did she say anything about where they might go?" He knew the anger in his voice, the urgency, might scare his mother into silence, but it colored his words, anyway. He'd never felt so desperately in need of an answer.

"To America," Ruthie whispered. She was sure this was what Leona said. She was sure she was right this time.

"Right, the northwest. She told me. Did she say where exactly, by chance?"

But when John looked over at his mother again, she was gone. Her body was still there, his frail mother in her too-loose dress, but her eyes were clouded over completely. She'd disappeared back into herself. He was alone.

He had made mistakes in his life. He knew that. He'd treated women badly, he'd not always been a good son and for most of his childhood he'd been filled with churning lava of hatred for his father and jealousy toward his dead brother. But he couldn't remember feeling worse during any of those times than he did now. This was a brutal itch of regret that strangled his insides and made him jump up from the stone bench and hurtle himself at the wall of baobab bark. Before he could think, he'd slammed his right fist into the tree trunk. The pain soothed somehow, and so he did it again and again. Finally he stepped back and clasped his right hand in his left. The bones throbbed and the tattered skin was slick with blood. He was too tired to care.

He sat on the bench until the horizon showed a thread of gray that gradually seeped into the night, turning the sky from darkness into dawn. A mourning dove cried from the branches of the baobab above him. A breeze shuffled the leaves above their heads. His mother still sat beside him, leaning her body into his, her head on his shoulder. She'd fallen asleep at some point in the night, and he was conscious that her nightgown was damp with dew. He'd need to get her home, warm and into dry clothes.

He realized he couldn't leave her here alone any longer. Not even with Sam and Daniel looking after her. She needed him now. He thought of his house in Karen and how she could have a little bedroom there and sit in the garden and, finally, relax in a place that was far enough from the ugly reminders of her marriage so that she could forget.

John stood up and lifted her into his arms. With every movement, his hand pulsed with pain. He ignored it. How light she was. Like a child. The truck's headlights had dimmed now, the battery dead. He couldn't drive her back to the house. He'd have to carry her. He paused for a second, shifted her in his arms and began walking. Making his way slowly, carefully, down the hill to home.

PART II

KHAMSA

Where Liberia hid in the shadows under the curve of western Africa's lower edge, Morocco was out in the light, pushing forward like a face upturned toward the sky. The boulevards were wide and flat, and the whole place felt bright and airy, clean. Jane didn't miss the moist breath of Liberia's jungles, which crowded too close to the city. She didn't miss the tangled bushes that, even in the city, could hide snakes and insects. Monrovia was hidden things that lay in wait and whispers from unseen sources. Rabat was the five-times-a-day call from the mosques whose distinctive square minarets dotted the skyline and the clear-as-glass skies that made the walls in the old city shine pink and gold.

When their plane landed in Rabat, the embassy expediter met them at the airport. He held a sign with Paul's name on it. Jane's shirt was damp with water Grace had spilled just before landing, and her eyes felt sandy from lack of sleep. Grace was a good flier. Even though she was only ten, she'd been on so many planes she couldn't count them. When she was one, Paul was assigned to a three-year stint at the embassy in Mexico City.

After that, it was Lima, Peru, then Kathmandu, Nepal, where they'd stayed for four years. Grace loved the takeoffs and landings, but this had been a long trip, and by the time they taxied across the runway to the airport, she was tired and sullen. In the last twenty-four hours, they'd flown from Washington, DC, to Paris and Paris to Rabat, with nearly ten hours spent wandering Charles de Gaulle airport in between.

"Salaam a lekum!" Paul said loudly and slipped in front of Jane to grasp the expediter's hand and shake it vigorously.

"Mehreba!" the man answered. "I'm Tarik."

Jane smiled at Tarik and nudged Grace to say hello. "You can shake his hand, Grace," Jane murmured. Grace dutifully reached out her hand and greeted the man under her breath. Jane noticed her daughter's grimace, slight as it was. She wondered if the wet spot on her chest was obvious. She felt dirty, and the bright light of midday made her more conscious of the fetid, sweaty airplane smells that rose from her skin and clothes.

Tarik drove them from the airport to the house the embassy assigned them. The boulevards around the old city were wide and smooth. Jane sat behind Paul next to Grace, who leaned her head against the window and appeared to fall asleep. Jane mindlessly stroked her daughter's arm and watched the city slide by outside the window.

This was their first posting back in Africa, and Jane couldn't help but dredge up memories of the last time they were posted together on this continent. In Monrovia, the trees and bushes all blended together in a smear of green. Jane was never curious about the flora there. But Morocco seemed more like Kenya, a place she remembered with mixed feelings but entirely without the anxiety Liberia pricked in her. Here, she could pick out familiar plants—thick stands of lavender lining a sidewalk, purple clematis climbing a streetlight and enormous carob trees that threw their deep shadows over the little tables of an outdoor café where men sat drinking from tiny cups. The car rolled to a stop at a red light, and Jane watched as a crowd of kids in matching school uniforms crossed the street in front of them. One little girl, no older than Grace, glanced in their direction and smiled. Jane thought of the girl's parents, somewhere in the city, who kissed their daughter goodbye this morning and sent her off to school—trusting the world to bring her back safely that afternoon. The idea of Grace being alone in the world like that made Jane's heart beat faster, and a wave of heat passed over her.

The house was large and airy, the outside painted the color of dried grass and surrounded by a large dusty garden. Jane envisioned lavender there, a carob tree that would shade their own patio table. Paul pulled their suitcases from the trunk, while Jane and Grace slid out of the car, dragging their purses and carry-on baggage behind them. Tarik fished through his pockets for the house keys and, when he found them, smiled and presented them to Paul. The door was thick wood, carved into intricate patterns. It was beautiful. As Paul slipped the key into the lock, Jane noticed a shiny piece of etched metal just above the door frame. It was the shape of a hand with two fingers stretched to each side, and three fingers in the middle pointing down. The etchings on the hand were detailed and flowery, abstract, but in the middle of the palm was something Jane recognized— the outline of an eye, wide-open with a tiny dot of black pupil in the center.

Jane turned to Tarik and gestured up to the metal hand. "What's that?" she asked.

"It's Khamsa…the hand of Fatima." He smiled sheepishly, as if he were embarrassed to explain the meaning to her.

"Some people, like the old people, believe it helps make you safe from djinn, the witches."

Jane thought of Liberia and the juju that killed the president and the evil that lurked in the mask she hated. "What do the djinn do?" she asked.

"They cause madness," Tarik answered simply, and then

grasped the handle of a suitcase and hoisted it inside. Jane felt the sensation of ice sliding down the back of her neck. She turned to watch Grace standing in the driveway, rummaging through her backpack. As Grace grew older, Jane became more watchful of the signs that her daughter might share Lance's disease. The notion terrified her.

Turning back to the door, she reached up and ran her finger over the etchings of the Khamsa. They were worn and smooth. It must be old. Who put it there, and why? She wondered if the hand was supposed to be hung and forgotten, as if its protection would swirl in the door frame and cover everyone passing under it, or if it was something like rosary beads or prayer wheels that had to be touched in order to work. Jane thought she shouldn't risk making the wrong decision, and so she reached out and placed her palm on the metal shape. She closed her eyes and imagined her daughter. "Be safe," she whispered, "be safe."

It was her job to control the world around Grace, her job to keep Grace sheltered from bad things and as far from the possibility of tragedy and darkness as she could. Maybe her own father couldn't have helped Lance, but maybe he didn't try hard enough. For an instant, Jane wondered if her cloud of anxiety was a gift—the wild animal on her back, claws drawn, a spirit animal, given to her for a reason. Her job was to embrace it, to pull all the bad things inside herself, like a sponge, and thereby keep them from Grace.

"I can take it down for you," Tarik said as he passed her again on his way back to the car. "It's just an old superstition."

"No," Jane said, turning to look Tarik in the eyes. She needed all the assistance she could get. She spoke slowly, clearly. It was important that he heard her. "No. I want it to stay."

Twelve years into their marriage, there were times Jane wanted to bite Paul, times she couldn't stand the sight of him. She wondered if other wives felt this way.

And even though she could still easily remember that first

moment she fell in love with him—the feeling of it, the intense, visceral way her heart filled up when she pulled back and looked into his eyes—she couldn't conjure that anymore.

Sometimes her anger at him took her by surprise. She didn't know where it came from, or where inside her the angry spring's source hid. She had a happy life, privileged. After Muthega, she hadn't wanted to track elephants anymore, so she pushed that dream away and, instead, followed her dream of mother-hood, and she took hold of the end of Paul's dream, too. They'd travel the world, he'd rise through the ranks and, one day, be an ambassador. She could keep herself occupied with the chil-dren they would have or the jobs at each embassy specifically set aside for "dependent spouses." The title was something of a joke; it was all wives. Dependent wives. Paul never pressured her to take one of the jobs, which Jane was grateful for. She had a masters in wildlife biology. One she used for less than a year, but still, she didn't want to work if she wasn't working in her field. There were days, though, after Grace got older and started school, that Jane felt she was wading through deep water or like a snake had wound its way around her neck and was slowly suffocating her.

Jane got pregnant only the one time. They tried for more babies, but none came. Jane didn't mind as much as she thought she might. She liked having only one child. She loved that the child was a girl. It didn't bother Jane when she and Paul and Grace arrived in some new, strange nation and woke up in a house they'd never seen before, and then had to make their way in a new city, meet new people. Since Grace was born, Jane always had her as a partner in adventure. When Grace was a baby, Jane sought out the English-language playgroups and made friends with the other women and their babies. When Grace started school, it was easy to meet the other international moms at events, through the parent-teacher association, on the soccer field, at scouts. Jane found she liked the life they'd created. The one Paul gave them. Somewhere along the line there was a shift. Jane thought about it a lot, but she couldn't pinpoint where it began. Slowly, though, her gaze turned from Paul to Grace. Grace became the one she orbited, and Paul took a secondary role.

As Grace got older, she spent nights at slumber parties or afternoons playing at her friends' houses. Jane used that time to catch up on reading, go for lunch with friends or dinners out with Paul and other embassy couples. Grace always came back, and she always needed Jane. Grace wanted to be with Jane more than she did with her own friends. The early afternoons after the slumber parties were Jane's favorite times. She would pick Grace up and help her unpack her overnight bag, and then they would curl up on the couch with cocoa and Grace would giggle and tell Jane the things they'd eaten at the party, how late they'd stayed up and which girls fell asleep first. Sometimes she'd drift off and Jane would feel Grace's weight on her legs. Grace relaxed into sleep so deeply that Jane could shift her over and not wake her up. Just like when she was an infant and, after a night nursing session, Jane could carry her back to the crib, lean over and lie her down on her back and watch her eyelids, fluttery and as pink as the inside of a shell.

It was a Sunday evening when Paul and Jane told Grace they were moving again. It was time. They'd been in Rabat for three years already, and Paul's tour here was finished. Grace had spent the day swimming with a friend at the club, and Paul and Jane picked her up and drove out to their favorite café, one with outdoor tables on a patio that overlooked the Bouregreg River. It was a quiet evening, still warm, and the breeze that blew off the water smelled like the fish the men hauled off their brightly striped boats in nets the color of the sand.

"Grace," Jane said, just after the waiter set a sweating, icy glass of Coke in front of her daughter. "We're moving to Nairobi, where your dad and I met!" Jane's tone was happy because she was happy. Their family moved—that's what they did, what they'd always done. This was their life. Jane and Grace would, as always, set up the house, hire a cook, a houseman, maybe a gardener. Jane would go with Grace to school the first day, meet her teacher, scope out the other moms. Jane and Grace were a team, still connected, if not literally by blood and flesh anymore, then by mutual devotion and shared interests. Jane had fond memories of Nairobi. The wide streets, the rows of jacaranda trees along the sidewalks and the cool, crisp air. That would be nice to return to. She thought about what it would be like to see the Rift again, to see if the rivers were full. She wasn't sure she wanted to see Narok again or the places she and Muthega had explored in that rattling Land Rover, but she pictured the silhouettes of elephants against the red evening sky, and suddenly she felt a surge of real joy.

So when Grace looked back at Jane and her eyes said instantly that she was angry, Jane was surprised.

"Hey, hon, you knew we would eventually—we always do," Paul said, and then, "Get this, your old man is going to be second in command! Whaddaya think of that?" Jane smiled at him vacantly, and a slip of a thought fluttered through her mind: Grace was thirteen now; she was growing up, turning away. Jane still saw her as the main character in their family play, but maybe Grace didn't see Jane—or herself—that way anymore.

Jane glanced back at Grace. "We're women of the world, Gracie! Right?" But a switch flipped in her daughter's face and she sat there for the rest of the meal, poking at her pizza, her mouth drawn, her eyes empty. That night Jane ducked into Grace's room to kiss her daughter good-night. She tried again to cajole Grace into seeing the excitement that she saw, that Grace had always seen before. But Grace began to cry. "I don't want to go somewhere new. I want to stay in one place. I want to stop. Don't you understand? I want to stop. I want a real home for once."

* * *

After that, Grace stayed silent, sullen. The days they all spent packing her Rabat bedroom were tear-filled and angry. As annoyed and hurt as Jane was by her daughter's shift in behavior, she was also terrified. She racked her memory to compare Grace's actions to her brother's at this age. He wasn't diagnosed at thirteen, but maybe there were signs? Maybe Grace was showing those signs and Jane just had to recognize them.

Jane was a nuisance to her daughter for the first time, and Jane's bewilderment and anxiety made her lash out at Paul in misplaced retaliation. The three of them spun like eddies in a pond, separate, divided, dragged down.

On Grace's first day of school in Nairobi, Jane woke up early, edged the new houseman aside and made Grace's favorite breakfast: French toast and potatoes pan-fried in butter. When Grace appeared, she was wearing the outfit they had assembled together the night before: a khaki knee-length skirt and a floral blouse opened over her favorite lavender T-shirt. "You look darling!" Jane told Grace. The truth was, though, that Grace looked like a different girl. Her eyes were dull, her hair seemed limp, even though the night before Jane had washed and dried it, pulling it straight, long and shiny with a big, round brush.

"Eat up, baby!" Jane said in a voice as happy as she could make it, because Grace's sadness shocked her. Jane wanted to push her own optimism into her daughter, make Grace's eyes light up again.

Grace cried herself to sleep some nights. She never let Jane see it. She pretended to be asleep if Jane poked her head into the bedroom, and she never cried when Jane was with her in the car, or even at dinner when Paul and Jane chatted about their days. They both tried to draw Grace into their conversation, but Grace only nodded quietly, barely speaking. Jane told Paul to let it go, that she'd come around. Jane thought she would. It was unlike Grace to hold a grudge, to be so withdrawn.

It was curious, too, that Grace's emotional absence changed the dynamic between the three of them. Without her as the central force for each parent to focus on, Jane and Paul were thrown back together in a strange way. For the first time in years they mostly talked to each other at meals. After dinner, when Jane and Grace would have worked on homework or watched a DVD together, Grace disappeared into her room. She didn't want help; she didn't want to snuggle with her mother on the couch and watch a movie. Instead, Jane and Paul circled each other warily in the evenings, trying to decide how to be alone with one another. After a while, they began talking to each other more, pouring glasses of wine and sharing the space more comfortably. It was nice, Jane thought one evening, to have this back. She hadn't missed it at all when it floated away from their marriage, when a distance neither of them understood or knew how to clip back had blossomed between them. Grace did it for them. When she ducked out of her place at the center, the two ends grew closer.

It didn't mean Jane didn't worry. She did. Constantly. She researched early symptoms of schizophrenia and kept Grace as close as she possibly could. She met with Grace's teacher to share her concerns, considered going to the school nurse. She didn't do that, though, because one day when she picked Grace up from school Grace had a smile on her face. She didn't want to talk much, and she was still sullen every night at dinner, but when Jane went out to the balcony after dinner to watch the sky darken, Grace came out and sat with her. It didn't last long. Something she said upset Grace, who then flounced back to her room. But the nugget of information Grace gave her that night made Jane want to shout with relief. A friend. Grace had finally made a friend at school.

RIPTIDE

The unraveling started with an early morning phone call. It was Thursday, a school day, and Adia was awake. She never slept in. Her life in the manyatta had trained her from birth to wake by dawn, and even though she and her mother lived in Nairobi now, that habit didn't change. The house was perfectly still. Adia could tell it was almost dawn because the stars were fewer; most had already flicked themselves back to wherever they lived when the sun came up. Adia always woke up early. Her mother didn't, though, and Adia knew to creep around the house silently so as not to wake her. This morning, just as Adia stepped up from her bed, the phone rang. Adia startled. Their phone never rang much—sometimes Leona's colleagues called, but their manyatta family, the ones Adia would love to talk on the phone with during the weeks she was here in Nairobi—didn't use phones. This early in the morning, the sound was both unexpected and harsh. Adia tiptoed out of her room and up the hallway toward her mother's bedroom, and by the time she reached the door, the phone was clattering to the floor. Her mother's voice through the door was harsh and annoyed.

"Hello? Hello? Who is this?"

Adia couldn't imagine who would call this early, and she leaned close to her mother's door to listen. There was a long pause. Adia wondered if her mother had fallen back asleep.

"What? Here? Mother...no."

Adia startled again. Her mother was calling someone else "mother." This was a revelation. At thirteen, Adia knew, of course, that everybody had a theoretical mother and father, but she'd never, not once, heard her mom talking about family. Adia assumed that she and her mother had that in common—without a father of her own, it wasn't a stretch to imagine her mother with no parents at all.

Through the closed door, Adia heard the phone slam back into the cradle and her mother whisper-shout, "Shit!"

Then the creaking of the bedsprings sent Adia racing, as quietly as she could, back to her own bed. She didn't want her mother to know she'd been listening.

Usually, Adia dressed herself for school and had breakfast alone. Gakaki, the houseman, always set a cup of hot tea, a boiled egg and a piece of buttered toast in front of her, and she'd eat while he sat on his haunches on the stoop outside the kitchen door slurping his own tea and smoking a cigarette.

This morning was different. Adia slid on a pair of jeans, which, she noticed, were feeling tight in the butt and ended an inch or so above her ankles. Adia didn't care about how her clothes looked, but she hated the feeling of being constrained. Too-tight jeans and T-shirts that tugged awkwardly made her feel conscious of herself, made her feel like she was a dog on a leash. Today would be more uncomfortable than usual. She pulled on her favorite hat—leather with a wide brim that her mother had worn for years and then passed on to her. Her boots were by the front door; she would put those on at the last possible second before running out of the house to catch the bus.

She hated shoes and wore them only because her school didn't allow bare feet.

When Adia walked into the kitchen, her mother was already at the table. She held a large teacup and breathed the steam into her open mouth slowly, evenly. She didn't acknowledge Adia. Gakaki sidled in quietly; he knew, too, that Adia's mother would be grumpy this early and that he should do what he could to be unobtrusive. He gently set Adia's plate on the table and then her tea, and then he stuck his tongue out at her and crossed his eyes, and Adia had to push her palm over her mouth, hard, to keep from giggling.

"We'll be having a visitor next week."

Adia glanced at her mother, who now had her eyes open and was sipping her tea through pursed lips. She winced a little when the hot liquid hit her tongue. Gakaki always boiled the tea just a little too long.

"Your grandmother—my mother. She wants to get to know you."

Adia paused with her fork halfway between her plate and her mouth. There were so many things she wanted to talk about, to ask her mother. But through the sudden chaos in her brain, only one question slipped out.

"Wait, what?"

Even though she heard her mother address the phone caller as "mother," she still couldn't quite believe she'd heard correctly. "I have a grandmother?" The thought that there was family in America never occurred to her. Her curiosity had only one focus—her father. This new information was a revelation.

At school that day Adia was distracted. She wondered how long her grandmother had known about her. From birth? If it was that long, why hadn't she come sooner? The idea of a family— people connected to her outside of the tiny, cool orbit she and her mother made—excited Adia. She quivered with the possibilities.

The school cafeteria was nothing but a small canteen that

sold sodas and chips, attached to a large, open-sided *rondaval* filled with picnic tables and benches. Most of the other kids at her school had parents who were diplomats, and their lunch boxes were full of imported cheeses, peanut butter and cookies and chips not available to people without embassy commissary privileges. Adia unwrapped her sandwich without thinking. Usually she was careful about her lunch and how she ate. She never knew what might end up in her lunch bag. Once Gakaki packed her a little plastic container of scrambled eggs. That day, she hunched low over it, because she didn't want the other kids to see. It was such a weird thing to have for lunch. He'd also forgotten to pack a fork, but she was so hungry she picked the pieces up with her fingers. She propped a book up on the table and pretended to read, but the book somehow tipped off her desk and when she reached out to grab it, her eggs spilled out of the container and onto the table. The girl sitting next to her shouted, "Gah! That's what was smelly! Adia's eating eggs!"

The other kids laughed and made retching noises, and one of the teachers on lunch duty peered over the top of his glasses and told her to make sure she cleaned it all up. Adia spent the next five minutes wiping egg into her palm, making sure she retrieved every bit. The rest of the afternoon her stomach grumbled. After that day, she tried to skip lunch entirely, ignoring her hunger pangs and trying to get by on just an orange or banana. She ate bigger breakfasts and drank a lot of water to keep herself full.

Today's lunch was a chapati, leftover from dinner the night before, rolled around a hunk of cheese. The chapati was torn and the cheese poked out the end a little. Adia sized it up and weighed her chances of eating without attracting notice. At least it didn't smell. Maybe nobody would notice. She was hungry.

"Is that a penis?" a boy nearby whispered. The kids who heard erupted into laughter.

"Adia's eating a penis!"

This time, the teacher didn't look up at all. Adia shoved the mess back into her lunch bag and opened her book. She didn't read it, though. She couldn't concentrate on the words at all. Instead, she tried to will the red flush from her cheeks by thinking about her grandmother. Her grandmother wanted to meet her. Her grandmother had wanted to meet her since she was a baby; her mother told her that this morning. Her grandmother would love her.

Adia didn't question the basic facts of her life. She didn't wonder why she and her mother lived in Nairobi or why she went to the international school with the sons and daughters of diplomats and development workers rather than a local school with kids more like the ones at home in the manyatta. She never wondered at the notion that her father was long dead, or if there were surviving family members of his that she could meet. She accepted those things without question. She accepted that she lived here with her American mother, but that she also had a Maasai mother in Loita. She accepted the things her mother told her about her father—he was a descendent of colonial Kenya, a "Kenya Cowboy"; he'd grown up in Maasailand like her. And he died when Adia was small.

She sometimes wondered if not having a father was the thing that made her different from the kids at her school. They were not like her. They came and went as their parents transferred into and out of Nairobi like migratory birds. She was a chicken that never went anywhere. Adia had plodded through the school since kindergarten—she was one of the few students who'd been there that long—but it didn't matter. She still never knew any of her classmates for more than a year or two before they disappeared forever. She was the silent, invisible ghost always left behind.

After a while she realized that her clothes and her food and her lifestyle made her too different for them to be friends with her, anyway. The other kids dressed in clothes brought from

Europe or America. They talked about movies and TV shows they watched back home. They had mothers who brought cake or cupcakes to class for birthdays. They referred longingly to places far away from here, places they called home. Adia didn't have any of those things. Her clothes were from the market or made by tailors from cloth her mother bought on Biashara Street. Her mother never came for birthdays or awards ceremonies or even for parent-teacher conferences.

Leona let Adia skip school the day her grandmother arrived. They drove together to the airport. Waiting in the meeting area, Adia watched the people come through the door from customs. There were so many. She had never seen a photo of her grandmother, so she had no idea who to look for. Instead, she alternated watching her mother's face and watching the crowds of people dragging suitcases behind them. Her mother's face was calm until, suddenly, it wasn't. Adia watched her mother's mouth curve into a forced smile and saw the natural light cloud in her mother's eyes. She was here! When Adia turned to see who her mother was looking at, she was stunned. This was not the person she imagined. The tall woman striding toward them with her own stiff smile pasted on her own stiff face was exactly the opposite of who Adia imagined was her mother's mother.

Her grandmother Joan arrived in a flurry of suitcases and a flapping safari jacket covered in pockets. She was tall and thin with perfectly white hair that started at her chin on one side and went all the way around to the other side without getting higher or lower. The ends were all exactly the same length. Adia wondered if she used a ruler when she cut it.

"Hello, dear!" Joan said as she stuck her face forward to give Leona a kiss. Adia noticed that the kiss never actually met Leona's cheek.

"Hi, Mom," Leona answered. And then she pulled Adia by the arm in between herself and Joan. Adia felt like a shield.

"Mom, this is Adia," Leona said.

"Well, there she is! Aren't you a tomboy!" Joan said. Adia couldn't tell if being a tomboy was good or bad in her grandmother's eyes. Joan leaned over to kiss Adia's cheek and, once again, Adia noticed that the kiss never made contact.

Her grandmother smelled like flowers and the pockets of her jacket were filled with hard candies and tissues. She had hands so pale that Adia could see bones and blue veins through them, and one of her fingers had a sparkly ring the size of a Band-Aid on it.

The best thing about her grandmother's coming was that the morning after she arrived, they all left for Mombasa. They didn't take the train, like Adia and her mother did when they went. Adia was relieved. The train was slow and hot, and mosquitoes billowed through the windows and feasted on them all night long. Adia didn't like the close feeling of breathing in the little four-person compartment they always had to share with two strangers.

Her grandmother bought tickets for them to fly to Mombasa on a little plane, and the lurch in Adia's belly when they sped down the runway and up, up, up into the air was exhilaration and fear and intense joy and it tickled her inside all over. But even better was the hotel. Usually Adia and her mother stayed in a little thatched hut near the water. The huts were plain but had a place to cook and take a shower and electricity and running water. Adia loved them because it felt like playing house and she could race between the ocean and the little porch all day.

The hotel Joan booked for the three of them was more beautiful than any place Adia had even seen. The hallways were large and open, filled with enormous chairs covered in cushions, and everywhere were potted palm trees and ceiling fans that made the palm leaves flutter. The hotel employees all wore bright white uniforms and perfectly white sneakers and moved quickly but so silently Adia imagined they were not really touching the glassy polished floor at all.

A bellhop pushed their luggage on a wheeled cart. Adia's grandmother's suitcases were clean and unscuffed and made of fabric that had pink flowers all over it. Adia wished the suitcase she and her mother shared was made of that fabric, but instead theirs was brown and lumpy and had a zipper held closed with a twisted paper clip. Grandmother Joan was not like her own mother, Adia thought. She was more like the embassy moms she saw at school sometimes. The bellhop, even, was more elegant than her mother, and his air of sophistication was alluring to Adia.

"When I grow up, I want to work here," Adia said, imagining the luxury of spending all day in that beautiful place.

Her grandmother stopped in her tracks and tipped her head back and laughed a laugh that was like silver bracelets clinking together in her mouth.

"Leona, darling, did you hear that? Your daughter aspires to be a maid in an African hotel!"

Adia smiled, but inside she felt shaky. She didn't understand the joke her grandmother found funny. Adia watched her mother turn and glance at Adia, and then at her own mother.

"She can do whatever damn well makes her happy, Mother."

Joan pursed her lips and shook her head so that the chin-length hair moved ever so slightly across the back of her neck.

"Leona, darling, lighten up! Of course we want our girl to be happy, but she's an American girl...with options!"

Joan turned to Adia and placed her hand on Adia's arm. Her fingers were soft and a little squishy, like the banana slugs that took over the garden when it rained, only with long bright red nails pointing out from the ends.

"You'll see," Grandmother Joan whispered to Adia. "When you get home, you'll see. There is a world of things a girl like you could do." Adia wondered what her grandmother meant. She had two homes—one in Nairobi with Leona and one in Loita with Simi.

The bellhop halted, and they all stopped in a little cluster behind him. He fumbled with a large key, and then rolled the cart into a room that would easily fit, in Adia's estimation, the entire *inkajijik*. She thought if she stood with her back against one wall, she couldn't even throw a ball hard enough to hit the opposite one. There were two big double beds and a shiny, glinting bathroom behind a tall, heavy door. The bellhop crossed the enormous room and pulled open a set of drapes that exposed sliding doors and a balcony. Adia gasped. The ocean stretched out brilliant and blue as far as she could see. It looked so close. She wondered if she could jump off the balcony and splash right into the waves.

"Well, I'm connected..." Joan said, opening a door Adia had thought was a closet, but instead led to a different room, equally big, with two more beds. Joan fumbled in her purse for a handful of bills and pressed them into the bellhop's hand.

"Just leave the pink suitcases in there, dear."

Joan looked at Adia and said, "They only work for tips, darling. You don't need to do that. You have options. When you're home, you'll see."

Leona turned from where she'd been examining pamphlets on the desk and leaned in close. She poked a finger toward Adia's face and said coldly, "Goddammit, Mother, she is home. Nairobi is her home. She's only ever lived here in Kenya. This is what she knows, and it's a perfectly wonderful place to call home, by the way."

Adia watched as her grandmother's face turned pale. Joan said nothing, but she turned and disappeared into the other room, closing the door firmly, but quietly, behind her. Leona went into the bathroom and slammed the door shut. Adia could hear her cursing under her breath as she peed. Adia's stomach was twisted into an unfamiliar knot. It made her think of the giant centipedes that curled into black shiny balls if you poked them. That was how they protected themselves, but her stom-

ach didn't feel protected. It hurt. She wanted to smack her
mother for being so rude to Grandmother Joan. How dare she
push away the only family Adia had. Adia glanced at each of
the closed doors, each with someone she loved behind it. She
didn't open either—she wanted air. On the balcony, she leaned
over the railing and watched people in bathing suits below. She
wasn't used to hearing people argue. She wasn't used to seeing her mom angry, and she wondered why, from the moment
Joan came into their house, the air around the two women felt
stiff, like cardboard. It scared her that Joan might leave again.

Later in the pool, underneath the surface of the water, it was
quiet. The space around her body felt soft and exactly the right
temperature to match her own—there was no border between
her skin and the water. Only when she pushed her feet hard
on the bottom of the pool and thrust herself upward to break
the surface and breathe in gasps of air did she feel her own skin
again, the breeze chilly and sharp against it. Those moments
of breath and air were as short as she could make them. Push
up, break the surface, exhale, inhale, exhale, inhale, hold it in
and down again, back through the water to the quiet, perfect
space below.

In the brief seconds Adia was in the air, she could hear her
mother's and grandmother's voices alternately scratching and
pounding like the surf from the ocean just beyond the pool
patio. Their voices made Adia's heart beat faster in her chest and
it hurt. She could tell her mother was angry. Her words were
quick and short and spiky, and her face hard and dark.

"I want to take Adia out into the bush," Joan said. "I want
to see where she grew up, where you lived."

"Mom, you'd hate it out there. Dust and heat and no dry
martinis."

"I don't mean I'm going to take her to live in a village somewhere. I mean on safari. There are safaris you can book. Nice
ones with hot showers and sheets and, yes, even cocktails." Joan

pulled her sunglasses up and squinted into the light. "There were brochures in the lobby. Some look quite nice."

Adia was at the far side of the pool, standing with her hand outstretched across the surface of the water. She was making tiny splashes with her palm. Then she disappeared below. Once, when Adia popped out of the water, she stayed up a little longer than it took to catch her breath. It was quiet, and she heard her grandmother say, "Lee, we have to talk about why you're so angry with me. I came to you. I came all this way to see you and to meet my granddaughter. I thought my making this effort, even after so long, would begin to bridge the gap. I want to bridge that gap. I'm old, and I don't want to die without repairing our relationship. Can you give me that?"

Leona's bathing suit was faded and stretched out. She'd been picking gently at the little fabric pills that clustered on the suit where it stretched across her chest. Her mother's words made the skin on her arms and legs bead with goose bumps. She felt exposed and pulled the large hotel towel around her. She pretended to watch Adia bobbing up and down in the water. This conversation was the opening to the dark tunnel of her past. Her breath quickened and the words she'd practiced in her head, over and over again through the years, scuttled away like sand crabs. She searched for a way to say what she wanted in a measured way, but all she found in her mouth was anger. It stirred and frothed, a rabid dog in her throat.

"You knew," she rasped. She never imagined that she would ever have this conversation with her mother. She'd fantasized about it but never thought the reality of it was possible. Now it felt like she wasn't thinking about anything at all, but that the words were pushing themselves out of her by their own power.

"You let my father do those things to me. I tried to tell you and you ignored me. You let him ruin me. I wanted to die. I wanted to cut myself into pieces. You destroyed my childhood.

I watched you do nothing to help, and then I finally escaped. I escaped halfway across the world and made a life for myself without any help from you. Now you're here? Now you want to talk? Well, guess what? Fuck you!"

Joan's mouth was an open black hole in her face, and the sunglasses had slid back down all the way onto the tip of her nose. She was perfectly still. For an instant Leona thought she'd killed her mother or turned her into stone—maybe she was a medusa with snake words. Leona's blood was streaming with adrenaline, and her heart beat wildly. During her speech, she'd felt separate from the body she inhabited, just a mind floating somewhere far above the quivering, angry woman spewing out feelings like pus from a wound. Now, watching her mother, Leona's two parts slowly seeped back together. She looked around. She must have been shouting. She hadn't meant to, hadn't thought she was, but people around the pool were watching them. Leona had the feeling of eyes on her, and then she saw that Adia, too, was standing stock-still in the water, staring at Leona from under her slicked wet hair.

Suddenly, Leona felt sad. This wasn't how she'd pictured it. She wanted to hurt her mother, yes. She wanted to punish Joan for the complicity she'd shown all through Leona's forty-two years. But it didn't feel good to finally shout what she'd held in for so long. There was no relief, no burbling up of happiness to fill the now-vacant space. Nothing like that happened. Just emptiness. A heavy emptiness. Leona didn't like all the eyes on her; she wasn't one for dramatic scenes, and the idea that Adia might have heard, that she would know…it was too much. She'd taken such care to construct a relationship with her daughter that would never allow light to shine on Leona's earlier life. Leona stood quickly, shoved her feet into her flip-flops and walked away before her mother could say a word.

The lobby was cool and deserted. Leona felt faint and dizzy. It wasn't like her to get emotional. She saw a chair tucked into

an alcove and sat down. She wanted to hide, and it felt good
to be folded up in this deep chair with its large, winged sides
that hid her from view. Leona closed her eyes and forced herself
to think about something besides the words she'd just spoken.

She focused on the bush. Should she let Adia go on safari
with Joan? Her first reaction had been to say no. When Adia
was born, Leona swore she'd do anything rather than expose
Adia to her parents. But really, with her father dead, the danger
was gone. Joan had been complicit, but never cruel. And Adia
seemed happy to meet her grandmother. Leona prickled with
a surprising jealousy when she saw how Adia hung on to Joan's
every word, desperate for the old woman's affection.

Leona opened her eyes and saw that the lobby was still empty.
The shelf of brochures was just across the hall. She knew there
were safaris her mother would be comfortable taking. She'd
heard of the luxury some of them promised, but she'd never
known details. Leaving her flip-flops behind, Leona padded
over to the display. There were plenty to choose from. Looking past the ones for parasailing in Lamu and exploring Mount
Kenya, she pulled out all the ones that looked suitable. Once
gathered, she brought the whole pile back to her chair and
curled up in it again.

They were all just variations of one theme: game watching
from the air-conditioned comfort of safari vans, and sleeping on
Egyptian cotton sheets in tents more Beverly Hills than bush.
Most of the safaris went into Tsavo and Amboseli. If Joan wanted
to go closer to where Adia was born, those wouldn't be good
options. Leona noticed only one that went closer to Loita. It
was a photo safari based out of a luxury camping site near the
Nguruman forest. Adia might even know some of the Maasai
guides; it was close enough to the manyatta that some of them
might work there. She could even escape and make her way to
the manyatta if she had to. Leona opened the brochure to study
the itinerary. Before she saw anything else, she caught sight of a

face in the upper right-hand corner, a photo of the proprietor, she assumed. She looked closer and blinked to clear the flashes of light that were exploding in her head. She tried to steady her breathing, but the flashes in her brain were so violent she thought she might throw up.

He wasn't dead. Even if the brochure was out-of-date, it couldn't be that old. When had she met his mother? Ten years ago? And his face in the photo was different—he'd clearly aged.

He wasn't dead and he wasn't far away. The whole time he'd been in plain sight. Maybe they'd crossed the same street in opposite directions. Maybe they been at the same bar one night, just hours apart. Had she seen him once and not recognized him?

There was a noise next to her and she looked up. Her mother stood there, her face a closed window.

"I just need to tell you."

"Jesus!" Leona said loudly. Her mother standing there was a surprise, and an unwelcome one that pierced the shock. But Leona was too exhausted to argue, or to refuse and stand up and walk away. The photo left her stunned in complete inaction. Her mother, now, was the least of her concerns. Leona nodded in the direction of another chair and watched as her mother, thin as a stem, struggled to pull the chair close.

"I was a bad mother," Joan said, lifting her hand against the argument from Leona that didn't come.

"I knew I was bad from the moment you were born. It didn't ever come naturally to me. I was terrified all the time when you were a baby. I could hardly leave the house for the first year because it all scared me too much. My mother didn't even come to help for the first couple of weeks, but then she had to go, and by the way, she was a bad mother, too." The words scraped Leona's skin. She didn't expect this—a plea for mercy, and she didn't want it. Seeing her mother as vulnerable now upset the entire balance of Leona's memories. But the older woman's words kept coming. They were a wave Leona was pinned under, and the only way to keep from getting sucked out to sea was to let it pass over her.

"Your father was a stern man. Not at all affectionate. He was always desperate for order, for things to be just so. He got mad one spring when the rows of tulips I planted along the walkway came up red and pink. He wanted only pink ones. He made me pull the red ones out and then go to the florist to buy replacements in little pots. Can you imagine? But I did it. I did everything he asked because I had nothing else. Where could I go? My parents would have been horrified if I'd gone back to them. I had no job, no skills. And then there was you, this daughter I felt completely unable to manage. We hired nannies and, after a while, I relaxed a little… I had to keep busy all the time, had to be out of the house as much as possible. That's where my freedom was. Yes, I knew. I knew but I didn't want to believe it. I couldn't allow myself to believe it, because if I did, and still I stayed? What would that have made me? A monster.

"Once I even asked him. I hoped that if he knew I knew, he would stop. He told me I was wrong, that I was imagining things, and that the depression was back and making me think things that weren't there."

She paused, and Leona looked up. There were tears in her mother's eyes, but Leona pushed back a pang of sympathy. This didn't change anything. Her mother could have mustered up the courage to help and she didn't. But somewhere, somewhere Leona couldn't identify or pinpoint, there was something new. Being a mother was confusing and hard. Children sometimes took things from you that you wanted or needed. She came from a long line of bad mothers. She hadn't yet broken the streak, and she saw, now, that her mother was nothing but a flawed human who, in the sea of motherhood, was weighed down by her own albatross. This feeling was new. Maybe not the burbling up of relief she'd wanted, but maybe a pinprick of light.

"When you escaped to college and grad school and then all the way to Kenya, I was relieved. I was glad for you. But, by the way, you didn't do it without help, did you? You've been living off the account he left you when he died. I'm glad."

Leona breathed deeply and exhaled. She couldn't believe that her mother, her reticent mother who hardly spoke more than the basic exchange of pleasantries while Leona was growing up, was saying all of this. She didn't know her own mother at all, she realized.

"When your father died, I missed him. I grieved. But I also felt a weight had been lifted from me." Here, Joan reached over and touched Leona lightly on Leona's hand—the one still holding the brochure.

"I saw a therapist. Can you believe that? It took me that long…all these years, to gather the courage to come to you."

Leona glanced away. Seeing her mother so exposed, so raw, made Leona feel as if she'd been dropped into a new country where she didn't understand the customs or the language. She couldn't meet her mother's eyes. This conversation was too big to consider now. She needed to let it absorb more slowly. Her mother was still leaning in close, watching Leona. Leona noticed the tight network of lines on Joan's cheeks, and the drapey quality of the skin across her neck. In her memory, her mother's face was smooth and expressionless, her constant makeup a mask, her thoughts always unreadable behind it.

"Well, Mom, I'm not sure how to react," Leona said, and her voice came out more sharply than she'd planned. Her mother's eyes flashed in surprise, and she leaned back, pulled her hand from Leona's arm. Instantly Leona knew she'd offended her mother somehow, and a bewildered feeling overtook her. Why was she feeling guilty for hurting her mother's feelings? It wasn't equal, not in the least, to how her mother had hurt her. Still, that she admitted she'd made a mistake somehow made Leona flush and, as a way to deflect the feeling, she separated out the brochure with John's photo in it and thrust the rest into Joan's lap. She slid John's into the space between the side of the cushion and the chair's arm. She stood up.

"I think you and Adia should go on safari together. I'm sorry I insulted you before. They do look nice. I want her to spend time with you."

The next time Adia popped up from under the water in the pool, she saw that both her mother and grandmother were gone. She was glad. Hearing them fight made her insides loose and scratchy, and when her mother cursed at Joan in that shrill voice that didn't seem like her mother's at all, Adia felt like she was tumbling in space. She'd barely gotten a grandmother and she didn't want to lose her so fast. Now the chairs where they'd been sitting were empty. The sun was pulled back and settling down on the other side of the sky, and the pool, which had been sunny and bright, was now shaded and cool. Adia climbed out of the water and stepped off the patio's cement steps and onto the warm, soft sand. Down at the surf, a few little kids were running back and forth along the frothy line where ocean met sand and up to where their parents stretched out on brightly colored beach towels. Adia walked as close to the little family as she could without their noticing and sat in the warm sand.

"Don't go in the water too far, kids!" the mother called at one point. "There may be riptides."

The oldest-looking child, a girl of about seven, plopped down on the edge of her mother's towel.

"What's a riptide?" she asked.

Adia knew. She'd studied them in science class. She whispered to herself, "A narrow stream of water traveling swiftly from shore out to sea."

She heard the mother say, "It's most important that if you get caught in one, you don't fight. The real danger is not in being in one, but in how you react to it."

Adia remembered that her teacher told the class that rip currents were caused by the shape of the shoreline itself, not by the moon or the sun or the particular undulations of the seafloor. The tides reacted to the particular way the shoreline behaved. The shore was in charge of the whole dynamic.

Adia watched the kids and their parents for a long time, trying to discern the pattern the children made between water and family. Who responded to whom? Which were the shoreline, Adia wondered, the kids or the parents, and which the tides? If she had a father and a mother together, like those kids did, Adia knew what she would be. She would be the water that answered the shoreline of her parents. She would swirl around their edges, delighted to be the third in their dynamic of two. They would be happy together—just like these parents seemed to be. Adia's parents would laugh and hold hands and be as steady as land. Adia, then, would be free to drift and return, drift and return, always knowing she had a safe, dry place waiting for her.

Later, at dinner, Adia watched her mother's face closely when her grandmother said, "I'm going to book a safari, the one that Adia liked the most." All three of them were rosy and exhausted from the sun and the water. Adia's eyelids drooped and she could hardly eat the hamburger the waiter had set down in front of her. Joan and Leona sipped wine and picked at their fish.

"Which one did you choose?" Leona asked Adia, briefly pushing the fatigue away and concentrating on her daughter's face.

"I forget the name," Adia said quietly, "but I picked it because grandma wanted to see our manyatta, and this one was the closest."

"What?" Leona asked, her voice shrill in the quiet restaurant. "I didn't see one anywhere closer to Loita than Amboseli."

"Really?" Joan said. "It must have dropped out of the pile you gave me. I found it sticking out of the chair cushion after you left this afternoon. It looks wonderful. Perfect for us. Adia, you've held on to it, right? I'll need the number."

Adia nodded. Earlier that evening, while they waited for Leona to shower and change for dinner, Adia and Joan sat on the balcony off Joan's room and looked through the various offerings. Adia picked the one closest to the manyatta, it was the only criteria she used. She'd been looking at the pictures when Leona called to them, saying she was ready and should they go down to the dining room? Adia needed her shoes and found them under her bed. She dropped the brochures on her bedside table. "Good girl. Give it back to me tomorrow and I'll try to book us in next week. Adia will miss a few days of school, but never mind. Of course, you're welcome to come along."

Leona felt her whole body shaking. She felt both cold and as if she needed big drafts of fresh air in her lungs.

Adia fell asleep fast, her dreaming mind full of ocean currents, pulling and pushing away from a wide shoreline. When she woke suddenly, she blinked into the dark and felt her body was a long piece of seagrass, waving in the depths of some dark body of water.

The voices came from behind the closed door leading to her grandmother's room. Adia couldn't hear words, just the rise and fall of quick, angry speech. She lay still for a moment, wondering if it would stop. When it didn't, she slid out of bed and crept to the door. She learned a lot of things by creeping up to doors lately, she thought. She pressed her ear lightly against the wood, holding her body stiff, not getting too comfortable, ready to spring back to her bed if she heard footsteps on the other side.

"No, you listen to me..." her grandmother hissed. "You can't keep everyone from her. Not me, not him."

Then her mother's voice. "I wasn't keeping her from him. From you, maybe, but not from him. I thought he was dead! I looked for him. I wanted to give her to him. But he was dead. This is as big a shock for me as it will be for her."

"But maybe this is the best way for her to meet him. Casually, not some big to-do."

"Jesus, Mom, I'm not sending Adia on safari to meet her dad. How would that work?" She mimicked a young girl's voice and said, "Thanks for a great experience, and by the way, I'm your kid!"

Adia's body stiffened with the word, the feeling of waving, dizzy, underwater rushed over her again. *Dad.* She said *dad.* At the sound of footsteps, Adia pulled herself away from the door. She leaped back under her sheet and pinched her eyes closed. She heard her mother rustle in the bathroom, turn on the light, flush the toilet. Then Adia heard her mother's bed creak, and the room was dark again and quiet. Adia was so used to being alone with her mother's silence that the idea of trying to pierce through it had never occurred to Adia. But that small word lingered in her brain—*dad.*

The idea of a father felt electric, and it kept Adia awake for hours. She stared up at the ceiling and watched the shadows bend and curve. When she was certain her mother was long asleep, she pulled the brochures from her side table, and slipped them under her pillow. When she finally fell asleep, the shoreline stretched out in her mind, infinite and pale against the dark waves swirling and churning with deadly riptides. *Drift,* the water whispered to her in her dream, *drift.* And the shoreline grew farther and farther away.

Adia woke. Her hair was tangled over her face and her skin felt warm and clammy. Her breath was hard and fast with fright, and in the dark she could barely see the last remnant of her dreaming self, almost invisible now in the vast sea, sliding out, alone, beyond the horizon line.

NAKURU

The first time they met, Grace didn't know what to think of Adia. She was strange, that was obvious. The only seat left in class on Grace's first day—already two months into the school year—was next to Adia, who looked totally different from the other kids, from all the kids Grace had ever known. She had long messy blonde hair and wore a lot of jewelry—beads and beads sewn onto leather bracelets and necklaces. She must have had six or seven around each wrist and around her neck, too. Grace had never before seen a white girl with so many beads. The other kids all looked up at Grace when the teacher introduced her, but the blonde girl just stared out the window and twirled a clumpy strand of hair around her finger. When Grace sat down, she noticed the other girl's fingernails were dirty and cracked in places, and that she chewed on the skin around them, so her fingers were covered in tiny cuts, bleeding a little. "I'm Adia," the blonde said when she caught Grace staring at her beaded wrists. "My Maasai family named me."

At lunch that first day, Grace sat at an empty table toward the back. First, she was alone, but then she saw the strange girl coming toward her. "I usually sit here," the beaded girl said. "I don't mind if you sit here, too, though." Grace hesitated—she understood already that Adia was an outcast in the school hierarchy and that by sitting with her Grace might be painted with that brush, too. She'd never been anything other than popular in her schools before. But now she didn't care. She was tired of all of this, the moving, the new houses, always being the new kid. She couldn't be bothered to get up and sit somewhere else. So what if the other kids thought she was weird?

Grace didn't talk much at that lunch. Instead, she listened to Adia. Adia talked as if she'd been holding words inside her like air in a balloon that popped. She couldn't hold back. Grace was annoyed at first. She wanted to be alone. But as Adia talked, she became more and more intrigued with her story. Finally, she stopped eating altogether and just listened. Adia was practically Maasai. She and her mom spent holidays in the manyatta. Adia had learned to herd the goats and start a fire using only sticks and her own breath. She'd learned how to grasp a goat by its feet and flip it onto its back so a man could slit its throat. She learned to drink the nourishing fresh cow blood the Maasai way—by piercing the skin of the cow's neck with a sharp spear, and then, after drinking her fill, pinching the skin back together so the cow could walk away with just a trickle running down its neck and the feeling of a bee sting. Both her parents were white; Adia said her dad was a Kenyan cowboy from a long line of white Kenyans. But Adia, as she said herself, was Maasai. By the time the bell rang for class to start again, Grace knew that Adia was the most interesting person she'd ever met and made up her mind to be her best friend.

Evenings in Nairobi were cool, mostly because of the altitude, and Jane often brought a cup of tea out to the balcony after dinner, wrapping up in an old gray throw and watching the bats leave their upside-down beds in the banana trees and go flitting around above her while the stars blinked awake. The rare occasions when Grace joined Jane made Jane want to cry with pleasure. Tonight Grace lay in the chaise next to Jane's and stretched her hand toward Jane.

"Can I share that blanket?" Grace asked, and Jane would have given Grace her own skin if she thought it would draw Grace closer again. Jane handed Grace the blanket and felt for her fingers as she took it. Jane wanted to touch her daughter, to trigger a desire in Grace to make her want to climb over next to Jane and huddle together under these foreign stars. But Grace just leaned back and curled up with the throw piled on top of her.

"Adia says people like us try too hard to make America wherever we go. And it's true, right?"

Jane was cold without the weight of the blanket on her, and the bats suddenly sounded like mice scratching the sky for food. Jane didn't like Adia. She didn't like the furtive way Adia glanced out from under her slack bangs or the awful clothes she wore.

"I know you're still new at school, and it takes time to settle in, but is Adia the only friend you have so far? She isn't like any of the girls you knew in Rabat. I mean…she seems, I don't know, so different from you. Like she needs to run a comb through that hair, and what's with the jewelry?"

Jane wanted Grace to giggle with her. She would have before. Jane knew her Gracie—Grace and Jane were the same. But Grace didn't giggle.

"I like her, Mom. She's different and cool, and she's nice. And I don't care about her hair and neither should you." Then she got up, tossed the blanket back on her mother and went inside.

A few days later, Jane offered Nakuru as her olive branch.

"Let's go for the day, Grace," Jane said. "I'll drive. We'll let your dad sleep in."

And then Jane added, "Bring your new friend. We'll pick her up on the way out of town. A girls' road trip."

Grace's face brightened, and Jane thought, who is she? But Grace never wanted to be alone with Jane anymore. Adia was the only hope Jane had of spending time with her daughter.

When Jane and Grace picked Adia up on the way out of town, it was early morning, and the girl sat in the half dark, hunched on her heels at the end of her driveway.

"Where's your mom?" Jane asked before Grace could even say hello.

"She's asleep," Adia said. "She hardly ever gets up before nine." Adia reached down and grabbed the straps of a lumpy, green, canvas backpack.

"My Maasai mom is meeting me at Nakuru. I have stuff to give her." She opened the back door of the car, tossed her bag in and climbed after it, snapping the door shut behind her.

"Doesn't your mom want to meet me?" Jane asked, ignoring her instinct to add, "Your American mom? I was looking forward to meeting her." Jane was stunned by a mother who would sleep in and let her thirteen-year-old daughter wait in the dark for a stranger to pick her up to take her away for the day. *Feral*, Jane thought, *she's like a feral child*. Adia's pants were dirty at the cuffs, and her T-shirt was stained and at least one size too small. Her ropey hair was shoved up into a large, leather hat that looked like it had seen more than a few dust storms. Jane watched Adia settle into the back seat next to Grace who, with her clean, brown ponytail, jeans and white sneakers, looked like a different species compared to Adia. When the girls threw their arms around each other, Jane shuddered.

They drove out of town quietly. The girls were still sleepy, curled up with their heads tipped against opposite windows. The sun was just crawling up the lower third of the sky when the road rose and suddenly seemed to drop out below them. Jane turned off onto the shoulder and they all got out to stretch their legs. The road wound steeply down and down and down, switchbacking all the way—hundreds of feet—into a huge great bowl in the earth.

"You guys never saw the Rift Valley before?" Adia asked, sensing Jane's and Grace's awe. Jane didn't correct her. Even Grace didn't know she'd once lived on the valley floor. She was vague about that period of her life—she didn't like to think about it much anymore. Adia waved proprietarily toward the horizon. "My Maasai family live out there." Jane looked over at Adia, and she saw the sun on Adia's darkly tanned arms and her dusty clothes. In this context, she looked of this place. Her clothes and hat and hair and jewelry made her look like a sliver of the savannah below them sprung into human form. For an instant, Jane wondered if she would have come to look like that if she'd stayed. If she'd met someone else here to marry and Grace had that man as a father, would she look like that, too? The road was rough and deeply pocked, and sometimes the edge just fell away. Jane gripped the wheel tightly and slowed to a crawl. But now and then Jane glanced up into the rearview mirror to watch the girls. Grace had closed her eyes again and leaned her head back against the headrest.

Adia directed Jane to a small road that seemed to lead to and from nowhere. "They'll be coming up this road," she said. "If you park here, we'll see them." They were close to the lake. Jane imagined she could smell the brackish water, the scent of feathers and guano. She was anxious to get there, to show Grace what she expected would be a magical sight and to tell her daughter how long she had waited to see it. But when they reached that spot in the road and Adia told Jane to stop, Jane was in equal parts stunned and awed. She saw Grace gaze at Adia with admiration as Adia hopped out of the car and used the front bumper to climb on the hood of the car, her lumpy rucksack next to her.

Jane leaned against the driver's-side door, drinking lukewarm water from her Nalgene bottle, and Grace lay across the back seat, her bare feet sticking out the window and her forearm slung over her eyes.

The Maasai women finally appeared through a break in the dust. It was like they unzipped a tent flap and stepped out—suddenly there they were. There were four of them, all with shaved heads and bare feet. All wrapped in loosely draped cotton cloths tied at the shoulders and wearing masses of the same beaded jewelry Adia wore. One of the women had an indolent toddler tied to her back.

"There they are," Adia said as she hopped off her perch. Then she strode up the road toward the women.

When they were close enough, Adia took off her hat and bent her head to each woman and they touched her hair, murmuring smoky, low words like a humming. Adia spoke to them in their language and untied the baby from the woman's back and held it like a mother would as she chatted—the baby perched naked on her hip, Adia's tan arm looking pale and angular against the baby's curved, brown bottom. Grace climbed out of the car and watched Adia with the gathering of women.

"Hey, Grace, bring me the pack." Adia glanced over her shoulder as if she'd just remembered that Grace and Jane were there.

Jane watched as Grace knelt in the dust, tugging open the straps and pulling things from the pack to hand up eagerly to the Maasai women, greedy for their attention. There was sugar, tea, tins of milk powder, OMO detergent and what looked like a large tub of Crisco. The women murmured and nodded, and one by one all the goods Grace brought out were tucked away in the folds of their wraps. Adia handed the baby back to its mother, who tied the girl deftly to her back again. Grace stepped back and watched as Adia and the women grasped each other's hands and said their goodbyes. Adia stood, her hand shading her eyes, and watched as the little band of women disappeared up the road, back through the curtain of dust.

Jane shut the car windows and flipped on the air-conditioning. She heard Grace's quiet voice say, "Are those the women you told me about? Your Maasai mother and the other wives?"

"Yeah," Adia answered, and her voice didn't sound strong anymore, but sad. "Simi is the one I told you about. She's my Maasai mom. I lived with them until I was six. Now I just spend summer vacations with them. Sometimes long weekends or when my mom is traveling. I wish she traveled more."

Jane thought of Grace's relatives—her grandparents, aunts, uncles and cousins on Paul's side, and silent Uncle Lance on hers. Grace had never met Lance and only saw her other relatives for a couple of weeks every other summer. Grace barely knew her American family, and unlike Adia, she had no other tribe. Jane thought that she and Paul never stayed long enough anywhere for Grace to make those kinds of connections. In a way, Jane and Paul had stolen something from their daughter that they could never give back. They flew away from everything. Grace had no one besides her parents, no place but where they were, and that was always temporary.

It wasn't like Jane pictured. Her imagination had it all wrong. Or maybe it was just too late. The drought had been too long, people said. It was entrenched all over Kenya now. People were hungry. Livestock was dying. *Shambas*, the family gardens people depended on, were nothing but rocks and dust, and when rain did fall, it fell too quickly and too hard to be absorbed into the bare soil. There were no grasses to hold on to the water, help it seep into the earth, so it spilled away, leaving nothing but volcanic rock and limestone—the earth's underbelly that could grow nothing of substance.

When Jane and Grace and Adia finally reached it, Lake Nakuru was shallow and dank, and it spread out at their feet like spilled paint swirled into browns and dark greens and grays. It seemed the flamingos were dying in great, pink waves. It was beyond what Jane imagined from the articles she'd read. The bodies of the dead lay half-submerged in the fetid water, their exposed backs baked by the sun, their lifeless necks, long as flower stems, drifting slightly in the gentle, shallow currents, their unseeing eyes watching over those forgotten eggs below them. The ones still alive were desultory and disappointing. They fitted themselves exactly in the drying shallows above the ancestor eggs. The earth was changing under their feet, water turning to mud, mud turning to dry land. But these birds stayed anyway, rooted to their home.

The dust that muted their pink feathers saddened Jane; the plastic water bottle she saw bobbing in the muddy edge; the cigarette butts half-buried in the slimy green algae that lined the shore. Jane had the sudden memory of her father standing near the jungle gym at the park so many years ago and telling Jane about acknowledging the moment they realized that Lance was gone. Things disappeared. Moments died, maybe her father was right to move on. Now Jane wanted to wave her arms and shout at the dreary flamingos left behind, to see them take to the air like the ones already gone, to imagine a new place for themselves. This wasn't what Jane had expected; it was not what she wanted to happen.

A group of European tourists climbed out of a zebra-painted pop-top minibus. They littered themselves along the path, red-faced and cameras clicking. They looked alien to this landscape. Fleshy, pale, breathing hard, like grubs plucked from under rocks, blinking into the sunlight. Jane wondered if she looked like them in the eyes of those Maasai women, or if Grace did with her shiny hair and fresh clothes?

"Comme c'est beau!" a woman in a wide-brimmed straw hat said to herself, breathing deeply in satisfaction, clasping her

manicured fingers. Jane wondered just what the woman was looking at. Nothing here looked beautiful to her.

Jane lifted her hand for an instant, wiped the dust off her forehead, and when she glanced back, Grace had stretched out flat, barely visible beside Adia. Adia, who hunkered, bored and blank as a shell, picking at her fingernails, her hat throwing her face into shadow, the skin on her arms as dark and dry as the dust at their feet. Adia—the only one who belonged to this earth. Jane felt a stab of resentment. She was happy that her daughter was feeling better and gave credit for that to Adia. But what did her daughter see in this girl? She was like nobody Grace had known before. She wished she could understand what her daughter saw in this strange girl.

Standing there, by the changing lake, she sent a prayer to the sky that her daughter wasn't really disappearing. "Don't let her leave me," she murmured. "Not like Lance, and not in a way that will never, ever change back."

It was a mistake to come to the lake, to the floor of the Rift. The landscape was so familiar it made her ache, and the memories came too fast. It hurt to remember Muthega and the women by the river and the dusty kids. It hurt to remember herself back then and how much stronger she was. But she'd still been too weak to stay, still too weak to swallow her fear and continue her work. After Muthega's murder, she told herself, and she told Paul, too, that what she admired most about the elephants was their deep maternal instincts. She said she'd lost her desire to work in the bush with them, and only wanted to emulate them.

It felt true at that time, and she hadn't missed the work in the years since. She'd followed another path—to be a mother to her own baby, to keep the child close, folded safely in the curve of her arm, her metaphorical trunk. Elephant daughters lived with their mothers for life, though. Human daughters didn't. They grew apart from their parents, up and away, and the mothers had to open their arms wide and release them. It took strength. Jane wondered if she would ever be strong enough to let Grace go.

FOREST OF THE LOST CHILD

The son of the shopkeeper always yelled his messages long before his feet reached the manyatta. Simi and the other women, gathered by the muddy trickle of the river, heard his voice and looked up from their washing. They could see a small billow of dust moving toward them.

"That boy has the voice of an elephant in pain," Loiyan muttered. She didn't smile, although the other women laughed. Simi noticed Loiyan's pinched face, and realized that she hadn't heard Loiyan enjoy her own jokes recently. Simi wondered if the other woman was pregnant again. She had three sons who were already *moran*, and a newly married daughter pregnant with her own first baby. Loiyan also had four children who still lived in the manyatta. All girls, two were toddlers, one was a serious girl of seven and the last was a baby, barely weaned. During the early pregnancies, Loiyan blossomed. Her cheeks grew round, her belly blossomed like a flower and her skin shone. Each of the first three babies was born quickly and easily. Loiyan was good at bringing babies into the world.

Then there was a tiny boy born too soon to live, his body

perfect and waxen and far too still, and it was then that Loiyan shifted. Just a bit. Her humor, Simi thought, was always a bit sharp. Her voice was always a little too loud, and her opinions a little too important. But there was always a brightness behind her barbs and her actions. She was quick and tough and never afraid. After the stillborn son, though, her personality grew uneven, a little darker, a little angrier. Some of the brightness had faded. Simi knew the pain Loiyan felt—she could remember her losses like they were still happening. But instead of that making it easier to talk to Loiyan, it became harder. Loiyan and Simi were never close, but the terrible thing they had in common seemed to drive them apart further. Loiyan no longer teased Simi; she didn't address her at all.

The pounding of footsteps came closer, and with it a cloud of dust that descended on the women. The boy bent over, breathing hard. He lifted water from the stream into his mouth with one hand and wiped his forehead with the other. "Simi," he huffed, "Adia is coming to Narok town tomorrow. She will have things for you. You can meet her there at midday."

He splashed water on his face and rubbed it hard. The sun glinted off the droplets like tiny shards of glass. Simi smiled at the boy and thanked him. "Go to my house and wait. I'll come soon and make you tea. You shouldn't go back to your father hungry and tired."

The phone in the little shop where the boy's father worked as both postman and shopkeeper rang often; so many husbands and sons were in Nairobi now that every day someone would call, asking the boy to deliver a message to one of the manyattas nearby. Simi, though, was the only one who had a daughter who called.

Simi turned back to the river to rinse the few items that were still soapy. She noticed Loiyan staring at her sideways. Even with all her children, she'd never be happy, Simi thought. Loiyan was a jealous woman. And for some reason she couldn't begin to explain, that made Simi feel sorry for her. Before she knew what words were going to slip from her mouth, she said, "Loi-yan, come with me tomorrow. Adia will have things for all of us." Loiyan looked down at the slow-moving water and sucked her teeth, but Simi knew she would agree.

Simi laid her wet clothes on bare, hot rocks and hurried home to make the shopkeeper's boy tea. She knew his family had little these days. The drought lingered, and there were children born now who couldn't remember ever seeing the land green—the descriptions their parents gave them were nothing more than fairy tales. But the families who still had livestock were doing well enough to feed themselves. Leona had kept her promise to the Maasai—in certain situations, for prescribed lengths of time, people could take their cattle and goats to feed in the highlands, where there was still grass to eat and water to drink. In the driest months, this left manyattas full of only women and children. Women and children who didn't have money to buy things from the shopkeeper. Women and children who did without sugar in their tea anymore and whose bellies often grumbled in the dark hours of the night.

Simi was the lucky one. Her Nairobi daughter never let a month pass without bringing soap and tea and sugar and fat to cook with. Adia was generous, and everyone in the manyatta benefited. This made Simi proud.

The next day, Simi and Loiyan began the walk to Narok. First wife, Isina, came, too, as well as her grown daughter, Nalami, who was visiting her mother. Both the other wives missed Adia almost as much as Simi herself did. The walk from the manyatta to Narok was long, and it was hot, and Loiyan carried her smallest baby on her back, wrapped in a *kanga*. Still, though, Simi was surprised at how slowly Loiyan walked, how heavy her breathing was, and wondered again if Loiyan was pregnant. She worried that they might miss Adia. By the time the sun was almost directly overhead, Isina had taken the baby from Loiyan and tied it securely to her own back. Loiyan hadn't argued—she gave up her burden wordlessly. This alone made Simi worry. Loiyan wasn't someone who easily kept from arguing.

The women stopped to drink water from a trickling spring just outside of Narok. Isina handed the baby to Loiyan, who sat, slumped and breathing hard, on a flat rock. The baby was hungry and wanted to nurse. Loiyan clasped her daughter to her breast, but even as the baby pulled and suckled, Simi could tell she wasn't getting much milk.

"Loiyan, are you sick?" Isina asked. It comforted Simi, somehow, that the other women noticed, too. Simi noticed beads of sweat dappling Loiyan's hairline, gathering together and sliding down the sides of her face.

"I'm just tired," Loiyan answered, and she stood, a little unstable, on her feet. She handed the baby to Isina. "Help me carry her."

It wasn't much longer until the woman noticed the outline of Narok on the horizon, the squat buildings, the uneven rooflines, and then there was a white car, new and shiny under the film of dust. There were two figures Simi could see: one sitting on the hood, one leaning against the car. Simi squinted to catch sight of Adia, and then she saw her daughter sliding off her perch and striding toward her. Her daughter. How lovely Adia always looked. And then they were standing together, talking. Even Loiyan looked better. She'd always had a place for Adia in her heart. All the members of the manyatta did.

"Yeyo, I have things for you," Adia said as she took the baby from Isina. Adia held the baby against her hip, and the child reached up and grasped a handful of Adia's hair and laughed. "My mother's worried about the grazing. Are the men back yet? She wanted me to ask you. It's important for them to stay there only for the time allowed. If they're still out there, if they stay past what they're allowed, they may not be allowed to go back next time."

Isina answered. "They're still there. None of them has come

back yet. We only have a few goats here for us to eat, no cattle. We cannot sell them or we'd have no meat, so we cannot buy the other things we need." Adia turned then and waved her arms. "Hey, Grace, bring me the pack." Turning back to Simi, she said, "I have soap and milk powder and sugar and *kimbo*. Some tea, too. And my friend. I want her to meet you, Yeyo."

The other girl began pulling items out of a backpack and handing them up to the women. Simi watched her carefully. She was similar to Adia—the same color skin, the same texture hair, but also so different. Her face was pale, and her eyes big and rounder, somehow, her fingernails were clean and white. Simi thought the girl looked a little frightened.

"We can't stay long," Adia said in Maa, and Simi felt a pang of disappointment. She'd have to say goodbye again so soon.

"Grace's mother is waiting. She's impatient." Adia smiled when she said it, but it made Simi angry with the other woman, that still figure in the distance, leaning against her car. She wondered if that woman had ever experienced any sadness at all. As Simi watched, the faraway woman put a bottle of water to her mouth and tipped her head back, drinking a long drink. Simi could imagine the feeling of cool, clean water in her mouth. It had been so long since the rivers were clear and cold.

"But I'll come again soon, Yeyo." Adia kissed the baby on her little cheek and handed her back to Isina.

Simi watched the car drive away. She thought she saw the round, pale face of Adia's friend pressed against the window, staring back at her. But then Loiyan made a small sound and sank to her knees. She was so close to Simi that her hair grazed Simi's calf as she fell.

"Loiyan!" Nalami shouted, and she knelt to hold Loiyan's head in her lap. She felt Loiyan's cheek and said, "She's too hot. It's a bad fever."

Simi wished they had some water, even a little, to wipe Loiyan's face, cool her down a bit, and to squeeze into her dry, hot lips. But the drought had made the smaller sources, the ones they might have found nearby, dry up and disappear.

Simi carried Loiyan on her back the same way Isina carried Loiyan's baby. Nalami was weighed down, too. She had the tins of *kimbo* and the butter and all the other things Adia had brought. The women walked slowly, and Simi had to stop often and gently slide Loiyan down to the ground and then stand up straight, catch her breath and stretch her aching back. Nalami's manyatta was not far, but the walk was slow, and the afternoon was hot and still. Worry weighed on Simi, too. She'd never seen a person faint and not revive quickly. Loiyan was still limp, her heart was beating and her breath was even, but her eyes were open and unfocused, and her jaw was loose and slack.

When the women finally reached Nalami's manyatta, it was evening. The sky was purple and the sun a dull red. It looked like an unhappy sky, a worried and bruised sky. By this time, Loiyan's baby, having slept during most of the walk, was wide-awake and hungry—crying for milk. Nalami's husband had three wives, one largely pregnant and another with children beyond weaning age. The pregnant woman might have milk. Otherwise the baby would have to eat *ugi* and maybe a little cow's milk, if some could be found. That would be a problem for Nalami to fix. Simi, meanwhile, carried Loiyan into Nalami's hut and laid her out on the bed. The *laiboni* would help now.

Simi didn't sleep well. It was too dark for her and Isina to make the walk home, so they slept on the rawhide bed in Nalami's mother-in-law's house. Simi wasn't used to sleeping that close to another adult, and every time Isina shifted, the movement woke her. It was still night when she gave up. Outside the hut, the sky was beginning to shift from darkness into dawn, and a pale, almost imperceptible orange light was the only indication of where the earth and the sky joined.

Simi and Isina left for home before the sun was fully up. Simi carried Loiyan's baby, who, still hungry from her sudden and unwelcome transition from mother's milk to gruel, fell asleep immediately, her cheek pressed against Simi's shoulder. She thought of Loiyan's other children, who waited for their mother to return. They would be sad and frightened. But Isina was carrying all the things Adia had given them, and maybe Simi could cheer the children up with sweet tea. None of them had had sugar in their tea for so long.

Two days later, Simi lay with Loiyan's baby in the shade of an acacia. The baby had begun to get used to eating *ugi*. She was a happy little thing. Simi had been caring for all of Loiyan's daughters for the last two days. Loiyan's older children had left the manyatta, the oldest daughter was married, and the three older boys were *moran*. These four little girls needed care, though, and Simi stepped in to provide it. The baby slept next to her at night, and the three younger ones slept nearby, like a pile of puppies cuddled together near the warmth of the banked fire. Simi loved hearing their sleeping breaths whenever she woke.

Now the baby was sitting next to Simi and running her chubby hands in the dust. Simi began to sing a song she'd made up when Adia was a baby. She was trying to pull the words out of her memory when she heard a shout. She sat up and shaded her eyes with the palm of her hand. There was dust, lots of dust in the distance. It was movement. A child darted from behind a nearby tree and raced past Simi to a large rock outcropping that had a view over the valley. From there he might be able to see what was within all that dust. Other woman, other children, appeared next to Simi. They gazed out at the brown cloud. Then the boy on the rock shouted. He jumped up and down and shook his fists in the air. It was a victory dance. He'd seen the cause of the dust and it was the men and boys, the livestock. They were coming home.

That night a cow was slaughtered. The *moran* danced and, after so long being so quiet, the manyatta was filled with noise and movement, people and animals and activity. Simi watched the dancing with Loiyan's baby in her lap, the two toddler girls leaning on her thighs. She couldn't remember when she'd last felt this happy, this full.

Several days later, Simi and some other woman were at the river again. The children milled around them, some helping pound soap into the dirty clothes, some splashing water on themselves and laughing. Simi was happy to see that Loiyan's seven-year-old was playing with a friend and that the toddler girls were splashing in the water. They asked about their mother sometimes, and each time Simi told them not to worry. Their mother was coming but, until then, she would care for them. "Don't worry," Simi told them, "I will care for you like you are my own until she comes. Don't worry."

Then the shout again, the pounding of a boy's feet, and the shopkeeper's son appeared, breathing hard and bending over, hands to knees.

"The *laiboni* sent news," the boy said. "It's Loiyan. She's dead."

Simi looked up to see if Loiyan's daughters had heard the boy and was relieved to see that the children were outside hearing distance; they'd moved to play farther down the river. *Etwaltwa*, death—a bad omen for someone as young as Loiyan to die.

"They took her outside the *inkajijik*," the boy continued. "The *laiboni* saw that death was coming. They didn't want to bring bad things to the manyatta."

Simi nodded. It was common. To have a death in your home meant having to move the whole manyatta to a different place. Often this was avoided by moving the dying person a distance away.

"Where is the body?" Simi asked the boy.

"It is there," the boy answered.

Simi didn't accompany her husband or co-wives to Nalami's manyatta. She stayed behind with Loiyan's children. She didn't want to see Loiyan's body rubbed with fat and taken to the forest. She didn't want to remember Loiyan that way. Tonight, when it just started to grow dark, hungry nighttime animals would come out of their lairs. If Loiyan was lucky, and enough fat was used to prepare her body, the hyenas would come first. They would feast. Hyenas, like the *oreteti* tree, were messengers between N'gai and the people, and they would return Loiyan's body to nature. For her part, Simi would keep Loiyan alive in the best way she knew how, by caring for her girls. A woman with children, after all, would live forever.

JACARANDA

Adia shivered with anticipation and a desperate need to pee. Her body's movement made the branches shake, and the feathery jacaranda leaves fluttered. A few lavender blossoms flickered past her as they fell to the ground. Adia caught one and rubbed it between her fingers until the petal turned to purple juice, and then she dabbed it on her lips. Sometimes the stain lasted for a while, like lipstick, unless she forgot and let herself chew her lower lip—a habit she was trying to break. Adia leaned forward and craned her body as far as she could without falling out of the tree. From this exact spot she could see the road. Right now it was empty. Grace wasn't here yet.

She'd never had a friend come and visit her before, and she couldn't wait. She'd imagined what it would be like to have someone else there, someone besides her mother and Gakaki. But instead of spending her weekends with friends, she'd climb the jacaranda tree and stay high up among the leaves and lavender flowers for as long as she could. Some days, after she'd been in the tree for hours, Gakaki would wander out to the garden and call her name.

"Miss Adia!" he would call. "Are you here?" But he never saw her up in the tree. He never looked very hard. He'd call once and then go back inside. If Adia climbed high enough, she could see into the window of her mother's study. She had to lean her whole body onto one large branch and rest her chin on her arms. It was comfortable like that and she could watch her mother typing her papers—or was it a book now? Often her mother would pause and lift her fingers off the keyboard to think, and twirl a particular strand of hair through her fingers. Adia tried staring at her mom really hard—letting her eyes bore into her mother's head. She tried not to blink and she concentrated so hard she shook—but it never worked. Her mother never felt Adia's presence. She never turned, sensing the eyes on her, to find her daughter's face.

These days, though, instead of trying to stare her mother into noticing her, Adia imagined her father. She had his face always in the back of her mind. She memorized the photo on the brochure, and she went over and over it, trying to see herself in him. She kept the brochure hidden in the biggest pile of clothes in the deepest of her dresser drawers.

Her mother still hadn't told her the truth. Right after her grandmother left, Adia purposely brought her father up in conversation. She'd asked her mother if he had hobbies. Did he paint? Ride horses? Take photos? At the time, she felt it was bold for her to ask these questions. Too bold, maybe. Surely her mother would see through what she was doing. But her mother answered with an abrupt adherence to the story she'd always told.

"You don't have a father, Adia. He died. I didn't know him long enough to know if he had hobbies."

When she was little, Adia's mother told her that her father was Kenyan, a rancher, or "Kenya Cowboy" as descendants of the British colonials were known. That made Adia proud. After that, she'd imagined her father often. She made him a brave man living in the landscape that she loved more than anything—the scrubby land near Loita. She imagined a man who would take her out on safari where they would sleep in tents and watch together as the sky turned orange and the enormous sun sank behind the horizon. They would light a campfire and let the glinting eyes of the curious animals not scare them at all. She wanted to be as brave and wild as this father she imagined, and she wanted to imagine him as the opposite of her mother. He wouldn't be taciturn or silent or always working. He would shout her name and climb the tree with her. He would smile every time he saw her. He would look at her when she came into the room. He would be interested in what she had to say. Now, Adia had a real face to think about. Her father was a safari guide—a man of the land, just as she hoped.

It was only because of Grandmother Joan that Adia knew the truth about her father. But Joan never spoke about him, either. Not when she and Adia went on their safari in Tsavo—about as far from the manyatta in Loita as they could get. To explain, Joan had only said that the other safaris were already booked up. This was the only one that had two spaces for the dates they needed. "Next time," Joan assured her, "next time we'll go to your neck of the woods." She and Adia had weekly phone calls since Joan left, but her father never came up in those conversations, either. That he was really alive, somewhere out there, was a secret they all carried separately.

When Grace came over to her house the first time, Adia was surprised to see her mom with her. Adia's own mother expected Adia to get where she needed to go on the city buses or the cheap overcrowded *matatus*. Adia felt a flush of shame when she saw Grace's mother get out of the car, slam the door behind her and then stand, looking the house up and down, slowly turning to take in the view of the dried-up garden, the patches of dirt, the old broken bucket on its side and the wicker table and chairs. Adia was in the jacaranda then, and she felt too stunned to move when she saw Grace and her mother approach the front of the house and then disappear from her view. She heard them call out, and then she spied her mother through the window. From this side of the glass, Adia couldn't hear if her mother said anything in reply, but she did see her look up, annoyed, and rise from her chair. Adia scrambled from the tree, then. She didn't want Grace's mother to meet hers.

When Adia rounded the house, she saw Grace's mother was tipped forward, her leather sandals' toes barely over the threshold of the front door, and she was craning her neck around the doorsill. "Hello? I've brought Grace to play with Adia."

Adia was breathless when she reached them.

"Hey, Grace! I was up in the jacaranda tree. Come on, I'll show you."

"Wait." Grace's mother put her hand out to touch Grace's arm. "I want to meet the adult in charge first. Adia, please get your mother."

"She's working."

"Well, maybe I'll bring Grace back when I can meet her. Grace, come on…"

"No, Mom!" Grace tried to twist away, but the hand on her arm gripped tightly, her mother's fingers turning her skin white.

"No!" Adia pleaded. "Don't go. I'll get her."

Adia left Grace and her mother at the door, and disappeared into the darkness of the house. She thought about lying, telling them her mother was gone, that Gakaki was in charge, that he was babysitting. But she heard her mother's study door open and the sound of footsteps in the hall. Adia had never considered her mother's appearance before, but now she looked critically. Her mom's hair was dark brown and streaked with silver. She wore it in two messy braids with a halo of escaped hair standing up in a fuzzy patch at the crown. Her face had tiny lines clustered around her lips and the corners of her eyes. She was barefoot and wrapped in a cotton skirt, topped by a white T-shirt that had a tiny drop of coffee exactly where her left nipple was. She glanced at Adia as she passed, smiled faintly and continued to the front door. Adia rushed to catch up.

"Hey," Adia's mom said. She smiled and used the back of her hand to rub at a smudge on her cheek.

"I'm Adia's mom. Leona. Nice to meet you."

She waved her hand vaguely around in the air. "Grace is welcome to come in. I'll be here the whole time." Grace's mother stood stiffly, her hand still on Grace's arm.

Grace's mother made Adia look at her house differently. Grace's house was neat, and Adia's house was anything but that. When you walked through the front door, it was into a hallway piled with shoes and boots and slippers. Three Cape buffalo skulls were nailed into the wall, their horns used as lopsided coat racks with piles of old jackets and flannel shirts and key fobs hung over them. Sometimes there were clumps of dried red mud from the garden that would crush under your feet if you stepped on them and then cover your heels with fine, red dust.

Leona didn't clean the house much. She didn't think about it. Gakaki ("That name sounds like a cat coughing up a hairball," Grace said with a giggle that first day when she met him) was supposed to clean, but he never seemed able to make a dent in it. Little cobwebs decorated the corners of the ceilings, and papers and books were piled on every surface.

It was more comfortable for Adia to go to Grace's. Even though Grace's mother and her stiff face and her questions made Adia nervous, she loved going to Grace's house. She felt, when she walked through the front door each time, that she was an anthropologist stepping into a whole new world, and it made her see the appeal in the work her mother was so passionate about. Being different, entering an unknown and exotic culture, was exciting.

Every time Adia went to Grace's, she found new mysteries—

the stacks of brightly colored boxes and packages of commissary food imported from the States, DVDs with television programs and movies that showed Adia the parts of American life she'd never even imagined before: happy families gathered in kitchens so shiny they looked unused, big fluffy dogs with no sign of mange that slept in special beds, piles of snow that kids threw at each other and made statues with. She could hardly believe the way people looked in the videos—perfectly clean, perfectly dressed and perfectly happy.

The biggest mystery, though, the biggest draw to Adia, was Grace's father. He wasn't there most of the times she was. He traveled a lot, Grace said, and he worked into the evenings most days. But when he was there, it fascinated Adia to watch him. He didn't look the way she pictured her own father. He wasn't broad shouldered or blond. He didn't have scars on his hands from bushwhacking, or a burned red neck. Grace's father was slight. He looked a lot like Grace, with his dark hair, narrow, straight nose and slanted cheekbones. He wore crisp white button-down shirts with shiny glinting cuff links. In the evenings, the few times Adia was there when he came home, she noticed that the first thing he did when he walked through the front door was set down his briefcase, then unbutton his cuff links and toss them in a little ceramic dish on a table in the hall.

He hugged Grace and her mom a lot. At first Adia found it uncomfortable. She wasn't used to seeing families interact this way. But then she noticed the TV families in the States were like that, too—smiling and talking together, hugging and kissing. She added that to the list of what her own father would be like. He would hug her and kiss her cheek hello and goodbye. He would look at her as if she was the most wonderful thing in the world. That's how Grace's father acted with Grace.

When they all sat down for dinner, he would ask Grace questions about school, about the things she was studying and what she liked best. The first time Adia ate dinner with the family, Grace's father poured the water from the carafe into all the glasses and said, "Gracie, honey, how did that math test go today?" Adia couldn't remember when, or if, her mom had ever kept close enough track of her schoolwork to know to ask that kind of question. She glanced at her friend. Grace rolled her eyes.

"Come on, Grace." Her dad seemed awkward, still standing behind Grace with the sweaty carafe in one hand. He leaned down to put the other hand on Grace's shoulder. "I know you were having trouble with multiplying fractions. Did the stuff I showed you help?"

Grace gave her shoulder a violent shrug and her father's hand flicked up like a bug. "God, Dad. Can we not talk about math now?" She kicked Adia's ankle under the table and made a face. Adia understood that she was to sympathize with her friend over the annoying, interfering parents, the myth she'd heard of but never experienced personally. Adia glanced at Grace's father and saw that he was stung. He caught her eye, though, and smiled.

"Our nickname for her lately is Grumpy Gracie."

Adia burst out laughing, and laughed a little harder when she caught Grace's dark expression watching her. Adia knew she'd crossed a line with her friend; she should have sided with Grace, not her dad, but it served Grace right, Adia thought. She had a father. She had an interested, kind father who asked her questions and smiled at her. She should treat him better.

Grace liked to have Adia spend the night at her house, but didn't like sleeping at Adia's. Adia didn't blame her and wished, actually, that she could spend more time at Grace's house. She wished she could stay there forever. Even Grace's mom eventually became less scary. She took them on road trips sometimes, on long weekends, and let Adia and Grace sing at the top of their lungs as they whipped along the highway down to the Rift, the back seat windows wide-open and the wind hit-

ting them hard, forcing them to shut their eyes and pulling the
words from their lungs.

At night, when Adia slept over, Grace's mom would have
them shut the TV off at 11:00 p.m. and get into bed. Sometimes
Grace grumbled and muttered curse words under her breath,
but she always did as she was told. She'd find her parents in the
living room, where they would be curled up at opposite ends
of the couch, each reading a book. Grace would lean down
and let each parent give her a kiss good-night and a hug. Adia
would stand next to the coffee table and wonder where to put
her hands. It wasn't the affection her friend received that made
her uncomfortable, but rather the desperate ache she felt inside.
Her father would do that, too, once she found him. It was on
the list now, in her imagination. He would hug and kiss her
good-night every night. She would sleep well, knowing he was
in the house, watching over her.

One night, Grace was talking about a boy from school that
she liked. It was late, and Grace was laughing about something
the boy had said, and so Adia heard it before she did—the rise
and fall of Grace's parents' voices from another room.

"Shh," Adia whispered from her nest on the floor. "What's
that noise?" In the dark Grace's voice trailed off and she was
silent. The Morse code of Grace's mother's voice tapped a constant discourse while her father's interrupted with deep inter-
mittent thumps, his words like things thrown against the wall,
thudded and mean.

"I guess it's my parents talking," Grace mumbled. "They're
just talking."

"Sounds like they're fighting to me," Adia answered. She
couldn't help but feel at once terrified that her perfect idea of a
family included parents who fought, and gleeful that the shine
of Grace's life at home might have a ding, after all. But she hid
the possibility of relief that Grace's life wasn't perfect, and she
sat up. She found Grace's hand and squeezed it.

"Grace," she said, thrilled with the thought that had only just occurred to her. "If your parents got a divorce, maybe your dad would marry my mom. Then we'd be sisters!"

Grace was silent. Adia could hear her breathing, and she could hear, too, that the angry voices from the distant room had quieted. The argument was over, presumably. Adia let go of Grace's hand and lay back on the floor. She hugged the pillow and pulled the sleeping bag close. She was just drifting off—listing in her head, as she did every night, the attributes she knew her father would have—but she heard what Grace said. She heard the tiny, choked voice from under the covers in the bed above her, and she let the message settle around her like dust. She didn't reply. She hoped Grace assumed she was asleep, that she hadn't heard.

"I would rather be motherless than have your mother."

In the dark, Adia was filled with the shame of knowing that she understood exactly what Grace meant.

She knew Grace was angry, and it scared her. Adia loved having Grace as a friend and she didn't want to lose her. She flipped through her mind for something she could say to make it better—to make Grace like her again. And then it slipped out; the secret she wasn't sure she was ready to tell. "My father's not dead, anyway. He might marry my mom. I know where he is."

It worked.

"Holy shit!" Grace flipped over to face Adia and leaned over the edge of her bed. "How did you find out?" Her face was so close to Adia's that Adia could feel hot breath on her cheek.

Adia shifted her body away from Grace and sat up. The sleeping bag slid down her back and pooled on the floor. The air was chilly, and Adia pulled it up over her shoulders again. She hesitated to explain. She knew the story made her mother look dishonest, and she didn't want to give Grace fodder that would deepen her distaste for Leona. But she couldn't think of a lie that would work. "I just heard my mom and grandma talking about him."

"And they said where he lives?" Grace was breathless. "Why didn't your mom tell you sooner?"

"My mom saw his picture in a brochure. He runs a safari business. She didn't know before now, either—she thought he was dead."

"I wonder if they would get married? If they met again?" Grace asked. And the idea of that made Adia shiver with wishing.

Grace turned over onto her back and was quiet for a minute. Adia wondered if she was asleep already. But then her voice rose again, quieter now, but firm, less breathless.

"You have to find him, Adia! I'll help you!"

Adia didn't sleep well, and when she saw that the sky was lightening, she got up slowly. She didn't want to wake Grace. She put her clothes on and shoved her pajamas into her backpack. She went to Grace's desk and scrawled a note: "Forgot! My mom wants me home for breakfast! Call me later!" She wondered if Grace would believe her lie. She thought they both knew that Adia's mom would be asleep until noon. That she never ate breakfast anyway, let alone worried if Adia had.

Adia crept past Grace's parents' closed bedroom door and down the stairs. She hoped Selestenus wouldn't be in the kitchen yet; she didn't want to risk Grace or her parents hearing them converse. But she was lucky—the whole downstairs was still and empty. No coffee percolating yet, no smell of eggs and toast.

Adia shifted her pack on her shoulder and slid back the bolt on the front door. There would be a night guard on duty; she'd have to get past him, but if she greeted him quietly, nobody inside the house would hear. She opened the front door and was about to step out into the chilly morning air when she caught the glint of something on the table by the door. Just where he always left them, Grace's dad's silvery cuff links lay in the ceramic dish. Adia looked at them for a minute; she picked them up—just to feel the smoothness of the metal, to run her fingers over the carved design on the face, to touch the place where they might rub against Grace's father's wrist.

She heard a noise and turned. From the kitchen the coffee-pot gurgled into life. The back door opened and shut again. Selestenus's footsteps echoed softly down the hall. Not wanting to be seen now, she slipped out quickly and quietly shut the door behind her.

The night guard was at the gate. Someone—Selestenus maybe—had brought him a steaming cup of chai, and he sucked it loudly as he opened the gate for Adia. He nodded his greeting and smiled like there was nothing unusual, nothing at all, about a young white girl walking up the road alone at dawn. Adia turned once to look backward, to see if there were lights on yet in Grace's house, if there was anyone who might know she was gone, who might worry. But the windows were dark. Even the night guard had disappeared back into shadows. Adia turned to the road. She slipped her hand in her pocket and felt the cool metal of the cuff links, smooth and firm. They felt good under her fingers. If she ever did find her father, maybe she'd give them to him. She was certain he would like them.

By the time Adia saw Grace again, early Monday morning at school, Adia had almost forgotten the secret she'd shared. But Grace hadn't. Adia was sitting at a table in the open-sided cafeteria when she saw Grace's mom's car pull up the circular driveway in front of the administration building. The car had barely come to a stop when the back door flung open and Grace leaped out. She shouted goodbye to her mother and slammed the door behind her. When she saw Adia, Grace broke into a run.

"Adia, I have the best idea!" Grace slammed her backpack down on the table next to where Adia was sitting and took a deep breath. "I'm pretty sure it'll work."

She paused to catch her breath and noticed Adia's blank expression.

"Your dad!" Grace said. "For when we go find your dad."

Adia loved having a friend. A best friend. Mostly, she felt she'd do anything to keep Grace happy so the friendship would stay intact. She never wanted to go back to eating alone, to having the other kids roll their eyes when she walked past. She didn't notice those things anymore, not since Grace came. But, for the first time since she'd known Grace, Adia regretted being open. She didn't know if she wanted to find her father now. Not yet. And she was pretty sure she wanted to do it alone— or even with her mom—when she did. But here was Grace, so eager and so excited, she'd planned the whole thing out.

"So," Grace said, "I'll convince my mom to let me spend the night at your house… I think she's getting used to your mom enough to say yes. And then we'll sneak out and get a bus to your dad's house. You can find out if there's a bus, can't you? You know all that stuff."

Grace's face was shiny and hopeful. Adia couldn't bear to disappoint her friend.

"Well, I know the bus to Narok." Adia hesitated, thinking. It would be fun to introduce Grace to Simi. "Then I usually take a *matatu* from there to Loita. I don't know where my dad lives. But he runs his safaris kind of near Loita. They may have heard of him, anyway." Adia knew this would buy her time. Maybe by the time they got to Loita, Grace wouldn't want to go farther. Maybe nobody in the manyatta would know how or where to find her dad, anyway. There was always that possibility. "We'd need more than just one night, though," Adia told Grace. "Ask your mom to let you stay with me for the whole weekend. Friday after school to Monday."

Adia could have told her mom the plan—not the whole plan, but the part about taking Grace to meet Simi. Maybe her mom would even have given them a ride to the manyatta. The secrecy

Grace imbued the plan with, though, deterred her. What would her mom care, anyway? She might not even notice—Adia had taken herself to the manyatta plenty of times.

It was dark when Adia shook Grace awake on the chosen morning a few weeks later. They needed to catch the early bus in order to make it before dark. She'd let Grace have her bed, and Adia had curled up on the bedroom floor in a sleeping bag. She knew Grace wouldn't be comfortable on the floor, although Adia knew well that any spiders or beetles in the house could just as easily crawl into the bed. What Grace didn't know didn't hurt her. Adia wondered what Grace would think of life in the manyatta—it made her feel nauseous to think that Grace might hate it, might find it too dirty and different. If Grace was uncomfortable there, Simi would be hurt, and the one person Adia wanted to hurt less than Grace was Simi.

They'd both slept in their clothes, so when Grace finally woke up, stretched and crawled out of bed, they didn't have much to do before tiptoeing down the stairs and out the door. It was dark and chilly, and the girls were silent as they trudged down the street outside Adia's house to the closest *matatu* stand, where they could get a ride to the bus depot. Miraculously, or maybe simply because it was so early, the *matatu* they found wasn't crowded. The girls each had a seat, and not long after they sat down, the fare taker swung himself into the van, banging the side to alert the driver, and they were off.

Grace didn't seem to mind the *matatu* or the crowds at the central bus park where Adia bought tickets for the Narok bus and then found a stall selling chai and *mandazis*.

"We have an hour," Adia said, waving Grace toward a low wall where they could sit. She handed Grace a cup of the sweet tea and newspaper-wrapped *mandazi*. "It's like a doughnut," she said. "You'll like it."

The girls didn't talk. It was still too early. They swung their legs against the wall and sipped their tea. Adia wondered if her mother was awake yet. If she would notice the girls were gone.

The bus left on time, which Adia assured Grace was highly unusual and extremely lucky. It was crowded, though, and Adia pushed Grace on through a throng of people and then shoved herself in, directing Grace to a window seat and then flinging herself down. The aisles would be full, too, with people and possibly livestock and poultry, she explained to Grace, so by sitting in the window seat, Grace would be protected from the possibility of having a chicken in her lap, or a runny-nosed baby.

"I see why you told me not to bring anything that wouldn't fit in my backpack," Grace said as more and more people filled the bus. There was no room to move. Adia was pressed against Grace, who was pressed against the window. Both girls clutched their backpacks to their chests.

"This is why I brought so much stuff to Simi when your mom drove us down here. When I'm on the bus, I can't really bring anything."

By the time the sun was directly overhead, the crowded bus had wound down the Rift Valley escarpment and was bumping along the pitted tarmac toward Narok. Grace had fallen asleep, her head bumping against the window every time the bus hit a pothole. Adia vacillated between excitement at seeing her friends and Simi again, and introducing Grace to all the people she most loved, and terror that it wouldn't go well. She didn't let her mind wander to the reason for the trip. Finding her father, meeting him in person, seemed so outrageous a notion that she couldn't even bring herself to imagine how it would unfold.

Grace remembered Adia's Maasai mother from the time they met in Narok. She was waiting at the fork in the road about a mile away when the *matatu* from Narok dropped them off. Grace couldn't understand how she knew when the girls would arrive, but Adia said she'd probably been waiting for a while. When Simi saw Adia, her face filled with an expression Grace couldn't imagine seeing on Leona—it was a face full of complete devotion. Grace noticed that Adia's own face matched. It was obvious Simi and Adia adored one another.

Grace ducked her head when Adia introduced her, the way Adia had told her to, and Simi touched the crown of Grace's hair and then said in English, "You are welcome here, like another daughter." Grace knew why Adia loved Simi so much; there was something about her. She made Grace feel immediately welcome and safe. Even in this completely unfamiliar world.

Grace woke up in the pitch-black of a thick, predawn night. The night before, the family, Simi's husband and some other people—Grace couldn't figure out the connections—cooked a goat to celebrate Adia's visit. Adia helped. She held the goat's four feet so when it was on its back and prone, it couldn't kick and escape. A man had delicately slit the animal's throat, and then held it upside down so the blood emptied into a large pot. Later, the same man removed the goat's skin in one whole piece, and cut rectangular pieces of it out. He then slit the rectangles in the middle, and slid one on Grace like a bracelet. She could still smell wood smoke in her hair and when she moved her arm, she could feel the goatskin clinging to her wrist. When she reached down to touch it, she could tell it was still slightly damp and malleable. When it dried it would tighten and stiffen, and it would hug her wrist. It was bad luck, Simi told her, to cut it off. Goatskin bracelets had to be worn until they broke off on their own.

Grace stretched and pulled the thin cloth *shuka* over her. She and Adia slept on the rawhide platform in the little hut where Adia was born. Grace hadn't slept well. Adia had fallen asleep instantly, and her heavy breathing and the sounds of the livestock just outside the hut kept Grace awake. She could have sworn that sometime deep in the night, she'd heard lions, too.

The people in the little village started their day early. Before
the sun gripped the sky and dragged itself upward to illuminate
the Loita Hills and the early spring grasses, Grace heard movement outside the hut. There were voices and sounds of someone
herding the cattle out of the enclosure to graze. A baby cried,
and there were clanks of metal pots being filled with water for
tea. Grace couldn't bear to open her eyes; she was too sleepy
still. But then Grace heard her friend's voice out there, too. Adia
was a different person here. Grace couldn't believe how seamlessly Adia merged into the Maasai language and Maasai life.

"Hey, Grace! Morning!" Grace rolled over at the sound of
Adia's voice.

"Come on, Simi's making tea."

Grace sat up and rubbed her eyes. She slipped a rubber band
from her wrist and made a ponytail in her hair. Then she followed Adia out into the morning sun.

Simi's house was smoky and warm. Grace could see Simi
through the murky light. She was blowing on the embers of
last night's fire, and tossing handfuls of tea leaves into the big,
dented *sufuria*. When the fire grew hot, she added fresh milk
and sugar to the boiling tea leaves. Next to the fire was a little
pot full of white porridge. As the tea boiled, Simi scooped out
spoonfuls of the paste into enamel bowls and handed one to each
girl. Grace watched Adia dig right into it. She used her fingers
to scoop out the stuff and roll it into golf ball–sized portions she
then flicked into her mouth. She made eating with her hands
look elegant, easy. Grace tried to mimic her, but the porridge
was sticky and it ended up all over her hands.

"Did you ask about your dad?" Grace asked. Then slurped
at the tea Simi handed her; an attempt to cover the unpleasant
flavor of the porridge.

Simi looked up from ladling tea into Adia's cup. Her eyes
were wide.

"Adia," she said. Her words were hesitant. "Your father, he is not alive."

Adia spoke in Maa. Grace wanted to tell her to speak in English, so she could understand. Instead, she interrupted. "He's not dead. He runs a safari business. Adia thinks he may have hired guides from here. Do you know?"

Adia looked stricken. She and Simi locked eyes and then, slowly, each turned to look at Grace. Grace was suddenly uncomfortable. Had she broken some cultural rule she didn't know existed?

Simi reached out and grasped Adia's arm. Adia looked like she might cry. They spoke to each other quickly in Maa. Grace sat back. She sipped her tea again, trying to pretend she wasn't there. Obviously her question was unwelcome.

Adia glanced at Grace. On one hand, she was angry with her friend. It wasn't Grace's place to get involved in this. Adia consented to bringing Grace here because she figured she could tell her that nobody knew of her father and then they could head back to Nairobi. But a small part of her, deep down, was excited. Grace pushed her to this, and now, maybe, it was the right thing to do.

"Grace, I had to explain to Simi that he isn't dead." Relief washed over Grace. She hadn't broken any rules, just good news. She thought Adia had told Simi already—Adia couldn't blame her for not knowing, especially when Adia and Simi mostly spoke Maa to each other.

"Anyway," Adia continued. "She does know a few *moran* who worked for a *muzungu* man a couple of years ago. She doesn't know if it's him or not, but she's going to find the guys and introduce me."

Leona hated the telephone. It always meant bad news. Especially when it rang this early in the morning. She opened her eyes. Jesus. It was only nine thirty. And a Sunday, too. Fuck.

It was probably her mother. Joan never seemed to remember the time difference. Mostly she called in the middle of night, which was okay since Leona stayed up late, but every now and again there was a wake-up call.

"Hello, Mom?" She coughed and told herself, again, she had to stop smoking. The voice on the other end wasn't her mother, though.

"Leona? Hi, this is Jane. Grace's mom."

Leona rubbed her eyes and sighed. It was a mother but at least it wasn't her mother.

"I'm just calling to check in with Grace. To see when she wants me to pick her up."

"Um. Okay." Leona sighed. She suspected it would be easier to just do what Jane was asking rather than trying to put it off, or ask if Grace could call her later. "Let me see." She put the phone down and shuffled down the hall to Adia's room. The door was closed and the room was quiet. Leona knocked and listened. Nothing. Expecting to see the girls fast asleep, Leona cracked the door open. Sun was pouring into the window, and the room was still. Adia's bed was unmade, as always, and the sleeping bag was piled on the floor, but nobody was sleeping. The girls were gone.

"Shit," Leona muttered. She wasn't worried about Adia and Grace as much as she was worried about what Jane would say.

Grace couldn't take her eyes off the men who crossed the ground in long strides—it looked like they were floating—to speak with Adia about the man they once worked for. Adia translated sporadically, but Grace barely listened. She watched the men's long fingers play on the pale ends of the *rungu* they each carried, a smoothly polished wooden throwing club they wore tucked into a leather belt around their waists. The men were each wrapped in bright red cloths—two pieces, one tied at the shoulder, like a sideways cape, and one wrapped around their waists. Their shoes were sandals made from strips of car tires, and they all wore bright beaded strips of leather around their wrists and necks. Grace had seen Maasai in books before, but the pictures had no smell, and the men were heavy with the scent of mud and ochre in their tightly braided long hair. When they first approached, they laid their spears down and Grace saw how sharp the tips were, how long the ebony handles were. She heard Adia say, "Yes, yes, John." And then the men unfolded their long legs and floated off again. Grace wished they would stay longer—having them so near was thrilling, like living in an exotic book. Grace felt a heavy emptiness in her chest as she watched them go.

"Okay, I think it's him." Adia sounded tired. "If we're going to go, we should go now. The bus for Solai leaves from Narok this afternoon."

"I can't put Grace on the phone now, unfortunately. The girls left already." Leona spoke firmly into the phone. She wanted to convey an air of authority, of confidence in her ability to survey a situation with her daughter and know everything was fine. Jane didn't seem convinced. In fact, she melted into a panic with a swiftness that startled Leona.

"Oh, okay," Jane answered. "Where did they go?"

Before Leona could think of a good lie, she told the truth. "I don't know—Adia has a whole litany of places she goes."

"You don't know where they are? When did you last see them?"

Leona realized she didn't know. She thought they'd been at the house the evening before. When she was out in the yard last night, curled in the wooden chair she'd dragged out there so she could stare at the stars and smoke, she thought she'd heard them. Hadn't she?

Leona assured Jane she'd call back soon. But when she hung

up the phone, she had no idea how to proceed, no idea what to do next.

A few minutes later, while pouring herself tea in the kitchen, Leona saw Gakaki emerge from his room. His quarters were set against the side of the house, a two-room concrete addendum to the house built when it was common for household help to live on site. Leona had offered him the rooms when she first moved in. Adia was too little to stay alone then, and she wanted him to be there when she needed to leave—alone—on short notice. She rapped a knuckle on the window and waved him over.

"Adia was packing things to eat," he said, when Leona asked when he'd last seen the girls. "She was putting food in her backpack. And water bottles."

Leona was relieved. She knew what that meant. Adia often woke early on weekends to take the bus to Loita. When she did, she foraged in the kitchen for snacks to eat on the bus. "Ah, they went to Loita," she said out loud.

"Miss Leona, I heard Adia and her friend talking of the father. Of Adia's father."

Leona's head swam and her hands began to shake. How on earth did Adia know? And why hadn't she realized this could never be kept a secret? Leona called Jane back and kept her voice light. No reason to worry this other mother who seemed to worry over nothing no matter what. "Yeah, they just went to meet Adia's friend. Yes, yes, they're fine. I'll have Grace call the minute they get back."

"Gakaki, if they call or come back, tell them to get in touch with Grace's mom." Leona didn't take the time to pee or fill up a water bottle. She just jumped in her car and started driving toward Solai. If she paused to think, even for a second, she would lose her courage.

BUFFALO

Sunday was shopping day, and John had paid the Muslim shop-keeper for the supplies and was loading them into his truck. The basics—milk, eggs, tea, a bit of sugar—and some luxuries like beer and Scotch whiskey.

He turned to push open the shop doors with his shoulders, but stumbled a bit when the door opened from the other side.

"Sorry, John!"

It was Daniel's wife's brother. John had met him several times before, but couldn't remember the man's name. He was successful, though—owned a beautiful plot of land just outside town where, rumor had it, he was planning to build a safari lodge. John had been meaning to speak to him about cross-pollinating—bringing his clients to Solai for discounted hotel fees. He couldn't begin that conversation now, though, because the man stepped into the shop and said, "I saw you have a visitor up at the house. I just drove past your gate and saw a *muzungu* woman there. A relative, perhaps?"

Startled, John fumbled one of the bags, and the shopkeeper's young assistant rushed to his side, "Mister John, *pole, pole...*"

he murmured as he slid a few of the plastic bag handles from John's wrists onto his own.

John looked up and saw the man still smiling at him.

"Yes," John said, not knowing what else to say, "a cousin. Distant. Lives in Uganda."

He set the bags in the bed of truck, lodging them tightly with the spare tire and an old tarp so they wouldn't slide around too much on the way home. *"Muzungu,"* the man had said. A white woman. Who on earth could it be?

John never intended to stay in Solai. After the night his mother confessed the truth about his older brother and about the fact that she'd told his daughter's mother he was dead, he'd shuttled back and forth from Karen to Solai every couple of weeks. The constant need to return to Solai made running his business from Nairobi hard, and so, eventually, he'd just stayed here. He'd transferred the business to Solai, and divided his time between that and taking care of his mother.

The road up from town to the house was pitted and pocked with hillocks and holes carved out by the recent rains. John's bottles of beer and whiskey rattled louder and louder in the back of the truck, the road growing worse the closer to the farm he got. And the louder the rattle, the more nervous John grew. He knew who he wanted the woman to be. But what were the chances? She was in America, had been for years. God knows he hadn't been with many other women since he'd moved here, and the ones he had found time to seduce were clients. All safely back where they'd come from, America or Europe. Too far away to make him feel hemmed in. This visitor was probably just a Jehovah's Witness or some other do-gooder. John reached up and felt the stubble on his chin. He glanced at his reflection in the rearview. The last time he shaved, he'd seen white hairs between the yellow ones. An image of his father flipped into his mind…pure white hair and beard. He'd looked like a child's image of God.

The afternoon was waning, and shadows were just beginning to lengthen. John pulled up next to a car parked in his
usual spot. It was a Renault 4, a common car here. But he had
to catch himself as he climbed out of the Land Rover; he almost
stumbled and fell. This was a dusty, dented one, old and worn.
His breath and heartbeat sped up. He leaned over and placed
his hands on his knees. He felt he might faint. Or vomit. He
remembered this car. He remembered watching it speed off,
leaving him standing alone and choking on dust outside the
Chabani Guest House. Now it felt as if every cell in his body
were shivering. He'd thought of Leona often. He dreamed about
his daughter, and he yearned to see her. But the hope that that
would ever happen had died in him a long, long time ago.

John rarely locked the house, and he was surprised when he
found the place empty. "Hello?" he called, just to make sure.

Ruthie had been dead over six months now, but the silence
still seemed new to John. She hadn't made much noise in her
decline, but the feeling of another human in the house was
something he'd felt. He missed it.

The car's driver, whoever it was, was nowhere in the house,
and there were groceries to unload. Passing the dented little car
again made his heart beat with anticipation. What was it doing
here, and where was the driver?

He gathered his bags and the boxes and the Scotch and piled
them on the kitchen counter. They were heavy, and he paused
and looked up. In the distance, up on the hill with the baobab,
he could make out the shape of a figure. There was a person up
there, a person sitting on the bench overlooking the headstones.

It didn't take long for John to stride up the hill. But as he
got closer to the figure, he felt himself becoming more and
more nervous. He was almost near enough to touch the person's back when he stopped. Should he speak? Simply sit down
on the bench, as well?

Then the woman turned. John felt a jolt. She didn't look

the same. Her face was smooth and curved into high cheek-bones; her eyes were clear. But the way her mouth was set; the movement of her hand to her chest when she saw him—John knew she was equally stunned to see him. She stumbled from the bench and stood. She was almost as tall as him, and John rarely met a woman he could look in the eyes without bend-ing his neck.

"John!" the woman said, and her American accent softened and rounded out her vowels.

"What are you doing here?"

His question was a stupid one, he scolded himself. There were days when the fantasy of meeting her again played out lov-ingly; they saw each other somewhere and she was apologetic, regretful. She'd made a mistake, she said in those daydreams of his, and she wanted to make it right. Other days his imagina-tion was clouded with anger and he'd see her somewhere and shout; he'd demand answers and shake her if he had to. He had played out every possibility there was. Except for this one. He was utterly empty of emotion and it rendered him speechless.

"I visited your mom here, years ago. I hoped she still lived here," Leona said. Her voice sounded like cigarettes. It reminded him, vaguely, of his father's. He felt a tinge of emotion then—anger. Resentment.

"You're about six months too late." He nodded sharply to-ward the newest headstone, still pale and bright, not licked by lichen or time.

"I hoped she still lived here so I could ask her where you were. But I saw a man when I drove up—Daniel, he said he was—he told me about her and said you'd be back soon, that I could wait."

"Well, you found me. Why are you looking for me?"

"Your daughter, Adia, she has run away. I thought she might have come to find you."

John felt his mouth go slack and his skin prickle. He didn't know how to stop his spinning thoughts enough to formulate an answer. "No," he finally managed, "I haven't seen her."

Leona sighed.

"She must have gone to Simi, then." Leona's voice was clear— she didn't seem at all upset, or shocked, by these circumstances. First, John wondered how she managed to be so controlled. Then he felt the bubble of anger rising in his throat, and the shout came quickly and loud, "I wouldn't even know what she looks like. I haven't seen her since she was a newborn."

"Well, she looks like you," Leona said. Still cool, still firm. "I need to find her. She's with a friend, and the other girl's parents are anxious."

She looked down, rummaged through a leather bag slung over her shoulder and pulled out a beaded key fob.

John was stunned by the heat that rose in his face. Was she kidding? To see each other after all these years and the only thing she could say was, essentially, hello and goodbye?

"Jesus, woman. You're just going to disappear like that again? I've wanted to see you—to see her—for years. I didn't even know you were in the country anymore, but even still, every time I see a girl who could be her age…every time I see a white woman who could be you, especially around here…" He paused. He hated being this emotional. He swallowed back a combination of tears and anger. "I'm not going to let you walk away. I want to meet my daughter."

She looked up at John. Her eyes were dark and rimmed with tiny lines. He wanted to touch her cheek. Or slap her silly. He still couldn't decide.

"Well, then, I could use your help. I need to drive to the manyatta, see if she's there. Will you come?"

John still didn't know what to think. He hadn't settled on the emotion that matched the situation. But he knew he didn't want to let Leona go away again, not without some answers.

And if he could meet Adia? The notion sent shivers down his back. He'd waited for so long.

"We'll go in my truck—it'll be better on the roads."

By the time they were outside the farm gates and on the way, the sun was just low enough in the sky that it glared directly into the front window. It was impossible to see, and John went mostly on instinct.

"I thought you were in America," John said. "And if you weren't, then why did you wait so long to find me?"

"She told me you were dead," Leona said simply. John glanced over at her profile.

He saw her start and then she screamed.

"Shit! Watch out!" She threw her arms up, instinctually reaching for something to grab on to.

John was shocked into alertness and he slammed on the brakes, bringing the truck to a screeching, quivering halt. There, less than twenty feet in front of them, was a large Cape buffalo. It stood stock-still in the middle of the dirt track, its enormous head low and heavy. It held one front leg slightly aloft, delicately. John noticed the leg was bleeding.

The buffalo grunted and shook its great, heavy horns. Then it was running and in seconds had thrown its full weight and battering-ram head into the front of the truck, shaking the frame, causing Leona to scream again.

"Fuck!" John shouted, and he flipped the engine off. He watched as the buffalo turned and galloped—fast for having a hurt leg, John thought—back to his starting point and then turned again, head lowered for a second run at the truck.

John twisted and reached for his rifle behind his seat. In one swift motion, he ensured it had a bullet in the chamber, cocked it and slid out of the truck.

"What are you doing?" Leona cried.

"Stay put."

He strode forward to meet the buffalo as it raced again toward them.

John was an excellent shot. It was the one thing of value his father had given him. It was necessary out here. His parents forbade him to be out on the land without his rifle, and John had used it plenty of times before. Never for the pleasure of hunting, which in fact brought him no pleasure at all, but for his own safety. He'd shot the heads off snakes and killed a hyena that approached him too fast one afternoon. He'd even come close, just once, to shooting his father. He remembered how powerful he'd felt as he held the older man's head in his sights. He knew he could hit him in one shot, and he knew that he'd be okay if he did—self-defense wouldn't be a lie. But in the end John lowered the gun and, instead, ran fast to Daniel's, leaving his mother alone at home to bear the brunt of his father's mood.

The first bullet hit the buffalo's chest, tearing away a chunk of flesh and causing the animal to stumble, grunt in agony and turn in the direction of the pain. He must have seen John moving, and John heard Leona scream as the animal, fueled by pain and fear, hurtled away from the truck and toward John.

John backed up as quickly as he could manage. He recocked the rifle—Christ but how he wished he'd counted the bullets in the chamber while still in the safety of the truck—and fell backward. He saw a wall of black buffalo descending on him, close enough that later he found the animal's blood on his boot. He fired again, and the buffalo fell. Immediately there was a thick silence. The only sound was a breeze through the grasses and the faint echo of the gunshot where before there had been hooves beating the ground and John's and the buffalo's terrified breathing.

The buffalo was beautiful. Huge and healthy, but for the broken leg. It was a shame he had to die.

Leona appeared next to him. She stood at the buffalo's head, looking down.

"Fuck! I thought I was going to see you trampled to death."

John looked up and saw Leona's hands were shaking. She had her sunglasses perched on the top of her head, and her eyes were wide-open and round with shock. She knelt down and stroked the buffalo's ear. "It's a beauty, though."

"Did you see its leg?" he asked. He hoped his voice would steady soon. In his mind he could still feel the ground shaking beneath him as the heavy animal came barreling toward him. Fear and adrenaline made his muscles weak and his blood pounded in his veins. He could hardly believe he'd felled it with that last shot.

"It was broken. He would have died soon anyway...a lion would have gotten it, a hyena. It would have been eaten alive..." He stopped. Leona already knew. She'd been in Kenya long enough to know. Life was hard out here for the unfit, the unhealthy. A quick death by bullet in the brain was far better than the alternative. He didn't need to tell her that in his own life he'd learned that death is often the kindest thing.

In this drought, the dead buffalo would give all the scavengers a rare meal. Tomorrow it would just be bones. Maybe he would go back and retrieve the skull as a reminder of the afternoon. He'd start a future soon, one he would write for himself. He was alive, and for the first time in ages, that felt like it might be a lucky thing.

The bus from Narok to Solai was far more crowded than the one they'd taken down the Rift from Nairobi the day before. Adia climbed on first and stood in the aisle, looking around for two seats together. Grace stepped up behind her, and stood so close Adia could feel her breath on the back of her neck when Grace said, "We can sit separately. I don't mind."

The bus was crowded. Only a few seats remained, and with the dozen or so people behind Grace, trying to board, Adia knew they had to grab any seats they could. They'd be gone in minutes.

"Okay, you sit up here." Adia pointed to a window seat just behind the driver. A prim, middle-aged lady sat along the aisle. Adia knew Grace would be safe from errant hands—men who thought it would be funny to pinch a young woman. "I'll take that one in the back."

Grace slid into the seat and adjusted her backpack on her lap. "No prob," she said and flashed Adia a brilliant smile. "I'll see ya on the other side!"

Adia squeezed into an aisle seat at the back of the bus. A large woman in a vivid pink dress and pink plastic shoes occupied the window seat. She held a baby, swaddled in a *kanga*, on her lap.

"*Jambo,*" Adia greeted the woman in Swahili, and then leaned back and closed her eyes. She didn't want to get into a conversation. For this reason, she felt grateful that Grace and she had to sit apart. Adia wanted to think, to calm her nerves and try desperately to figure out what to say if, when, she saw her father.

The bus rattled and bounced along the heavily pocked road to Solai. The lady in the pink dress fell asleep and her head lolled onto Adia's shoulder. Adia opened her eyes then and glanced down. She smiled at the baby who stared back at her with big, shiny eyes. Adia looked up and saw Grace's long brown ponytail waving in time to the bus's jolts. She was proud of Grace. Grace hadn't complained once about the buses or the *matatus*, and she'd seemed comfortable in the manyatta. Adia had been terrified to introduce Grace to that part of her life, and the relief she felt now, knowing that it had gone so much better than she could have anticipated, was warm. She looked out the window at the golden land sliding by. She couldn't be down here, at the bottom of the Rift, without feeling lucky. This was her home. The most beautiful place in the world.

Suddenly, Adia saw the pink-dress woman's head jerk forward and smack the seat in front of them, hard. Adia saw the baby

bounce and, without thinking, she flopped her head and chest
and arms down, covering the baby and pinning the tiny body
to the mother's bright pink lap. She felt a pain slice through
her skull and vaguely realized that her head, too, had slammed
into the metal bar at the top of the seat in front of her. She registered the glass flying over her head, and the horrible, uncontrolled movement of the bus, but, oddly, she didn't feel fear.
Later, she'd play this moment over in her head until she could
name what she felt—utter acceptance. She was going to die.
It was this that frightened her most in the weeks and months
to follow. The ease with which she gave up. Then the movement stopped as suddenly as it had started. The air, the people,
the vehicle, Adia's thoughts were all completely still and silent.
Nothing moved.

Adia tasted blood and ran her tongue over her teeth. One was
jagged and broken, and her mouth filled quickly with blood. She
watched the blood fall to the dirty bus floor and make a little
pool. No one spoke; no one breathed. Adia looked up and saw
the green lights on the dashboard flicker and dim. She couldn't
see Grace's ponytail. She hoped Grace wasn't scared.

She looked over at the pink-dress lady and saw that she was
still, too. Her head thrown back and resting on the cracked
bus window. There was blood on the window. Then the panic
rushed in, a tsunami of terror, and Adia could hear herself
screaming. Underneath her arms, something moved. There
were those shiny eyes and there was that baby's mouth, open
like Adia's own, screaming and screaming loudly and long out
the broken window and over the pitted dirt of the road and over
the dry grasses waving in the wind as if nothing had happened
at all. Then Adia realized they weren't the only ones crying and
screaming, but that others, too, from where they were, were
moaning and sobbing into that clear, wide-open Kenyan sky.

The baby's mother moved then, she slowly lifted her head
from the window and Adia watched her eyes as they made a

shift from dazed and unsure to horror as she realized what had happened, and then how they slid into relief as she noticed Adia leaning into her lap, still clutching the baby. Adia sat up then. Her head hurt, and her back did, too, and so did her still-bleeding mouth. She managed to reach down and pull her backpack out from where it had wedged under the seat in front of hers, then she picked her way gingerly toward the front of the bus. There were bodies she stepped over. Broken ones and bleeding ones. Some moved a little, some made terrible sounds, but the worst were the ones that were completely still. Adia couldn't see Grace at first. She saw the prim woman Grace sat next to. There she was—she was a still one, flopped like a doll over the seat clear across the aisle from where she'd been. Her eyes were wide-open, and she looked perfect, but Adia noticed the slight off-kilter look to her back. Backs didn't bend that way.

Then Adia saw Grace, curled like a bug near the driver's seat. Her silken ponytail gliding across the dirty bus floor. Adia knelt down to tuck Grace's hair over her shoulder. She leaned down and whispered in her friend's ear, "Grace! Grace, it's okay. I'm here." Grace's eyes were closed. Maybe she was sleeping. Adia felt like escaping into sleep, too. Adia bent herself over her friend as she'd done the baby. The baby had survived. The baby was all right. She ran her palm across Grace's cheek, and then she closed her own eyes. Maybe none of this was happening at all.

The bus shook and the voices of the people wove themselves around Adia's consciousness. Men were shouting, people were lifting bodies out of seats and carrying them past Adia and Grace. The bus was crowded now, so crowded and noisy. After a while, a man leaned down and grasped Adia by the shoulders. He said something. His hands were rough, his grip strong. Adia pulled herself from him and clutched at Grace again. She wouldn't leave Grace. This was not Grace's world; she'd be scared when she woke up surrounded by unfamiliar faces and a language she didn't understand. The man said something else, he wrested Adia away from Grace and lifted her up, high above her friend and the dirty bus floor and the broken people who still littered it. He lifted her down the bus steps and into the sunshine.

"You are lucky, *toto*! You are lucky because you lived." Adia heard his words, but they rattled in her brain without finding footing. They didn't make sense at all. She tried to push past the man and board the bus again, but he was large and had long arms and a passive face. He gestured to a woman who stood nearby, and the woman came closer and took Adia's hand.

"Come here to sit with me. Help will come soon."

Adia let herself be led away. She was tired. More tired than she'd ever been. She wanted to sit under a tree with her head in this kind woman's lap and fall asleep until everything was normal again.

Adia and the woman sat. Adia was thirsty and tried to open the straps of her backpack to get her water bottle, but somehow she just couldn't make them work. Her fingers had forgotten how to function. Another woman approached. It was the mother in her pink dress holding the baby. One of the mother's eyes was crusted over with a thick layer of blood.

"They need *kangas*," the mother said to the woman next to Adia. "The flies are too bad now. They have to cover the dead."

The dead. The dead. Those words, too, flipped into Adia's brain without taking root. They echoed and echoed and she looked up and saw that, yes, there were lines of people lying on the earth as if they were sunning themselves on a beach. Those were the dead. A couple of women had gathered extra *kangas* and market bags and were carefully covering the bodies to keep flies from licking up the drying blood. One of the women who'd just draped a cloth over someone stood up and moved, and in the space she'd vacated, Adia saw a pale arm peeking out from under a plastic bag. No. That was wrong. She stood and walked to the line of people and pulled the bag off the girl who lay underneath. It was a mistake. Grace wasn't dead. Grace wasn't dead. Grace wasn't dead. Adia sank down and stretched out next to her friend.

"Jesus!" John cursed loudly, and Leona pulled up her sunglasses and looked in the direction he was pointing. Up ahead in the distance, the road was crawling with people. There was a crowd. Where did they all come from? Leona wondered for a split second, until she registered the black smoke billowing up and heard the people shouting and crying. By then, they were close enough to see that a large, crowded bus had collided with a truck loaded down with supplies headed from Nairobi to Narok and too heavy to be easily maneuverable. Both vehicles were badly damaged. The front of the bus was crushed and the windshield shattered. There was blood on the glass, and the swarms of people, the survivors, were frantically pulling bodies from the bus—some seemingly alive, some dead, all broken.

John swerved the truck to the side of the road and jerked to a stop. Leona and John flew out of the car and ran toward the bus. They saw the *muzungu* body. Then another. A young girl, her hair matted with blood and her limbs completely still, and a blonde girl lying so close to the first, and so still, that together they looked like a carving. Something like electricity snapped in Leona's brain and a deep shock of fear tore through her so violently that she stumbled and fell. She couldn't gather the strength to stand, and so she just watched John stride ahead of her, speaking in rapid-fire Swahili, demanding information, asking if someone had called an ambulance. Leona had been a distant mother, unemotional, but she knew the singular curve of that blonde girl's shape, she knew that body almost as well as she knew her own. John didn't know, Leona thought. He didn't know that girl was his girl, that the way her expressions folded on her face sometimes reminded Leona of him. That the blood on her face, the salty blood he was dabbing at with a handkerchief, was as much his as it was hers. That girl was the two of them, swirled together. Leona didn't pray. She was impatient with the concept of God. But just then, at that moment, she closed her eyes and murmured a wish. "Please let them have a chance to know each other. Please don't let her die." And she imagined the wish, her breath made into whispered speech, floating up to the outer limits of the sky, where maybe, just maybe, God would hear it.

GIRL IN THE SHAPE OF AFRICA

Letting go a little was Paul's idea, but Jane agreed. Part of her knew she had been holding Grace too tightly for too long. Paul and Jane had both had mostly regular American childhoods; being independent was part of that. Their parents hadn't been their friends, like Jane was with Grace. When she and Paul grew up, they taught themselves to ride bikes and spent whole weekends only seeing their parents for meals. That's the way it was for all kids back then. Jane told herself she was more protective of Grace because they lived overseas—Grace was not at home, and dangers were different here. But Jane knew, somewhere inside herself, that that wasn't really the truth. This was Grace's home, after all. Jane was the one in strange territory. Jane clung to Grace because she needed her daughter more than her daughter needed her.

When Adia began spending the night at their house, coming over after school to do homework, Jane felt like she was doing a service for the girl—feeding her nutritious food, making sure she minded her manners. She didn't entirely trust Adia, who'd foraged in the pantry for food without asking permission, and Jane still wondered if it had been she who'd taken Paul's cuff links, but Jane thought it was better, much better, to open her home to Adia, rather than have Grace going to Adia's house more than she did already. Jane's skin crawled at the thought of that grotty place.

But when Grace finally did beg to spend the weekend with Adia, Jane said yes. Jane knew there wouldn't be as much supervision as she herself would provide. She'd seen Leona's distracted parenting, the way she let Adia traipse around the city on *matatus*. And Grace had even mentioned that Adia caught buses into the Rift Valley to visit her Maasai friends sometimes. All alone. Jane couldn't imagine doing that as an adult, let alone allowing her child to. But she told herself to trust Grace. She'd raised her right, hadn't she? Grace would make responsible choices over the weekend because she was a responsible girl.

It was evening and the balcony was cool. Jane was sitting in the chaise, trying not to worry over the fact that she still hadn't heard from Grace, and that Leona hadn't called back, either. Paul had stepped out onto the balcony, too, and handed her a glass of wine. "The bats," he said, and Jane nodded—they were blooming from the innermost branches of the banana trees like velvet flowers and speeding across the sky. Paul reached down and caressed Jane's shoulder. They were rarely alone anymore, and even through her fear, a tiny ember of gratitude lit inside Jane. She didn't want to cry now, not from fear or thanks for her husband's gentleness. When the ringing phone jarred the silence, Jane started so violently that Paul's hand was flicked off her shoulder. "You're as nervous as a cat," he said. "I'll get it."

The noise, the gasp-turned-cry her husband made, would, for years, visit Jane in her dreams, shocking her awake at least once a week, stealing sleep for the rest of those nights. She always thought that if there were one moment in her life when she would have chosen to be deaf, it would be that moment.

She'd never heard Paul sound so helpless, so broken. It was as if she were an auditory witness to the second his life dipped into darkness.

Someone ran to the nearest village to find transport to Narok. Luckily, someone there had a motorcycle and sped off to alert the clinic that wounded and dead were coming. Another flatbed truck appeared from the horizon and had room for the bodies. The dead were gently laid in the truck; the wounded that could sit hunched in the truck bed, too. Then a smaller car, a tourist Jeep, pulled up. John was busy guiding the remaining survivors into the spaces on the truck, so Leona just gestured at him, called in a voice scraped raw that she would take this girl to the clinic in the Jeep. He didn't need to know. Not now. For the first time since Leona had pulled Adia from Simi's grasp all those years ago, Leona wanted her daughter to herself.

The two tourists in the Jeep, and their driver, were silent. The tourists had ashy, shocked faces, and their staring eyes kept returning, time and again, to the odd and bloody girl. Leona had to close her eyes because she was afraid that she'd suddenly leap up and smack them. Their sad faces and their pity. She hated them. Now and again Adia became overcome and leaned down, face in hands, and keened. A whistling breath escaped her lips, and she rocked back and forth, not sobbing so much as moaning. It was a dry, heaving call, something from another world.

It was dark by the time Grace's parents arrived. They came with a little team of people from the American embassy. By then, Adia was curled in a corner of the crowded clinic's waiting area, fast asleep. Leona sat on a bench that rocked on uneven legs and occasionally stood, forced herself outside to buy tea from a stall, where the milk was boiled over a charcoal brazier that gave the tea a smoky taste. Leona had just returned to the bench with a fresh cup and sat, exhausted, with her head tipped back against the wall and her eyes closed. She wondered where John was.

A woman's voice, strained and raspy from sobbing, cut through her thoughts.

"This is what happens…this is what happens when you aren't careful!"

Leona lifted her eyes and saw a face hanging above her, big and red and raw as meat. It took her a moment to recognize the face as the one belonging to Grace's mother. Now the face was as swollen and haunted as Adia's was before she drifted off.

"This is what happens!" The woman sobbed through the gasping of her breath and the tears and mucus that slicked over her face and choked her words so they were staccato, hemmed in by quick, ineffective breaths. The sounds felt like stones pounding Leona's ears. Leona stood up, her legs shaking. She saw that the noise had woken Adia, and now the girl was trying to stand, her face stricken and gray.

"They were too young to have that kind of freedom. You may not care about your daughter, but I care about mine. I'm a real mother!"

Adia pulled herself up off the floor and moved to Leona's side. She took her mother's hand and squeezed it. The squeeze was welcome but unfamiliar. They didn't hold hands, Leona and Adia. They hardly touched at all. There was a man behind the screaming woman now. Dark and slight, he wasn't crying but looked as empty as a shell. Leona thought he must be the husband, Grace's father, whom she'd never met. His face was slack with shock, his eyes red-rimmed and bewildered. Still, he was calm. He pinched the woman's shoulder blades and whispered into her ear until she turned and stumbled away through a doorway into a room behind her. The people who'd come with her followed. Later Leona discovered they were the embassy doctor, the consular officer and the duty officer.

★ ★ ★

Once Grace's parents arrived at the clinic, there wasn't a reason for Leona and Adia to stay. Instead, Leona led Adia through the nighttime streets to the Chabani Guest House. Leona couldn't quite believe they were back here—and stranded—after all this time. Without a car, they'd be dependent on the same bus to Solai that Adia and Grace had ridden. But Leona couldn't parse out their options or make a plan. She was too exhausted. Instead, she tucked her daughter into bed and went to the bar for a beer. Matthew, the barkeep, was there, and his familiar face was comforting. After she emptied her bottle, too fast and on an empty stomach, she told Matthew that if he saw John, to tell him she was there, too. Then she'd climbed, light-headed, off the stool. She was not in control anymore. She didn't want to be, either. It was too hard and too lonely. Under the fluorescent light outside the door to their room, Leona looked down and noticed there was blood—Adia's blood—on her shirt. She fought the urge to lift it to her lips and taste it.

In the morning, John was there. Leona stepped out of the shower and dressed quietly. She didn't want to wake Adia, who had slept fitfully, once even waking herself up with sobs. Now, although relaxed in sleep, her face was still swollen and red. The light tapping on the door startled Leona. She pulled her dirty T-shirt over her head and cracked the door an inch, not knowing who to expect. John's face was scrubbed clean and pink, his hair combed with a wet comb. The look of hope on his face told Leona everything she needed to know.

"I'm sorry," John whispered as Leona stepped into the hallway and pulled the door closed behind her. "It never crossed my mind that it was her." His face looked as excited as a boy's. "I immediately went into emergency mode and it never occurred to me. Matthew told me last night. I couldn't sleep. Is she okay?"

Leona was prepared to be, she expected to be, annoyed by this early morning visit and its emotional impact. But instead she felt a ripple of relief shiver through her. This was what it was like to share the burden of something heavy.

"She just wants to sleep," Leona whispered. "She's been sleeping on and off—mostly on—since we found her."

"What a crushing thing to happen to a kid." John's eyes were dark with sadness. "She'll be grieving this for a long time. What about the other girl? Her parents…" John trailed off. Then he said, "I just can't imagine." In his mind he thought suddenly of his own mother, who had also lost a child. How did she get through it? How would the parents of the dead girl he'd loaded into the back of the truck yesterday get through it? The body he'd carried was so light, the face, bloodied as it was, so smooth and young.

John looked at Leona. Her hair was wet from her shower, but her clothes were rumpled and dirty and a little bloodied.

"Of course we'll go back to Solai today," John said. "She'll recuperate at my house. Nairobi is too far to take her in this condition."

The ride from Narok to Solai was quiet. Leona was right; Adia curled in the back seat with her eyes closed and didn't say a word the entire time. John didn't know whether she was asleep or just hiding from the bone-crushing pain of her new reality. He understood that desire to hide. He'd felt it himself a time or two.

John slowed down when they passed the buffalo's body. Had that only happened yesterday? It felt like years ago. He didn't stop—there was still flesh on the animal's bones, still vultures feasting. He didn't want the skull anymore. Today was the real beginning of his life.

When John pulled the Land Rover up the last hill, Adia roused.

"Where are we?" she whispered.

"Home," John answered.

Leona turned in the passenger seat to look at her daughter. She watched her daughter's face, the tanned cheeks, the strong jaw and the hollow sad eyes. The saddest eyes Leona could remember seeing. They were a puzzle, the two of them—two pieces that never seemed to fit. It was her fault, she knew that. She'd never really tried to be a decent mother. She took a deep breath, and she felt the familiar feeling of guilt sliding under her flesh like bits of broken glass. She wasn't, she hadn't been, brave enough to be a good mother. She hoped she was brave enough for it now.

Leona closed her eyes tightly. She was aware that John was still there with them, his wide shoulders almost brushed hers. But he was their third, her daughter's father, and he had a right to be there when she told Adia the truth. "I've been keeping a secret, Adia," she said.

"I already know, Mom," Adia said quietly. "My father's not dead. Grace and I were trying to find him."

Leona reached out and clasped Adia's hand. "You found him, Adia." Adia's face was calm, and she turned to look up at John, who'd shifted so he could face her. Adia didn't move her hand from under Leona's, but her lips curved up in the barest feather of a smile and she watched John as she said, "Grace and I were coming to find you. She would be so happy." Then her face crumpled again, and she began to cry. "I just can't believe it."

Leona sat there holding her daughter's hand tightly. She wished she knew what to do.

"Let's go inside and eat." It was the only thing she could think of to say.

Leona remembered where the kitchen was, and soon began opening cupboards and taking things from the fridge. She pulled out a frying pan and eggs and was cracking them, mixing them with a little milk.

That's how John found them. Adia sitting at the table, and Leona at the counter.

"How's her cooking?" John asked Adia.

Adia looked at him, and then at her mother, who she'd never seen acting quite so maternal.

"I don't know," she answered. "I can't remember the last time she cooked."

John smiled at her and pulled three glasses off a shelf. Then he bent down and retrieved a bottle of whiskey from a cabinet.

"Then we'll probably need a drink."

He poured two glasses half full of whiskey and placed one on the counter for Leona. He splashed a bit of whiskey in the third glass and then added water. He set it on the table in front of Adia. "It'll help a bit," he said.

The sky outside the window was golden. Leona watched shadows playing on the grass underneath the magnificent baobab. "I sat under that tree with your mom," she said. "Years ago. She told me you were dead. I believed her."

"She was confused like that for ages before she died. Alzheimer's," John answered. "She told me that she told you I was dead. She said you went home after that, to America. I never looked for you. I never thought I'd find you. But still…something…something made me do a double take, get my hopes up, every time I saw a woman or a girl who could have been you and—" now he turned to Adia "—Adia, a good Maasai name."

Then Adia spoke. "We've been in Nairobi the whole time. Mom found out you were alive recently, a few months ago. Your brochure was in a hotel. She didn't tell me, though." Leona winced and flipped the eggs onto plates John had set beside her.

They sat together at the kitchen table and ate the omelets and toast in silence. Afterward, Adia said she wanted to go to sleep. John led her down the hall to a little guest room and showed her where the bathroom was.

"I hope you sleep well," he told her. "Tomorrow, or sometime when you're ready… I look forward to beginning to get to know you."

Leona washed the dishes and wiped the table of crumbs. She was surprised at herself—she didn't usually like doing domestic chores, but here, in this house, with the wide-open savannah outside the window and no sound but the tinny chatter on the radio she felt relaxed.

When the last dish was washed and placed in the drainer by the sink, Leona stepped out the kitchen door. She remembered, years ago, walking up this path to the baobab, watching Ruthie and Adia holding hands and walking together in the distance. Now Leona walked alone up the hill to the tree. The breeze was cool and just strong enough to make the grasses whistle. She crossed the crest of the hill where the headstones were casting their evening shadows.

"I think we need another drink." Leona started when she heard John's voice behind her.

"Didn't mean to scare you," he said, "but there's been a lion around here in the evenings." Leona saw he had a rifle under one arm and a bottle in one hand.

"Guns and drinks," she said. "That's a combo."

Underneath the baobab, the bench was cold and the light dim and green, like being under water. When they weren't speaking, the silence fell thickly around them.

"We'll have to share," John said, and twisted the bottle's top. "Scotch."

He opened the bottle and handed it to Leona. They sat side by side on the bench, and the cool of the concrete seeped through John's pant legs. It was always chilly here, and the light was always murky. Leona nudged his shoulder with hers and passed him the bottle. He registered, again, the fact that their shoulders were almost the same height and that he could see her eye to eye with no effort. He liked that about her.

They drank quietly, watching the leaves above them turn blacker as the evening collected around them. After a while

Leona stopped shuddering after each taste, and he stopped being shy about gulping it down. The bottle was more than halfway finished before they spoke.

"So these are your dead," Leona finally said.

She stretched one leg in front of her and, with her foot pointed, tapped the larger gravestone with the tip of her shoe. John knew the alcohol was working its magic on her brain and her tongue. She smiled a little at the three gravestones at their feet.

"There's a tiny one and two big ones. It's so sad to have a tiny one."

John cleared his throat. Again, he found himself speaking words he'd never uttered aloud before.

"The largest is my not-so-dearly-departed father, the newest is my mother, and the smallest my older brother, died in early childhood. I hardly remember him."

He thought about biting back the rest of the story, but he kept going, piercing through the shell of secrets that marked his life.

"My mother killed him, actually. I only recently found out. It was an accident. Ran him over in a truck."

The alcohol stirred the horrible absurdity in his brain. It wasn't funny. Nothing about his childhood was funny. It was one fucking nightmare after another, he thought. But he felt a laugh in his chest. It was all so awful.

"Oh, God. It's not funny, is it?"

Leona watched his face closely. She looked so kind then, so young and open. He wondered if she'd looked that kind when he first met her. She hadn't the last time he saw her. Not even close. He'd never told anyone about his childhood before. Not even the women who'd wanted to marry him. But this woman was different; this was the woman who had his child. And now he wanted nothing more than to drain the sickness from himself, to pull it all out from the darkness and fling it into the world. He didn't want it anymore.

"She hit Thomas—that's what my brother was called—because she was frantic to leave my father. He was a terrible, mean drunk. She was so desperate to leave that she was going to leave the two of us, Thomas and me, behind."

He took a final swig from the bottle and then hurled it as hard as he could. It shattered on the largest of the three headstones. He felt Leona wince beside him.

"It was, needless to say, an unhappy childhood."

He glanced at Leona and saw that her eyes were steady and serious. She wasn't recoiling in horror, as he thought she might. She smiled gently at him, and her teeth were brilliant white, even in the gathering dark, and perfectly straight. American teeth, he thought. She reached out and touched John's hand.

Her hand on his brought him back to where they were. It sparked a yearning in him that made him feel lonelier than he'd ever felt. The women he'd been with lately, the shiny, doll-like tourists, they were only scratching an itch. He didn't know them, and they seemed more interested in him as a novelty. He'd been in Solai for years now, and apart from the groups of tourists he met at the airport and took on safaris, he hardy saw anyone else. Not anyone he hadn't grown up with, anyway. He'd pushed his need for touch, and for understanding, behind him in service to his mother.

"Yes, and we're drunk, girlie. But not to worry…this place has seen more drunks than it can count."

He paused and then continued. It felt important to tell his story, to get it all out. He wanted Leona to know him, the dark parts, the sad parts that had never before seen light.

"Before my dad was put in the dirt here, when I was still a kid, I used to come up here all the time. I'd curse my dead brother for being the one who got away. I wanted to be the dead one. I wanted to be the one who didn't have to see my dad breaking my mother's bones, or see how my mother let it happen time and again. I didn't want to think that my mother was the kind of person who'd have left me if she could—I was just a baby—with that bastard. I thought he was the lucky one—lucky dead Thomas.

"Then my father died. I dug his grave myself. I wanted to put him in the ground. It made me happy to know he was dead."

John thought of his father's slow death, how relieved he'd been when his father was buried in the ground, unable to hurt anyone anymore.

"I was happy my dad died, too." Leona's voice was clear and free of guilt. "He was a bastard, too. In a different way." She didn't elaborate. This was a subject still too uncomfortable to talk about. She didn't talk about it. Not at all. But she wanted to give this to John. A gift of understanding.

Talking to Leona was easy this time. John saw what he'd recognized in her all those years ago—they were both broken people. Broken in ways they could understand in the other. They could see the pieces of each other lying deep on the other side of the walls they'd put up. As in a foreign country where the language is utterly incomprehensible to those who'd never heard it before—they shared an understanding none of the other people in their lives did. They were the sole inhabitants of this land, speakers of a unique tongue. They could see each other's failings and potential. It was inevitable.

John felt like talking. He felt like the words he was sharing, finally, would find a home, a place to settle and then blink out, like ash. They weren't hard and permanent. They could escape into the night sky and never bother him again.

It was late when they walked back to the house. Leona stood outside Adia's door for a moment and then opened it slowly, wanting to check in on her. She assumed Adia was already asleep—wrung out and exhausted by tears and terror. Leona doubted she'd have come in if she'd known Adia was awake; she felt she wasn't qualified to guide her daughter. For so long Leona prided herself on keeping her own grief contained, boxed up and reserved. All her emotions were controlled, most of the time, anyway. She crept across the dark room to Adia's bed. She sat on the edge of the mattress and then lay down next to her girl. She was so close she could feel the Maasai bracelets on Adia's wrists, feel the bones just under her skin and even feel the pulse of blood through her daughter's veins.

"Adia," she whispered into the dark. "I love you."

Leona was surprised when Adia rolled over and burrowed her face into her mother's arm. She wasn't asleep after all, and Leona felt embarrassment. She wasn't sure she'd ever said those words to her daughter. She wasn't sure she'd ever felt them as keenly as she did now. At this moment, she would have lived through all of it again for the chance to be a different kind of mother.

Leona squeezed her eyes shut tightly and saw lights shooting across the insides of her eyelids. The silence that had infected her since childhood was a habit now, ingrained in her blood, written in her DNA, embedded in her flesh. She didn't want her daughter to live this way. She wanted Adia to find comfort in connections, to feel, always, the warmth of sharing time and space, and her deepest self, with others. To make that happen, Leona realized, she had to let her own silence leak out. She had to break herself open so her daughter could see inside.

That night, Leona lay in the same bed she'd slept in before. She didn't sleep well. Her mind spun with images of John. She was surprised at how she remembered his smell. He smelled like dry dust and sun and sweat, a heady combination. Her head filled with memories of the first time they met, of the sensation of his arm brushing against hers while they cooked earlier that evening. She turned over and over in her head the secrets he'd told her under the baobab. She rarely found herself physically drawn to men, but John was different. The whole time they'd sat together under that tree earlier, she'd wanted to touch his skin, to feel his warmth on her fingers.

PART III

MOFFAT'S WIFE

Death in Kenya—in all of Africa, really—is common. After years on the continent, Jane knew that. Livestock is trotted to the butcher and, without preamble, right on the sidewalk in front of the shop, the animal's neck is slit and then the carcass is hung upside down to bleed out. Shopping in the open markets means walking on blood-slick ground through rows and rows of skinless heads and headless bodies lined up on tables, flies laconically licking from the dead beasts' empty, staring eyes.

Just after their arrival in Nairobi, Jane was out in the suburbs with another embassy wife. The other wife told Jane about a shop she loved and how she had to show Jane the traditionally dyed fabrics you could buy there. The other woman was driving and she drove much faster than Jane normally did. Suddenly a dark shadow flashed in front of the car and Jane heard a thud.

"Christ," the other woman muttered, "damn dog came out of nowhere."

Jane turned and saw the bloody spot on the road where the dead dog lay, his fur burst open like a too-ripe fruit.

Jane wasn't naive. By the time Grace died, she had been in

Africa long enough to know that animals weren't the only living things that blinked out of the world so easily. Humans died
constantly, too. They died of disease, of hunger, of age, of a
million different things. They died in *matatu* accidents and on
airplanes. They died at the hands of other people like all those
men she'd secretly watched on the beach in Liberia. Life, especially here, Jane knew theoretically, was fleeting and fragile.
But she never thought that it would happen to her.

The days and weeks after Grace died were blurred. Jane didn't
remember those days when the ghosts came to her—was that
her own stepmother? Her father? Was that shadow Jane's oldest friend? Who had told them the news? She couldn't imagine
dialing a phone, let alone speaking the terrible words aloud.
They slid their palms down Jane's cheeks, smoothed her hair,
asked if she was hungry—how could Jane be hungry when her
baby was dead? How could her body need food or water or
sleep? Jane couldn't imagine wanting anything ever again. She
was dead, too. The weeks turned to months; they went to the
States for R & R and returned. Nairobi wasn't home, but Jane
didn't care. Home didn't exist for her anymore.

After they had Grace cremated, Paul wanted to take the re-
mains to America. That way, he said, she'd be at home.

"We can visit her grave," he'd said.

Jane couldn't eat, wasn't sleeping, barely speaking. She wanted
to disappear. But she was firm in this: home was no set place
for any of them anymore. They'd been nomads for too long.
Grace would stay with them.

During the long afternoons when the sun slanted through the
flame tree at the edge of the garden, illuminating the dust in the
air, Jane often found her heart racing and her breath choked in
her throat. The anxiety came almost daily, but still it surprised
her. The tingle in her limbs rushed up from her fingers to her
shoulders, her toes to her thighs, and blossomed into popping
flashes of light behind her eyes. She'd struggle up from her chair,

clasping the edges of the table for support and for the feeling of hardness under her fingers. Gripping the table seemed to draw her back to earth, back to reality, and then, as suddenly as it came, the panic disappeared. She'd sit back down, arrange her legs under the chair, take a sip of lukewarm tea and stroke the edges of the saucer.

Worse than the attacks that found her in the afternoon, though, were the dark breaths of despair that crept up on her while she slept curled like a leaf around her husband in the middle of the night. They gripped her out of nowhere, her dreams tossed up into the darkness, and she'd wake strangled for breath. She still couldn't believe that Grace was gone. Jane supposed it was better to have the anxiety wake her from her sleep than the other possibility—the times right after Grace died when Jane would be asleep and then wake up feeling calm, happy even, because she'd forgotten. The crash of memory, when she realized again, was devastating. This was better, marginally. But the nights she woke up like this were so dark, so long. She hated hearing Paul's even breathing in those moments, so content and relaxed he was. She hated how he slipped into sleep so easily.

When she was asleep, she could escape reality, but upon waking it crumpled her like paper. It was a physical pain she lived with constantly, a feeling of bone-deep agony.

"Let's go to Nakuru," Paul said one evening at dinner. "Have a safari, see the lake again." A distraction from the grief, he'd said.

It was a year since Grace had died, and her ashes were the one thing Jane would take if there were a fire. People always used to ask that question. It was even one of the choices for the application essay for her college. She'd answered it but couldn't remember what she said. The days of having to think—really think—what the choice might be were over. Now her answer was ready-made, always at the tip of her tongue. She'd leave everything else behind, even Paul, and take only her daughter.

She'd hated the lake when she was there with the girls. But maybe it would help, she thought, to see if the lake looked healthier now, if somehow it had changed for the better. Maybe it would help to see the birds again. The lonely way they floated above the eggs they'd lost reminded Jane of herself.

Paul stood behind Jane at the edge of the soupy water. She heard him clear his throat and shift his boots in the dirt. Jane had hated him every day since Grace died. Hated the way he tried to comfort her and how he wouldn't lay blame. Jane wanted to be punished. She should never have ignored her instincts. She'd been right all along—the world was a dangerous and terrible place and anything could happen. She cursed herself daily for letting down her guard, but Paul refused to hurt her.

"I want to be alone a minute," Jane said, and she heard that her voice was shriller than she'd intended, anger always too close to her surface.

Paul didn't answer, but he shifted away. Jane could hear the change in the air behind her and felt his absence. She hadn't wanted to leave their home to come here. Not even for the day, as Paul had planned. She was a snail ripped from her shell, too soft and exposed. Jane hated Paul for finding it easier than she did to get on the Rift Valley road and drive away, to trade the comfort of grief for the distraction of this wild, desolate place.

There was a flat rock nearby and Jane sat down on it. It was warm beneath her. She felt like lying across it and letting it absorb her so she'd disappear. But as brackish as it was, the water beckoned. Jane unlaced her boots and pulled them off. She peeled her socks from her feet and rolled her pants up to the knee. The mud under her toes was slimy and colder than she'd expected. Jane shuffled her feet carefully, half expecting to feel the smooth roundness of eggs underneath, and not wanting to crush them. The living birds clucked and cawed nervously as she edged closer to them.

A flash of pink caught Jane's eye and she looked up. A lone bird near the edge of the lake had raised it wings. It stood still for a moment, and then began running, its spindly legs and the knuckles of its knees carrying it fast across the shallow water. Then a split second of stillness and it seemed to hang in the air, its long legs now gracefully stretched behind it. And it was off, wings silent in the sky and powerful. In seconds the escaped bird was nothing but a dark spot, too high, too far to see anymore. Jane wondered if that bird had left anything behind.

She turned to catch Paul's eye. She hoped he'd seen the bird in flight. It was beautiful. He grinned back at Jane from the shore. He'd seen it. Jane waded a little farther into the murky water. Paul was the kind of bird who'd have the courage to fly away. He knew how to spread his wings and hang, silent, in the air. Jane wondered if he'd leave her behind, preserved but empty. There were times, in the months after Grace's accident, when she wished he'd leave. She'd been a ghost, and like a ghost, she'd wanted to be invisible, to nurture her pain alone, to let it cover her like mist so she could disappear into it.

Now, in this place, the water licked Jane's calves. She felt nothing but the physical sensation of the sun on her shoulders, the slight wind that flicked a hair across her cheek. She took off her hat and tipped her head back. The sky was white and flat. There was no rain there, just high, thin clouds and somewhere, somewhere far enough away that it could look only forward not back, was the flamingo she'd watched leave.

Suddenly, Jane wanted to run through the water as fast as that bird had. She wanted to wave her arms and shout at the limp, left-behind birds until she scared them into flight. She wanted to see them take to the air, drink the newness of the sky and imagine a new place for themselves.

She wished she'd brought the small silvery urn with them. She thought of it, sitting on her bedside table next to her books, her reading glasses and a vase filled with roses from their garden. She thought Grace would like it here, to be sprinkled on the surface of the water and to sift, slowly, down to nestle into the silt below. She'd rest among the other lost eggs and be watched over by the birds. Maybe, soon, the rain would come back and spill down the sky for days and days on end. If that happened, Nakuru would fill. The flamingos that hadn't left yet would shake the rain from their feathers and raise their necks so their beaks would point skyward. Grace would swirl around their feet and they would watch over her.

Africa had, in Jane's mind, cemented itself into a shadow land—dark and veiled and seething with things that frightened her. Insects and snakes and newsreel images of civil wars and starvation, of guns and hunger and disease—of accidents that happened in the blink of an eye, ones that changed everything. But she was linked to this place, now, deeply and irretrievably, and she couldn't face going back to the States. She told Paul, when it was time for him to transition to a new post, to bid on another African country. Jane knew they couldn't stay in Kenya forever—Paul's job wouldn't allow that—but she wasn't ready to leave Grace's place behind, either. Grace was Africa now, too, and Jane wasn't ready to make the continent nothing but conversation for cocktail parties. She was trapped, linked to the place by the worst moment of her life. So when Paul was offered Lusaka, they didn't hesitate to accept.

But Jane didn't expect the shock to her system the move caused. She didn't expect the anxiety, the visceral instinct she felt, her body, veins and tissues all leaning away from here, cringing away from this strange place, pulling her thoughts back toward the familiar, always. Like the way a plant in a gloomy room curves and stretches toward the distant band of light it craves. Jane felt physically the yearning toward her daughter, toward the past when things were still okay. She was not moving on; she was not beginning to accept. She was in danger, she knew, of being cemented in this, a beetle cast in amber, forever preserved in a terrible moment.

She tried to explain her feelings to her husband; she tried to tell him how stunned she was by the unfamiliarity of everything she encountered. Everything was different now that she didn't have Grace to explore the new place with her. The air itself smelled repugnant to her, and every morsel of food, every sip of water, tasted dusty and old. She didn't know if it was the new country or her grief that colored everything here. Paul smiled sadly when she told him all of this. He'd held her hand and said, "You'll get used to it. It will become less hard. I promise." And what choice did Jane have? His work was here now. It was a distraction for him and it was working for him. His feet were finding ground. If she left, she would leave alone.

The other American embassy wives were so different from her. They had kids or jobs to go to, things to wrap themselves around. They seemed breezy and confident and comfortable here. They spoke of Lusaka like they spoke of their children— pesky and frustrating, but beloved. Jane tried to socialize at the beginning; she tried hard to conjure the person she had once been, but when she went to the spouses' teas and to the meetings of the International Women's Group, she found her words stuck behind her lips. Her roots had been clipped; she had nothing here—no job, no friends, nothing that was hers alone. Even her words had been pruned. She was aware that some of the other embassy families knew about the accident, about Grace. Embassy communities were tight-knit, and even though the people within them moved around constantly, that meant that all of them knew people in common—news of tragedy spread fast through the expatriate grapevine. Jane never spoke of it to anyone, though, and nobody brought it up with her. Paul encouraged her to speak with the embassy doctor; he could arrange counseling, maybe an antidepressant. But Jane couldn't imagine crying and talking about it with a stranger.

★ ★ ★

Jane's whole purpose while Paul was at work became avoiding the houseman. The houseman's name was Moffat. Moffat sounded like soft old slippers shuffling along through the rooms of the house. Moffat's mannerisms bore a disconcerting similarity to Muthega's—he spoke in the same way, and he provided a similar service—helping Jane with things she didn't necessarily need help with. He was kind, too, like Muthega was—giving rides to the women and candy to the kids who thronged around the truck. Moffat's kindness made Jane angry. Sometimes people would come to the door selling fruit or fish, and Moffat always opened the door. Jane never gave him money to buy any of the things, but he always crouched in the doorway and chatted.

Although Jane and Paul had always had household help in every post they'd taken, Jane realized that she'd never been home so much. She'd been busy, out and involved, helping at Grace's schools, working out at the embassy gyms. This was not how she'd been since Grace was born, terrified to leave home, forced inside by fear, like an animal too used to captivity to find the courage to escape, even when the cage door was wide-open. For the first time, Jane found it disorientating to have a stranger underfoot all day. She tried to avoid him, but it was hard.

The house had only two levels: the bottom one was a wide-open swath of living room, dining room and kitchen, and the top was just a line of three airy bedrooms and a bathroom laced like beads along a wide, empty hallway. Moffat seemed determined to dust and mop in every nook. Jane wanted to make herself invisible when Moffat was in the house, so when he arrived each morning, she acted busy and distracted and greeted him while hurriedly gathering up books and papers and pens and a large mug of tea. When she scooped up all she could hold—books and papers in one crooked arm, mug of tea clutched in the other hand, she escaped to the backyard table, where she sat shuffling her pile of novels and books on native flora, or she hunkered down in the weeds and poked at the dirt with her trowel and tried to force away the image of a pair of tiny hands in hers. Grace had helped in the garden since she could sit up.

One day, Moffat didn't come. Jane felt his lateness without looking at her watch. She sensed she'd waited longer than usual to gather up her books and her tea; she noticed a slight difference in the intensity of the light that streamed through her kitchen window. She wondered what happened. She thought she should try to get in touch with him. But how? Jane had been to his house only once when she and her husband dropped him there in the car one rainy afternoon when his bicycle chain was broken.

It was late morning when Jane heard the familiar click of the gate latch and then the scrape of metal against the concrete walkway. She stood up from her patch of weeds in the yard, laid her trowel aside and wiped the dirt from her hands. She saw Moffat and a woman she didn't recognize walking slowly up to the front door.

The woman was tall and sinewy, and under the puffed sleeves of her blouse her bare forearms were lean and muscular. She wore a piece of colorful fabric wrapped tightly around her waist like a skirt, and it hugged the hard bloom of her pregnant belly tightly. Jane walked around the side of the house to meet them. "Come in," she said, gesturing to Moffat like he was an expected guest. She wondered how one was supposed to talk to the houseman when he appeared at the front door, late and with a guest. Should she be stern? Beatific? She led the pair into the living room and sat down in an armchair. She was embarrassed about the mud smeared on her legs and under her fingernails.

Moffat and the woman huddled on the couch. "This is my wife, madam," Moffat said. Jane was surprised. Moffat looked ancient and mousy. His wife looked elegant and clear-eyed, and sitting ramrod straight on the couch, she towered over Moffat.

There was a pause, and Jane wondered if she should offer the couple tea. She thought yes, she would, and moved to get up. Just then Moffat and his wife rustled and spoke to each other in hushed voices. They looked at Jane expectantly and she sat down again.

Moffat's wife leaned over to rummage in a small bag at her side and then drew out a white envelope. She handed the envelope to Jane and sat back. Suddenly Moffat's wife looked tired. Jane had a flash of empathy. She'd never been so tired as when she was pregnant. She could have slept and slept.

Jane held the envelope in her hands for a moment. It felt empty except for a small lump in one corner.

"Madam," Moffat began, "we had a thief in our house last night." Jane listened while the story unfolded, the envelope cool between her fingers.

A pair of robbers had slid into Moffat's house before dawn that morning. They came in through the plastic sheet that covered up the unfinished part of the roof. Jane wondered what the robbers were after. She'd seen Moffat's house herself. There was nothing to steal there. "My wife heard the thieves before I did, madam—she fought with them." Jane glanced at the tall woman on her couch. "There was a fight, madam, one of the thieves, they bit my wife." Moffat pointed to the envelope in Jane's hand.

"Oh, yes," Jane breathed, and slit it open with a finger, dumping the contents into her palm. Moffat's wife sat still and calm on the couch. Her thin body, straight but for the round stomach and the knot of brilliant cotton on her head, made her look like a wilting flower.

Jane looked at what lay in her palm, confused. It was a small mushroom, no bigger than her thumb tip and the color of warm earth. She wondered what to say. Why would they give her one brown mushroom? And what did the mushroom have to do with their story of the thieves? She raised her head to ask, and when she did, she saw Moffat turn to his wife and nod abruptly. Moffat's wife pulled aside the colorful fabric of her headscarf to reveal her upper neck. It was streaked with blood. Moffat said, "Her ear, madam." Jane looked at Moffat's wife and then back at the mushroom in her own hand. It wasn't a mushroom at all. It was the smooth fleshy lobe of Moffat's wife's ear.

Jane swallowed and tried not to recoil as she shuffled the bitten-off ear back into the envelope. Her hand felt as if it had been burned in the place where the ear had sat for those long seconds. She wanted to cry.

"Madam, we need a ride in your car to the hospital. My wife needs to see a doctor. In the fight, we think the baby could be hurt."

"Why did you save the ear?" Jane's thoughts were jumbled; she couldn't make sense of what Moffat was asking. She thought of the flesh in her palm and swallowed, tried not to blanch.

"The ear is proof of this fight, madam. I can show the police. I can show you so you know I was not lying when I didn't come to work this morning on time."

"Um...and the baby?" Jane asked, swallowing her tears of horror and longing for her chair in the yard, her trowel and her weeds. She rubbed ineffectively at the dirt on her hands.

"Yes, madam, my wife is worried about the baby. The thieves, they kicked her."

"Oh, my God!" Jane said. Her voice sounded too loud. Moffat and his wife were so calm. She, on the other hand, felt completely out of control—like she was shaking from the inside out. She'd just held someone's ear in her hand. She tried to measure her response, to calibrate her voice to match those of her visitors. "Of course," she whispered, "let me get my keys."

★ ★ ★

The teaching hospital lay on the outskirts of Lusaka. Jane drove hesitantly. She hated driving now. She was nervous; the streets were rutted with deep holes, and people, animals and other cars tended to appear without warning. How easily accidents could happen. She sat stiffly and gripped the wheel tensely, leaning forward with concentration.

The sun was in her eyes, and she fumbled to pull down the shade. She crawled along through the traffic, unsure where to go, which turns to make. Occasionally Moffat leaned forward from where he sat in the back seat with his wife, and pointed one way or another, and Jane dutifully turned.

The halls of the hospital were filled with people. Jane felt nausea rise—this place was too similar to where she'd seen Grace, broken and gone. She didn't think she could stay. But Moffat guided Jane and his wife to a space on a wooden bench set against a wall. He motioned to them to sit. "I'll try to find the doctor, madam—you can sit here." Jane and Moffat's wife sat. The space on the bench was small. Moffat's wife was pressed up against Jane on one side, and on Jane's other side was an old man with a shriveled arm. The man appeared to be asleep, his head lolled back against the wall, his mouth slightly open and his eyes shut. Jane sat stiffly, trying not to feel the closeness of Moffat's wife's pregnancy. She couldn't bear to think of the hollowed-out space in her own body.

As other people sat down, the space between the women got smaller and smaller, and Jane felt herself being squished. The old man's wilted arm lay like a flower against her leg, Moffat's wife's elbow was almost in her lap. The hallway grew hotter and hotter and the air grew thick and smelled of unwashed skin and the fetid breath of the sick.

Jane felt herself growing light-headed and angry. This place was making her anxiety raise its head. This wasn't good for her—to be reminded. Why did Moffat make her do this? Why was she stuck in this horrible hospital hallway pressed skin to skin with all these strangers? These Zambians were staring at her unabashedly, probably wondering—as she herself was—what she was doing here. It occurred to Jane that she should be frightened—Africa was dangerous, after all—but she felt too annoyed to be scared.

Jane was distracted by a fluttery touch on her arm. Moffat's wife was looking up at her, wiggling her fingers lightly on Jane's arm to get her attention. "Yes?" Jane asked, more sharply than she'd intended.

The women spoke words that Jane couldn't understand. "I'm sorry," Jane muttered, "I don't speak Nyanja." The woman motioned to the bench they were sitting on, and then made a gesture of leaving and returning. "Oh, yeah, you want me to save your seat. I'll try." Jane couldn't think of a way to do that. She shrugged. "I'll try," she said again.

Jane spread out when Moffat's wife left. She slid down and let her knees fall open. She pushed her elbows back so they touched the wall behind her. She made herself big. It suited her mood to poke the old dead-armed man in the side and to glance up angrily at the lady standing nearby with a sagging toddler in her arms, eyeing the vacated space with big, glassy eyes. It was a side effect of grief—this anger, this self-involvement. Before, she would have felt sad to watch this woman and her sick child. Now, though, she couldn't spare the emotion on someone else's pain. She hurt too much herself. But she felt an odd sort of kinship with Moffat's wife, whose ear she'd held in her hand and who had entrusted her with her valuable spot on this bench.

Just when Jane thought she couldn't hold off the press of people anymore, she saw Moffat's wife returning. She edged through the crowds belly-first and caught Jane's eye. She smiled and held up her hand. In it was a smooth, ripe orange, a bright blister of color in the dark hallway. Jane smiled back and folded herself smaller so the woman could sit next to her again.

Moffat's wife began to peel off the skin of the orange, sending light sprays of scented spritz into the air. It smelled delicious. Jane tried not to stare, but her mouth watered. She was suddenly thirsty and hungry. Moffat's wife nudged her with an elbow. Jane looked up and saw the peeled orange in her outstretched hand. Moffat's wife smiled.

"No," Jane said, hesitating, "you go ahead, pregnancy makes you hungry." She knew the woman couldn't understand her words, but it seemed worse to stay silent. Moffat's wife pulled back her hand and in one swift motion split the orange in two right down the middle. She pressed half into Jane's hand. Jane looked down at the plump, cool half she held. She wondered if the orange was dirty. She watched Moffat's wife use her thumb to dislodge a section from the half she held, and slip it between her lips. Jane could almost feel the sweet juice and pulp sliding down her own throat as Moffat's wife swallowed. Moffat's wife reached out and, before Jane could refuse, grasped Jane's hand and pressed it, palm down, on the tight rise of the flesh of her stomach. Jane closed her eyes and felt the baby thump. When she opened her eyes again, Moffat's wife was smiling up at her.

"I had a baby, too," Jane said. She knew Moffat's wife couldn't understand, but it helped to say the words out loud, to claim them again, after so long.

"I lost my baby." Jane's eyes filled, and her breath shortened. The panic rose in her body again, setting off the flashes of light in her head and the breathless feeling of drowning. Jane closed her eyes and tried to count her inhalations and her exhalations, regulating her breath. She felt Moffat's wife pluck the orange half from Jane's hand. Then she felt the soft edge of a section against her lips. Moffat's wife held the piece of orange up to Jane's mouth, her slim, dark fingers so close to Jane's face that when she opened her eyes, she could see the rough skin on her knuckles.

The orange was cool and sweet. It filled Jane's mouth with juice. She opened her eyes and tried to smile. "Thank you," she whispered.

Just then Moffat pushed through the crowd and reached out to take his wife's hand. Moffat's wife stood, and Jane saw the way the two looked at one another. Had she and Paul ever had that expression? That look of instant understanding and devotion? The moment, so many years ago, when she sat in the car sobbing as Paul held her flickered into her mind. He did then. There was a time, not so long ago, when they'd understood each other.

Moffat spoke quickly to his wife in Nyanja and then turned to Jane. "Madam, they will see my wife now."

Jane shucked the sleeping old man's flaccid arm off her leg, where it lay, heavy and immovable. She stood up. Like water pushed into a void, all the bodies on the bench slid over to fill the space she'd vacated. She took a deep breath to dispel the fear that bubbled up at the thought of exiting the crowded hospital and finding her car and then her way home without Moffat and his wife to help her.

Moffat's wife looked up at Moffat and whispered something to him.

"Madam," Moffat said, "we can take you to the car. Maybe the doctor will wait for us."

Jane smiled in relief and nodded. She wouldn't have to push through the throngs of people in the hallway alone. But when she turned, she glimpsed Moffat's wife's neck, the bare brown expanse of skin and the stain of dried blood visible under the colorful headscarf. She caught the look of worry on Moffat's face. She remembered the feel of the unborn body sliding under her hand when Moffat's wife pressed her fingers to her belly, and she remembered, with a spasm of sadness, how thrilled she'd been when she felt the butterfly wing of her own baby's movement deep inside her, and how that baby grew up to be her daughter—who would always be her daughter. She thought of Moffat's wife, so pregnant, fighting off the thieves in the night. How brave she was.

"No, I can manage." She looked Moffat straight in the eye. She thought it was the first time they'd had eye contact. His clear eyes belied the old-man slope of his shoulders, the wrinkles on his forehead.

After the smells and crowds of the hospital, Jane's car was quiet and still. She took a deep breath and closed her eyes. Her heart beat fast, and she felt sweat sliding down her back. But she was a grown-up. If Moffat's wife could fight robbers, she could drive herself home. She could do this. She drove slowly and concentrated on not getting lost; she registered the garbage on the streets, the animals wandering past and the grubby barefoot kids with streaming noses. She was careful; she edged around the possibilities of living things darting out from any corner. When she finally pulled into her driveway, she felt like celebrating. She raised her fingers to her nose and inhaled the scent of the orange that lingered there. It was such a familiar and beautiful smell.

Jane locked the car and followed the path around the house to her backyard. She didn't bother to go inside the house. She didn't want to lurk in the dim rooms right now. The sun felt good on her shoulders, and the air smelled sweet. The weeds still choked the flower beds; the bare patches of lawn still looked mangy in the late-afternoon light. Jane's books and her teacup still sat on the outdoor table. But she didn't sit down. She felt a sense of energy she hadn't felt for years. She pulled her clippers from their case, slid her gloves onto her hands and breathed deeply the scent of the rich, perfect earth into her lungs. She knew Moffat's baby would be all right. She'd felt it under her own hand, and she wanted to make sure to have flowers to bring when the baby was born.

It would be slow, she knew, pulling out all the weeds and preparing the soil. Gardening was a process; you had to go through it one step at a time, like being pregnant, she thought, or like grieving. It took the time it took. But she would make this garden grow, and later when Paul came home from work, he wouldn't find her caught inside. He would find her out here and he would look at her like she was real, like he knew her and was welcoming her back to him. This time she would see it. She would let him look deeply at her, and she would look back at him that way, too.

A ZEBRA TAKES ITS STRIPES
WHEREVER IT GOES

"They're sending me away."

Adia and Simi sat together under an acacia.

"My grandmother thinks it's time for me to live in America, to learn to be an American. But it's not even near where she lives. It's the place where she went to high school a million years ago. On the east coast. So I won't even be near the one person I know in the whole country." Adia picked up a pebble and tossed it away. "She's worried because I haven't been going to school since Grace died."

Saying this out loud made Adia's eyes fill, tears threatened. "I couldn't go back to school, not without her."

Simi knew the story already. Leona wrote from Nairobi, weeks after the accident, asking Simi what to do, telling her that Adia wouldn't get out of bed, refused to go to school. For a few weeks, Adia had come to stay here, in the manyatta. A change of scenery would be good—they all thought so. But Leona had called Joan, too, who suggested a more drastic change of scenery—a whole world of change. Even John, when Leona mentioned the possibility of sending Adia away, had been positive.

"I can't see how it would hurt," he said, but he was reticent. He didn't know if his vote would even count, and he was relieved when Leona said that Adia would come back for holidays, that of course she'd come to Solai. She wanted John in Adia's life. That wasn't a question anymore.

Noni, the baby, now eighteen months, sat in Adia's lap, chewing on Adia's hair. Not far away, the toddler twins, Naeku and Naisiae, drew in the dirt with sticks.

"She told my mom to use my dead grandpa's money. I guess he left Mom a lot, and she has a bunch left. My grandma convinced her to use the money for my education."

Since her visit to Kenya, Joan called Adia every month. "You're my only grandchild, and I want you in my life," she said almost sternly. But Adia felt warmth under the formality, and she looked forward to the calls.

"You'll get used to America," Joan said. "You'll meet lots of new friends and you'll love the school, it's absolutely gorgeous." She told Adia stories about how it was when she was a student there, years and years ago, and tried to convince Adia that it would be fun.

Naeku screamed, and Simi and Adia looked up in time to see Naisiae pulling Naeku's stick away.

"Children are a blessing," Simi said wryly. And Adia laughed. "You love it, Yeyo!" This adoption was never made official. After Loiyan died, Simi just continued caring for the children. None of the other wives minded—they all had children, too, and even grandchildren, of their own.

Today, Kiserian, the eight-year-old, was at school. Simi didn't wait to enroll her. She didn't ask her husband—she simply walked the child to the school building a few days after Loiyan died and paid the fees. It was a story Simi hadn't even told Adia. She was determined to send the girls to school and didn't

want to ask her husband for money because that would allow
him the chance to refuse. Simi made a promise to herself in
the heart of that *oreteti* tree so long ago. She found the necklace
that night, and she wasn't bitten by a snake or eaten by a leopard. N'gai had encouraged her. She would not risk having her
husband forbid her dream from coming true. Instead, she left
the girls with Isina early one morning. She didn't have money
to pay for school. She had only one way to get it.

Two hour's walk down the Mara River was a *muzungu* hotel.
Simi had seen it several times before from a distance. It was a
large building that spread along the river like a snake. There
were more glinting glass windows than Simi could count, and
a large stone terrace on one end with lots of tables and chairs.
That's where Simi went. She walked until she was close enough
to see the terrace with the tables and the chairs and the tourists eating things she'd never seen before. They drank colored
drinks from tall glasses. Simi stopped. The *muzungu* tourists sat
at those tables, and people brought them things to eat and drink.
She wasn't sure she'd ever seen so many *muzungus* in one place
before. Any bravery she'd felt that morning was gone. But she
couldn't let fear stop her. She knew this hotel had a shop inside.
Years ago, she'd spoken to some women who lived near here
and they'd said that the shops even sold jewelry. They laughed
when they told her that they could spend just an hour making
a bracelet or a necklace, they could use the cheapest beads and
create the simplest designs, and these shops would give them
money. They'd set the ugly necklaces and bracelets on little tables and then the tourists would buy them.

"The *muzungus* don't care if the thing is cheap and badly
made." One of the women laughed. "They will buy everything."

Simi desperately hoped that was true. Not looking up, and
trying to pretend that none of them could see her, Simi walked
quickly around the stone terrace. The tourists' voices were loud.

Around the other side of the building Simi found herself standing on a large, circular road with zebra-striped vans parked in a row. These were the vans she remembered from her childhood, the ones she'd wave at, hoping the faces in the window would see her, call out to her those English words she'd craved so much then. Two men dressed in khaki uniforms stood smoking in a shaded spot next to the building. They greeted her in Swahili.

"I am here to sell something in the shop," Simi said. "Can you tell me where to go?" One of the men chuckled. "They won't like you to go in there, sister. But I can tell the shopkeeper to come and see you."

The men dropped their cigarettes on the ground and crushed them under their boots. Then they turned and walked toward a huge glass door, one shaded by trees and flowers in pots bigger than any Simi had ever seen. One of the men turned back to Simi, motioned for her to wait and then they opened the great door and disappeared.

Simi waited. She squatted in the shade where the men had stood and examined the vans parked so neatly on one side of the driveway. Beyond them, in the distance, were purple hills that hid the horizon. Simi wondered how far away those hills were. She waited longer and felt herself getting sleepy. It was midday. She thought of Loiyan's girls back in the manyatta, and this thing she wanted so badly to do for them. Just then, the door opened and several people came out. There was one of the men she'd spoken to coming through the front entrance and leading several tourists across the driveway. Two of the tourists were women, both with nut-brown skin the same shade as Simi's own, two were men and then a boy about Kiserian's age.

Simi called to the man. He glanced over at her, and then spoke to the group of people. She couldn't hear what he said to them, but then he turned back and called to Simi, "They don't want to buy anything today. You should go home."

Simi stood. She wasn't sleepy anymore. She was hungry and

thirsty and she was here for a reason. She wouldn't leave until she had what she wanted. The man and the tourists were beginning to get into one of the vans. The driver held the door open, and the young boy climbed in first. Simi didn't want the man to leave before she spoke to him. She hurried over and he looked up. One of the women looked at Simi, too. She said something to the driver, and he answered her.

Then he turned to Simi and said, "I am taking these people on a game drive. That is what they came here for. Don't waste our time."

Simi looked directly into the man's eyes, but she chose her words, and her language, for the woman standing just behind him. She spoke in the clearest, boldest voice she could find, and said in English, "I have a rare necklace to sell. My mother was the best jewelry maker in the manyatta. The necklace is old, and it's more beautiful than anything in that shop. If you haven't told them I am here, then you are a bad employee. This will be the best necklace in the shop."

She'd hoped the man would be struck by her words, maybe ashamed. She knew he was lying. He grinned, though, and only said. "Go away, woman. This is not a place for you."

"Wait a minute, Jackson." The woman spoke to the driver, who looked surprised. But her eyes were on Simi.

She continued, "Did you try to see if they'd sell this woman's necklace?"

Then the man looked annoyed, not ashamed. "They do not sell this kind of thing here." He spoke in a loud voice, mimicking authority.

"I've seen the jewelry in there." The woman's voice reminded Simi of Leona's. The woman smiled at Simi. "Can I see the piece?"

Simi reached up and unhooked her mother's necklace. She held it up. It was warm from where it had lain against her neck. The woman gently took it from Simi's hands and looked at it carefully. "It's beautiful," she finally said. "Your mother was an artist." She smiled warmly. "It must mean something to you. Why do you want to sell it?"

Simi hoped the woman would understand the reason she gave. She was being a dishonest wife by not asking her husband for the school money, and maybe this woman would disapprove.

"I have four daughters. They are mine now because their own mother died. You see, I want to send them to school, but I need money for the school fees. If I ask my husband, he may refuse. Then my daughters will never get an education." She looked away. Sharing all this with a stranger made her feel exposed. But she was desperate. She examined those distant purple hills and pretended she was far away from here.

"What is your name?" she heard the woman ask. She answered.

"Simi," the woman repeated. "Simi, I think your daughters are lucky." The woman turned and poked her head into the van where the other tourists sat. It crossed Simi's mind that the woman would jump in the van and drive away—her mother's necklace still in there with them. But the woman wasn't getting into the van. She was speaking to the men. Simi could hear her own story being recited in the woman's voice. Then one of the men spoke. Simi cold hear his gravelly voice, but she couldn't make out his words.

"Okay," the woman said, and pulled something off one of the van's seats. Then she reappeared again and stood smiling at Simi.

"I want to buy your necklace," she said. Simi glanced at the driver. He'd gotten into the driver's seat, and Simi could see his face through the window. He looked angry.

The woman spoke again. "Can you tell me how much the school fees are?"

Simi did a quick calculation in her head. "Two hundred shillings for one year," she said.

"And there are four girls? That's eight hundred shillings for

one year. That's…less than a week's groceries at home in At-
lanta." The woman opened a wallet and looked inside. Then
she leaned back into the van and spoke to the others. Simi saw
them rustling. They gave something to the woman.

When the woman turned back to Simi, she was holding a
handful of money. "We'll pay for five years for each girl." Simi
looked at the money. It was a lot.

"Is it an okay price for the necklace? It's four thousand shillings." The woman looked a little worried. Simi felt faint. It
was more money than she'd ever seen. She'd hoped to sell the
necklace for the two hundred shillings needed for Kiserian's
first year. Now she could send all the girls for five years. She felt
dizzy and looked in the woman's eyes. She wanted to assure her.

"This is too much," Simi breathed. "It is so much money."

The woman smiled. She looked happy. "It's a beautiful necklace. And I want those girls to go to school. Please take it."

Simi tied the money into a knot of her wrap.

"I can help you put it on," she said, and the woman handed the
necklace back to her and turned, lifting her hair out of the way of
the clasp. Simi fit the necklace around the woman's neck. She'd
never touched a foreign person other than Leona and Adia. The
woman's skin was soft, and though her hair was straight, Simi
noticed little curls of hair just like her own at the woman's nape.
When Simi secured the necklace, the woman turned around to
face her. The blue and green beads looked beautiful.

"Thank you," the woman said, "I'll take good care of it."
Then she smiled once more and climbed into the van next to
the others. She slid the door shut and the driver, still annoyed,
Simi assumed, roared off with a squeal of the tires.

Simi walked home quickly. She was excited and happy, and
also terrified that someone would rob her. But she couldn't stop
smiling. She would miss the necklace, but when she'd given
it to N'gai the first time, he didn't want it. He gave it back to
her for a reason. She had to make sure that dream came true.

Now, sitting under this tree with Adia and three of her other daughters, Simi felt a deep sense of pride. She looked at Adia and said, "You are brave. And you are lucky. You have this chance to go to America and get a good education. It's a chance the other girls will never have. You have to take it. But you are not going alone, Adia. We will be in your head. You will be learning all those American things for us, too. Bring it back to your yeyo and your sisters."

"It's not just that," Adia said. "I'm scared to go. I'm not brave. I've never been anywhere but here. And I just barely met my father. If I go, I won't see him for a whole year..." She trailed off, and then said, "And Grace." Adia's voice cracked and her eyes filled. "I feel like if I leave Kenya I'm leaving Grace, too."

Simi patted Adia's arms and murmured. "You know that the dead cannot die if we remember them, Adia. Grace will always be with you, too."

Later that afternoon, two goats were slaughtered. Adia was going to America, and that was a reason to celebrate. Adia sat with the other manyatta children. She was the oldest one now. The Maasai girls her age had mostly been circumcised and married; the boys she grew up with were *moran* now. Simi watched her oldest daughter helping Kiserian with her homework. They bent their heads together over Kiserian's exercise book, Adia showing Kiserian how to form the letters of the alphabet. Simi felt deeply proud. There were times, years and years ago, that she could never imagine she'd be blessed with one child, let alone five. There were times she thought she might not even be allowed to stay in the community, a barren woman like her. But all those years were over, and now everything was different. Everything had changed. Sometimes Simi woke thinking it couldn't possibly be real, that this must be a dream. But it was a dream tinged with sadness. Simi never thought Loiyan would be someone she thought fondly of, but she found she missed her. The twins didn't speak much about their mother, and Noni would probably never remember her, but Kiserian talked about her mother with love and sometimes tears. Loiyan had been a dedicated, loving mother.

The younger girls fell asleep early, their bellies full of meat. Simi and Adia sat by the fire. They didn't talk much. The fact that Adia was leaving tomorrow, back to Nairobi and then on an airplane to America, hung between them. Simi thought about what she'd said to Adia earlier that day—that she should welcome this change, that she should be happy to get such a good education. The truth was muddier. Adia hadn't come from Simi's body, but her existence, from the moment she was born, altered Simi's life in ways she'd never have anticipated. She hated knowing she wouldn't see Adia for so long, and that she would be so, so far away.

"Yeyo," Adia said. "I'm really sad to leave. I'm going to miss you and everyone here. I'll miss the Loita Hills and the sky and the way the grass smells. I lost Grace and now I'm losing everything else."

Simi stood up and gestured for Adia to follow her outside. She walked to the edge of the manyatta, where light from the fires in the little homes couldn't reach. The air was chilly. The stars were out. It was a clear night, and the moon was almost a perfect circle. The air smelled like livestock mixed with dust, wood smoke and charred meat.

"I love that smell so much," Adia said. "I never want to forget it."

Simi sighed. "You cannot worry about that," she said. "You know they say 'A zebra takes its stripes wherever it goes.' You don't ever really leave your home behind. It is the stripes of the zebra…it will follow you like your own skin does."

Simi looked up at the moon and remembered again the way her mother told her an education could never be taken away. She remembered the sad time after Leona took Adia and how she stared at the moon one night and felt that, even though she had that education, everything else had been taken from her. The moon was watching her again tonight, and this time, she wouldn't be sad. Adia was her oldest daughter, but not her only one anymore.

In the morning, Simi and the girls walked Adia up the road to where she could catch the *matatu* to Narok, and then the bus to Nairobi. Simi felt the wait was far too short, and too soon, Adia was wiping her tears and saying her goodbyes.

Simi pushed her blonde daughter up into the open door. She'd made a promise to Adia's other mother, and she would honor it. It was hard, though, feeling Adia's spine through her thin T-shirt, knowing she was pushing her daughter into something neither of them really wanted. Then Adia was on the van, perched in a window seat, her face pressed against the glass. Simi saw the pink splotches on her girl's skin, and thought she might die from the weight of sadness.

Adia thought she might die, too; she fought the desperate need to tell the driver to stop, to let her off. Instead, she watched Simi and her sisters through her smudged window and waved until she couldn't see them anymore. Then she just watched the landscape flying by. She wanted to drink it, to ingest it. She wanted to tuck the whole sweeping savannah into her cells, into her brain, where she could remember it forever.

A couple of hours later, as the bus chugged up the side of the Rift Valley, she turned and looked back at the wide expanse of land far below her. The light was pearly in the late afternoon, and she could barely make out the smudge of greeny-gray that marked the Nguruman forest, and just below it, the place where the manyatta was. Adia sighed and turned around to face forward, toward Nairobi. She wanted to be like the zebra, carrying this home with her, wherever she went, in the very pores of her skin.

CAPTIVITY

The animal was wild. Adia knew that immediately, though she'd seen nothing exactly like it before. It was bigger than a serval cat, maybe the size of a cheetah, but thicker, somehow, leonine, with a wide yellow face and white fur lining its ears. It was a predatory cat—it moved like a lion through the foliage; shoulders rolling purposefully with each step, eyes focused straight in front, head slightly down so the spine was a line, flat as a horizon. Adia took in the details without really thinking. As a child, her Maasai friends taught her how to share space with untamed creatures. She'd been close enough to lions and leopards to reach out and pet them if she'd been stupid enough to try. She'd been close enough to hyenas to smell the rotting meat on their breath and sense the damp blood of zebra on their chins. Adia instinctively slowed her own breathing, taking in air carefully, making herself as motionless as she could. She knew how to behave in the wild.

The animal stilled. It was watching something Adia couldn't see. It flattened its chest into the earth, leaving its backside still as a stone and showing Adia it had a thick, long tail. It was stalking something. Adia had seen kills before; she'd killed animals herself, in fact. The Maasai only ate goats and cows occasionally, but when they did, they slit the animals' throats, collecting every drop of blood and every scrap of meat—utilizing every part. Even the smallest bits of wet skin were slit down the middle and worn as bracelets that dried to a fuzzy rawhide around the wrist or ankle. Adia wasn't squeamish about that sort of thing, so it was with curiosity, not horror, that she watched the tawny creature leap up suddenly and pounce. The bushes were too high for Adia to see exactly what it killed, but she could hear the grunts the cat made and the struggle of its prey.

The bushes stopped moving, the sounds quieted and the cat emerged again. A large gray rabbit was clutched in its jaws. The cat didn't stop to eat. Adia was surprised. She wondered if it was more like a leopard. They liked to drag their conquests up into trees before feasting. The rabbit was huge, and the cat paused to drop it and reposition it in the grip of its teeth. It was close to Adia now, just a few feet away. The breeze was in her favor, and the animal didn't sense she was there. She was invisible. With a perfect view of the animal's profile, Adia could see clearly that its sides heaved with the efforts it had put forward. Adia saw the telltale drooping of its underside, the way the belly widened and stretched. She saw the cat's swollen teats. Whatever the animal was, it was female, and it was pregnant.

"Are you Adia?" the woman who picked her up at the Philadelphia airport asked. But she pronounced it "Ay-die-ah." And the way her thick lips curled into a smile made Adia swallow her correction. "No, it's Ah-dee-ah," she wanted to say, but couldn't. She didn't correct the woman—the dorm mother, Adia later understood—at all during the forty-five-minute drive to the school, and so the name stuck. Here in America she immediately understood she wasn't herself anymore; the name assigned to her was strange and ugly to her ears. She'd never been shy about speaking up before now; she didn't know what it was, exactly, about the unfamiliar place that made her feel mute. She only knew that she was different here, too.

"You're from Africa?" a group of girls she met that first day asked, their eyes wide with curiosity. And then the cocoa-colored girl who was her roommate asked, "Then how come you're white?"

The question made Adia stammer and she hated the apologetic way strings of words she'd never even said before stumbled from her mouth. "I'm American. My mom is American...that is...my dad is Kenyan... British Kenyan... He's Kenyan but, you know, white... I have an American passport...even though I've never been here before. I've never been to England, either. My real home is Nairobi, but I like it better with the Maasai. In the manyatta."

"The *manyatta*?" the cocoa girl asked, and her voice made the word—the word that Adia loved most in the world—sound ugly in her mouth. "What's a *manyatta*?" But she threw back her head and walked away, laughing, before Adia could explain.

Her name wasn't the only thing that was different here. The light in America was different, too. It was thin and hard, somehow, like a pane of glass. Adia was used to a different kind of light, a softer version. Back home, the light cupped around you like a palm. It held you near, but was yielding. You could push your way through it, you could pull it around you, consider it a comfort. This new light, this American light, didn't look at the people it illuminated. It didn't move like the Kenyan light did, which always changed and shifted like a living thing.

The sounds were also different. Adia was used to silence. Sometimes, back home, Adia climbed the jacaranda tree and heard nothing but rustling leaves and starlings. This boarding school was never silent. The wooden hallways echoed with footsteps and voices from early morning until lights-out on the dorms at 10:00 p.m. And then there were other noises, too.

There was the noise of her roommate shifting in the upper bunk and causing the bedsprings to squeak, and the uneven legs of the bunk shaking and thumping the floor. There were late-night bangs and clanks from the radiator and the vague traffic sounds from the road outside the school's gate.

These new sounds—the shouting of laughter from other rooms, the scratching of pencils in notebooks during study hall, the faint, muted voices from the dorm mother's TV slipping through the wall—they all made Adia feel lonely and stranger than she felt already. The sounds made her hate the sources a little. She didn't want to get used to these people, these lives, these shiny, clean girls. She didn't want to become one of them. And yet, she was lonely.

She heard Grace's voice in her head, always, and cried herself to sleep with the ache of missing her friend. She hated the way the memories wouldn't loosen their grip. And she'd learned something that Grace was wrong about, something important, and it deepened her grief that she couldn't tell Grace—that she'd never be able to tell Grace what she finally knew to be true—that it wasn't really better to be motherless than to have Leona as a mother. Adia would have given anything, now, to be high in the jacaranda tree watching her mother through the window, or listening to the quick tapping of her mother's keyboard through a closed door. She would have given anything to see Simi now, to curl up next to her in her dark, smoky house, listening to the far-off sounds of hyena and Simi's heavy, sleeping breath.

It was hard to be away from home, and making it worse was the silence that blanketed her from the inside. She could barely make herself open her mouth; she felt herself melting into the walls and the floor and even the air. People looked past her; they didn't hear her or notice her absence or her presence. Only the letters from her mother and John, Simi and even Joan made her seen. When a letter arrived, if only for the time it took her to read it, Adia felt like herself.

In the free time between classes and meals and study hall, Adia escaped outside. She was more comfortable without the walls around her, or the waves of other people. When she first found this path down to the little lake in the woods abutting campus, she thought it felt like swimming the way she did in Mombasa. The air in the woods was like water swirling her hair around her face, and the silence a good silence—a heavy and infinite thing that pressed on her like arms holding her tightly. Here, the air smelled wet and cool, and the light was cloudy and green. She could hear the breeze in the treetops and the calling of unfamiliar birds, she could smell decaying leaves on the path and damp earth that she pressed into with her boots as she walked. She could put aside the feeling of being invisible and, instead, reach out and touch things that didn't recoil from her: the rough bark of the trees, the pinecones that smelled sharp and soapy. She could breathe here without the chaos of all those eyes and voices that never looked at her or spoke to her.

Three weeks in, Adia woke before dawn one Saturday and lay in her bed, watching the rectangle of sky out the window. She traced her finger across the wool blanket she'd painstakingly packed from home. She could hardly bring anything with her—just two suitcases—but she'd insisted on this. She'd had it her whole life, and in its fibers she smelled smoke and the faint scent of sheep. She loved that it smelled like her manyatta home. She'd heard her roommate complaining to another girl about how Adia and her stuff "smelled like a barn," and once she came back to the room to see her school supplies, the folders and stapler and blotter she'd bought from the school store, pushed way over to one side of the long shared desk that stretched across the wall under the window. Embarrassed, she sniffed and sniffed everything she owned, but couldn't figure out what smelled bad. She tried to make her things and herself smaller, even more invisible, so her presence wouldn't bother her roommate. She crammed all of her clothes into her dresser, and left the shared closet empty of her things. She meticulously stored her books and papers in the drawers at her end of the desk and kept them tightly closed. She kept the offending wool blanket folded as tiny as she could make it and pushed far under her pillow.

Careful not to wake her roommate by jostling the bed frame, Adia slipped out of bed and into a pair of jeans and a sweatshirt. She picked up her boots and closed the door quietly behind her. The wide dorm hallway was empty and still and Adia took a deep breath and padded silently down the stairs to the outside door. It opened when she pushed it and a surprising surge of happiness jolted her into a smile. She slipped the boots onto her feet and ran. She was free. She sprinted past the playing field and down the path toward the lake.

The trees made the dawn darker but Adia wasn't frightened. She ran until she couldn't breathe without gasping. Then she stopped and looked around. Her breath was loud in the early silence of the woods. To her left, the lake shimmered under the barely rising sun. Adia turned and found a tree with roots large enough for her to sit comfortably between. She leaned back against the tree and closed her eyes. She wanted to imagine herself into a different place. By the time the cat appeared, Adia had been sitting between those roots for hours.

When she saw it, Adia stood slowly, gripping the tree trunk for balance. That's when the cat made its kill. Now the dust-colored animal held the rabbit tightly in her jaws and began her slow, shoulder-rolling walk down toward the lake and slunk between two bushes and out of sight. The leaves closed behind her like a door. Adia knew it was stupid, especially since she was alone, but she was bored now, and achy from sitting so long. Plus, the animal had made her kill already, and big cats were less dangerous when they weren't hungry. Adia crept along the same path the animal took. She tracked it easily. The late stage of the cat's pregnancy made her slower, less agile. Adia stayed conscious of the breeze, and shifted as the wind did, ensuring the animal wouldn't smell her. Adia forgot about her roommate and the silence inside her and the feeling of being completely invisible. By the time she heard shouts, the sun was high in the sky.

Adia pushed through the underbrush in the direction of the voices. Judging by the screams, something terrible had happened. The lake was calm and smooth, the sun dappling the surface. A few kids in canoes slipped across the water, trailing tiny splashes that glinted in the sun with each stroke of their paddles. The long dock and the boathouse were frantic with bodies. The few teachers on weekend duty were herding the kids not already in canoes to the farthest end of the dock. One teacher stood waving her arms above her head to signal the canoes across the lake to come back. Adia wondered why they all seemed scared. When the teacher on the dock saw her, he yelled, "There's a mountain lion! Get out of the woods."

"Did you hear?" her roommate asked her that night, just before lights-out. She was breathless. "There's a lion in the woods. A bunch of people saw it by the lake."

Adia looked up from her book. She hadn't heard her roommate speak to her—at least not without sneering or clipping her words angrily—before, and she wondered if this change was a cruel trick. Like someone holding out a cookie to a child and then snatching it away again.

"Yeah, I know. It's pregnant."

"Pregnant, how do you know?"

"I was out there really early this morning. I saw it make a kill, and then it got closer and I saw it. It's really pregnant, too. Like any day now."

"You saw it? You got close? You're fucking crazy. Crazy or lying."

There it was—the cookie snatched from Adia's hand. She should have known. But talking to her roommate—to someone—surprised Adia by feeling good. Her voice liked the air it slid through, outside her body, and her face liked being looked at. Something deep inside her blinked awake.

"I can take you to find her if you can wake up early enough tomorrow. She's not hard to track."

It was odd being out in the woods with someone else. Adia found it slower going; her roommate stumbled in the dark and kept grabbing Adia's arm in fear. She made too much noise, and Adia imagined how her Maasai friends would mercilessly tease this rustling, stumbling girl.

"How did you learn how to do this?" she asked once, and Adia was about to answer when she heard a slight sound, a muffled sort of huff. The sound of breathing.

"Shh!" she whispered as quietly as she could. She held her finger to her lips and motioned her roommate to stop, to stay where she was. The huffing was clearly audible. Adia tested the wind with her finger. She knew it would be unwise to go any farther. The Maasai, as brave as they were, weren't foolish, and tracking a predator in the dark like this would never happen back home. She suspected the animal was feeding, which was both good and bad. It wouldn't be hungry enough to see the girls as food, but it would be protective of its kill.

"We should turn around. It's right beyond this bush." Adia said the words under her breath.

"What the fuck, Adia? We came all the way out here. Are you wimping out or bullshitting me?"

Adia felt her roommate's moist breath on her ear. Something deep within her pulled taut at her chest and Adia had the feeling of a rush of cold water through her blood. It was that feeling that made her ignore her instincts, take a deep breath and push forward as slowly as she could.

"Fine, come on." Adia slipped carefully through the branches, spreading them with her hands and moving her body slowly.

"Look! There!" Adia was on the other side of the stand of bushes now, and she had a clear view. Her roommate sidled closer to her, and, to Adia's surprise, reached for Adia's fore-arm and squeezed it.

"Holy shit," her roommate whispered.

The lion was roughly thirty feet away, and in the shadowy light the dawn was bringing, they could see her clearly. The cat was lying prone in the hollow base of a rotten tree. Her head was resting on the ground, and her legs were outstretched. The sounds were not the huffs and grunts of a cat enjoying its kill, but rather the sounds of pain. The cat raised her head and chuffed. She rolled over and struggled to a standing position. She stood, trembling, head down, legs splayed.

"I told you, she's pregnant. She's having her babies."

Her roommate's eyes grew wide and the two girls knelt in the dirt and clutched one another's hands as they watched.

In America, there were rules Adia had to learn. There were rules about when to be certain places, when to eat, when to study and when to turn off her light at night. Adia had to clean her room in a certain way on a certain day, and she was forbid-den from leaving the grounds without permission. She had to ensure she remembered the rules the school imposed. Forget-ting meant she was singled out and reminded, or given extra study hall or a demerit as punishment. The official school rules were hard enough to understand and follow, but the unwritten social rules were far more complicated and dangerous. There were certain invisible lines that shifted and moved that you had to keep your eyes on. Crossing these lines meant the punish-ment of sidelong looks and the subtle shifting away of sweat-shirted bodies in the halls or cafeteria, and the pervasive sense that made you feel your own body, any touch from you, was poison to everyone else.

After watching the lion together and slipping safely back into their room before the dorm-mother caught them, Adia felt a sense of camaraderie, of having shared a danger and survived, with her roommate. When the bell rang for breakfast that morning, Adia was eager to finally have a place to sit, to chat with the other girls and actually eat hot food, drink cocoa and orange juice, instead of escaping the cafeteria with pockets full of bread and fruit. She hadn't eaten a hot meal in days. She followed the crowd of girls into the enormous room and weaved herself around the chairs being pulled out and the plates of eggs and pancakes being carried precariously between tables. There she was! Adia made her way toward the table where she saw her roommate just sitting down. There was even an empty chair. Adia reached for it and gripped the back, ready to pull it out and sit down. A thin-faced girl with sleek blonde hair looked up.

"Not so fast, lion tamer. That chair is reserved."

Adia glanced at her roommate, who sipped her glass of juice and smiled into the middle distance, refusing to look at Adia.

"This table isn't for zookeepers," the blonde said. Adia's roommate laughed.

Adia froze with embarrassment, all the hope and the flicker of happiness drained out of her. She made herself turn; she bit her lip to stop any tears and didn't even try to grab a yogurt or a bottle of water. She only wanted to leave. At the door of the dining hall, she turned once to see if anyone was watching her go. Just then, the dean of students stood. Spoons tapped glasses and a hush fell. Now it was too quiet for Adia to open the creaky door unnoticed.

"Some of you know that a cougar was seen in the woods. Everything is fine, nobody was hurt and these animals don't want to hurt you. They're way more scared of you than you are of them. That said, we're responsible for your safety so, for now, no one, absolutely no one, goes to the lake or the woods until the animal has been caught," the dean said loudly. "We've called the Park Service, and they're going to do what they can to remove the animal."

Adia wondered if that meant they would hunt the cat down

to kill it, or simply catch it and take it elsewhere. The lion had brand-new babies. Four had been born while Adia and her roommate watched, three healthy and one stillborn. Adia's eyes welled up and her breath constricted.

The lake was shiny under the clear sky and the moon was almost full. Adia was grateful. She'd forgotten to bring a flashlight, and although the lion didn't really worry her, she did think about the possibility of snakes. She wasn't sure how many poisonous ones might be in this part of the States; she didn't like the idea of chancing it. She found the dock and walked all the way out onto it, her footsteps on the wooden planks dull and hollow. She lay down on the wood and looked up at the stars, wondering what time it was in Nairobi, in Loita. What would everyone she loved be doing? She shivered. September was cool here. She sat up and pulled her backpack close. She wanted her blanket.

The shot was loud, close enough to make Adia shriek in surprise. She stumbled to her feet, but kept her body low, and still. Another shot rang out. Then she heard footsteps and a voice from the woods just behind the dock where she hunched.

"Got it!"

Adia's heart pounded in her chest, and adrenaline surged through her. She didn't think at all. She pulled her pack onto her shoulders and ran toward the sound of the guns and voices. She felt fingers grabbing at her forearm and felt the nearness of bodies as she passed the thin beach into the low bushes that bordered the lake. She shook the hand off and kept running.

She scrambled through the thickening trees, heading in the direction she'd last seen the mother cat. She was grateful, again, for the moon illuminating the tree roots and rocks, and she leaped over them, running all the way to the hollowed-out tree.

Her breath was ragged and painful in her chest, and she stopped just beyond the small clearing where the tree was. There was no sign of the mother cat. She kept her eyes wide and tried to look in all directions at once. If she was wrong, the mother could attack. Nothing was more dangerous than a mother with babies, and she could be lurking anywhere, ready to pounce.

The three cubs were snuggled into a little pile of kitten fur in the farthest curve of the tree trunk. They were still blind from birth, and they mewed and stretched their tiny arms, paws splaying with needle-sharp claws. Adia knelt down and reached into the tree. Their fur was so soft. One cub blindly took the tip of her pointer finger and began to suckle it. Wishful thinking, Adia thought.

The men found her quickly. She'd only been there a couple of minutes when they crashed loudly through the bushes nearest her and said, "You could have been killed!" One of the men pulled her up by her shoulder and she saw they wore uniforms. Matching hats and jackets, matching badges on their chests. Their flashlights cut the gentle darkness like knives.

"You killed her! You killed her and she has babies!"

"What, now?" one of the men said, and the other knelt down on the ground and shone the beam of his flashlight into the hollow tree.

"By God, would you look at that?" he said quietly. "Kid's right. We've got ourselves a couple of cubs right here."

"Better take 'em out. We'll have to deal with them. Make some calls when we get back."

He looked at Adia and added, "Yeah, had to get her out of here, so you kids can have your woods back. Been a problem around here lately, anyway. Couple of dogs got taken last week up at the houses down the street. Don't want you all getting hurt."

The light was coming up slowly, stretching out above the trees, filling in the spaces between the dark branches and coloring the woods a watery gray. The light here, in the midst of these trees, wasn't the hard-as-glass light Adia still hadn't gotten used to. This was the kind of light she understood, malleable and soft. Adia watched as the men pulled heavy gloves over their hands and reached in to grasp each of the cubs, one by one, and carried them to the truck parked on the lake road. One of the men pulled a small, empty cooler from behind the passenger seat and opened it wide. The two men nestled the kittens all together in the bottom. When they opened the back of the truck to load the new cargo, Adia saw the body of the mother lion slack on a tarp. She stepped close enough to see the scars pitting the short fur on the lioness's cheeks and around her wide-open, bead-green eyes.

"We'll take 'em somewhere nice, girl," one of the men said. "They'll be treated well, I promise."

Adia thought of those cubs growing up motherless, and she started to cry. Once the sadness was exposed to the air, she couldn't turn it off. Huge, painful sobs rushed through her like waves. She thought she'd never cried so hard and so suddenly and so loudly. She hoped the babies wouldn't be taken to some zoo or animal sanctuary. She hoped they would be let free. Wild. She hoped they would never come back here, but instead find a place far, far away from people. She pawed the tears from her eyes, wiped her face with her sleeves, but the sobs kept coming.

"They'll be fine," one of the men said, shifting his weight from one booted foot to the other. He glanced uncomfortably at his partner. "You just take care of yourself now, girl."

"Wait," Adia said, and her voice was ragged and cracked. "Let me wrap them up."

She slid her pack down her arm to the ground and pulled the blanket out. It smelled like everything she loved, and she knew she'd miss it. The men watched as she leaned into the truck and carefully tucked the rough cloth around the little cats. They wiggled and mewed and nestled together. They would need to be fed soon.

Adia watched the men climb into the truck and disappear up the dirt road, away from the lake. When she couldn't hear the engine anymore, Adia picked up her empty pack and walked slowly up the wooded path to the large empty lawn that stretched out across the length of the school's main building. Lights were turning on in windows; she could hear voices and other sounds, hair dryers and laughter. She turned her back to the building and sat down in the damp grass. They would find out soon she wasn't where she was supposed to be.

The open green extended all around her, up to the imposing building behind her and down all the way to the woods where the sun was cracking the sky open now, and the rays were long through the trees.

Her face was raw and pink, and she knew the tears weren't yet gone. She didn't care. She was tired of invisibility. She stretched out on her back and watched the sun continue to rise. She was cold without her blanket, but she didn't need it anymore. She pressed her bare palms against the grass, and dug her fingers into the dirt beneath her. She bit her lip and tasted blood. It mixed with the leftover tears that crowded her throat. The sobs came again and she didn't try to stop them. She didn't care who saw her. She didn't care who heard. She was a wild thing, testing out her fangs.

A FATHER, FOUND

Leona loved that first moment she could see the curve of the hill up to the house in Solai. How long ago it had been since she'd come here first, but how satisfyingly familiar the land was. There were the chipped concrete posts that marked the driveway; there in the distance was the hill and the silhouette of that massive baobab. After all these years in Kenya, Leona was still impressed with its size. She'd never seen one as big.

They rounded the last curve of the track and pulled up next to the stone patio.

"Here we are." Leona flicked the engine off and wiped her sweaty palms on her jeans. "Your dad's probably inside."

"It feels weird." Adia spoke hesitantly, but with a smile that belied her excitement. "So weird to have a dad."

All that year, while Adia was in America, she lived for the letters she received from her mom and Simi, Joan and John. John's were her favorite. He wrote her funny memories of his boarding school life and descriptions of the tourists he took on safaris. Adia wrote back about how much she missed Kenya. She saved every letter she received from Kenya. She tucked them in a box she hid at the very back of a dresser drawer. The idea that her roommate might find the letters and read them made her nauseous with fear. When she felt most alone, Adia took the box out and carried it down to the lake. Sometimes even in the middle of the night. She read and reread the letters so often she could almost recite them. John's were the ones she reread first.

Now, though, with him bounding out of the house and across the patio toward Leona's car, Adia felt shy. She opened the door and stepped out hesitantly. John didn't feel the awkwardness. He flung his arms around Adia so tightly Adia's feet left ground.

This is what it feels like. The thought flashed into her head without prelude. *This is what it feels like to have a father who loves you.* And she sent up a silent thank-you to Grace. All of this was because of Grace, and Adia never, not once, let a day pass without thanking her friend.

That night, tucked into the narrow bed she'd slept in twice before, Leona couldn't sleep. She'd grown used to Nairobi and the urban night sounds. Here, it was all different. She heard elephants growling low and deep as they lumbered up the hill, and the whooping of hyenas somewhere in the distance. Finally she slipped out of bed and down the hall to the kitchen. Maybe tea would help her sleep, or warm milk. She loved the view from this window, how wide and open the world looked from here. In the silvery dark of the half-moon, the grasses and trees, the anthills that rose narrow and as tall as a man from the earth, all looked magical. Leona had been feeling restless recently. Her teaching job was not as exciting as it had been in the early years, and the work she'd been passionate about—preserving Maasai herds by increasing grazing land—had gone as far as it could go. Things were still very bad—the land was still dry and the animals still hungry, but there was nowhere else for them to go, the green lands were shrinking as the dusty ones were growing.

She stirred her tea in her cup and thought about Adia, how

she'd been pulled from Kenya and sent to make a life somewhere as foreign to her as the moon. She wasn't sure, if their
roles were reversed, that she'd be able to do the same. When
she got back in bed later, she curled up under the blanket, and
in that second between waking and sleep, she had a flashing
thought—she'd never been as brave as her daughter. She'd lived
her whole adult life hiding from the things that scared her most.
Not animals or loneliness, but the far more dangerous risk of
connection—of allowing herself to know and be known, all
the way through, even the darkest parts.

The next morning, bleary from lack of sleep, Leona padded across the patio to a wicker chaise. The paving stones were
smooth under her bare feet and she clutched a mug of coffee
in her hands. She hardly ever woke up early, and she wanted
to take the opportunity to see the sunrise. She didn't see John
until she'd settled herself down. When he spoke, she jolted in
surprise, sending a splash of coffee down her sweater.

"Ah, fuck!" He apologized, "I didn't mean to scare you. I
thought you'd seen me!" He rummaged in his pants pocket,
pulled out a handkerchief and handed it to Leona. Then he
leaned back in the chair and was quiet.

Leona watched the orange orb slip from behind the horizon
and climb up the sky, tossing orange-and-yellow light across
the wide-open land as it moved higher and higher. It stunned
her, and without pausing to think, she said, "I saw a photo of
you once, that time I first came here. It was in the dresser in
the guest room. A photo of two little boys. I assumed one was
you—it looked just like she did when she was a baby. But maybe
it was Thomas. I didn't know about him then."

"You saw that picture?"

"It was in a dresser in the guest room. There were baby
clothes in there, too. Lovely things." She paused and looked at
John, and then down the hill to where giraffe were beginning

to nibble their breakfast of acacia leaves, and a tawny eagle called from somewhere she couldn't see.

"Where's that photo now? Adia might want to see it. She should know about her family."

John nodded, but didn't answer. Leona continued, pushing hard against her own reticence to talk, her own discomfort at probing the deeper parts of other people with her questions. She was good, so good at this in her professional life, but it terrified her when it meant something personal. Still, she was determined to pave the way for her daughter to have a real relationship with John, and since Adia didn't know what questions to ask yet, she had to ask them.

"If possible, I'd love for her to see that photo. Or any others that you might have of you as a kid, or of her relations on your side."

"I have all that stuff somewhere. I packed it up when Mother was dying. I didn't want to look at it then, and I assumed I would take the sentimental stuff to the Karen house. Never occurred to me I'd stay here."

"Why did you stay?" Leona asked. "The business?" She knew he'd done well, and the town of Solai had become a bustling place, with markets catering to the tourist industry that, though not as big as elsewhere, was all due to John's work.

"No," he said. "The business is good, yes, but it would be better in Nairobi, or elsewhere, Tsavo maybe, Amboseli. I stayed because, once I got here, once I learned about my mother and the awful life she lived here…I didn't want to leave her alone again. The way she stayed for Thomas? I think that's why I stay, too. For her."

Adia woke late, a combination of jet lag and adolescence, and when she made her way to the kitchen to find breakfast, John was sitting at the table, buttering bread for his lunch.

"You're awake!" He grinned. "Sleeping beauty."

"Where's my mom?" she asked. It was one thing to read

John's letters and write letters back to him, and to imagine what it would be like to be with him, father and daughter, but now, here, Adia felt shy and awkward. The only father she'd ever really seen being a father was Grace's dad. And he and John were not the same at all.

"In Solai, gone to pick up groceries and put gas in her car. Make you some toast?"

Adia's stomach was empty. She was starving, but it felt weird to sit here, just her and John. She didn't know what to talk about.

"I'm okay. Going to go for a walk, I think." She motioned out the window. "Maybe up to the tree."

"Perfect," John said. He popped the last bite of bread in his mouth and wiped his hands on his shirt. "I'll come along."

Adia didn't try to make conversation as they walked, and John didn't, either. Not really. Now and again he'd tell Adia some memory from his childhood, how he'd climb anthills and race to his friend Daniel's house and try to beat his record every time—counting steps out loud to scare any animals out of the way and taking bigger and bigger leaps across the red earth. Adia didn't answer, but she listened, and she tried to imagine this man as a boy—younger, even, than she was now.

At the top of the hill, though, Adia turned to John and smiled, "I love this tree," she said. She ran her fingers across the pulpy wood. The baobab, the "tree of life," was as porous as a grass stem. Its roots absorbed water in otherwise dry places from deep within the ground, and the fibrous wood held it tightly.

"I love it, too," John said. "It's one of the biggest I've seen. When I was at boarding school I had dreams about this tree. And when I moved to Nairobi to start work I missed it. Every time I came back to visit I'd take a photograph. I must have a hundred now, all taken at different angles, different times of day. If I can find them, you can take the ones you want with you when you go back to school. It'll help you remember, like it did me."

After his mother died, John felt inert. He'd expected the opposite—to finally feel free from all obligations, no family left, just him. He'd imagined himself moving back to the city, starting to meet women again, maybe even finding one to fall in love with. He felt maybe he was ready for marriage. But it didn't happen like that, and instead when Ruthie died, he'd felt as if his insides were nothing but an empty hole. Hollow and static. He was pulled under waves of grief that rose and fell like the ocean, and couldn't be predicted. On safari one day, with a family of Brits here on holiday, he'd felt strong, in control. But then he watched the little boy look up at his father with an expression that made John feel as if he were breaking into pieces.

"I thought I'd leave here," he said. Adia was still standing next to the tree, picking at the bark with a finger. "But right around that time was when your mother came, when I found you."

"When Grace died," Adia said.

"When Grace died," John confirmed. "And that's the kind of thing that makes life so damn confusing, doesn't it? Because here's this awful tragedy—your being hurt and losing your best friend, but me finding my daughter. The one I'd wanted ever since she was born."

Adia turned away from her inspection of the bark and faced John. "I wanted you, too. I imagined having a dad forever."

"And there you have it." John smiled. "We wanted one another and we found each other. It doesn't erase the fact that Grace is gone. Nothing will ever do that."

He patted the cool, stone bench next to him. "We have a lot to learn about each other, don't we? I've had no practice being a dad, no role model, either."

He smiled, and put his wide, warm hand on Adia's shoulder. "But we'll work out how to be with one another."

Adia felt a tightness in her chest uncoil, just a little, and felt her back relax. Her stomach growled loudly, and John laughed. "I'm already failing! Any dad worth his salt would have made sure his daughter ate something before dragging her out on a walk and giving her a lecture!"

It was almost dark when Leona's car bumped back up the driveway. She'd stretched her errands out for as long as she could; she stopped and had tea at a bakery, browsed at a tiny shop that sold books and wondered how Adia and John were managing. She hadn't told John she would be gone for so long or why she was really leaving. But she wanted to spend time alone, quiet. And she thought John and Adia would be able to talk more easily if she weren't there. Now, as she pushed the car door shut and hoisted her bags out of the trunk, she wondered if it was a mistake to leave them alone together. Maybe they'd avoided each other all day, not talked at all. Worse, maybe they'd discovered that they had everything in common, maybe they wouldn't want her back, wouldn't need her at all.

Leona piled her bags on the patio. She wasn't ready to go inside just yet. Instead, she walked around the side of the house and partway up the hill. The gathering dark made it too dangerous to walk far alone. In the near distance she heard a hyena. There were animals out now; this was their time. She turned toward the house again, and saw that, through the darkness, the brightly lit windows shone.

She had a sudden memory of her childhood home and how, sometimes, after school in the winter, she'd walk up the street from the bus stop and wish to see the windows in her house lit up, warm and welcoming and with someone there to take her in.

She stopped and turned to look back up the hill, where the baobab was silhouetted against the sky. The sky folded itself around the enormous tree and grew darker and darker until Leona couldn't see anything anymore. Not the branches, not the leaves, not the lonely headstones. Even the sky itself, for that moment, was invisible to her. It lifted itself like a lid, and air rushed in.

Leona turned back to the house. In the light of the kitchen window, she saw John and Adia. They were sitting at the table. John had a box at his feet and what looked like photos, some framed, some not, spread across the table between them. Adia was holding one, large and in a gilded frame, and John was pointing at it. Leona imagined him telling his daughter the stories of these people, her family, and his. She only knew the saddest stories of John's life, but surely he had happy ones, too. And if not, maybe it was because the happy moments in his life were still ahead, spreading out like the sky. Maybe the same would be true for her, too. She hugged herself against the chill air and began walking back down the path. She had come a long way, so had Adia, and Simi, and so had John. They all had. There were pieces of all their lives that were broken and ugly, but new ones were emerging. Adia had two mothers and a father now; Simi had more daughters than she'd ever dreamed she could have.

Leona considered herself and her daughter and John, in that moment the three of them inconceivably together in the wide-open land they all loved so much. Things slipped into the places where they were supposed to fit, and despite her fears and her refusal, time and time again, to love, she was here. She was here and she could feel herself opening. It took courage to relearn everything, to let her darkest spaces crack open to the light. It took bravery.

Leona smiled into the dark and quickened her pace. She let out a deep breath. She was ready to be brave.

★ ★ ★ ★ ★

BEHIND THE BOOK:
HOW NOSTALGIA BROUGHT
THE BRIGHTEST SUN TO LIFE

ADRIENNE BENSON

At the end of the movie version of *Out of Africa,* when Karen
Blixen is leaving Kenya, she says, "If I know a song of Africa,
of the giraffe and the African new moon lying on her back, of
the plows in the fields and the sweaty faces of the coffee pick-
ers, does Africa know a song of me?"

I always cry at that point, because I know exactly what she
means. Clichés about Africa aside, the landscape in Kenya is
arresting. It changes with the seasons and with the mood of
the sky. My family left the US when I was four, and with only
one brief stint back there, we'd been in Africa for a total of ten
years by the time I returned to the US from Kenya at sixteen
because of my dad's job as an international aid worker with
the US government. We'd lived in two other African countries—Zambia and Liberia—but Kenya was where I lived the
longest (five years) and it was the place I felt most connected

to. It was where I began the adolescent individuation from my parents, where I first claimed experiences for myself and where I began to see the very tender and tiny shoots of the adult I'd later become. All of this meant that Kenya, and her dramatic landscape, was the place lodged most firmly in my heart when I returned to the United States to begin a life in a "home" I didn't really know.

People like my characters Grace and Adia and me are Third Culture Kids (TCKs)—kids who spend significant portions of their formative years outside their parents' countries. They are not immigrants—they are always expected to repatriate to their passport country. In the world of the TCK, goodbyes and leaving are not only par for the course, but are also something to be excited about. TCK culture swallows grief. Moving somewhere new is considered an adventure, not an end that should be mourned; grieving is discouraged. Well, as I learned, when grief is sublimated and memories age, nostalgia flourishes.

In the way Adia was born of the special kind of loneliness expatriates can feel, *The Brightest Sun* was born of a nostalgic ache I've wrestled with for the thirty-one years since I left. The word *nostalgia* itself is a hybrid of the Greek words for *homecoming* and *pain*. As a writer, my therapy of choice for mental pain is to catch the things that hurt and put them on paper. I find it helps to clear the darker spaces inside me and empty the little throbs that collect in my mind like dust bunnies under the sofa. So when I heard Leona's voice in my head, I knew that she was only the eye of a needle, and that the thread she'd pull through the story was one that would also empty me of the nostalgia I'd harbored like a phantom limb for so long. So I set her in that same stunning landscape I couldn't forget, and I gave her a baby, Adia—a little TCK to watch growing up in between two cultures.

I knew kids like Adia, clearly foreign but allowed to root for an entire childhood in a single setting. Even though they knew they'd have to leave, and that they'd still face the struggle to find place, they displayed a deeper sense of belonging than those of us who moved more frequently. Adia's story isn't mine, so once I'd conjured her, I saw a place for something more like my own story. That's where Grace came in—her TCK experience is more closely aligned to mine. But you don't have a TCK without a parent who chooses to uproot. Grace gave rise to her mother, Jane, who has pushed aside her own needs and given up a career in order to accompany her husband, a diplomat, to his various international postings. Further, you can't have expatriates without a foreign nation for them to live in, one peopled with individuals who each have a deep and complex history and culture of their own. That's Simi—the steady one who never chooses to be foreign, but instead grows foreign simply because of her inability to be what her community demands.

The struggles the three women and two girls in *The Brightest Sun* face is really the struggle to define, and it's a universal struggle: to define yourself as a mother or daughter, to define yourself in relation to where you live and to define your place in the world—literally and figuratively. It's that struggle, ultimately, that I undertook and it's that struggle that inspired the book.

I'm not Karen Blixen. I know that Africa doesn't have a song of me. I know that the deep nostalgia I feel for aspects of my childhood are not reflected back by the places I lived, or by shadows underneath the baobab trees, or by the delicate dawns when the grasses glitter with dew. Any trace of me in Kenya, or Liberia, or Zambia, or Cote d'Ivoire is long gone. But fusing those memories and nostalgia and imagination into this novel was part of my personal journey. I knew I needed to claim that space in between—the little sliver of Venn diagram where "American" and "other" meet. That's my place. I knew I wanted to bring the life of that "in-between" expatriate child to the page, to set it down and introduce it to people who don't know it. Those kids, and the adults they become, are my people, after all. And though Africa will never sing of me, I'm okay with that—my song isn't purely an African one anyway, nor is it American. Instead, it's the anthem of the sojourner, of all the placeless kids whose home is everywhere and nowhere. It's the song of kids who dream foreign smells and foreign tongues and who, when the plane taking them away banks and turns, trace on the window the dark shapes of hills they may never see again.

ACKNOWLEDGMENTS

People say writing is solitary. But writing a book for publication, and making that book into a real, tangible thing with a good story, believable characters, correct spelling and commas all in the right places takes a village. I'm lucky to have, somehow, been adopted into a literary village full of creative, smart, dedicated and kind professionals—people without whom this book wouldn't exist.

I've wanted to write a novel since I was seven, but it wasn't until the summer I turned forty that I tried. That summer, I accidentally opened an envelope addressed to my houses' previous owner—an inadvertent act that changed my life. The flyer was stamped with the George Washington University logo, and advertised the university-sponsored Jenny McKean Moore Community Workshop, a writing workshop led by actual, working writers. I applied, I got in and I was so nervous the first night I almost threw up.

The Brightest Sun was born in that first JMM workshop, and honed in a second workshop I took three years later. It was born because of the encouragement my two instructors—the first real writers I'd ever met—generously gave me, and the faith they had in my ability. Their support sustained, astonished and inspired me. I also met and stayed in touch with another participant, Terri G. Scullen. Over the course of the next four years, Terri read draft after draft after draft of this book, and not only had the kindness to remain my friend, but also gave me invaluable ideas, helped me attack the story and cheered me on. Terri, an amazing writer herself, was this book's most constant and most exuberant supporter.

Writers need readers for those first drafts, readers with critical eyes who can see the good and help point out the bad. I was lucky. I found a group of smart women who called it like they saw it, were generous with their time, gave excellent feedback and always had good snacks—Lisa Burke, Justine Hedgepeth, Laura Kaiser and Heather Prichard, I owe you multiple margaritas. Sharon Samber, I owe you Scotch (and probably money). Carol Hawk, friend since third grade and hawk-eyed reader, for your patience and insights, I owe you, too.

Finally, the pros that pulled me into the club I'd yearned for so long to join. Matt DiGangi of Bresnick Weil Literary Agency took a chance on me, made me feel like a professional, helped me keep the faith through the submission process, made me laugh and, ultimately, sold the book to the incredible (and possibly magical) editor Liz Stein of Park Row Books. Liz saw what the book should grow into and gently led my writing there. I am deeply grateful to her for the countless hours of work she put into this project. I'm also grateful to the rest of the team at Park Row for so professionally and seamlessly doing all the other hard work necessary to bring a book into the world—from copyediting to printing, from marketing and publicity to designing a cover so beautiful it made me gasp. This is a dream come true for me. A dream that took buy-in and faith from lots of other people and that is what stuns me the most—the willingness of so many others to help make this happen. I'm more grateful to all of you than you may ever know. Thank you. Thank you. Thank you.

ABOUT THE AUTHOR

Adrienne Benson's earliest memories include roasting green mangoes over bonfires in Lusaka, Zambia; climbing walls to steal guavas from the neighbors; and riding in the back of a VW van for weeks on end, watching her mom and dad navigate African border crossings and setting up campsites among thieving monkeys and vocal lions. A USAID worker's daughter, she grew up traversing sub-Saharan Africa, finding homes in Zambia, Liberia, Kenya and Côte d'Ivoire. At sixteen, she made the hardest border crossing of all—the one that brought her "home" to America—a country she barely knew. She's been a Peace Corps volunteer in Nepal, lived in Ukraine and Albania, slept in more airports than she can count and is now happily ensconced in Washington, DC, with her three kids. Her writing has appeared in Buzzfeed; the *Foreign Service Journal*; *Brain, Child*; the *Washington Post*; the *Huffington Post*; *ADDitude* magazine; and several anthologies. *The Brightest Sun* is her first novel.